A Reliance
Sinclair
Novel

IMPULSE ON

HEATHER TEXLE

ON IMPULSE IN

A Reliance Sinclair Novel

HEATHER TEXLE

UNTIL IT LOOKS RIGHT
MINNESOTA

Sign up for bonus content including
On Instinct, a free *Reliance Sinclair* story at
heathertexle.com

For Justin.
It's okay to tell people I'm a writer now.

Chapter 1

I glanced at my cuff. Nineteen hundred hours. It wasn't like Jarrett to be so late.

A gray-haired security guard looped by the fruit stand again—the third time in ten minutes. He eyed me from across the aisle of packed earth. An excess of gut spilled over his belt to hide his badge, but I knew an off-duty officer when I saw one. His stiff-backed walk was born from years of lugging around a two-and-a-half-kilo blaster strapped to a nine-kilo utility belt.

That prickly feeling flared up at the base of my neck. I tugged my cap lower over my eyes, but realized the action only made me look more suspicious. The fruit merchant noticed, too, and sidled closer to my side of the stand to keep an eye on me.

"You must be exhausted from standing in front of my stand for so long. Can I interest you in a cantaloupe? Or a honeydew?" he asked, and shoved a pale-yellow melon under my nose. "They arrived from Saper this morning. You won't find fresher in the market."

I waved off the melon. "No, thank you. My friend will be here soon."

"Ah," he said, undeterred, and snagged a pre-portioned container from his right. "How about some hellaberries? A perfect snack while you wait."

The plump little berries looked good, and it had been a while since I'd had fresh fruit. "How much?" He named a price that made my head spin. "Maybe some other time."

"Dates, perhaps?"

My thigh cramped. I shifted my weight. "No, nothing. I'm good."

"Tourists," he mumbled, and set the container back down in the shade of his bright-blue canopy. He mopped the sweat from his sun-weathered brow with a cloth tucked into his apron. "Your friend doesn't appear to be here, and your scowl scares away my customers." Then he made a shoo-shoo motion with his hand. "Wait somewhere else."

I stepped to the side.

Shoo-shoo.

I took another step. And another. My hip bumped into the spice table at the next booth. Baskets of rosemary, turmeric, hyssop, and thyme wobbled precariously, earning me a glare from the owner.

Satisfied, the fruit merchant called out to the passing crowd. "Dates! Sweet dates, dried dates, stuffed dates! Get the best date of your life right here. Dates so good they'll make you lie to your husband!"

Two women laughed and nudged each other in their sides as they crowded me farther out of the way. The one in the green bell-sleeved top selected a container of dried dates. She raised her arm to let the sleeve drop back and waved her cuff over the merchant's payment hub.

I spotted a sturdy metal crate near the back of the fruit stand and slipped around to stand on it. Jarrett was tall and blond. Thanks to his Ritruvian heritage, he usually stood a head taller than most people. Looking around, though, I didn't see him anywhere on the block.

The security guard crossed to my side of the aisle. Flat eyes traveled from my hands to my waist, scanning for weapons, then to the set of my shoulders before stopping at my face. Definitely an officer. Probably picked up a side job as security for a little extra money.

I held still. No sudden movements to worry him.

"Move along, ma'am," he said, jerking his head toward the end of the block while giving me The Look. "There's no loitering here."

I ignored the "ma'am" comment. On a bad day, I could still pass for thirty; twenty-seven if I put a little effort into it. Definitely not a ma'am.

The guard hooked his thumbs on his belt and rocked back on his heels like he had nothing better to do than follow me around all day.

I jumped down and wiped my palms against my pants. "No trouble. I'm waiting for someone."

"Looks to me like you've been scoping out this stand for a while now. I don't see that you've made any purchases yet today. You weren't thinking about stealing any of this fine produce, were you?"

"What? No." Jerkwad. "I'm just standing here. There's no crime in that. It's a public place."

"All the same, it'd be best for you to be on your way."

I bit my tongue before retorting with something I'd regret. It didn't matter what planet you were on; it was always the same. To them, you were either a good guy or an asshole, and this off-duty officer had already decided I was an asshole.

Same to you, buddy.

Lifting my hands in surrender, I stepped out from the shade of the stall's canopy and squinted into the harsh glare of the late afternoon sun. Cerulean-blue-and-white-striped canopies flapped above me, providing puddles of shifting shade for the merchants hawking their wares beneath them. The scent of warm fruit and spices filled the air.

To my left, a man used a long knife to slice open pomegranates before turning them over to pound out the ruby seeds with a wooden paddle. Beyond him, a sharp-eyed grandmother tracked a brood of youngsters darting among the stalls. To my right, a skinny pickpocket jostled her way through a throng of unsuspecting shoppers, taking full advantage of the security guard's focus on me. She must have felt my gaze, because she craned her neck around until she made me. Quick as could be, she disappeared down a break between buildings.

If the guard was more interested in harassing innocent pedestrians than protecting shoppers from nimble-fingered thieves, that was his problem. I wasn't about to rat her out.

Striking off to the right, I waited until I'd walked two blocks before activating the holoscreen on my cuff. I swiped my hand over a patch of specialty material on my jacket below my elbow. It turned translucent, allowing a shimmering holographic screen to project in front of me.

"Felix," I said, activating the voice control on my cuff, "pull up my last comm from Jarrett Viorel."

"This is the twenty-fourth time you have opened this comm. Is something faulty with your memory? Should I perform a health diagnostic screen when you get back?"

"Just show me the message."

It was short and to the point. *Meet me in the Brin market at the melon stall. Eighteen hundred hours. Tell no one. Watch your back.*

Two months ago, I'd asked Jarrett to dig up information on my former partner. I hadn't heard from him in weeks, then a week ago he sent me that message on an encrypted line and hadn't responded to any of my follow-up comms. The markets on Andaress-4 were only open on Saturdays, so he had to have meant today. I'd wrapped up the fraudulent insurance claim that I'd been investigating and hauled ass to get here in time.

Why such a cryptic message? Why hadn't he wanted to meet at his apartment like we usually did? And why hadn't he shown?

I readjusted my cross-body bag on my shoulder, grimacing when it pressed the leather of my jacket more firmly against my already sticky skin. If I cut through the market, I could be at his place in ten minutes.

Ducking between two stalls, I ignored the sweet fragrance of ripe honey dates, apricots, and Andaress pomegranates. My stomach rumbled, reminding me I hadn't eaten since dinner the night before. Maybe after I sorted out whatever had Jarrett so on edge, we could snag dinner at a cafe near his place. I could even pick up a few pieces of less-expensive produce to restock the *Soteria*'s galley.

It took me ten minutes to traverse the length of the market. Most of the stalls sold rich, fragrant spices transported in from the agricultural city of Saper, but mixed in with those were dozens of Brin salt merchants selling everything from powder-fine grinds to chunks of translucent-white crystals the size of my head. An abundant supply of salt was the main reason the Andar Salt and Spice Company terraformed this planet and the only thing keeping it from falling off the galaxy charts and into oblivion.

Jarrett lived on the west end in a two-story building overlooking the textiles section of the market. A tailor's shop and a small electronics repair store occupied the ground level while four apartments squeezed into the upper level.

I slipped through the narrow walkway between buildings, my feet sure-footed on the familiar path to the rear stairs. Out of habit, I sidled to the inside edge where the worn treads wouldn't creak beneath my weight.

A narrow balcony ran the length of the white building. Four faded-blue doors marked the entrance of each apartment. Jarrett rented the largest unit on the far end, which had a kitchenette that jutted out into the balcony. Not that he used it.

As I passed the second door, a small dog rushed to the entrance, yapping loudly. Its nails scrambled against a hard floor. A shadow passed by the opaqued window, but the owner didn't come out.

When I reached the last door, I held my cuff to the door reader to request entry but found it was already unlocked. Years of training had me drawing my blaster from the lower back holster hidden beneath my jacket. I released the safety before nudging the door open with my foot.

The heat hit me first, with the stench barking right on its heels. Rotted compost, feces, urine, and rancid meat. My stomach soured at the fetid odor, bile rising in the back of my throat. The climate control must have been disabled, because it was a sweltering thirty-six degrees Celsius. I switched to short, shallow breaths through my mouth and did my best to ignore the foul taste of the air.

"Jarrett!" I called out, trying not to gag. "It's Reliance. Are you in there?"

No answer.

I eased in, back to the wall, and swept my eyes across all four corners of the room. His furniture lay overturned, the cushions split open. Seeing no one, I pivoted around the corner to clear the shoebox-sized kitchenette. There, too, cabinet doors hung open and drawers had been yanked off their tracks and dropped to the floor, their contents scattered everywhere.

Someone had tossed the place.

The bathroom and bedroom were at the front of the building overlooking the street. Working counterclockwise, I moved around an overturned desk, being careful not to tread on the busted console laying smashed on the floor. The smell got worse with every step.

His bathroom was minuscule, a two-meter by two-meter square with barely enough room for a gray-water toilet and sonic shower. It, also, had been tossed. A sheet of clear plastiglass hung over the sink, the mirror function busted from a fist-sized crater in the center.

That left the bedroom.

I paused at the closed door, listening for sounds of movement. When I heard nothing except the thumping of my heart, I pushed the door open, blaster raised.

"Shit!" Protocol forgotten, I holstered my weapon and ran to my friend. He sat slumped in a chair, his face bloated and discolored in death. Black fleshflies swarmed over his eyes, lips, and cheeks, gnawing on the soft tissue areas and hastening decomposition. That they had already matured past the larva stage told me Jarrett had been dead at least four days. Why hadn't anyone reported his death? His partner? His coworkers? Surely, someone must have missed him.

Blood, darkened from oxygen until almost black, soaked his shirt and pooled where it had dripped from his fingers to the floor. Carefully, I peeled back the matted hair at his temple, revealing a blaster burn. Something high-end, judging by the bright-red spidering of the veins, well-defined edges, and localized charring of his flesh. Specialized tactical teams carried that kind of firepower. Military and mercs, too.

A small radius at the point of entry indicated a close-range shot. The gaping exit hole said it had been cranked all the way to lethal.

Jarrett's fingers, once graceful as they flowed through his cuff controls, were bent backward at the joints. Burn marks covered his forearms. Another blaster hole mangled his thigh right above the kneecap. He hadn't only been murdered. He'd been tortured.

My hand cupped the side of his face that still bore some resemblance to the man I knew. "Oh Jarrett, who did this to you?"

I blinked away my tears and stepped back to analyze the room, berating myself for contaminating the scene like a first-year rookie. It may have been over a year since I'd left the Department of Enforcement of Criminal Affairs, but I still remembered how to process a damn crime scene.

"Felix, start visual recording." I spun in a slow circle, letting the lens capture the entire room from ceiling to floor before taking a closer view of Jarrett—of the body. "End recording."

Felix was the mobile extension of my ship's computer. He would upload the information to the main system for further analysis as soon as I got within five kilometers of the *Soteria*. Later, I could blow it up on the bridge's viewscreen for analysis, but for now I wanted to take in what the camera couldn't.

I circled the perimeter of the room, avoiding any visible splotches of blood. The window opaquing had been engaged, blocking the view from street level. Below, the clatter from the market was loud enough that a herd of Brionite hairy coos could have trampled through the apartment without being heard.

Jarrett's attackers had strapped him to a chair from his kitchen table set. Shrink ties cut into the bloated flesh at his wrists and ankles. They were high-end and not something Jarrett would likely own. They must have brought those with them. That indicated premeditation.

I hesitated, analyzing my gut reaction. *Attackers? Plural?*

Jarrett was thirty-three—a year older than me—and fit for a techie type. He'd grown up on Ritru-6, a planet with a marginally stronger gravitational pull than the Earth standard. That, along with some genetic tweaking, resulted in most Ritruvians having increased bone density and muscle mass. He also enjoyed the well-developed ego they all seemed to share. And like all DECA agents, he passed strenuous physical exams that included basic self-defense components. Not an easy mark.

I squatted beside the body to scrutinize the dried blood beneath. Besides the puddle below his hand, fat, round drops dotted the space between his feet. Smaller bits of spatter trailed out in short lines. They'd struck him in the nose and mouth for sure, but the blaster burn made a mess of everything else. Then he'd hung his head between his knees.

Standing, I stepped into an obvious void where the blood had landed on the assailant instead of the floor. This was where the shooter had been positioned. I raised my hand, mimicking holding a blaster to Jarrett's temple.

My eyes traveled over the body to the opposite wall. Level with Jarrett's head was a fine mist pattern of blood. That would be from the kill shot. Three sides fanned out in a rough circle with the droplets concentrated in the middle and lightening at the edges. The fourth side, though, ended in a harsh line. Another void.

My gut was right. A second person had been standing there when the killer pulled the trigger.

"What were you on to that was worth your life?"

Jarrett was a tech genius. We'd met as rookies twelve years ago on a smuggling case on Brione-5. I'd gone undercover and royally fucked up. He'd done some computer magic to salvage something from the six-month-long sting and probably my job as well. It turned out the smugglers we were targeting kept astonishingly detailed records.

For that matter, so did Jarrett. If he had discovered something worth being killed over, he would have documented it.

I walked back into the living space. His console lay in pieces. The thin plastiglass screen had been shattered and two side bars cracked open. Someone had extracted the delicate hardware and ground it into the tile. I didn't know enough about consoles to tell if the data storage had been stolen, but I could tell there would be no recovering any information from that.

All the hiding spots that leaped to mind had been ransacked: chair cushions, cabinet drawers, clothes closet. No, Jarrett was too smart for that. He'd pick somewhere with easy access and so mundane no one would ever look at it twice. He might even keep it on his person. I went back to the bedroom.

"Sorry about this," I apologized and searched his pockets. Empty.

His cuff lay on the floor across the room—obviously removed to prevent him from summoning help. I picked it up and held it against his wrist to release the DNA lock. I scrolled through the log. Nothing stood out, but I created a link to my cuff and instructed Felix to copy the files.

While that worked, I checked behind Jarrett's ear and along his hairline for a microdot. Undercover agents sometimes used the sticky discs to pass along small bits of data to their handlers. That reminded me of another case we worked together. Our informant had been a low-level drug mule who smuggled stardust into the prison two doses at a time in the hollowed-out heels of her boots. Jarrett thought it was rather clever.

I slipped off his right shoe and clawed back the inner material. It came up easily, as if someone had loosened it before. There, nestled into a smooth groove inside the heel, was a data dot. Whatever information Jarrett had been willing to die for was likely on that dot.

A forceful knock on the front door interrupted my success. "This is the D-E-C-A. We have a report of suspicious activity at this location. Come out with your hands up."

Chapter 2

I IMAGINED HOW I looked through the officer's eyes: armed, standing over the victim, and holding incriminating evidence. I'd royally screwed myself in the ass by not calling it in right when I'd found him.

If the data dot contained what I thought it did, Jarrett had likely bent a few laws digging up that information for me. It would take them days or even weeks to clear me. By that time, the trail would have gone cold. If it hadn't already. The only way to find the ones responsible for Jarrett's death was to do it myself. I owed him that much.

"Clear right!" the DECA officer called to his partner. Two sets of footsteps circled the living space in opposing directions—standard procedure.

"Doorway left," the second officer called at the bathroom entrance. "Clear!"

I palmed the data dot and sprinted for the bedroom window. With no time to disengage the locking system, I struck the corner of the pane with the butt of my blaster and winced as the sound of shattering glass announced my location to the two officers. I raked away the remaining milky-white shards with the barrel and stuck my head through the opening.

"Halt!" a female voice commanded as I threw one leg over the sill.

Two stories weren't an impossible drop, but it still hurt when I landed. I absorbed most of the shock with my knees and tucked into a roll. In seconds, I was up and shouldering my way through the crowded street. The officer wouldn't risk shooting into the throng of people, even with the blaster on stun. A bystander being hit would be a public relations nightmare. She leaned out the window to watch me and then yelled my direction to her partner.

As soon as I was out of the officer's line of sight, I darted into a group of people gathered around a merchant's stall. "Felix, begin timer."

I threaded my way through to the center of the group, stripped off my black leather jacket, and shoved it in my cross-body bag. Underneath, I wore a simple, white, short-sleeved shirt. My hat and hair clip followed, letting my coffee-brown hair fall loose around my shoulders.

A young woman placed her order with a guy selling some kind of slow-roasted, cubed meat on a stick. A bright-orange shawl lay bunched up at the top of her shopping bag—a concession to the late afternoon heat, no doubt.

My hand slipped in and out without her notice. I tied it around my waist at a jaunty angle, like a skirt, to alter my silhouette. Finally, I flipped my messenger bag around to expose the smooth back-side, tied a quick knot in the strap, and slung it over one shoulder like an oversized purse. By the time I came out the other side of the knot of pedestrians, I'd gone from Suspect-on-the-Run to Woman-out-Shopping.

Both officers converged at the intersection behind me. They were hard to miss in their black tactical pants and forest-green jackets. The woman climbed on top of a merchant's folding chair to see over the crowd. She raised her hand to shield her eyes from the sun.

I kept my pace to a brisk walk since running would only draw their attention. As the officer's head turned in my direction, I fell in step beside a portly man in his midfifties and accidentally-on-purpose bumped into him.

"Oh, excuse me!" I placed my hand on his pudgy forearm. "That was so clumsy of me."

His expression of annoyance morphed into an appreciative leer while his eyes dropped from my face down to the front of my shirt.

"No trouble at all," he assured me. "The path is rather uneven here."

It wasn't, but I took his arm when he offered it. A couple was less conspicuous than a single woman. He commented on the streak of hot temperatures they'd been experiencing, and I responded with something equally inane. It took all my willpower to keep from looking behind me.

"Perhaps you could help me," I said. "I'm looking for a cafe near here. It's supposed to have excellent raki dumplings." They were a local specialty, and chances were good that half the restaurants in town served them.

He smiled. "You must mean Zee's. It's around the corner. I'd be happy to escort you."

"Oh, would you?" I beamed up at him.

Fifty paces later, I disentangled myself from my prop outside the front door of a tiny restaurant sandwiched between a holovid store and a place advertising guided tours out to the salt flat. Not my idea of a holiday, but to each her own.

The man cleared his throat and pulled himself up to his full height. "Since we are here, perhaps you would let me buy you dinner?"

Crap, I'd laid it on too thick. "I would, but I'm meeting my husband."

"Your husband?" he stammered, thrown by this unexpected revelation.

"Mm-hmm." I smiled. "But thank you so much for showing me the way. I wouldn't have found it without you."

He stared after me as I slipped into the cafe, his expression somewhere between confusion and indignation.

"Felix, time."

"Two minutes forty-six seconds. May I ask what we're timing?"

"My freedom."

"What did you do now?"

"Nothing. I can't talk right now. Mute." I flagged down the nearest server. "Excuse me, do you have a back entrance I could use? I think that man is following me."

The server glanced out the window at my former escort, who was still staring at me. "Do you want me to call law enforcement?"

"No, no," I assured her. "I'm probably overreacting, but it doesn't hurt to be careful, does it?"

She gave me a knowing nod. "Isn't that the truth? Here, come with me, honey."

Through the window, I saw the two DECA officers take position and scan each passing pedestrian. I ducked my head and followed the server through the kitchen to a back alley. It reeked of old garbage and urine.

As soon as she disappeared back into the restaurant, I broke into a fast jog. I'd slipped by the initial perimeter, but I wasn't in the clear yet. Because of the restricted parking around the market, I'd left my bike a half-klick away.

"Felix, unmute. Time."

"Five minutes, twenty-three seconds. Are we speaking again?"

"Mute." He'd make me regret that later.

Sticking to the labyrinth of alleys, it took me another five minutes to reach my bike. Too long. By that time, the DECA officers would have contacted the Andaress-4 Central Command. How long did that give me until they grounded all planet-to-orbit transports? Thirty minutes, if I was lucky, and luck hadn't been my friend in a very long time.

My hoverbike purred to life, rising two meters off the ground while I secured my helmet. The UV-reflective face shield had the added benefit of blocking my profile from the city cameras. I glided into the skylane and matched the speed of other LAVs—low altitude vehicles—until I reached the Brin city limits. Then I swung north toward the barren salt flats and punched the throttle to full blast.

The setting sun transformed the stark-white desert floor into a golden sea. A plume of salt dust arced behind me. It would be visible from kilometers away, but there was no helping it. Cutting through the salt flats was the fastest way back to the port city of Salin where I'd docked my ship and the only way I'd make it off the planet before the authorities performed a ship-by-ship inspection.

"Felix, display timer as a visual." The software in my helmet connected with my cuff and the timer displayed in the upper-right section of my visor. 13:58. It would be tight.

The city appeared as a tiny speck on the horizon and grew larger as I neared. Sunlight glinted off the metal and plastiglass surfaces of the buildings. Salin sat at the edge of an ancient salt-water sea that was drying up, due in part to the large desalinization plant on the west side of the city. A tangled mass of pipes and storage tanks rose into the sky. I remembered the spacedock was near it and veered left.

"Felix, unmute. Scan all frequencies for the words homicide, barricade, detaining ships, fleeing suspect, in pursuit, or Jarrett Viorel. Use the decryption program JV10. Report in audio."

He didn't respond. I swore to the great dark void that I'd kill whichever programmer thought giving simulated emotions to a ship's computer system was a good idea. "Felix, I'm in a jam here."

"Scanning . . ." Felix replied, his synthetic voice sounding hollower than normal through my helmet but still as pouty. "Your search yields one hundred and twenty-six results. Shall I play them in chronological order?"

"No. Limit search to the last fifteen minutes and sectors eight and nine."

"Seven results."

"Transcribe and display. Continuous update."

Text scrolled across the bottom third of my visor. "Next. Next. Next. Wait! Stop. Go back and play the third one."

A woman's voice came on. "This is Officer Patel. We have a homicide at the intersection of Eighth and Market. Suspect fleeing on foot. Female, midthirties, black jacket, cap. Last seen heading west on Market. In pursuit."

Midthirties! Officer Patel needed her vision augmented. "Felix, add Officer Patel to the search. Prioritize her communications. Play."

"Patel to Dispatch. Lost visual of suspect . . . Patel to Dispatch. Unable to track the suspect. I'm returning to secure the scene . . ."

"Dispatch to Officer Patel. Lead Agent Grayson Wright is assigned to this case. Coordinate efforts with him."

"Pause," I instructed Felix and slowed the hoverbike to merge into traffic. My close-quarters cutting technique didn't thrill the LAV behind me, and the pilot gave me the traditional three-fingered hand gesture to express his displeasure. I returned the sign as I accelerated past the next vehicle. My eyes flicked to the timer. 20:22.

"Felix, I'm coming in hot. Begin preflight check."

"Initiating preflight check. Systems coming online."

The spacedock came into view. Nothing more than a glorified parking garage, but all ships capable of interstellar travel landed there to refuel. Central Command controlled arrivals and departures and handled customs issues for incoming cargo. Normally, all great things. I loved Central Command. Happy to work with them. Except for today. Today, they were going to be a giant pain in my ass.

"Felix, lower the cargo door and patch me in to Central."

"Central Command." The woman's tone was curt and efficient.

"Hey, Central. This is Captain Reliance Sinclair of the *Soteria*, requesting permission to launch." I counted the seconds waiting for Central to respond.

"You're cleared for takeoff in ten minutes, Captain Sinclair. We're waiting on a passenger ship ahead of you to vacate the launching zone."

"Thanks, Central. Sinclair out."

I slowed to a near crawl as I passed through the security gate. Above me, an armed security drone swept for explosives and contraband. My heel bounced against the gearshift.

"Come on, come on," I muttered as pilots ahead of me leisurely split off in either direction toward their own ships. Now wasn't the time to draw attention to myself.

The guard inspected my bike, scanned my cuff, and waved me through.

The *Soteria* was docked at the end of row G. Felix already had the rear cargo door lowered, so I flew straight in and landed the hoverbike in its stand on the port side. I cut the engine and tossed my helmet on the handlebars.

I scrambled up the metal-rung ladder to the upper deck and sprinted down the short corridor to the bridge where a thigh-high metal cat greeted me. "Talk to me, Felix."

The computer interface switched over from my cuff to the ship's avatar. "Preflight check is complete. Electrical systems go. Guidance systems go. Communications go. Environmental levels go. Oxygen and nitrogen tanks at eighty-seven percent. Batteries at twenty percent. Sinnafuel cells at thirty-four percent. Recommend additional fueling before takeoff."

Well, that wasn't going to happen. "We'll have to tighten our belts."

"Reliance?"

"Never mind. Close the cargo door and begin cabin pressurization sequence." I woke the console from standby mode, synced my cuff, and aerial scribed in my authorization code. The dashboard lit up. "Update on frequency recordings."

The playback continued with a man's voice, low and with a Ritruvian accent. "Wright to Patel. Pull surveillance feeds from satellite 62AC-B . . . Patel here. We found her, sir. She's on a hoverbike heading toward Salin. Officers redirected to the city's southern limits. Sending you visual recordings now . . ." I checked the time stamp. They were seven minutes behind me.

I felt the rear hatch lock into place and began the launch sequence. The floor vibrated when the engine engaged, then the entire ship rocked back and forth as the thrusters lifted us the first meter off the ground.

"Come on, baby, you got this," I coaxed. The *Soteria* was as space-worthy a vessel as they came, but that didn't mean she wasn't a drama queen. She eased out of our hangar into the open air.

Felix jumped into the copilot's chair, his metal-scaled tail curling around the armrest to secure him to the seat.

Agent Wright's voice came on over the playback, sounding rough and annoyed. "Patel, she's not going into the city. She's making for the spacedock."

I powered up the boosters and eased us down the row to the launch pad.

An announcement from Central Command interrupted the recording. "All ships are grounded until further notice. Power down and await further instructions. I repeat, all ships—"

The roar of my engine drowned out the rest as the *Soteria* lifted off and blasted toward the sky.

My body slammed into the seat. "Harness, harness," I said, clicking the straps into place.

Energy rolled up from the engine, shaking the walls, floor, and chairs. That was always the worst part. The force increased, and I felt like a dry, brittle leaf clinging to the end of a dead stick in a gale-force wind.

Red lights blinked across the dash. My baby was not happy about the cold start. Teeth rattling, I forced my skull away from the head-rest and input manual adjustments to keep the princess ship from throwing a full-blown tantrum.

Within minutes, the sky transitioned from evening blue to deep indigo and then the blackest of blacks. When I broke through the thermosphere, I went from a cacophony of noise and lights and being tossed about so hard my bones felt as if they might shatter—to nothing. It was as if I'd gone deaf; the silence was so absolute. And then, for the briefest moment before artificial gravity kicked in, I was weightless. It was my favorite part of flying.

Today, however, I had zero time to enjoy it.

"Star chart, now. And prep the warp drive. Skip the safety checks while you're at it."

Felix threw a sector map on the main screen. His heterochromia eyes stared at me without blinking. "There are seven recommended safety—"

"I said skip it, Felix. Authorization Sinclair-Foxtrot-Mike-Lima-Ten-Four. And stop judging me."

The drive kicked on, sending a shiver of anticipation through the ship. My panel lit up like the sky on Exploration Day. I aerial scribed in the commands to make the warning signals go away. Then I peered down one last time at the blue-white ball of Andaress-4.

"I promise I'll find who did this to you, Jarrett, and I will make them answer for it."

The indicator light for my warp drive turned from red to blue, signaling it was ready. I turned back to the sector map to choose a destination, and my screen went dark. So did my control panel, the main cabin light, and the auxiliary lights, plunging the bridge into total darkness.

"Felix, what just happened? Where's my power?"

Felix didn't respond, and I stuffed down the fear threatening to overwhelm me. No power meant no lights, no comms, and no air exchange. Heat would also become a problem, as the thermal control system ran off the batteries.

Hoping it wasn't a full-system failure, I felt around for the lever that would release the backup interface from its nesting place within the desktop. It was created for emergencies like this and connected to an independent power source. I found the lever on the outside wall near my knee and pulled. A tray dropped, coming to rest centimeters above my lap. My fingers brushed over the square buttons, trying to recall which ones did what. I hadn't used a physical keyboard since I tested for my pilot's license as a teenager. My fingers struggled to find the correct keys.

Not that it mattered. Nothing I tried worked. Not flicking the power toggle back and forth, not stabbing my finger at the buttons, not even kicking the stand with the toe of my boot. That only left one other option.

Gah! I'd been so close. Another minute and I would have been out of the system. I hadn't thought such a backwater planet like Andaress-4 would have remote ship-disabling technology. Salt thieves couldn't be that big of a problem to justify the expense.

Darkness settled around me like a living, breathing thing. It had a weight. A presence. Without my console screens, I couldn't even see the light of the planet. My fingers felt stiff, and the tip of my nose itched with cold. I told myself that was ridiculous. The ship wouldn't lose heat that fast. Even though it seemed longer, it had only been a few minutes.

Logically, I knew it was a power move, carefully timed and orchestrated to manipulate my emotions. That didn't make it less effective.

Finally, my main screen lit up with an incoming communication link. The staccato notification sound echoed throughout the bridge.

I squinted in the sudden light, waiting for my eyes to adjust. When I was sure my face wouldn't betray my emotions, I accepted the comm.

The hard-edged face of a man appeared on my main screen. Midthirties, clean shaven. He had a regulation uniform, a regulation haircut, and a regulation stick shoved so far up his ass I was surprised he could still sit in a chair. Intelligent eyes gave nothing away, and there was an air of authority about him that likely made all the little rookies swoon and piss their pants in turn.

"Captain Sinclair," he said. "I don't believe we've met. I'm Lead Agent Grayson Wright, and I'd appreciate a word with you."

Chapter 3

"WHAT CAN I DO for you today, Agent Wright?" I kept my face neutral but let a hint of impatience color my tone. No one enjoyed being detained by the authorities, even one as attractive as Agent Wright.

"You left the spacedock after Central Command grounded all flights."

"Did I?" My eyes widened in faux surprise. "Weird. There must be a glitch in my comms."

"They seem to work fine now."

"Hmm, that's so strange." I opened the screen in front of the copilot chair and initiated a systems check, using the control panel beneath the desk and out of Wright's view. Diagnostic code scrolled by faster than I could read. "Thanks for letting me know. I'll have that looked at the next time she's in for repairs."

Grayson Wright leaned forward until his face filled the screen. His neck and jaw muscles clenched, making the veins pop to the surface. I had that effect on men.

"You're wanted for questioning in the death of Jarrett Viorel," he said. "We launched a DECA ship to escort you back to the Salin spacedock. Officers will seize control of your vessel and transport you to the precinct for questioning. Do you understand?"

Oh, I understood all right. That move was straight out of the Department's handbook. Once they dragged me back to a holding cell, they'd let me sit for hours or even days, while they tore the *Soteria* apart looking for evidence that didn't exist. Well, except for the data dot I'd taken from Jarrett's shoe. Credits to crispers it related to the work Jarrett did for me and was what got him killed. I stood the best chance of figuring it out, and I sure as hell couldn't do it from the inside of a holding cell.

My copilot screen stopped scrolling. I opened the subfolder and cursed under my breath. Sodding agent was using the satellite to scramble my navigational instruments. Even if I got full power back, without the nav system, the *Soteria* couldn't get a three-dimensional fixed point of our starting location. No starting point meant no ending point. Between the universe expansion, rotation of the galaxy, and orbits of billions of planets, the risk of flying through a rock or burning ball of gas at warp speed was too great.

I smiled at Wright, showing a lot of teeth. "Now's not really a great time. Any chance we can reschedule for next week?"

"This isn't up for negotiation, Captain Sinclair. We will bring you in. By force, if necessary." His look would have quelled many suspects. I had one of those looks myself, although his was better. It came naturally with that whole alpha-male thing he had going on.

"Is your eye twitching?" I asked, squinting. "Because you might want to get that looked at."

Wright made an indecipherable grunt, and I could practically *feel* him trying not to blink those hazel eyes.

He leaned back and checked something off-screen. "We disabled your navigation system. However, you can still land your craft using line of sight."

An alert flashed across my screen, warning of an approaching vessel. Wright wasted no time getting that ship into orbit. I minimized the warning and got to work blocking the interference from the satellite. Luckily for me, the Salin DECA office hadn't bothered updating their software in the last year, and I knew a backdoor into the system. Well, not luckily. A rather clever smuggler had once exploited the same weakness against me, and I kept a copy of the program she'd used. For educational purposes, of course.

My heel drummed impatiently against the metal floor as I waited for the virus to upload. In a few minutes, that satellite would be nothing more than a two-thousand kilo hunk of space trash—at least until they called in a repair crew.

"Grayson—can I call you Grayson? I'm sure this is all a big misunderstanding."

"You fled the scene of a homicide."

There wasn't any point in denying it. Every security camera from Jarrett's apartment to the spacedock had recorded my wild ride back to my ship. All Wright needed to do was request the footage.

"Jarrett was my best friend. I didn't kill him."

"Then why run?"

Typical asshole agent with space dust for brains. "Jarrett died at least four days ago. I didn't even arrive on Andaress-4 until this morning. You can check the docking records."

Wright's blond brows knit together. "How do you know when he died?"

"Fleshflies," I explained. "They'd already hatched. But you'd know that if you'd done your job. Jarrett worked for DECA. He was one of your own. Didn't anyone notice when he didn't show up for work? How is it I'm the one who found him?!"

"You're not in a position to be asking questions."

"At least I'm asking them. He lay there for four days while his killers had plenty of time to escape. *Four days!*" I sucked in a sharp breath, cutting off the rest of my retort. First Cavender, now Jarrett. The law enforcement agency was corrupt or incompetent, or both. Either way, I couldn't rely on DECA to bring Jarrett's murderers to justice. He deserved better than that.

Wright's voice sounded tight. *Guilt? Shame?* "Be that as it may, you will begin reentry procedures or my officers will board your ship. Don't make this more difficult than necessary."

A light flashed on the side of his screen, momentarily bathing half his face in pale red. The accompanying alarm signaled that the virus had wormed its way into the satellite's system. His fingers flicked through the air in front of his console, the silver nerve impulse cuff around his forearm translating the aerial scribes into digital commands.

Off-screen, a feminine voice rattled out a string of curses that would make a freight hauler proud.

"Agent Leahy, report."

"There's a void-be-damned bug in the satellite, sir. I'm losing control."

"Get it back."

"I'm trying. It's going to take a minute."

"Problems?" I asked sweetly.

A creative string of obscenities poured through the communications link. I swirled my little finger to refresh my diagnostics screen as the rest of my lights powered on. I smiled for real this time. "Gee, I'd love to stick around and chat, but I've got places to go and things to do. You know how it is."

"Sinclair, don't—"

I waved my hand in front of the console, cutting off Agent Wright's reddening face.

"Felix, put up the feeds from the external cameras. I want to see that DECA ship. Then show me a list of all the star systems within range, given our current fuel supply. And get that warp drive going again."

My side screen flickered black and then a dull gray ship appeared in the center. It was a skiphopper, designed for interplanetary system travel. Fast and agile, they held two people and were ideal for patrolling low-orbit space. Central Command probably had one on standby for situations like this. I'd flown one a time or two and liked how they handled.

"Calculating closest stars," Felix said. "We'll run out of battery before fuel. The dock workers never got around to hooking me up to charge."

"Of course they didn't. That's what I get for telling them I'd be on the planet for a few days."

Three star systems popped on to my screen. I picked the middle one, a white dwarf with no habitable planets. "Do we have enough energy to get to Beta Rahn?"

"Yes, if I run on minimal power."

"Good, plot a course. Get us as close as possible without frying us." The Beta Rahn system didn't have any Goldilocks planets, but I could park myself in the star's orbit and charge the batteries long enough to get to somewhere more hospitable. There should be enough sinnafuel left for one, maybe two, jumps.

A visual of our plotted course popped up on an auxiliary screen. "The warp core will be ready in thirty seconds."

More warning alarms flashed on the copilot's screen as the skiphopper moved to intercept. The crew wouldn't risk boarding the *Soteria* while she was still mobile, but they might do all sorts of nasty things to keep me from leaving, like scattering mines in my path or using their rail guns to damage my ship. I used a precious bit of fuel to maneuver out of their direct path.

Agent Wright hailed me over the comms. I swiped my hand across the screen, declining the request.

"Talk to me, Felix."

"Twenty seconds."

I punched through a series of commands that would ready the ship for warp travel.

"Ten seconds."

Wright hailed me again. The man was persistent.

The skiphopper swung around, using its superior speed to dart in front of me. Weapon flaps opened along the forward section of its hull.

"Shit." Inertia would carry me right into the line of fire. I burned my port thruster and prayed I had enough fuel left to make the jump. If I didn't, well, the warp bubble would collapse somewhere in the void. There were worse ways to go, but stuck between stars and thousands of light-years from civilization was high on my list of things to avoid.

"Five seconds. Four. Three."

The warp core went from gently vibrating to rattling the ship from stem to stern. I clenched my teeth to keep them from clacking. Pressure built until my ears felt like they were going to pop.

The DECA ship fired. Felix tracked the slug, displaying its course on my screen. The round was only the size of a loaf of bread, but even pebbles caused massive damage at high speed. Something that size would easily breach the hull. The blinking light advanced toward the *Soteria*, but all I could do was watch.

"Two. One."

I held my breath as the icons for the slug and my ship occupied the same fraction of a centimeter on the screen.

My body slammed into the back of the chair as the warp drive kicked in, hurtling us forward as it built the warp bubble. I rocked to the side, the shoulder harness jerking me to an abrupt halt. Not my most graceful moment as a captain, but nothing blew up, caught fire, or got sucked into the vacuum of space. I counted that as a win.

The skiphopper wasn't designed for travel outside of a single planetary system, so I didn't need to worry about immediate pursuit. Even if Wright sent a ship after me, it would take him at least a day to requisition a larger ship, supply it, and pick up my trail. That might take him two days. I had breathing room.

"Felix, damage report."

"All primary systems operating within normal parameters. Fuel at twenty-six percent. Estimated level at arrival: twenty-one percent. Batteries at thirteen percent. I recommend restricting your movements to the bridge and shutting down all nonessential systems in other areas of the ship to conserve battery life."

I stared at the map on the main screen, the little ship representing the *Soteria* following a direct path to Beta Rahn. The clock beside it estimated eighteen hours until arrival. We'd be lean, but we'd get there.

"Reliance, did you hear me?" Felix's huge, metal paw reached delicately across the space between our seats and tapped on my armrest.

I unbuckled my harness and stood up. "Engage autopilot and alert me to any issues."

"Reliance? Where are you going? We need to conserve energy."

"Just . . ." My voice came out sharper than I'd intended, even if he was just an avatar. I grimaced and tried again. "Give me a minute, okay? Then we can shut everything down like you suggested."

Adrenaline flowed freely through my veins, but I'd crash soon. Before that happened, I needed to secure my hoverbike in the hold and make some safety checks. The slug may have damaged a noncritical system.

I walked down the short hall between a storage closet and environmental control system and climbed down the ladder to the lower level. The maintenance console was near the rear hatch. I opened the protective door and set it to run a full systems diagnostic.

A visual inspection of the interior revealed a few toppled containers from the rough jump and a broken gasket on a pipe leading from the gray-water tank. It looked like I'd be enjoying sonic showers for the foreseeable future. A minor inconvenience, but hot showers were one of the few luxuries I indulged in.

My hoverbike lay on its side, new scuff marks gracing its red shell but otherwise in working order. I reactivated its anti-grav, tipped it up, and slid it into its rack along the wall. It needed to recharge, but that would have to wait. I added it to my growing list of things to do.

The diagnostics would take four or five hours to complete. That gave me time to change into something more comfortable, find a bite to eat, and maybe even catch a couple of hours of sleep. It had been—I did the math—twenty-one hours since I'd last slept.

My shoulders slumped. All the energy in my body suddenly drained out the soles of my boots like an uncorked barrel. It left me empty inside save for a burning knot of pain in the hollow of my chest. Tears, unbidden, slipped down my cheeks.

Why didn't Jarrett say how urgent it was? I'd have dropped everything to get there. I could have stopped them. I could have done . . . *something.*

And to top it off, I really fucked things up with DECA. Agent Wright would find me. No doubt about that. I didn't have the skills or credits to live on the run forever. Not that I would want to, anyway. That life would be even lonelier than what I had now.

Evading arrest and incapacitating the satellite had been stupid, but I didn't see what other choice I'd had. The best I could hope for was evading capture long enough to find the people who killed Jarrett and see them answer for their crimes. And then I would have to answer for my own.

Chapter 4

As I DROPPED OUT of warp in the Beta Rahn system, an image of two bluish-white stars appeared as bright dots on my screen. The binary stars were orbited by five planets, all of them far too hot to sustain life.

I passed Beta Rahn-5, the outermost planet. Details about its topography, mineral composition, and notable features accompanied its image. Fuel companies had mined it and its neighboring planet, Beta Rahn-4, several decades ago for sinnalite, the energy-rich material that made faster-than-light travel possible. Everything of value had been stripped, refined, and hauled off to more civilized corners of the galaxy.

The inner three planets didn't even warrant that much attention. There was no reason for anyone to be here, and more importantly, no reason for Agent Wright to suspect I'd chosen this system. He wouldn't know I was low on fuel and power.

Beta Rahn-B—the nearest star—grew steadily larger over the course of the next thirty minutes. I switched to manual control when I passed through the orbital path of the innermost planet. The ship could operate solely on voice or digital commands, but I preferred the false sense of security that having my hand on the yoke gave me. Traveling at near light speed was always tricky. Even with the computer handling all the mathematical computations, the unexpected was always a possibility. Debris too small to be mapped could drift into the targeted landing area or a blast of stellar wind might knock us off course.

Felix padded onto the bridge, dragging an electrical wire the length of my arm. He jumped into the copilot's chair and dropped the wire. One end dangled loosely over the edge. "Approaching destination coordinates," he said, and batted at the swinging cable.

"Where did you get that?"

No answer. Fucking cat.

"It better not be from anything important." I leaned over and gave it a tug. His paw snapped out, pinning it to the chair before it fell.

My stomach wambled as the reverse thrusters fired, dramatically reducing our speed. The ship settled a safe distance from the star. If I stayed here, the star's gravitational pull would eventually suck the *Soteria* so close that it would burst into flames. However, I only planned on being here a few days.

"Extend both booms. We need all the sails this time."

"Confirmed."

The ship groaned as the side doors opened. Four telescoping poles extended out, two on either side. They jerked to a halt, sending a jolt through the ship. Long strips of silicon-infused fabric slid out between them on tracks. They drew taut and glinted a burnished copper when I adjusted them to absorb the maximum amount of stellar energy.

Sinnafuel provided the massive amount of energy required to break orbit and generate the warp bubble, but that much energy would fry the nonpropulsion systems, so batteries powered everything else. I'd planned on staying on Andaress-4 for a few days and using one of the cheaper slow-charge options at the Salin spacedock to top off.

"How're we looking?"

"Main batteries are charging. Estimated time to full charge is one hundred forty hours and thirty-seven minutes."

"We only need enough power to get us to the next charging station."

"Where will that be?"

"I haven't figured that out yet."

That was the big question. I had to assume Jarrett's murder related to the work he was doing for me. If that were the case, whoever ordered the hit probably came from another planet, because Jarret was my only connection to Andaress-4. That was good, because it would be almost impossible to investigate on that planet with Agent Wright dogging my every step. It was bad, because it left several dozen other planets as viable options.

Sensing a long night, I climbed down to the common area on the lower level to grab something to eat. A quick peek in the refrigerator confirmed nothing new had magically appeared since the last time I looked. I pulled out a frozen mycoprotein patty and threw it in the zapper to heat. Those were getting low, too, so I mixed a scoop of sugar, a nutrient pack, and five ounces of water into the proofing vat and added a pinch of fungi spores.

Lightweight, shelf-stable, and cost-effective, mycoprotein was a tasteless wonder of space travel. Later tonight, I'd 3D print the batch into pasta to go with the bottle of tomato sauce sitting in the back of the pantry.

The zapper dinged. I used my one-and-only fork to stab the patty out of the tray, dropped it on my one-and-only plate, and doused it with sweet chili sauce. Then I poured myself a generous glass of twenty-year-old, double-barreled whisky from a bottle hidden in a drawer below the utensils. If any night deserved a drink, it was tonight.

Back on the bridge, the captain's chair creaked as I sat down. I cut off a chunk of patty with the side of my fork and tried a bite. It needed salt.

I raised my glass to my lips, hints of butterscotch and honey hitting my nose. The whisky stung the back of my throat before mellowing to smoother notes of caramel, vanilla, and oak.

"All right, Jarrett. What did you find?"

Six files from the data dot filled my screen. My hand hovered in front of the console, unsure of where to start. None were helpfully titled, *"Read Me First!"*

I pointed twice in quick succession with my index finger, and my neural impulse cuff sent a command to open the first file. It was the DECA report from my last case with Hal Cavender. It made sense that Jarrett would have started there. The first few pages I recognized. As the junior agent, it had been my responsibility to fill out the reports.

Ruana Sorelsdotter, twenty-five, worked as a financial adviser in Clava. She'd died on her way home from work one night, alone, in an alley, her pockets rifled and purse stolen. No sign of injury or trauma. If I closed my eyes, I could still picture her face—eyes wide and unfocused, lips parted, as if her death had come as a surprise.

The medical examiner removed the body for autopsy while Cavender and I searched her house. I started in the bedroom and bathroom, looking for anything obvious: signs of living beyond her means, an angry partner, drug abuse. The only thing I found was a sheet of postoperative medical tabs near her bed. Not exactly hard core. Still, I called out the find to my partner, citing the full name, date, prescribing doctor, and hospital in case he found anything related.

Right after, Cavender received an incoming comm and stepped outside to answer it. When he returned, he summoned me into the living room. I stepped out, holding the clear evidence bag with the tabs inside. I remembered thinking it was my last bag, and I needed to get more from our LAV. It's funny which details your mind holds onto, even when you wished it would forget.

When I looked up from the evidence bag, Cavender had his blaster trained in my direction. Its high-pitched whine indicated it was charged and ready. At first, I'd thought someone must have snuck behind me. I'd spun and dropped into a crouch, drawing my weapon while giving my partner a clear field above me. But no one was behind me. His blaster clicked a split second before discharging. It had been my only warning.

His shot went high, tearing into the wall where my torso would have been had I not dropped low.

Reflex and training took over, snapping my arms up into position. He froze, shock wiping his face of all expression. Then he crumpled to the floor. Smoke wafted from the burn mark in his green DECA jacket. Three marks, actually. Center mass, like we trained.

It had stunk. A mix of ozone, charred meat, and melted synthetic material that I had never smelled before or since, except in my dreams.

The craziest part was that I didn't even remember pulling the trigger. How could I not remember pulling the trigger?

My hand trembled from the memory, threatening the safety of the amber liquid in my glass. The remaining alcohol burned the entire way down to my gut. I coughed, wiped my sleeve across my mouth, and contemplated a second round to get me through the rest of the file.

Another agent took over the case after that. Internal Investigations carted me off for interrogation. Even though they cleared me of any wrongdoing, working for the Department hadn't been the same after that. No one ever discovered the reason Cavender turned on me. He was a solid agent with a clean record.

It had happened so fast. There were days I questioned whether I had read the situation correctly.

No one willingly partnered with me after that, and if I was honest, the underlying feeling of suspicion and distrust went both ways. If Cavender could betray me, then so could any of them. Eventually, I resigned and sold my house. I used the credits and my savings as a down payment on the *Soteria* and took a job as an insurance claims investigator. It let me work independently and still use my training from the Department.

Turning back to the Sorelsdotter case, I flicked my finger to scroll down. Beneath my preliminary notes, the new agent had included her own. She listed the cause of death as natural, resulting from venous thromboembolism—a blood clot. Case closed.

Jarrett had also included three of Cavender's cases from before we became partners: two from Clava on Brione-5 and one from his post at Púki on Vesen-1. A quick read revealed nothing out of the ordinary in any of them.

The next file was a copy of Cavender's financial records. That was more interesting. He had two decades on the job over me, so I expected his salary to be higher, but wowza.

Out of curiosity, I checked his weekly pay stubs. They weren't much more than mine had been. Perhaps he had made some good investments. I jumped to that section. Typical stuff. He invested through the same company as me, as did most DECA personnel. Next, I checked his deposits, and there things got interesting.

Cavender had four large deposits from a company named RMZ Incorporated. Each deposit could have purchased three of my hoverbikes.

"Felix, run a search on RMZ Incorporated."

"Unable to connect to the interplanetary network." The big cat sat in the copilot chair. He adjusted himself, moving several centimeters closer to me. "This system doesn't have a subspace relay station."

Of course it didn't. "Save the search and run it when we get to the next system."

I reviewed the entries again, looking for clues. Something about the dates caught my attention. I mimed pinching all four case files between my fingers and dragged them over to the copilot's screen. Each deposit coincided within two days of one of Cavender's previous homicide cases.

"Hal, you sneaky little bastard. You were on the take."

"On the take? Please define."

I flinched. Felix's speaker was right next to my ear and two levels too loud. "Jeez, cat, when did you get so close? It means he was being bribed."

Felix had one green eye and one blue eye. He blinked them, storing the information. His vocabulary program had required a lot of updating when I first got him.

The final document on Jarrett's data dot was a business license showing KaLo Research as the parent company of RMZ.

"Add KaLo Research to the search list. I want new articles, business filings, complaints, staffing—anything that pops up." It was doubtful a public search would turn up anything Jarrett hadn't already discovered, but I might get lucky.

Cavender died a year ago. Whatever he had been paid to cover up must have been big. Big enough that whoever was behind it was still tying up loose ends.

His four homicide cases shared a connection beyond him being the lead agent. Figuring out what linked them together was my first step in solving the case.

The next document was the file for Cavender's case on Vesen-1. If I recalled correctly, he'd worked there about five years before transferring to Clava on Brione-5. He and his wife were originally from Brione-2 and wanted to be closer to her elderly mother.

The file included all the usual reports. Subject was Kelthea Zairesh, a young woman, midtwenties, never married, and in good health. DECA officers received a call for a welfare check from the house's automated security system. Subject was dead on arrival. The autopsy listed the cause of death as complications from a recent surgery. No similarities jumped out at me. I needed to go to Púki and find what wasn't in the file.

"Felix, how long until our batteries are charged enough to get to Vesen-1?"

"At the current rate, sixty hours, forty minutes."

Three days was too long.

I ran my finger along the rim of my empty glass, making a squeaking sound, much to Felix's fascination. "How about Ceti?"

"Thirty-four hours, twenty-eight minutes."

"Add another day for travel, and we're looking at fifty-eight hours."

"Fifty-six hours, nine minutes. Approximately."

I leaned back and folded my arms across my chest. It was a shit plan. I knew a man in Ceti. An opportunistic, pompous, crazy, would-sell-his-own-mother-for-the-right-price kind of man.

But one who happened to owe me a favor. He might be willing to help for the right price.

Felix's blue eye—the one with his optical scanner—made a soft whirling noise as it zoomed in and out of focus on my glass. His paw darted out with a quick tap, tap, tap and the glass crashed to the floor.

"Dang it, Felix! That was my favorite glass."

Chapter 5

Four days later, I landed the *Soteria* at the spacedock on Ceti, one of twenty-three moons around Nephali-4 and a popular travel destination. My sinnafuel was down to eight percent, and the batteries were near drained. I docked in Gate K on the opposite end from my usual hangar in the business section and transferred payment for an express refueling and charge. If things didn't go well, I wanted to be prepared for a quick exit.

"Felix, transfer data on completed searches for RMZ Inc. and KaLo Research to a blank data dot. Also, include a copy of the scan from Jarrett's apartment and the recordings made immediately after."

"Completed." He jumped down and stretched, head down and mechanical butt in the air, then reversed. I asked him why he did that once, and he'd said it kept his nuts from seizing. Whatever that meant.

A tray slid out from below my main screen. I removed the pea-sized device and placed it in a travel case beside a copy of the data dot I found in Jarrett's shoe. The original was in a hidden compartment in the ceiling of the cargo panel, accessible only by turning off the artificial gravity while in space and floating up to it.

"Now calculate jump coordinates to Valla for every hour for the next two weeks. Store location marks with Level 5 security protocols. Don't make them too hard to find."

"The recommended security protocols are Level 3 or stronger."

"Acknowledged. Proceed with Level 5. We're not actually going to Valla, but I want anyone looking at your logs to think we are."

"Where are we going?"

"Sorry, buddy, I can't tell you. Anything stored in your memory banks is retrievable."

He circled back around to sit at my feet. He stared up at me, unblinking. "Reliance, why would someone be pawing through my memory banks? Are you leaving me?"

"For a few days. You're too easy to track."

Static buzzed from his speaker, which I interpreted as his version of a human *humph*. "I was built for stealth."

"You were built for economy class private transport."

He stood, whipping his tail side to side. "If you're going to be gone, I'll run the scrubbing bots on the outer hull. We picked up some space dust going through the asteroid belt around Beta Rahn. I may not be *stealthy,* but I can at least be clean."

With that, he clomped off down the hall, his feet clanging against the metal floor loudly.

"Hey." He swiveled his head to look at me over his shoulder. "Before you go, delete the last five minutes from your logs. That's an order."

Felix's bicolored eyes flickered, and then he continued on to the lower level.

Fuck me.

I'd already packed my bag with a clean shirt and pair of underwear, a jacket, my cosmetics bag, a mini first-aid kit with extra migraine tabs, five meal bars, a reusable water pouch, and my pitiful stash of emergency legal tender. Everything a girl on the run could need. I added the container of data dots and exited the *Soteria*.

Tourists clogged the walkways, unloading travel cases and looking confused until their cuffs' holographic maps linked to Ceti's network and showed them which way to go. A boy about nine or ten let out an excited squeal as he jumped a full meter straight up and descended at three-quarter speed. One of his mothers patiently took him by the hand and steered him out of the main walkway.

Weak gravity made Ceti a popular vacation spot, especially for adrenaline junkies. People came from all over the sector to go rock climbing or skydiving. I'd heard sunset parachuting at the edge of the lava fields in the southern hemisphere was an experience you never forgot. And, of course, there were the casinos.

Once I broke free of the crowd, I took a circuitous route to the Gaming District a klick and a half away. My strides were slow but long, eating up the ground with minimal effort. I settled into an easy gait that let me pass other pedestrians, but not so much as to draw attention to myself.

Even with the sun high overhead, the golden planet Nephali-4 shone brightly in the sky. It was a gas giant, with four thin ice rings and octagonal storm clouds on either pole. I'd seen holos of Saturn from the Sol System that looked similar, although none of its moons were terraformed because of their temperature. I guessed the season to be late summer, but being so near the equator made it difficult to tell. Within minutes, my leather jacket grew too warm to wear and a sheen of sweat coated my lower back and arms.

The industrial area around the spacedock gave way to a smattering of low-rent apartment buildings and small businesses. Ahead, one-hundred-story luxury casinos created a jagged skyline that slowly consumed the sky as I drew closer. Foot traffic also picked up, and I was soon bumping elbows with tourists and locals alike, probably out looking to grab a midday bite. Ceti was known for its cuisine, which it imported from all over the sector. Chefs dreamed of opening restaurants in one of the casinos, but even the dinged-up hovercarts on the street corners offered mouth-watering options.

Although I didn't spot anyone following me, it was impossible to ignore the constant prickling sensation at the back of my neck. I was probably being paranoid, but the feeling propelled me past the hovercarts and the tempting smells emanating from them. I turned onto a quieter side street and the unease dissipated.

Five minutes later, I pushed open the lead-barred door at Sedwaro's Treasure and Trade. The smell of other people's homes hit me immediately. Shelves of antiques, secondhand goods, liquidated resale products, and homemade crafts assaulted my eyes. Pottery, dishware, chairs, lamps, knickknacks, used clothes, artwork, old toys, baskets, and tools. Every shape, color, and texture imaginable crammed next to each other until they bled into a homologous blob of stuff.

"Rel!" exclaimed the short, wiry man in a tomato-red suit. "How good to see you!"

"Hey, Seddy."

Sedwaro hurried around the end of the plastiglass counter to greet me, ringed fingers clasping one of my hands and pumping furiously. "You're stunning, as always."

"It's good to see you, too. How's Jonathan?"

"Ah"—he waved a hand—"you know. The restaurant keeps him busy, too busy. He asks about you."

I laughed. "Tell him I said hello."

"Are you on Ceti long? Should I send him a comm and have him reserve a table for the three of us?"

"Afraid not. I was hoping we could talk privately if you have a minute."

"Of course, of course. But first, tell me—and be honest—do you like my new hat?" He tweaked the short edge of a bright-orange felted cap. The band was a paisley print that echoed his red suit. "It's called a stingy brim. Isn't that marvelous? A stingy brim."

Seddy's hair had taken a permanent vacation a decade or two ago. His hat collection could fill my entire bedroom on the *Soteria*, and maybe the copilot's room, too.

"It suits you. Better than that beefboy hat you wore last time."

He looked puzzled for a moment, then laughed. It was high, nasal, and ended in a snort. "You must mean my *cow*boy hat. Never fear, I sold that little beauty for quite. a. profit." The last three words he punctuated with a jaunty jab of his finger. "Now then, what brings you to my humble shop? Did you bring some more of that fine Clava whisky to trade?"

"That was for you to drink. You don't have a liquor license to sell it."

He winked. "For decorative purposes only, of course."

"Of course."

"Is everything all right with the *Soteria*?"

Seddy sold me my ship last year. I still owed him a hefty sum on it, even though I made steady payments. "She's good. The avatar's personality could use some tweaking."

He chuckled and placed a hand on my lower back to guide me down a narrow aisle. "You know it uses adaptive learning technology, right? It emulates its personality after the crew."

"In that case, I'm screwed."

At the back sat a tiled bistro table nestled among a few other large furniture pieces and a rack of coats more popular when my grandparents were young. Seddy fussed about pouring two steaming cups of raspberry tea. I declined his offer of milk but added two lumps of beet sugar to my cup. When he finished, he settled into the seat across from mine.

"So what brings you to my shop? Looking for some jewelry? Or something to make your ship feel like home? I just picked up a set of rugs from Earth, handwoven by little old ladies on a mountaintop. One hundred percent organic wool and dyes. Come, let me show you."

He started to rise, but I placed my hand on top of his to stop him. "I'm sure they're lovely, Seddy, but I can't purchase anything today."

"Oh? Is this a social call, then?"

The fuchsia liquid sloshed in my cup, and I set the cup down before it spilled. "I need credits, fast. I'm here to pawn the *Soteria*." Even saying the words hurt. "She's a quarter paid off. Give me five hundred thousand credits and hold her for a month. If I don't come back, you can resell her. She's worth three million easy."

Seddy removed his stingy brim hat and fiddled with the band before putting it back on. "This is a big ask. You haven't finished paying me for the initial sale. It's bad business."

"It's an excellent investment," I pressed. "The ship is already here and docked. You don't have to store it on site. You don't even have to move it. Plus, I'll pay you five percent interest. It's easy money."

He scoffed and pushed his cup to the side. "Even if I wanted to help you—and I do—I don't keep that many credits on hand. The best I can do is three hundred thousand at fifteen percent."

"Fifteen is extortion."

"Eh." Sedwaro shrugged his thick shoulders. "I am not the one who needs the credits."

"You owe me, or have you forgotten about that little run-in you had on Brione-5? If it weren't for me, you'd be pouring that tea with a bionic hand after Greggar caught you cheating at his mah-jongg tables. Four hundred fifty thousand at eight percent," I countered.

"Four hundred, ten percent. I shouldn't even do that but, you are correct, and I am particularly fond of my right hand."

I pretended to mull over his offer. The truth was, I didn't have anywhere else to go, so the old man had me over a barrel. All ships carried identifying transponders that were simple to track. Every planet or moon I landed on would have a record of my activity. It wouldn't take long for Agent Grayson Wright to find me. My best bet was to ditch the *Soteria* and rely on public transportation.

"Throw in a new cuff, one programmed with a false identity chip, and we have a deal."

"No, no. That is out of the question." He waved both hands emphatically. "Selling such a cuff is illegal. I am a reputable businessman."

I noticed he never said he didn't sell them, only that it was illegal to do so. "Cut the crap, Seddy. We both know you run a strong side hustle. Why do you think I'm here?"

Sedwaro's eyes narrowed suspiciously. "You're sure you're not still with Criminal Affairs? I'd hate to think you would deal dishonestly with me when I'm only trying to help a friend in need."

"Seddy, right now DECA wouldn't register a complaint from me if I told them the Butcher of Bellarouxdonda was asleep on my couch."

He sat back. "That bad? All right, all right, we have a deal. Sedwaro"—he flourished his hand in an exaggerated fashion—"honors his debts."

I couldn't help but laugh, and Sedwaro joined in.

He patted my hand and stood up. "Let me poke around in the back. I think I have just what you need."

"Thank you," I said, as he retreated to the back storage room.

I heard something large scrape across the floor, the pop of a touch-latch door opening, and then the telltale chime of a retina scanner accepting authentication. Sedwaro returned with a low-end nerve impulse cuff coated in a glittery, bubblegum-pink polymer case.

"Shit, did you steal this from a kid?"

He waved his hands dismissively. "Kids lose their cuffs all the time. Why parents keep shelling out good credits for them is a mystery."

I picked it up gingerly between two fingers. It had rainbow-furred kittens on it that sparkled in the muted light of the shop. "What kind of profile is on it? I can't pass for a seven-year-old."

"You worry too much. The DNA identifier has been wiped clean. The profile is set to a twenty-five-year-old woman, brown hair, slender build. Pull your sleeve down and no one will notice." He gave me an appraising look. "But maybe don't let anyone get too close."

I fought the urge to futz with my hair. Okay, so I was having a rough beauty week. *Things had happened.* Did everyone have to keep rubbing it in?

"Fine, if this is all you've got. Transfer the credits to the new cuff, but I need two thousand in legal tender." Interplanetary transports required electronic payment, but once on a planet, I should be able to get by using hard currency. The more I could stay off the network, the better.

"One thousand LTs is all I have on hand. I made several large purchases this morning before you arrived. If I had known . . ." The tone of his voice convinced me of his sincerity.

"Then one thousand will have to do."

For my end of the bargain, I tapped my cuff and projected a holographic screen. It took me a minute to unlock the security protocols to access the original loan documents, title, and registration verification that I'd organized while waiting for the *Soteria's* batteries to charge. Seddy politely turned his back while my financial information displayed on the glowing screen. Having my cuff linked to a ship's computer meant its graphics were better than average, but there was no getting around the lack of privacy with a holoscreen.

Once I accessed the relevant screen, Seddy confirmed they were the correct documents and accepted the transfer. He used his own screen to call up his banking program while I feigned interest in a display of creepy porcelain doll figurines. With a few flicks of his wrist, he transferred three hundred ninety-nine thousand credits to the black-market cuff. Then he pulled a hideous brass vase from a shelf, rummaged inside, and pulled out a stack of LTs. This poor, humble merchant act certainly made for great business.

"Our deal will be complete when the next payment is due," he said. "If you are not here with my credits, I will resell the *Soteria*. Agreed?"

"Agreed, and I consider your debt to me repaid."

"Where will you go?" he inquired.

"To Valla." I named a moon in the next system over that enjoyed a rather disreputable reputation.

He looked as if he were rethinking the deal, but he patted my shoulder as I stood. "Then I wish you luck."

I hated lying to Sedwaro, but eventually Wright would track the *Soteria* here. If I had any hope of finding Jarrett's killers before he caught up to me, then I needed to set down layers of disinformation to throw him off my trail. In my early days as an officer, I'd tracked many suspects to Valla who intended to disappear into the crowd. It was a believable destination for my next stop.

We shook hands, and I exited Sedwaro's Treasure and Trade through the front door. I retraced my path back to the main road that ran between the Gaming District and the spacedock. This close to the casinos, surveillance cameras dotted the corner of every building and surveillance drones patrolled the air above.

I window-shopped at a few stores and purchased a bag of miniature apples at the last one, being sure to use my real accounts. It had been a month since I'd eaten fresh fruit, and I savored their sweet, tangy juice as I strolled by several other stores.

Once I felt sure multiple cameras had captured my image, I made my way back to the spacedock. This time, however, I entered at the northern end, where the commercial transport ships docked. Security scanned me for weapons, explosives, flammables, contagious diseases, and contaminates that would be dangerous to interstellar travel. I felt naked without my blaster, but I would never get through the checkpoint with it, so I'd left it on the ship. The woman running the show didn't look up from the miniaturized holovid she was watching, instead relying on the machine to alert her to any problems.

My bag passed by on the belt. I grabbed it, headed over to the ticket console, and purchased a ride on the first flight to Valla—again, using my real account. When Wright found my trail on Ceti, I wanted to give him every sign Valla was my destination. The ship departed in two hours, so I sat on one of the padded benches in the lounge. Subdued amber lighting and soothing music kept nervous fliers calm. There weren't many families. It was mostly singles and young couples, looking like they'd had too much fun and too little success at the tables, and wanted to be left alone to recover in silence. I feigned boredom, closing my eyes and leaning my head back to let the cameras get a clear shot of my face and outfit.

A chime sounded fifteen minutes before boarding. Several people got up, taking one last opportunity to stretch before the long flight. I stood and stretched, then leisurely made my way to the public restroom.

On the way, I passed a man slumped in his chair, deep asleep. In his lap lay a paunchy hat that had been popular a decade ago and was now coming back in style. I bent down as if to speak to him, lifted the hat, and walked away with it tucked between my body and my bag.

Thankfully, the restroom was empty. "Felix," I whispered into my cuff.

"You aren't being pursued again, are you? Should I ready the engine?"

"Ha-ha. Once the sinnafuel tanks are completely full and the batteries are recharged to one hundred percent, lock down the ship. It might be a while before I get back."

"Confirmed. For how long?"

"I don't know, but if it's longer than a month, Seddy will come for you. Don't give him too hard of a time, okay?"

"Reliance?"

"Take care of the ship." I turned on the holoscreen and flicked my finger to navigate to the main control page. From there, I severed the link from the cuff to Felix and the *Soteria* and reset it to factory settings. The delicate electronics crunched beneath the heel of my boot.

It hurt more than I thought it would to throw it in the trash. That ship had been my home for the better part of a year, and Felix my constant companion. Telling myself that I'd be back once I found Jarrett's killers and cleared my name rang hollow, even to my own ears.

Pink wouldn't have been my first choice, but I slid the black-market cuff onto the thickest part of my forearm, powered it up, and set the authenticator to key onto my DNA sequence. It asked for an identifier, and I assigned it the first thing that came to mind: Sparkles. Not the most creative name, but I hoped to not be saddled with the fuchsia monstrosity for long.

Then I got to work on my second quick change of the week.

In my cosmetics bag was a bronzing brush that came with six settings. I cranked it to the highest option and brushed it over my face, neck, and hands to give me a tan like I'd spent the last week having fun in the sun instead of stuck inside a windowless ship. Next were my eyes. Several coats of mascara and thick eyeliner winged at the corners and smudged to make it difficult for the camera to lock onto my nodal points. I selected a bluish-purple hue from the eyeshadow brush and applied it all around my eye sockets to replicate the effects of an all-night bender.

I damped my chestnut-brown hair with water to make it appear darker and sleeker and twisted it into a knot on the top of my head. Combined with the hat, it looked as if I had short hair and a narrower head. To bulk up my frame, I rolled my extra shirt into a rope and laid it across the back of my shoulders. When I added my jacket and popped the collar, it hopefully altered the overall effect enough to fool anyone reviewing the security feeds.

The public transport to Vesen-1 was scheduled to embark twenty minutes later. I paid for my ticket with the new cuff and took my place in line, keeping my head tilted down. When the side hatches opened, everyone rushed in to secure the most desirable seats. It was a twenty-two-hour flight with three stops, cramped seating, and a pervasive smell of unwashed bodies and recycled air.

I found a seat near the center of the ship on the third level, far enough from the restrooms not to be bothered by the foot traffic, but close enough in case of an emergency. It took a lot of power for a ship this size to travel at warp, and the effects on the body were ten times worse than on a little ship like the *Soteria*. Stomachs were typically the first organ to object, followed by the bowels.

The man next to me reclined until his chair was almost flat, strapped in, and started snoring before they'd sealed the doors. It would have been smart to follow his lead, but I was too amped up to sleep.

Finally, everyone onboard was strapped in, and the engines spun up. This far from the mechanical section, it was more of a hum than the roar I was used to. We lifted off, sluggish at first, but quickly picked up speed. My ears popped twice on the way into orbit. There was a brief moment of weightlessness before the anti-grav kicked in, and the sound of six hundred bodies smacking into the back of their seats as the behemoth launched into faster-than-light speed.

A teenage girl rushed to the restroom but didn't make it in time. Like a chain reaction, three more people made use of the motion-sickness bags tucked beneath the seats.

I closed my eyes and focused on my breathing. No alarms had gone off. No security personnel had boarded the public transport vessel. There was no way of knowing if my trail of disinformation and quick change would be enough to fool Agent Wright, but it was the best I could do. All I could do now was move forward with the plan.

In an effort to distract myself, I reclined my seat and counted rivets on the ceiling. My thoughts turned to what I would do once I got to Vesen-1. Cavender's homicide case there was the first instance Jarrett had found of Cavender receiving a payoff. My idea was to reexamine the case and figure out what Cavender had been paid to do. "Follow the money" had proved a solid investigative technique since before the time of space travel. The tricky part would be doing so as a civilian. Before, I'd always had the full resources of DECA at my disposal. Now, I didn't even have Felix or the *Soteria*.

I hoped it was enough.

Chapter 6

Icy wind snatched at my purloined hat and snaked down the back of my neck. The temperature hovered between negative five and negative ten degrees Celsius—too cold for my unlined leather jacket that cut off right below my waistline.

Above me, evenly spaced pinpricks of light peppered the morning sky—an expansive grid of orbital mirrors that reflected light and heat down to the surface. Even though Vesen-1 was the closet planet to its star, it still sat at the outer limits of the Goldilocks range. In addition, its exaggerated elliptical orbit made for short, hot summers and long, cold winters. It had only been terraformed in the last couple of decades as a research station for geothermal energy. I blew on my fingers, deciding the jury was still out on whether the new mirror technology worked.

The first phase of my plan involved a shopping trip. I swiped my hand down my sleeve, making the material transparent, and opened a holoscreen to connect to Púki's planetary net. Sparkles was a full seven generations behind Felix. My aerial scribing felt slow and cumbersome in comparison. Fingers frozen, I called up the site for tourist information.

A semitransparent map projected itself in front of me. Snow flurries shimmered with light as they passed through the holoscreen, making it glitter like electric static. I turned my back to the wind, trying to block the worst of the interference.

After scrolling around the map, I settled on McGillacuddy's, a chain I was familiar with from my days at the Department. A flashing yellow line appeared over the map, showing the fastest walking path. I memorized the street names and then swiped my hand up my sleeve, turning the material opaque again and covering the glittery-pink affront to good fashion.

Another gust of frigid wind caught me unaware. It hurt the skin on my face. I huddled into my jacket, bent my head into the wind, and took off at a determined pace.

The buildings in Púki were short and squat and painted in an array of bright primary colors, like a child's coloring tablet. They lent a bit of cheer to what would otherwise be a drab palette of black rock, gray sky, and white snow.

By the time I got to the store, my nose was runny, and the apples of my cheeks felt raw. The automatic door closed behind me as I basked in the sudden warmth of being inside. The early settlers had tapped into the geothermal activity of the volcanic planet, providing a cheap, if somewhat sulphuric-smelling source of heat and energy. As a result—and perhaps in sheer retaliation of the bitter cold—Vesians cranked up the heat and left it there.

I stomped my feet to clear my boots of snow and attempted to wipe them dry on the doormat. McGillacuddy's catered to military, law enforcement, and private security personnel. Some items—such as weapons or blaster-resistant armor plating—required you to show your government ID to purchase them, but many were available to anyone off the street.

I beelined for the law enforcement section, leaving a trail of wet footprints. The selection was small, but weather appropriate and specific to the local DECA office's dress code. I picked out a black shirt, gloves, cap, and green jacket with DECA written across the back. It wasn't a part of the standard-issue uniform but a layering piece an officer might add as a supplement using her own funds—particularly if she worked on the night shift when the temperatures often dropped below freezing. My black cargo pants and boots matched the standard-issue ones closely enough that I decided they would do. Besides, unless I was a rookie, walking in wearing all new clothing would be an instant red flag.

I held up Sparkles to the store's automatic payment scanner and held my breath while the funds cleared from the dummy account. It beeped, signaling a completed transaction. Say what you will about the man, but Seddy's merchandise was top-notch.

There was a fitting room in the back, where I changed into the new clothes. I twisted my brown hair into a low bun that sat beneath the band of the corp-style cap. Heavy makeup was often against regulation, so I wiped my face clean using the inside of my dirty shirt. At a quick glance, I'd pass for a DECA agent, but it wouldn't hold up under scrutiny.

The warmer jacket and gloves made the cold bearable. Near the city center, I found a public transport depot with lockers I could key to my cuff and access any time of day. I paid for a day's worth of time and cached my messenger bag inside.

Phase Two would be more difficult. I knew from the case file that the medical examiner who performed Zairesh's autopsy was Doctor Lora Miller. She worked at the city morgue, located a few blocks away in the precinct's basement. My plan was to pose as an internal investigations officer, reviewing old cases as part of a routine performance review for Cavender's former partner, Officer Gigi Okeke. They worked the Zairesh case together. I wanted to discover if there was anything unusual about the case to point me in a better direction.

Across the galaxy, coffee shops and precincts enjoyed a symbiotic relationship, and this one was no different. I ducked inside and ordered two large artificial coffees and a box of pastries. Balancing the cups on top of the bright-pink box, I stepped back outside to wait in the cold.

It took ten freezing minutes to pick out my mark. A young officer, still all shiny and full of unbridled enthusiasm, hustled from the covered LAV parking area toward the front doors. I timed my pace to put me a few steps behind him as he reached the entrance. The door buzzed open in response to the code embedded in his cuff.

"Hold the door!" I called out, panting and acting flustered. I made a show of juggling the pastry box from one hand to the other, almost spilling hot coffee down the front of his freshly pressed uniform.

He caught the cup before it toppled off the box. "Got it!"

I crowded into his personal space, social norms dictating he keep moving to create room between us. He stepped into the building and held the door open with one hand high above my head. I spun underneath his arm, "accidentally" brushing my derriere against the front of his pants.

"Ugh, thank you! That was almost a disaster." I held the second cup up and used my pinkie to lift the lid on the box. "Want one? I bought extra."

His pupils dilated at the selection. "Oh, no, ma'am. That's unnecessary."

"Go on. Take one," I prompted.

The young officer didn't need more encouragement. "Well, if you insist." He selected a sugar-crusted donut filled with a mix of dark purple hellaberries and bright lemon curd. He handed me back the coffee and took a bite. "Mmm, thith ith delitheth. Thankth."

He was still chomping away when I excused myself to "get to my meeting." As soon as I was out of his sight, I set the box and one of the cups onto a table beside the lift. The other coffee I held onto as a prop for the overworked, underpaid officer I was about to portray.

Precincts followed similar layouts from city to city and even from planet to planet. Morgues were in the basement. Out of sight, out of mind and where no one would stumble into one by accident. Because . . . dead people.

I got into the lift.

"Floor, please," said the automated voice. It was programmed with a Ritruvian accent, which made me smile. I always found it a bit on the sexy side, as far as accents went. It reminded me of Jarrett. And Agent Wright. My smile evaporated. Just because two men grew up on the same planet didn't mean they were anything alike. Even if they sounded similar and both chose to go into law enforcement. Wright was not my friend.

"Lowest level," I said, regretting that I hadn't snagged a donut before abandoning the box. It had been a hot minute since I'd eaten.

The lift descended, then stopped. As the door whooshed open, the pungent smell of antiseptic hit me hard. I exited into a poorly lit hallway with bare walls.

I activated my holoscreen, opened a program for aerial scribing notes, and entered the basic facts of the case along with some official-sounding gibberish. Then I minimized it for later. I didn't want the medical examiner thinking this was my first stop.

The basement level appeared to be organized in a neat grid fashion. I wandered down several hallways that led to equipment rooms, evidence lockers, and storage facilities before finding the morgue at the end of a long corridor. Thankfully, there was a front office area, and I didn't have to go into the actual exam room, because one dead body was my quota for the week.

"Hello?" I called out.

A woman wearing a light-blue lab coat came through a back door. She was tall, with an athletic build and gray hair threaded through tight, black curls. Blue-rimmed fashion spectacles perched at the end of her nose. She peered over them and gave me an assessing look. "May I help you?"

"I'm looking for a Doctor Lora Miller."

"Well, you found her."

"Do you mind if I ask you a few questions? I'm doing a performance review on Officer Gigi Okeke and reviewing a few of her cases to make sure she dotted all the i's and crossed all the t's. She's up for a promotion."

Doctor Miller furrowed her brows. "I only know Officer Okeke in passing. Not sure what I can tell you, but you can ask."

I blew on my coffee and took a sip before projecting my screen with the fake form. "Officer Okeke was assigned to Case Number 856035-B. An adult female by the name of Kelthea Zairesh found DOA. You're listed as the medical examiner. It says the cause of death was 'complications from recent surgery.' Can you elaborate?"

The doctor leaned back against a stool and folded her arms across her chest. "Zairesh. Let me think. Was this about three years ago?"

"Yes. Do you remember the case?"

"Mm-hmm. I had to perform a brain dissection to determine the COD."

"Is that unusual?"

"Around here? I'd say so. Most homicides are pretty straight-forward: blunt force trauma, blaster burns, an occasional stabbing. Zairesh had no outward signs of trauma. She was young and healthy. It took me a while to figure it out."

"What was your conclusion?" I asked, taking another sip of coffee.

"It isn't in the report? I wrote a whole supplemental on it."

I made a show of flicking through my fake form. "No, I'm not seeing it. Maybe it got misfiled?"

Doctor Miller sighed. "Wouldn't be the first time. Zairesh had a medical device surgically implanted at the top of her brain stem." She pointed to the back of her head. "The surrounding tissue be-came infected, and her body rejected the device."

"Did you run additional tests?"

"No," Doctor Miller said. "That's the other unusual part. The lead agent closed the case soon after I gave him my preliminary findings. He said the family requested cremation as soon as possible for religious reasons. The cause of death was obvious, so I saw no reason to object."

"You're sure it was the lead agent who ordered the cremation?"

"Yes."

"Would that have been Hal Cavender, Officer Okeke's partner at the time?"

"Yes, that's right."

"Thank you. Do you remember the name of the surgeon who operated on Ms. Zairesh?"

"No, but it might be in my notes."

"Would you mind looking?"

Doctor Miller linked to the wall console behind her. She navi-gated to the precinct's database. When she tried to open the file, it prompted her for her credentials. She aerial scribed them in and the file opened. She adjusted her glasses and read through the text.

"The surgeon's name was Doctor Lourde from Brione-2." She paused, then swiveled on the stool to face me. "I'm sorry. How is this relevant to Officer Okeke's performance review?"

"The case was closed with only a preliminary investigation. I want to make sure a thorough job was done."

"Mm-hmm. What did you say your name was again? Officer . . .?"

And that was my cue to leave. "You know, you're right. I'm sure I have all I need to complete Officer Okeke's review. Everything looks to be in order."

I tapped off my screen and turned toward the door.

"Hold on. Show me your ID."

No way was I stopping. I made it all the way to the door before I heard her call security. Then I dropped my coffee and ran.

The polished regolith tiles were slick beneath my feet. I sprinted full-out, knowing I needed to reach the lift before they started a lockdown procedure. Overhead, emergency lighting flashed in time with an alarm. I hit the first intersection and spotted two security officers on their way to the morgue. They saw me, shared a glance, and broke into a run.

Skidding around the corner, I retraced my path to the lift. My breaths came in quick, short bursts. Dang, too much time in space had done a number on my lungs. Behind me, heavy boots pounded. The officers yelled at me to stop. I pumped my legs faster, willing the stitch in my side to go away.

I took a left and quickly realized I'd made a wrong turn. Nothing looked familiar. No choice but to keep going.

One, two, three doors zipped by, but I didn't dare take the time to see if any of them were unlocked. I kicked myself for not identifying multiple exit routes when I had the chance. Rookie mistake.

Camouflage had always been my preferred method of escape. Give me a crowd, and I could disappear in seconds. Swap a dark shirt for a light, a redhead for a brunette, a solitary person for a roman- tic couple—the eye focused on what it wanted to see and ignored everything else. Down here, though, in the cold, sterile basement of the precinct, there was nothing to blend in with. There was nothing but white walls and gray floor tiles.

I stole a glance behind me. The male officer must have peeled away to cut me off at a junction. His partner, however, had her blaster drawn and was gaining on me. I weaved left and right, trying to keep my pattern random to make aiming at me more difficult. She squeezed off a shot and a section of the wall in front of me exploded with a pop of electricity and the smell of ozone.

At the end of the hall, I took a sharp right and gambled on the first door I saw. It swung open and the automatic lights clicked on.

"Lights off!" I hissed. The room plunged into darkness, and I eased the door shut without a sound.

I crouched by the wall, straining to hear my pursuer over the thudding of my heart. Footsteps, fast and light, raced past the door. Good. That bought me a minute. If she'd go around the next corner or into another room, I could slip out and double back to the lift.

In seconds, my eyes adjusted to the dark. The only sliver of light came from the crack beneath the door. I was too far below ground for there to be any windows, but I looked around, hoping for a second exit. No such luck.

The room was smaller than the bridge of the *Soteria*. Shelves lined the walls on either side, stacked with buckets and bottles of cleaning detergents that made my nose scrunch in self-defense. A hospitality bot stood sentry at the far end, charging on its pad. I groaned inwardly. Of all the rooms I might have picked to hide in, I'd chosen a damn supply closet.

I listened carefully for the sound of another door opening. The officer stopped about halfway down the hall, near as I could tell. Silence. Then I caught snippets of a murmured conversation. The male officer must have come from the other direction. They would know I had to be in one of the rooms along the hallway. It was only a matter of searching each one until they found me.

I scanned the shelves for inspiration. There were disinfectants and other harsh chemicals that could blind them, but I didn't want to injure the officers, just get away.

Down the corridor, a door slammed open. Scuffling sounds as they cleared the room.

My thoughts raced, debating if I should make a run for it. One officer probably waited in the hallway. They would have opened the door and stepped back to let their partner enter. Standard operating procedure. The second officer would've rushed in, blaster drawn, looking for any excuse to pull the trigger.

The woman shouted something I couldn't decipher.

Indecision rooted my feet to the ground. The door to the adjacent room banged against our shared wall. I jumped and sucked back a gasp. There was nowhere to go. I counted to five in my head. Visualized them sweeping the space, finding nothing.

"Clear," the man said.

Shadows caused the light under my door to flicker. I faced the door and raised both of my hands high in the air.

Right on cue, the door burst open, flooding the storage room with blinding light. The female officer swept her gun muzzle left to right before settling on me.

"Hi," I said.

"Get your hands up!" Her hands shook with adrenaline from the chase and repeated room clearings.

"They are up." I wiggled my fingers.

"Don't move!" The officer's voice ratcheted up until she was practically screaming. My guess was they didn't get much action down here in the lower level and this was her first foot pursuit in a long time. "Down on your knees!"

"Which is it? Don't move, or get down on my knees?" I asked.

She jabbed the blaster in a downward motion. Her finger slid into her trigger guard. A soft, high-pitched whine from the weapon indicated a full charge.

Slowly, I lowered myself down to one knee, then two, keeping my hands high.

"Easy now, I'm cooperating."

"I'll cuff her," the male officer said from behind his partner. He placed a hand on her shoulder to squeeze by.

She jerked, startled, and squeezed the trigger in an involuntary motion. I watched as the energy blast slammed into my chest.

Everything went dark.

Chapter 7

I CAME TO WITH a splitting headache in some kind of window-less break room. There was a banged-up table, six chairs, and a counter with a machine that brewed artificial coffee and . . . was that my box of donuts?

Restraints bit into my wrists where they were secured together behind a chair. My chest felt like it'd been kicked by a mule. Damn blaster packed a heck of a punch. Thankfully, it had been set to stun, or I wouldn't have woken up at all.

The male officer stood with his back to me, aerial scribing into a wall-mounted console. His hair was a natural orangish-red—a rarity these days—cut regulation short. He had a ruddy complexion with a heavy speckling of freckles covering his neck and hands.

I shifted to ease the cramped muscles in my lower back. He turned at the sound.

"Good, you're awake. I don't suppose you want to make this easy and give me your name?"

Not likely. "I am Empress Poppycock of the planet Balder-dash, at your service." I leaned as far forward in the chair as the cuffs allowed in a mocking bow.

"Ma'am, this is serious. You're being charged with trespassing, impersonating a DECA officer, and resisting arrest. Care to try again?"

"Hmm, would you believe I was the long-lost daughter of Delma Sterling?"

Red's eyebrows dipped, making little furrows appear between them. "The holovid actor? Sister, maybe. If she has a daughter your age, I'll eat my boot."

Everyone was a critic.

Red stomped over to my chair and ripped off my cap. He held his cuff a handspan from my face. "Tiki, scan for facial recognition."

A narrow beam of light passed over my face. "Scan complete."

Red marched backed to the console and initiated a data transfer. "My partner bet me five credits you're already in the system. She's upstairs getting a head start on processing right now."

With his back turned, I twisted my head to the side and rubbed the nape of my neck against the coarse material of my jacket. The bun unraveled, letting my hair fall past my shoulders. I arched my spine and strained my head back as far as it would go. My fingers combed through the ends until they felt something hard—a hairpin I'd used to secure the bun.

Working quickly, I bent the pin straight and added a forty-five-degree angle to the end and broke two of my nails in the process. It was awkward maneuvering the makeshift pick into place with my hands behind my back, but through trial and error, I found the lock on the left restraint and inserted the bent end. Luckily, these were basic restraints that officers kept on them as part of their standard kit. The thin metal rings were inexpensive, lightweight, and easy to carry, but they were only meant to be used temporarily. If he'd bothered to switch to augmented restraints—as protocol dictated—I wouldn't have had a chance at picking them.

Across the room, the console chugged away at the facial recognition program. It started with the local database and would move on to the interplanetary sources after that. Since this was my first time on Vesen-1, my image shouldn't be in their system.

Wiggling the pick around, I felt the thin metal plate of the internal latching mechanism. I slid the tip under and levered it up. It clicked softly. Pressure eased around my left wrist as the ring split open. Careful not to make too much noise, I wiggled my hand free. I caught the loose end of the restraint in my right hand so the metal wouldn't rattle.

"No matches found," reported the console.

Red swore. "Tiki, expand search to interplanetary databases."

"Searching."

I lunged from my chair. Three long strides and I was across the room. Red heard me, his face swiveling toward me in surprise. It had been a rookie mistake not to use the augmented restraints and even bigger one not to search me for weapons or tools. He paid for that now.

On the next step, I leaped, launching myself onto Red's back. My legs wrapped around his waist, ankles locked on each other to keep him from bucking me off. I wedged the inner crook of my elbow under his chin and grabbed my opposite bicep in a rear chokehold.

Red sputtered as I increased the pressure. His attempted call for help came out as a gurgled gasp of air. He grabbed my arm and pulled, trying to break my hold.

I gritted my teeth and beared down. Time was on my side.

When clawing at my arm didn't loosen my grip, Red shifted tactics. He threw himself backward and rammed me into the wall.

It knocked the breath from my lungs. I fought against my instinct to let go and continued to squeeze his carotid. He lurched forward, doubling at the waist, then flung himself backward again. This time, I thought I felt something crack when I hit the wall. A rib? It felt like a rib.

"Come on, big guy." I grunted and leveraged my open hand to the top of his head to increase the pressure. I couldn't see his face, but I imagined it had to be a dark shade of pink by now.

Red's knees wobbled. His muscles slackened, and I knew he had passed out before we collapsed to the floor.

I rolled off and checked his pulse. Satisfied he was still alive, I tapped his cuff. "Tiki, turn off power save mode. Stay active until further notice."

"Acknowledged."

I removed the neural impulse cuff from his arm and tucked it into my pocket. Then I searched his pockets and utility belt, removing anything that could be useful and chucking them out of reach. The restraint key in his front pocket unlocked the remaining bracelet on my wrist. I cuffed Red's hands behind his back and around the leg of the heavy six-person dining table. He could get out, but he'd have to work for it.

"Search complete," the wall-mounted console reported. "Positive match to Captain Reliance Sinclair. Wanted on an interplanetary warrant for homicide, fleeing the scene of a crime, tampering with government equipment, and resisting arrest. Considered armed and dangerous. Approach with extreme caution. Notification sent to Lead Agent Grayson Wright of Salin, Andaress-4."

So, Wright knew I was on Vesen-1. Fan-freaking-tastic. My disinformation trail would be pointless now and getting off-planet would be trickier this time.

I sighed. One problem at a time.

Two holos of me popped up on the display. The one on the left was taken from a surveillance drone just outside Jarrett's apartment. I looked shady as hell. Next to it was one taken two years ago after a grueling day of physical trials when they'd promoted me from officer to agent. My hair was sweaty and plastered to my face, I had a split lip from sparring, and exhaustion left matching pale-blue saddlebags beneath my eyes.

"Really?" I said to Red's unconscious body. "Did Wright intentionally pick the two worst holos of me out there? I mean, what about a little professional courtesy? Jerk."

Red didn't respond, which was probably a wise decision on his part. After I figured out who killed Jarrett, I was going to treat myself to a spa day. Clearly, I was overdue.

Moving on. I'd blown my cover as a DECA officer. I needed a new disguise and scoured the room for inspiration. It didn't offer much. Red hadn't taken me to a holding cell or even an interrogation room. He probably didn't want to carry me across the entire building.

I rummaged under the counter and pulled together a box of kitchen supplies. In all my time doing undercover work, I'd never posed as hospitality staff. It wasn't my most creative idea, but it would have to do.

My new jacket and cap had DECA emblazoned on them, so they got tossed in the reclamator where they would be broken down into their base elements and stored for recycling. I untucked the bottom of my black shirt to give myself a more casual, rumpled vibe and scrunched up the sleeves far enough that Sparkles was on full display. No self-respecting agent would be caught dead with a glitter-infused pink kitty cuff. Then I retied the laces of my boots so that the laces hung loose and pulled my pant legs over the tops to make them appear more like shoes. I flipped my head upside down and finger-combed my hair to add volume. When I righted myself, it fell into a deep side-part, partially obscuring my face.

I used Red's cuff to unlock the secured door, picked up the box of kitchen supplies and a donut, and scurried out into the hall like I was behind on my duties. Since Red and his partner had apprehended me, the alarm had been silenced. I kept my head down and shoulders hunched—traits often exhibited by much of the younger support staff around the sometimes-brash and egotistical officers.

A man wearing a lab tech shirt nodded to me as we passed. "Are there any donuts left?"

"Sorry," I said, holding up my chocolate-glazed confection. "Last one."

"Damn. Too late, again."

"Better luck next time."

He kept walking down the hall, and I didn't encounter anyone else and got into the first lift I found.

"Floor, please," the automated voice asked.

"Main level."

The platform rose silently while I polished off the donut. It came to a halt, and the door slid open to reveal an atrium. Natural light spilled from a three-story wall of windows into an indoor garden. Plants and trees were artfully arranged around a central fountain.

This wasn't a typical precinct design, but I surmised the addition of indoor green space was due to the long, harsh winters of this planet.

I cut through the center of the atrium, following a winding path dotted with rowan and apple trees. An older man with captain bars on his uniform sat on a bench eating his lunch. He nodded as I walked by. I gave him a weak smile and doubled my pace.

At the end of the path, I spotted an exterior plastiglass door. I dumped the box of kitchen supplies on the nearest bench. Sweat beaded on my forehead. Instinct urged me to make a break for it, but I reined it in with a firm hand.

Twenty paces from the door, an alert went out to every cuff linked to the building's network, including Red's. All around the atrium, pale-blue projection screens blinked on.

I lifted Red's cuff. A three-dimensional image of my face appeared. It was from the scan Red had taken a few minutes earlier. Beside the image in big, bold text were the words BE ON THE LOOKOUT. Excellent. My very first BOLO.

Tiki interrupted my internal eye roll. "Building lockdown initiated."

"Shit," I swore and sprinted for the door. The lock engaged right as I slammed into the opaqued plastiglass. Flashing Red's cuff to the reader had no effect. I tossed it aside and looked around for options.

One bench had pots of rosemary and lavender arranged on either side. I grabbed the nearest one and hurled it at the door. The plastiglass shattered, triggering a screeching alarm. Wasting no time, I stepped through the hole and into the frigid air.

Voices from inside grew louder as officers zeroed in on the broken door. I didn't hang around for them to arrive.

The sun had come out, making the brightly painted buildings pop in the snow like sprinkles on a birthday cake. I melted into pedestrian traffic, zigzagging down several blocks, and then offered to hold the door for an elderly lady as she shuffled through the secure entrance of her lemon-colored apartment building. She thanked me and thought nothing of my stepping in behind her.

On the top floor, I found a gathering area for residents with multiple tables, couches, and a holovid projection area that was almost life-sized. I cleaned up in the restroom. There wasn't much I could do to change my appearance, but I braided my hair and let the thick brown rope hang over my shoulder. Then I curled up on a couch to wait while the heat died down.

Four hours later, I stood in front of a rickety dresser inside a legal-tender-only motel room. I craved a hot-water shower, but the room only came equipped with a sonic model. Chilled from standing naked in the open air but at least feeling clean, I'd hurried into my spare shirt, socks, and underwear. The dirty ones I scrubbed in the sink and hung to dry.

I'd retrieved my bag from the locker and stopped at an apothecary before selecting a hotel. I pulled my purchases out of my pack and spread them on the dresser.

"Sparkles, mirror, please."

"Here you go!" said the singsong synthetic voice with a feminine tone. I needed to adjust that setting to something less chipper.

A real-time hologram of myself appeared. The graphics weren't as well-rendered as they would have been with Felix, but they'd get the job done. I combed my damp hair straight and parted it on the side. Then I sectioned it off into two ponytails that fell well past my shoulders. With shaking hands, I used the scissors to cut a decimeter off each one.

The hologram had a split-second delay, so I watched my real hair fall to the dresser and then the holographic hair follow it into a shimmery pile. Long hair had never been a defining feature for me, so it didn't devastate me to cut it. However, I had been wearing it long for the last few years, and its sudden absence was a bit discomforting.

It took another ten minutes, but I shaped the cut into something resembling a chin-length bob.

Next was color. I took out the new stripping wand I'd purchased, poured the chemical solution into the handle, and waited for it to do its thing. When the light turned green, I selected a lank of hair and clamped the wand as close to the roots as I could get. Then I pulled the wand down through to the end, revealing a streak of platinum blond. I repeated the process until my arm wanted to fall off and my head looked like dandelion fluff on a windy day.

For the last step, I opened the packet containing color-additive powder. Purple was trending this season all across the galaxy. Last month, one of my insurance claimants had sported hair in a striking shade of indigo. So striking that I couldn't remember much else about his physical features. I was hoping the color would have the same effect on me.

Now that Agent Wright had confirmation I was on Vesen-1, he wouldn't be reviewing old recordings trying to pick me out of a crowd; he could request local officers begin active searching before he arrived. I needed a disguise that could fool sensors and facial recognition software if I wanted to get off the planet.

I sprinkled the purple powder over my white tresses and used my brush to work it through to the ends. The package said I had five minutes to change my mind and rinse it out before it permanently set. Turning my head from side to side, I examined my holographic image. It wasn't half bad. My face appeared more angular with the fresh cut, and the purple complemented my skin tone and brought out the lighter flecks of gold in my otherwise brown eyes. Tomorrow I'd add a dramatic makeup palate and a few other tricks to complete the look. Goodness knows, I'd seen them all in my time at DECA.

Hungry and exhausted, I dug out a nutrient bar and the last handful of miniature apples from my pack, and I sat on the bed to eat. There was no headboard, so I rested against the bare wall and ate. Staring at the wall, I noticed a slight disturbance in my vision.

"Great. That's just what I need. A migraine."

I stuffed the rest of the bar into my mouth and got a migraine tab out of my pack. The medication did wonders, but only if I caught it soon enough. I placed the tab on my tongue to dissolve, not caring for the chalky fake-fruit taste it left behind.

My original plan had been to reexamine Cavender's case, interview witnesses, and find out who would benefit the most by hiring him to sweep the investigation under the rug. There wasn't enough time now with Wright on his way. I needed to be a ghost by the time he got here.

The other two cases in Jarrett's files were both from Clava on Brione-5. Two deaths, three months apart. I'd really hoped to avoid going back there. While I had a few friends, most people were relieved when they discovered my new job as a claims investigator would keep me off-planet. It had been a tidy solution to a messy problem.

"Sparkles, when's the next public transport to Brione-5?"

"That would be tomorrow at 0600 hours Universal Standard Time, Terminal 3. Should I book you a ticket?"

"No, that won't be necessary."

"You got it!" she chirped.

Tomorrow. Tomorrow, I would reprogram the cuff or go insane. I missed Felix's steady voice. I missed my ship and my work. It wasn't much, but it was reliable, and it was mine.

It would be an early morning, but the sooner I got off Vesen-1, the better. In the meantime, I needed to lie low and keep my face and new disguise off the net.

The migraine tab hadn't kicked in yet, so I turned off the lights and practiced one of my visualization exercises to manage the pain. In my mind, I packed the pain into cargo boxes and loaded them on a ship. Then I launched the ship into orbit and charted a course straight into a burning star.

A combination of exhaustion and medication overtook me, and I fell asleep before the ship burned to a fiery crisp.

Chapter 8

Sleep came in fits and spurts. In the morning, dark circles ringed my eyes, but it didn't matter. My hair wasn't the only thing getting a makeover.

By now, every officer in Púki would have a copy of Red's scan from the precinct. Indigo hair might fool the human eye, but it would be useless against a camera. I'd gotten away with it on Ceti because local law enforcement hadn't been actively looking for me. That wasn't the case now.

My biggest hurdle would be slipping past the facial recognition programs at the spacedock. They worked by identifying key facial features from a scan and matching them against live feeds. As soon as they got a hit, the closest officers would be dispatched to apprehend me.

Therefore, the next step was to camouflage my real features. I went for a more heart-shaped face, using contouring to give myself the appearance of a wider forehead, thinner nose, and pointier chin. The bob would enhance that silhouette. Selecting Void Black on my eye color brush, I drew a thick, rectangular bar across my eyes from hairline to hairline and added a row of artistic dots across the top. Color-blocking makeup wasn't exactly trendy, but some people in the counterculture sphere wore it. The dark band would make my eye spacing and brow bones difficult for the computer to pick out.

My lips tended toward the thin side, so when I picked up the hair color, I also picked up a collagen booster. I pressed the pad against the center of my lower lip and flinched when the tiny needles jabbed into my skin. I kept the injections focused on the middle of my lips to create a round, pouty shape. Then I stained the centers an iridescent shade of Hellaberry Blue that almost matched the bluish-purple color of my hair.

As a final measure, I took a roll of gauze from the mini first-aid kit and wrapped my knees. I left them loose enough not to hinder my ability to run, but tight enough to alter my gait without my having to think about it. Gait detection could identify me just as quickly as facial recognition. I didn't know if the local office used a gait-analysis program, but it was a possibility. They had plenty of recordings of me walking around the precinct to compare it to.

Unfortunately, my clothing selection was limited to the jacket and two shirts I'd brought with me, and the extra shirt I'd purchased at McGillacuddy's. I looked at the long-sleeved black shirt hanging over the door to the bathroom, then at my scissors. Heaving a sigh, I cut off the bottom decimeter, turning the shirt into a crop top. I tried it on and knotted the loose material in the back so the fabric pulled tight against my skin. Then I cut a few strategic slits across the chest area and rolled the fabric so flashes of skin peeked through. The sleeves I kept long. Paired with my cargo pants and boots, it had an edgy vibe that matched my new hair and makeup.

Disguise complete, I stuffed my meager belongings into my bag and left for the spacedock. By the end of the first block, I desperately missed the warm jacket I'd ditched at the precinct. I opted not to wear my leather jacket, although I seriously reconsidered that two minutes into my walk. If Agent Wright had tracked me to Ceti, he may have recordings of me from there wearing the jacket. While I doubted he was already here, he could have sent the images ahead. Better to make a clean getaway, if I could.

I stumbled into Terminal 3 snot-nosed and shivering fifteen minutes before the flight to Brione-5 was scheduled to depart. The ticket reader accepted payment via Sparkles, and thirty minutes later, we were lifting off. Only then did I allow myself to relax.

Two cramped and smelly days later, we landed at the R. Burns Interplanetary Spacedock in Clava, the capital of Brione-5, and my hometown. I inhaled deeply, taking in the salty sea air, and sneezed. Fall was my favorite season, but the native mountain fireweed kicked up my allergies. On the plus side, it was warm, for which my bare midriff would be eternally thankful. Daytime temperatures would stay around twenty-three degrees Celsius for another month before dipping down to below freezing for the winter.

Brione-5 was a beautiful planet, as close to a mirror of Earth as you could get, with a temperate climate, abundant potable water, and large swaths of arable land for crop production: ideal conditions for terraforming. In fact, food was its primary export. Ten large metropolitan areas already dotted the two continents and more were in the works. The planet didn't enjoy the same prosperity of rare earth-metal-rich Brione-2, but the economy was growing steadily and at a sustainable pace. I'd enjoyed living here and missed it more days than not.

Maybe if I'd left on better terms, coming to Clava would feel like having a home-field advantage. I could talk to my friends at the Department, see what they remembered about the cases, ask them to run background searches. But it had been a spectacular shitshow when I'd left. My boss hadn't fired me, but she might as well have. No one wanted to work with the person who had shot her own partner. They'd made that abundantly clear. My being implicated in yet another murder would only reinforce their opinions. Jarrett was the only one who'd kept in contact, and look where that got him.

I needed to be creative in searching for a connection between the three cases, while avoiding situations that would alert authorities as to my whereabouts. My new disguise would only go so far in hiding me.

Sparkles linked to the city net, and I looked up the contact information for the next of kin to Thomas Rhinehardt, the victim from the second file on Jarrett's data dot. His brother, Sean, lived in downtown Clava. I sent him a communication, requesting to meet in person to talk about Thomas but kept the details vague.

The third case file was for Silar Culpepper. He died three months after Thomas Rhinehardt. Silar's wife, Waverly, still resided at the same address. I sent her a communication and received a reply almost immediately. She was home and could meet with me right away.

I ordered an auto-LAV and gave the computer the address as I climbed in. It lifted off, joining the stream of air traffic heading toward one of the residential sections on the east side of the city. Twenty minutes later, it dropped me off in front of a single-family home in a pleasant neighborhood.

Children's toys littered the path to the front door. Some had grass growing between the parts like no one had played with them in months.

I knocked, and a slim woman in her midthirties answered. "Waverly Culpepper? I'm Reliance Sinclair."

Waverly smiled and held open the door. "Come in. I've been expecting you." She led me through a narrow kitchen to a small but comfortable sitting area. "Can I get you something to drink? Coffee? All I have is artificial, I'm afraid."

"Coffee would be lovely," I said, taking a seat.

Waverly went back to the kitchen and returned with two steaming mugs. "I only have half an hour, then I need to leave for my shift at the clinic."

"You work at the rehab clinic?" I asked. Clava, like all major cities, had its problems with drugs. It was soul-sucking work. Many patients were frequent fliers, and not everyone wanted to be helped. I'd spent a fair amount of time there my first couple of years in the Department.

She nodded. "I had trouble making ends meet after Silar died. My job as a nurse at the hospital doesn't cover everything. I started picking up extra hours at the clinic about a year ago. It helps."

"I'm sorry for your loss. You have children?" I nodded toward the holo sitting on a shelf of Waverly, two boys, a girl, and a man I assumed to be Silar Culpepper.

Waverly tucked a strand of limp, black hair behind her ear and followed my gaze to the holo. A smile ghosted her lips, then disappeared. "Yes. They're with my mother now. She watches them during the week. I don't like them being home alone for so long."

"You have a beautiful family."

She pointed to the image. "We took that the summer before Silar passed. It's one of my favorite holos. He still looked healthy then." She inhaled audibly, straightening her spine and turning her focus back to me—back to the present. "Your message said you wanted to talk about Silar. How did you know him?"

"I didn't, but I'm an insurance claims investigator. I have a few questions regarding the manner of his death." Not a total lie.

"You're from the insurance company?" Skepticism filled her eyes. "You sure don't dress like any of the other insurance people."

"My apologies. The transport company lost my luggage on my flight here." I showed her my claims investigation ID.

Her shoulders lowered, but suspicion still sparked in her eyes. "All right. I thought this was all settled, though."

"Don't worry, this won't affect any payout you've already received. You mentioned Silar was in poor health, but I thought he died in a physical altercation."

Waverly cupped her coffee and stared into the warm, brown liquid as if searching for inspiration. "Silar started getting severe headaches about two years ago. Vision loss and sensitivity to light, that sort of thing. Occasionally, he got a nosebleed. He used to borrow my sleeping mask, and I teased him he looked like one of those old-time superheroes. You know, from the vids they made us watch in historical literature class? The ones that wore skintight bodysuits?"

I nodded, vaguely recalling some hokey 2D vids I saw as a kid.

"Then the tremors started," Waverly continued. "First in his hands, then his arms and legs, until his whole body shook at times. It got so bad our youngest was scared to be in the same room when it happened." Her breath hitched, and she paused, collecting herself. "The doctors didn't know what to make of it. They ran every test they could think of. Experimental stuff, too. It got so bad that Silar couldn't work anymore and had to quit his job. We cashed out our savings, our retirement, got a second mortgage on the house. My parents chipped in, too. Nothing helped."

"That must have been incredibly difficult," I said. "Brione-5 doesn't have the most advanced technology, but our medical facilities have always been good."

"Oh, I don't blame the doctors. They tried. They hadn't seen anything like it before. One of them even contacted a colleague of hers on Brione-2."

"But this disease, or whatever it was, wasn't what killed him?"

"No, well, indirectly perhaps. Silar was mugged on his way home from the hospital. The agent said he'd been struck by something heavy from behind that fractured his skull. He died instantly." Waverly's voice quavered, and I felt like the worst kind of jackass for making her relive her husband's death. "They took his cuff and a few LTs. His wedding band. Nothing worth much. We weren't rich."

I reached over and placed my hand on hers. "I'm so sorry. Did they catch the assailant?" Cavender's last update to the file marked it as a cold case, but that had only been a month after Silar Culpepper's death. Jarrett might have had an old copy.

Waverly wiped a finger under her eye. "The agent said it was a random act of violence, and that those were the hardest to solve. They never even found a suspect. How can that be? Right in front of the hospital like that? I know for a fact they have cameras and security drones doing regular flybys. I see them every day when I go to work. It doesn't make any sense."

"Did Silar have any enemies? Grudges with coworkers, run-ins with a neighbor? Anything like that?" Waverly shook her head. I continued. "Money problems? You said the tests were expensive. Could he have borrowed money from an unlicensed lender?"

"A loan shark? Never." The widow was adamant in her refusal.

"Did anyone suspicious come around after? People claiming to be old acquaintances or wanting to look around the house?"

Waverly arched one eyebrow. "You mean, besides you?"

"Fair point. What about Agent Cavender? Did he ever check in on you?"

"No, and come to think of it, I believe I saw he died about a year ago. It was on all the local news vids." Waverly's eyes widened. "Do you think that's why they never found the person who murdered Silar?"

We were getting into uncomfortable territory. I didn't want Waverly searching old news stories after I left, because my name would be all over them. That was one homicide that didn't need investigating.

"The Department should have transferred all of Officer Cavender's open cases to another agent at the time of his death, but it's something I'll look into." I set my half-empty cup on the coffee table between us and stood. "Thank you for speaking with me. I don't want to take any more of your time."

"You'll let me know if you find out anything?"

"Certainly, but I want to caution you not to get your hopes up. I might not find anything new." Or anything she'd want to hear.

I walked until the Culpepper house was out of view, ordered another auto-LAV, and waited. My cuff vibrated, alerting me to an incoming message. It was a written communique from Sean Rhinehardt, whom I'd messaged earlier.

It read: *The Black Hole. 1900.*

The Black Hole was a bar in the business district, near the heart of downtown Clava. It catered to the business crowd—happy hours, client schmoozing, and the like.

I had a few hours to kill, so I directed the auto-LAV to drop me off on Eat Street so I could grab a quick bite. It pained me—like physically pained me—to walk by Andy's Pizzeria and not stop in. Slices so big you needed to fold them in half to eat. Sweet tomato sauce. Fresh mozzarella. Not that dehydrated, reconstituted stuff they sold at the market. And spicy pepperoni that might actually come from real pork. Andy claimed it was a family recipe passed down from his great-great-grandmother, an Earthling born in New York City.

My mouth watered thinking about it, but Andy's had been one of my frequent haunts when I lived in Clava. People there would recognize me, and I couldn't afford that right now. So I consoled myself with a few deep sniffs as I passed by: hot bread, roasted garlic, oregano, and grilled cheese. *Hnnnng.*

Instead, I stopped at a sandwich shop three doors down, which I knew had been cited for a few minor health code violations. It had a high employee turnover rate, and all the locals avoided it like the rat-infested shithole it was. Which meant it was unlikely anyone I knew would venture inside.

Not wanting to risk food poisoning, I ordered a bottle of water and two bags of prepackaged veggie chips, paid for them with LTs, and took them to a booth tucked in the back. I'd made it through the first bag and a sizable way into the second, when Sparkles alerted me to an incoming communication. The ID didn't match the ones I had for either Waverly Culpepper or Sean Rhinehardt, but no one else had Sparkles's ID. To be safe, I set the call to audio only before answering.

"Hello?"

"Reliance Sinclair." The man's voice sent shivers down my spine, and I tried not to think about that.

How the effing void did he get this ID? I tamped down my emotions into a hard little ball in the pit of my stomach. When I was sure none would leak into my voice, I said, "Lead Agent Wright, I don't recall giving you my number."

"You didn't make it easy on me. I had to convince a mutual friend to give it to me. Sedwaro sends his regards, by the way. Nice chap. Terrible poker face, though."

Seddy. My fingers curled into fists at my side. He must have rolled over and shown his belly the second Wright showed up at his door. Not that I blamed him. He didn't ask me to drag him into this mess.

"I hope you weren't calling to ask me for a date. If so, I'm afraid you've wasted your time. My dance card is completely full. Maybe next week?"

"I didn't realize I had competition. How many men do you have after you, Ms. Sinclair?"

"A lady never kisses and tells. And it's Captain Sinclair."

"Yes, about that. We impounded your ship on Ceti. Don't worry, though. I'm happy to come pick you up on Brione-5."

I muttered something unladylike under my breath.

Agent Wright chuckled. "What was that? I didn't quite catch it."

"What makes you think I'm on Brione-5?" I asked.

"Sedwaro was kind enough to give me the number of the account he deposited your money into. That's frozen now, by the way. I hope you're comfortable, because that auto-LAV was the last purchase you'll be making for a long time."

"So much for professional pride."

"Don't be too cross with Sedwaro. I threatened him with aiding and abetting a known fugitive."

"Seddy had nothing to do with what happened on Andaress-4, and you know it. And for the record, I had nothing to do with it, either. Go back home, Agent Wright. Find Jarrett's actual murderers." And let me do the same.

I disconnected the call, removed Jarrett's data dot, and threw Sparkles into the nearest reclamator. No longer hungry, I tossed the rest of the veggie chips in, too.

This was bad. I hadn't thought Wright would get to Seddy so soon. He must have had his entire team running searches around the clock to have picked up the transponder log on Ceti. I knew for a fact that Sedwaro had dock workers on his payroll. They should have given Wright the runaround for at least a day. I revised my evaluation of Agent Wright and determined not to underestimate him again.

The question was, where was Wright? On Ceti, Vesen-1, or on his way here right now? I needed to be off this rock by the time he arrived. That raised the question of where I would go next. These were the only three case files Jarrett had left. If I didn't start connecting some dots soon, I'd be at a dead end.

No matter where Wright was, I felt confident he wouldn't pinpoint my exact location within the next three or four hours. There was no reason to cancel my meeting with Rhinehardt's brother. An auto-LAV was out of the question. I could pay in legal tender, but I didn't want to use my remaining hard currency on a luxury. Also, I had no way to place the order without a neural interface cuff.

It looked like I was walking.

Chapter 9

THE BLACK HOLE WAS a swanky, upscale lounge in the financial district masquerading as a dive bar: scarred and ring-marked tables that didn't wobble; strategically placed dim lighting that created an intimate but nonthreatening atmosphere, and a selection of craft beer you wouldn't find in any establishment ten blocks to the west. It was the kind of place you took out-of-town clients to show them an "authentic" slice of Clava without the hassle of leaving downtown.

I bellied up to the polished bar. The bartender finished rinsing a glass, set it upside down to dry, and wiped his hands on a towel.

"What'll it be?" he asked.

"Whisky, neat with a drop. Not too high on the shelf."

"I've got an eight-year Lonnie Powell."

"That'll do."

It was a local brand. Whisky was a source of great pride for the planet. Forests planted by the second generation of settlers had only grown large enough to support logging in the last one hundred years. Several distilleries had opened, crafting their own oak barrels to age the liquor. Few terraformed planets had the natural resources available to do that yet.

The bartender set a glass in front of me and poured in two fingers of honey-colored liquor. I added two splashes of water from the tiny dropper and swirled the liquid, letting it breathe and admiring the legs that slowly trailed down the inside of the glass. The fragrance bloomed—warm and spicy with notes of sinnafuel that burned the back of my nasal passages.

"I'm meeting someone here, a guy named Sean Rhinehardt. You know him?"

The bartender jutted a bearded chin toward a man sitting on a stool. "That's Sean at the end there, in the gray suit."

I paid for my drink in LTs and took it down to the empty seat beside Thomas Rhinehardt's brother. From the rosiness of his warm-beige skin and the smell of alcohol wafting off him, he'd beaten me here by an hour or two.

"Sean?" I asked. He looked up from the gambling game he was playing on one of the bar's consoles installed at every seat. "Is this seat open?"

"You the one who wanted to talk about Tom?"

I nodded, and he waved a hand for me to sit down.

"Can I buy you another drink?" I asked. I was already twirling my finger in the air, signaling the bartender for another round.

Sean eyed my purple hair and cut-up crop top. He emptied his beer. "No offense, but you're not exactly what I expected."

"I've been getting that a lot today."

The bartender set a frosty mug in front of Sean. Foam sloshed over the top and dribbled down the side. I dug out a few more LTs from my bag and tossed them on the bar.

"So, what do you want to know?" His words slurred together, and he took a long pull of his beer.

"I have some questions about how he died and about how the Department handled his case afterward."

"What's it to you?"

"Call me a concerned citizen."

Sean ran a hand through his cobalt-blue hair. It was short at the bottom and curly at the top with powder-blue highlights threaded throughout. An expensive style. His suit, while rum-pled, was cut from a soft Brione wool and tailored to fit. I guessed he worked at either an investment firm or a law office in one of the high rises.

"Tom was a good brother, a good son. It about killed our mum when she heard the news. She worried about us moving downtown.

Wanted us to stay out in East Town by her. Said the crime here was too high. Turns out she was right."

"I heard Tom took his own life." Ate a bullet is what the report said.

"That's a lie. Tommy would never do that. He had too much going for him. No reason to check out." Sean took another drink and emptied half his glass.

"No reason?"

"We were close. He would have said something." Sean took another drink. "Money was good. He'd been promoted to Senior Vice President. Nice girlfriend. They'd been together about a year. I think it was serious. What more is there?"

"Senior VP?"

"Well," Sean said, "he worked over at Saratomlin as financial analyst—stocks, bonds, pensions, that kind of thing."

The bartender stopped in front of us to stock a tray of clean glassware beneath the bar. "Tom was a regular, even gave me an investment tip from time to time. Damn shame what happened."

"It sounds like a stressful job," I said.

Sean finished his beer, and I signaled the bartender to bring another mug. "Tommy thrived under pressure. He talked about work like it was one of those VR games. Moving money from this account to that account, gaining half a percent here, a quarter percent there. I'm good and all, but Tommy, Tommy was a freaking genius."

I sipped my whisky, enjoying the accompanying heat that pooled in my belly, and assessed Sean's state of inebriation. His skin was flushed, and his eyes were bloodshot. When he reached for his glass, his movements were loose and slow. Well-lubricated.

"Sean, what do you think happened to Tom?"

He swiveled to face me and leaned one elbow on the bar for support. "What's any of this matter to you?"

The bartender set down the second beer, folded his arms across his chest, making it clear he wanted to hear the answer, too.

"My friend thought there was something suspicious about Tom's death. He died before he told me what it was, and I owe it to him to finish investigating."

Sean looked into his beer like it held all the answers at the bottom of the glass. "Someone killed him. It's the only explanation."

"Who would do that?"

"Tazza Industries," Sean spat out.

"The tech company? They make ship parts, right?" Some of the *Soteria*'s communication hardware came from it.

"Yeah, and a lot of other stuff, too, like medical devices. And weapons."

"Here we go, again," the bartender said and removed Sean's empty glass. "I think you've had enough for the night."

Sean's face pinked, and he pounded a fist on the bar. "You never believed me, not even after he died. What will it take to convince you, Cress?"

"Convince you of what?" I interrupted.

Cress placed Sean's glass into an empty sink and wiped a wet rag across the bar. "Don't listen to him, ma'am. When he's had too much to drink, he likes to spin his conspiracy theories."

"I love a good conspiracy theory. What have you got?"

Sean shot Cress a triumphant look, but the bartender shook his head. "It's your time to waste."

"It started after Tom got that big promotion," Sean began. "Saratomlin paid for him to get an Insight so he could work the big cases faster. That's when he started getting headaches."

"Wait," I held up my hand. "What's an Insight?"

"You know, that thing that's like having a cuff in your brain."

"Cuff in your brain?"

"They've been out for a year or two," said Cress. "Real expensive. Some techies from Tylo came in with them once, and it's all Tom talked about for the next month. Here."

Cress aerial scribed something into the console and spun it to face me. An ad played showing people shopping, working, and playing without having to wear cuffs to interact with computer systems. A snazzy graphic illustrated how a small chip implanted at the base of the neck could read neural impulse signals faster and more accurately than an external cuff strapped to the forearm. Big letters flashed across the bottom of the screen: *Insight. Look to your Future.*

It would be a revolutionary concept if it worked.

"It says you can only get the implantation done in Tylo."

The bartender shrugged. "Could be. I recall Tom mentioning something about Saratomlin springing for his travel expenses to Brione-2."

"Mind control is what it is," interjected Sean, wobbling on his seat.

Cress pulled out a cutting board and began slicing three lemons. "All I know is, I'm not jamming something inside my brain when a good old-fashioned cuff does the trick. Technology for the sake of technology. It doesn't make everything better. Take that whisky there. It's made the same way they've been making whisky for a thousand years. Sometimes simpler is better."

It was a favorite argument, especially for people who spent their whole lives in one city. More advanced didn't always mean better. Often, it just meant the thing was expensive and difficult to fix when it broke. It was the same reason combustion guns were still popular, even though blasters had been around over a hundred years. They were cheap to produce, easy to use, and got the job done.

"So, Tom got one of these Insight things and started getting headaches. What happened after that?"

"He went back to the implant clinic in Tylo," Sean said. "They were accommodating at first. Ran all kinds of tests and gave him some meds. None of it helped. The headaches kept getting worse. Tom wanted them to remove the implant, but they said they couldn't without risking severe brain damage. He contacted the IBMD to lodge a complaint, to see if he could sue Tazza Industries or something. A rep came by and filled out a report. The next day, a DECA agent showed up and said he looked into it. If Tom went ahead with the complaint, Tazza Industries would sue *him* for defamation. Can you believe that? Tom was going to go ahead, anyway. He was bullheaded that way. Next thing you know, they find him in his bedroom with the back of his head blown off! The man didn't even own a gun. Now, how do you explain that?"

Tears shone in Sean's eyes, but he sniffed them back. Cress poured him a glass of water and told him to drink it.

The Interplanetary Board of Medical Devices usually took complaints seriously. They also handled their own investigations and didn't request help from DECA. My gut told me something was off.

"This DECA agent, did he also handle the investigation into your brother's death?"

"He said he knew Tom from the IBMD report and requested to head it. To make sure it was done right."

I bet he did. "Do you remember his name? Was it Hal Cavender?"

Sean blinked a few times. "Yeah, that sounds right."

"Thank you, Sean. You've been very helpful." I turned to the bartender. "Cress, do you mind if I use this console for a quick comm?"

"Knock yourself out."

"Thanks." I aerial scribed Waverly Culpepper's ID number. She answered immediately. Behind her, I could see the hustle and bustle of the busy rehab clinic.

"Reliance?" she asked as the video feed linked.

"Hey Waverly, there's something I forgot to ask you before. Did Silar have an Insight neural implant?"

"Yes, he'd had one for about a year. He got it through work. Why?"

"Maybe nothing." Maybe everything. "I'll get back to you as soon as I know more."

I disconnected and rotated the console back toward Sean. It looked like I'd found my next lead.

Outside, the cool, autumn air whipped bits of hair across my face and chilled the strip of exposed flesh between my shirt and pants. I dragged a finger across my forehead to tuck the errant strands behind an ear and continued walking down the street. There was a park up ahead that I used to visit when I needed to decompress after work. It was a good place to think.

The sun had set an hour ago, and only a few stars twinkled overhead. The brightest one sat low on the horizon, but it wasn't a star. It was Brione-2, glowing a dark amber in the deepening night sky. I stared at the pinprick of light, wondering if the answers to my questions were there.

Zairesh, Culpepper, and Rhinehardt all had implants that either malfunctioned or caused negative side effects. I knew Culpepper and Rhinehardt had Insights, but the maker of Zairesh's implant was unknown. All three died. My former partner investigated the cases and had done a shoddy job, at best. At worst, he'd deliberately tampered with evidence of the implants malfunctioning.

I thought back to the last case I had worked with Cavender—back to the day I had shot him. The memory was still raw and painful, but like a sore tooth, I couldn't keep from poking at it. That day, I had searched Ruana Sorelsdotter's bedroom and found a sheet of postoperative steroid tabs. Could she have also received an Insight? She was wealthy enough to afford one.

Perhaps Tazza Industries had paid Cavender to sweep the Sorelsdotter case under the rug, too. Is that why he shot at me? Was it all a cover-up for a faulty device?

Is that why I shot my partner? Why I had gotten Jarret killed?

If Tazza Industries was behind the cover-up, it was a bigger problem than I had thought. It wasn't some two-bit player trying to bury a bad business deal. It was a tech giant with virtually unlimited resources.

An ache formed in the center of my chest, like a gravity well of emotions caving inward. Exhausted, I veered off into the grassy park, hoping nature would soothe the pain. I slumped down on a cold bench, not sure what to do next.

Taking on a corporation like Tazza required a team, connections, funding, the ability to obtain and execute a search warrant—it required DECA. I could just imagine Agent Wright's face if I brought this to him without proof and only the barest scrap of a lead. Maybe if I hadn't run. But I had, and there was no putting the genie back in the bottle.

I sniffed. Damn fireweed allergies.

My options weren't great. As much fun as it was, I didn't want to live on the lam forever. It had never been the long-term plan, anyway. Eventually, I'd have to turn myself in, but I hoped to take Jarret's murderers in with me.

Wright would be here within hours. If I waited on this bench long enough, he'd find me, arrest me, and take me to the local precinct for booking before hauling me off to Andaress-4. I didn't mind the arresting part so much, but I really didn't want to be dragged through my old station in restraints.

A better option would be to go to Andaress-4 and turn myself in. Between that and giving them all the information I had, a judge might be lenient with me. After all, I was legitimately innocent of the murder charge. However, resisting arrest, impersonating an agent, assault and battery, and damage to property was another matter.

But that plan required credits, and all of mine—thanks to Agent Wright—were currently frozen in a dummy account. And the legal tender I had wasn't enough to purchase a ticket to Brione-2, let alone the Andaress system.

I scrubbed my palms up and down my thighs, feeling the coarse weave of the fabric grate against my skin. My fingers stretched, then curled into tight fists.

Jarret gave his life for me, and I couldn't even do this for him. I was a terrible friend.

And a terrible person. That implant killed people, and the company was getting away with it. Didn't I have a duty to expose the truth?

Brione-2 winked at me through the flickering atmosphere. The answers were all right there, only a couple of hundred million kilometers away. Barely worth warming up the warp drive. But I didn't have a ship, credits, a valid ID, or any of the things I needed to get there.

I could go to a news outlet or the media, but who would listen to a wanted fugitive?

There was the Interplanetary Board of Medical Devices. An anonymous tip might get them to investigate and revoke their certification, but there was no guarantee it wouldn't get swept under the rug like Thomas Rhinehardt's complaint.

If hard evidence existed that the implants caused the deaths of Zairesh, Rhinehardt, Culpepper, and Sorelsdotter, it would be at Tazza Industries headquarters in Tylo. It needed to be strong enough to force DECA to take my claims seriously.

That was a lot of assumptions, and I still needed to get to Tylo first.

There was one possibility I hadn't explored. I swallowed hard and wet my lips as even the mere thought left a foul taste in my mouth, but I didn't see any other options.

May the void take me, but if I wanted to get to Brione-2, I needed to talk to Lady Ilymechina, and hope she didn't still hold a grudge.

Chapter 10

My first two years at DECA were spent undercover. The Department liked to use rookies who hadn't yet developed the ubiquitous attitude of seasoned officers. After a few years, we all stood the same, walked the same, talked the same—even smelled the same if you believed the criminals.

I chuckled to myself. If only my old training officer could see me now.

They had assigned me to a task force tracking the head of an intricate smuggling operation. She went by Lady Ilymechina, although I doubted that's what it said on her identification card. Despite having access to every camera feed in the city, we hadn't managed to get a single image of her. She often wore clothing made of illegal ov-ex material, which interfered with recordings by causing the pixels near it to become overexposed. Her crew included body doubles, guards, and moles within the Department who tipped her off on raids.

My team was tasked with infiltrating her network from the ground up. That was when I first met Jarrett. He handled the tech end of the operation—communications, recordings, and tracking activity over the network.

I posed as a low-level buyer looking for pain killers. As far as I knew, Lady Ilymechina didn't deal hard drugs, but if you wanted pharmaceutical-grade tabs without a script, she had a reputation of providing a quality product that *probably* wouldn't kill you if taken in the correct dose. We'd also linked her to bootlegged alcohol, counterfeit merchandise, and illegal tech.

It took me six months to work up enough cred to meet her face-to-face, and that happened purely by chance. The plan had been for me to set up a meeting between my dealer and a more experienced undercover officer posing as my cousin, the foreman of an agri-operation in an outer district. My "cousin" wanted to purchase a large amount of pharmaceuticals to sell to his laborers—large enough that my dealer would need to take the offer to someone higher up the food chain.

Everything went according to plan until one night my dealer told me to meet him at a club for a buy. Lady Ilymechina happened to be there. My dealer introduced us. I—being the arrogant, dumbass rookie that I was—arrested her.

And promptly threw close to a year's worth of investigation down the drain.

The media had a field day with it, plastering her face on every news program and tabloid site for weeks. She became the face of smuggling on Brione-5. Not exactly desirable in her line of work.

The Clava city attorney tried to make a few charges stick, but everything we had was hearsay or circumstantial. Her crew was fiercely loyal; not a single one flipped. Two even confessed to crimes I knew they didn't commit to keep Lady Ilymechina's record clean. In the end, she walked away free and clear, but no longer had the luxury of working from the shadows.

Even though the Department wouldn't assign me to any official op, I'd kept tabs on her over the years. A copy of all the information I'd gathered was cached in a storage locker here in Clava along with backups of all my other important information in case something happened to the *Soteria*. Unfortunately, I'd stopped tracking her once I left the Department. My information was over a year old. I could only hope she still frequented her regular haunts, which brought me to the butcher counter at the grocery store.

My knuckles rapped on the counter. A song played over the store's speakers that I hadn't heard since my early twenties. It reminded me of decompressing with my team after a long shift, usually at Andy's with pizza and beer.

An older man, whipcord thin and balding with pale, ashy skin, came through a swinging door. He wiped his hands on the front of his apron, leaving pinkish-red smears in their wake. "What will it be, honey?"

"Seven snake tails." I hoped they hadn't changed the challenge question.

He looked me over, taking in my ripped crop top, indigo hair, and color-blocking makeup, and jerked his head to the side.

I slipped around the end of the display case and into the refrigerated back room where they stored the meat. Whole fish and slabs of red meat were laid out on stainless-steal tables, waiting to be butchered.

A walk-in freezer took up one wall. I stepped inside and waited for the door to shut, shivering and watching my breath form little puffs of frozen air. The vibration on the floor was my only warning before the concealed platform lift descended, carrying me with it.

The heavy thump of bass enveloped me as I stepped off the platform into the dimly lit nightclub. Lights along the walls shifted in color and intensity, throbbing to the music like a visual heartbeat. An elegant host greeted me wearing a black-and-white gossamer shift that left nothing to the imagination. She handed me a mood bracelet after extracting a hefty cover charge. LTs only.

It was still early by club standards. Only a couple dozen people were on the dance floor. Another handful clustered near the bar or at high tops scattered around the edges. I slid into a padded booth with a good view of the room and flagged down a server for a regolith rocks. Thinking of my empty stomach, I added an order of fried potato crispers and paid for them out of my dwindling supply of legal tender. Then I settled in to wait.

The Snake Den took its name from being run by the Seven Serpents gang. The butcher—who was also the manager—reserved the right to refuse entry to anyone he didn't like, and he didn't like a lot of people: officers, recovery agents, attorneys, judges, health inspectors, government employees, ex-wives, or anyone with the first name Zoe. He took his divorce hard.

Numerous borderline activities occurred here, but while DECA raided the nightclub several times a year, nothing worse than low-level possession ever came of it. The nightclub didn't advertise, and the only way to find out about it was through word of mouth. Judging by the pricey new stage and bar display they'd added since my last visit, it seemed to work for them.

As the minutes ticked by, a steady stream of people exited the semisecret lift and joined the party. I sipped my glass of regolith rocks and tried to name the songs the experience jockey, the EJ, played, but living on a spaceship had its disadvantages—not keeping up on current music trends being one of them.

The current song blended seamlessly into the next as two women passed by my booth on their way to the dance floor. Their mood bracelets glowed neon blue, showing they were activated, and both women grinned as the EJ signaled everyone's bracelets to release a minuscule dose of mood-influencing drugs—just enough for the EJ to move the crowd toward whichever experience they'd crafted.

I inhaled deeply and caught hints of rosemary, sweet clover, and pomelo. Those, along with the soft lavender and turquoise lights, smooth music, and cool climate-controlled air blowing on my arms told me the EJ was still warming up. By the end of the night, they would treat patrons to a full journey of emotions, from loneliness to lust to heartbreak to desire. The rush of the ups and downs was addicting in its own right, but the mood-influencing drugs would amplify the feelings tenfold.

After my first glass, I switched to a sweet, nonalcoholic drink, both to preserve my wits and my LTs. Two hours later, I tipped my third glass of soda water back and shook it, trying to dislodge the last ice cube stuck to the bottom. The crispers were but a distant memory, and I was losing hope that Lady Ilymechina would show.

The lift doors opened, and my eyes automatically scanned the newcomer at the front of the club. My heart stuttered when I recognized Iko, one of Lady Ilymechina's underlings. He'd been a scrawny, pale, conniving little sneak when I'd been undercover, but a lot could happen in ten years. Now, his tall frame was packed with muscle, and he held himself with the air of confidence of someone used to getting his way.

Iko leaned in to whisper something in the host's ear. He'd grown his black hair out and wore it tied back with a thick leather cord.

She nodded, then sent a communication on her cuff. Moments later, two bouncers cleared the customers from a round booth at the back of the club. Waitstaff hustled to clear away glasses, wipe up spills, and shine a disinfectant light over the table and chairs.

As they finished, the lift doors opened again, this time carrying Lady Ilymechina and two women I didn't recognize. The tall, lithe one on the left dressed like a guard in a gray bodysuit made of synthetic material I knew to be slash resistant and lined with force-distributing webbing. Her dark hair was slicked back and plaited, except for a short fringe of bangs that stood out against her light-olive skin. She carried a high-end blaster holstered at her waist and a telescoping baton clipped to her belt. I bet if I ran a background check on her, I'd find a list of military contracts or mercenary work.

The woman on the right could have been Lady Ilymechina's sister. They shared the same high cheekbones and wide-set mahogany eyes, but where Lady Ilymechina's black hair was styled in an intricate set of braids, this woman wore hers loose in a soft brown cloud around her head.

I shrunk down in my seat.

Lady Ilymechina stepped out last. Her dress was an iridescent black, like oil on water, and it hugged her curves like a second skin. A daring slit clean up to her hip revealed a stiletto knife strapped to her thigh. The opal hilt shimmered a translucent blue when she stepped off the platform.

The host inclined her head and led the group through the crowd of revelers to the velvet-covered booth. As they passed by, I got a look at the back of Lady Ilymechina's dress: open backed, emphasizing her slender waist, with three delicate chains strung between the sides. Suspended between the chains was a solid gold snake stretching the full length of her spine, a symbol of her status and power as the head of the Seven Serpents.

Food and drink were served. As the night wore on, people approached the table, sometimes to pass something to Iko and other times to receive something, but always discreetly. If I hadn't been watching carefully, I wouldn't have caught it.

An hour ticked by, then two. Dancers spilled off the packed dance floor and into the space between tables. Body heat alone raised the temperature by several degrees. My ass hurt from sitting on the bench. If I held out much longer, my bladder was going to protest. But I wanted Lady Ilymechina in the best mood possible, so I waited until her business slowed before approaching her table.

A fast-paced song blared out over the speakers, shifting the colors of the room into golds and ambers as I threaded myself between pairs and trios of sweaty dancers. All around me, wristbands pulsed brighter, eliciting an excited gasp from the group. Two large hands gripped my hips from behind and urged me to move with the beat.

"Dance with me," a male voice shouted into my ear to be heard over the music. His pelvis rolled against my backside, promising a good time.

"Later!" I yelled back, twisting out of his grip and skirting by the next group. Unfazed, my would-be dance partner gyrated his way to the next-closest person, who appeared more receptive to his offer.

I broke free of the throng of bodies several meters from my destination and put on my game face. If I showed any weakness, these snakes would eat me alive.

Iko and the bodyguard watched me as I approached. The open end of the round table had no chairs and was where her minions had anxiously stood during their business meetings all night. The bodyguard sat to the left, followed by Lady Ilymechina, her doppelgänger, and finally Iko on the right.

I snagged a chair from the next table and dragged it with me. When I stepped within a meter of the velvet booth, sound dampeners kicked in, reducing the music volume to a conversational level. I dropped the chair and straddled it backward, resting my arms on the back but keeping my weight on the balls of my feet. "Hello, Ily."

Iko's jaw clenched. "Make tracks, hellaberry head."

"Everybody's a critic," I muttered under my breath. The purple hair was actually growing on me. To Lady Ilymechina, I said, "I need to speak with you."

"My lady doesn't speak to anyone she doesn't know."

"Oh, she and I go way back."

The smuggler arched a sculpted brow over piercing blue eyes. "Is that so? You don't look familiar."

She whispered something to her companion, who laughed. The bodyguard watched us impassively.

Iko jerked a thumb toward the door. "Today's not your day, sweet cheeks. Time to leave."

I ignored him, imploring my case directly to the woman in charge. "Please, hear me out. I need your organization's particular specialty. You're the only one who can help me."

"Are you deaf, lady, or stupid?" Iko's nostrils flared as he took in quick, deep breaths. His fingers coiled and flexed into loose fists. I recognized the prefight indicators but kept my expression neutral.

"I'll only take a few minutes of your time, and if you're not interested in the job, tell me so and you'll never see me again."

Iko slapped both hands down on the table, causing the glasses to rattle and slosh amber liquid over their sides. He leaned forward as he pushed himself up, but I was ready.

Before he shifted his center of gravity back over his feet, I grabbed a handful of fabric below his neck and yanked down with all my strength. I used the leverage to pull myself up and followed through with a downward elbow strike between his shoulder blades. His chest hit the table, rocking it forward. My hand slammed down over his ear in a cupped position, pinning his head down and sending a shock wave of air down his ear canal that was sure to cause dizziness and pain.

I took advantage of his momentary disorientation and transferred my hold from his shirt to his wrist. He wiggled beneath me, but I leaned more of my weight onto his back and head.

My lips lowered to his ear. "I am neither deaf nor stupid nor much of a lady, asshole."

The high-pitched whine of a blaster spinning up had me looking up to find the barrel of the bodyguard's blaster pointed steadily at my head. Her gray eyes were hard and emotionless. She could pull that trigger and not suffer a moment of regret.

"Now I recognize you," Lady Ilymechina said, holding up her hand to stop her bodyguard from shooting me. "You're the brash little officer who arrested me, all full of piss and vinegar."

"Reliance Sinclair. Guilty as charged." I flashed a smile, but no one laughed. "Too soon?"

Lady Ilymechina tapped a nail against her glass. "That didn't work out very well for you, did it? I seem to recall hearing about a demotion."

I released Iko with one last shove on his back and sat back down. At least I had their attention.

"Back to walking the beat. I was stuck in a uniform for eight years after that mistake."

"You're not looking for an apology, are you? Because I don't do those."

"Already we agree on something."

Ilymechina didn't quite smile, but her eyes twinkled with amusement, and she motioned for her guard to lower the blaster. "If it is not to offer me your humblest and most sincere apology for dragging my good name and likeness through the proverbial mud, I must ask, what brings you to me tonight?"

I pointed to one of the half-empty glasses of alcohol on the table—probably Iko's from the daggers he shot at me with his eyes. "May I?"

Lady Ilymechina waved her hand. "By all means."

I downed it in one shot. I didn't need the alcohol to steady my nerves, but it served a higher purpose. A person who did you a favor, even a small one, was more likely to do you a favor again. Lady Ilymechina had stopped her bodyguard from shooting me. That was favor number one. And then she gave me a drink when she didn't have to do so. That was favor number two. It was my paltry attempt at priming the pump.

"I need you to smuggle something to Brione-2."

"Usually, things come from there to here, not the other way. What is it?"

"Me."

She laughed. "Assuming I am even in the smuggling business, which I do not admit, what makes you think I would take a DECA officer anywhere? And you, in particular?"

"I can pay eight hundred in legal tender." It would almost wipe me out of LTs, but I was running out of options.

Lady Ilymechina laughed and waved a hand at the packed dance floor. "Do I look desperate? Eight hundred LTs won't even buy you a ticket on a public transport."

"All right, then do it because I know how you get stardust into the Clava prison. That's quite the money maker for you, isn't it? Low risk, high margins, captive market."

Iko's face flared bright red, and he pounded his fist against the table. "You little—"

Lady Ilymechina cut him off with a sharp look. "A little stardust never hurt anyone, and for many, it makes the confinement at least somewhat tolerable."

"Even so, I'm sure DECA would be interested in knowing about your arrangement with Chief Warden Stiles." I placed the data dot I'd retrieved from my storage locker earlier on the table between us.

My informant had never said as much, but she'd alluded that someone high up had their finger in the pie. Stiles was always at the top of my suspect list. I never got the go-ahead to pursue a full investigation, because the Department protected its own. Still, there was enough information in that file to raise questions if released to the public.

A slight widening of her eyes was Lady Ilymechina's only tell that my guess had hit the mark. "If you had proof, you would have taken it to your boss already. You have nothing."

"I no longer work for DECA. Haven't for about a year now. Normally, I wouldn't concern myself with what you sell or to whom you sell it, but I'm in a bit of a bind here. I need off this rock, fast, and I will burn every bridge to make it happen."

"Or I could have you killed and solve the problem that way. Iko would probably be willing to oblige."

If looks could kill, Iko had been practicing for the last five minutes.

"Lady, you kill me, and I swear you will have so many agencies up your ass, they'll be making reservations. There's a reason I'm not taking public transport."

She sat in silence, as if weighing the veracity of my words. I steeled myself not to squirm under her scrutiny. Finally, she turned to the woman sitting beside her.

"Dominique, if you would."

The woman took the data dot and placed it in her cuff. She opened the files, analyzing and assessing the data quickly.

"This is circumstantial at best." Her lilting accent softened her hard consonants. I placed her from one of the Fleur-de-lis systems: Avignon or maybe Corsica. "But it would ruffle feathers that we have taken great pains to keep smooth."

Dominique removed the data dot from her cuff and placed it back on the table. Lady Ilymechina's nail tapped against the side of her glass but stopped when she caught me staring.

"The eight hundred and this will be the last of our dealings. You will not go to the authorities, and you will never attempt to blackmail me again."

"I swear, DECA won't hear about it from me, and you will never see me again."

"Perhaps something can be arranged," Ilymechina said, relaxing back in her chair. "Dominique, do we know of any ships heading to our sister planet?"

"One moment." Dominique said. A furrow appeared between her dark brows as she swiped through screen after screen. "We may have room aboard the *Fortitude*, but it would be a tight fit."

"I'll suck it in," I said dryly.

"You can't be serious," Iko groused.

Ilymechina looked at him like a parent scolding a wayward child. "I never joke about business."

"Great. When do I leave?" I asked.

Iko's heavy brows slashed downward in a scowl. "Not soon enough."

"Tomorrow at sunrise," Dominique said. "The *Fortitude* is the first scheduled departure of the day."

"Thank you. I'll be ready." I stood to leave, but Lady Ilymechina motioned me back down.

"Not quite yet. There is still the matter of insurance. I have only your word that you will keep your mouth shut, and frankly, that isn't good enough. We have cargo arriving on the same ship, and you will help unload it."

I thought it over. Whatever they were bringing in was illegal. By helping, I would be an active participant in the crime and give Lady Ilymechina leverage over me. Morally, I would be responsible for whatever harm resulted from its presence. I had to weigh that against the possibility of not getting to Brione-2.

"What's in the shipment?" I asked.

"Not your concern."

"Will it kill people?"

"An apple can kill someone by choking them. But no, the product is not meant to cause harm."

A heaviness settled inside my chest as I rose. That left a lot of wiggle room. "We have a deal."

Chapter 11

"Here." A middle-aged woman with strawberry-blond hair shoved a buttery scone under my nose. "No jam, but there's butter on the table if you want it, and coffee if you can stomach the artificial stuff."

"Caffeine's good." I nodded my thanks and took my breakfast to the common room to eat.

Lady Ilymechina had instructed me to arrive at one of her drop houses at three in the morning. My internal clock was so screwed up, I couldn't tell if it was very early or very late. Too much planet hopping in too short a time. I hadn't slept since my transport to Brione-5 and spent the last several hours sitting under a tree in a park. My back hurt, my ass hurt, my feet were cold, and my neck had a knot the size of my fist. Hopefully, this morning would go smoothly, and I'd be in Tylo by the afternoon.

Ten people crowded around the table, talking and laughing. The furniture was cheap and mismatched, likely salvaged, much like the people using it. Iko was the only one I knew by name, although two others looked vaguely familiar. They chatted gamely with each other. Spirits were high, even at this insane hour, and I had a sudden pang of longing for the easy camaraderie they shared.

I sat in an empty chair on the opposite end as Iko and slathered butter over my scone. Warm and flaky, it smelled delicious. I swiped at a drop of drool that escaped the corner of my mouth.

"Thanks, Ms. B!" a young guy called over his shoulder before sitting down beside me and depositing a small hoard of scones on the table. He was lanky, with disheveled hair and light skin speckled with red acne over his cheeks like freckles. Dirt stains covered his coat, although the material looked high-end and matched what the others wore.

He was a kid. Seventeen, tops. He smiled at me as he reached for the butter.

"Haven't seen you here before. You new?" He chomped down on his scone, showering crumbs on the table.

"Just passing through."

"Name's Willy. I joined about a month ago. It'll be nice not being the new guy, even if it's only for a day."

"They treat you well?"

He shrugged. "Typical new-guy razzing. It's all right. Better'n living on the streets, I s'pose. No one messes with me as long as I get my work done, and the food's good."

I bit into my biscuit and hummed my agreement.

"Ms. B. says she's gotta fatten me up before winter so I don't catch my death cold."

"You always eat with the gang?"

Willy buttered a second scone and shoved half of it in his mouth. "Only 'fore a gig. The Lady says we do better if our stomachs aren't growling the whole time. I'm thankful, though. Beats what I was eatin' 'fore." He stuffed the other half in and licked his fingers.

"Do you know what we're doing this morning?"

"We're—"

"Doing what we're told and not running our mouth," Iko's dark, unblinking eyes beared down on Willy until I thought the poor kid was going to pee his pants.

Willy's cheeks flamed in embarrassment. "S-sorry, sir. Just makin' conversation."

"Ms. Sinclair, here, is a bona fide agent of the Department of Enforcement of Criminal Affairs."

"*Former* agent," I corrected, but the room had already quieted. All eyes swiveled toward me.

One man spat in my direction. "Once a ribbit, always a ribbit."

"It's been a long time since I've worn a green uniform. I've got no beef with anyone here."

Iko flexed his hand and curled his fingers into a fist. "Well, maybe some of *us* have a problem with *you*."

"Don't blame me because you're as slow as Vesian moss growing on a rock. How's the ear, by the way? Still ringing?"

He lunged, but I was already out of my seat, ducking below his swinging arm. Willy fell backward, crab walking to get out of the way.

Damn, I needed to learn when to keep my mouth shut.

Iko spun, and I danced back out of his reach. Someone shoved the table and chairs out of the way to clear a space. Voices raised as people placed hasty bets.

Iko circled to my right. I mirrored his movements, relaxing back into a loose fighting stance. His shoulders shifted, telegraphing his next move would come from his left. People usually led with their dominant side. A southpaw.

I spotted the lumbering haymaker before his hand formed a fist. It missed me by centimeters. I slipped to the outside, parrying his forearm to keep it moving past me, and checked him with a quick jab to his unprotected ribs.

Iko's elbow shot back, catching me in the deltoid. I staggered. My entire upper arm smarted, but I shook it out.

The crowd shouted encouraging words. None of them for me.

"You got her, Iko!"

"We'll have frog legs for dinner!"

"Twenty LTs says she doesn't make it five minutes!"

"What are you waiting for?" I baited. "Don't let 'em down."

Iko was the kind of guy who didn't think while he fought. He went on pure instinct, and not the amazing in-the-zone kind of instinct of skilled fighters. He took whatever opening presented itself as soon as it occurred. That suited me fine.

The big guy charged like a wild boar and with an equal amount of grace. I tried to jump to the side, but a foul-breathed woman blocked my path. He crashed into me, sending us both to the floor in a tangle of limbs and curses.

Iko came out on top. He had me by a good twenty kilograms, and the sheer mass of his body pinned my back to the cold floor. Slowly, he worked his way around until his torso paralleled mine.

By the void, he was heavy! I bucked my hips to dislodge him, but to no avail.

Switching tactics, I locked my legs around his waist in a closed guard position. It brought our pelvises in to uncomfortably close proximity.

A grin split his lips. "All you had to do was ask, sweet cheeks."

"I'm more of an action-oriented kind of girl." I grabbed his shirt with both hands and yanked him down so we were chest to chest.

Instinctively, he braced one hand against my breastbone to push himself away. I switched to a double hammer fist and slammed both hands against his bicep like a club. His hand slipped forward, and I trapped his arm flat against my body. At the same time, I uncrossed my feet, twisted my hips, and swung my foot over his head, forcing him into an arm bar. It was a classic move, and frankly, it surprised me he didn't see it coming.

He struggled to break free, even though the pain in his shoulder must have been excruciating. I lifted my hips, increasing the pressure so he'd take a hint.

"Yield," I bit out between gritted teeth. I didn't want to tear the tendons and ligaments in his elbow if I could avoid it.

His face strained with the effort of keeping silent. Blood flushed to the surface, turning his skin an alarming shade of crab-apple red.

"Enough!" Lady Ilymechina called from the doorway.

Iko stopped resisting. I released my hold and pushed free with my legs until I had enough space to stand up. We were both sweating and panting hard.

"Iko, take a walk outside. And you"—she stabbed her finger in my direction—"come with me."

The crowd grumbled, disappointed she had cut their morning fun short, but set to work righting the furniture and cleaning up the spilled food.

I followed Ilymechina in silence up a set of narrow stairs to a sparsely furnished bedroom. Today, she wore black pants with a blue embroidered top that fastened from her throat to her navel, then flared open down to her knees. A golden snake ring wrapped around her middle finger. Her hair was down, the dozens of small braids held back by a matching embroidered band around her head.

She leaned against a low dresser with her arms crossed, giving me enough time to process how monumentally stupid I had been to let Iko provoke me into a fight. They didn't need me, but I needed them.

"Look," I started, "I didn't mean to—"

She waved her hand, shushing me. "Iko can be a real ass sometimes. Once he gets an idea in his head, it takes a sinnalite-powered excavator to dig it out. And he hates officers. Got pinched a few years back and spent time inside. He never got over it."

"Are you calling off our deal?"

A long moment dragged by while the statuesque woman studied me. Her full lips narrowed into a thin line. I felt like I was back at the academy preparing to be dressed down.

Finally, she sighed and walked over to look out the window. "No, I am a woman of my word. In this business, I cannot afford to be anything less."

"Thank you."

She scoffed dismissively. "Change into something that will draw less attention."

"All I have is what I'm wearing."

"You look like you're going to a shitty club." Lady Ilymechina looked me up and down. "I'll have Rizpah give you something to wear. You're about her size."

"In that case, I'll pay you now." I dug in my pack for the thin wad of legal tender and handed it to her. I'd set aside a hundred to get me through the next few days. After that, I didn't know what I'd do. "You can have the data dot once I'm on the ship."

"Agreed. Rizpah will accompany you. You may give it to her."

As if summoned, the lithe bodyguard appeared holding a stack of clothes. Lady Ilymechina took her leave, and I quickly changed. The pants were long in the leg and tight in the thigh, but once I got them on and moved around, they stretched to a comfortable fit. They were plain gray, serviceable, and utterly forgettable.

Rizpah handed me a cuff, an empty backpack, and a lightweight, hooded gray jacket. It was the same style and material as the jacket Willy wore, but much cleaner and smelled of fresh laundry detergent.

"Ov-ex?" I asked, shrugging into the jacket and zipping up the front.

"Yes, everyone has one. They'll help shield us from the cameras. The cuff is new, cheap, and unregistered. It has basic programs, but don't go through a security check with it. Toss it if you're compromised."

"Got it." I slid the flimsy cuff onto my forearm and powered it up. The material was stiff and guaranteed to chafe my skin. After it cycled through its startup routine, a giant holoscreen popped up, easily the size of my entire torso.

"Shit, are we trying to land spaceships with this thing?" I flicked off the holoscreen while it did its thing.

"You're not worth the cost of something better. Try not to use the holoscreen in busy areas."

I followed the two women downstairs where Lady Ilymechina handed out the day's assignments. Only six of us were on the crew going to the spacedock. The rest had other jobs to attend to.

My team took two separate LAVs to the spacedock. I rode with Dominique and Rizpah. Iko, Willy, and a man who went by Goat followed behind us.

The sky had shifted from black to midnight blue with the barest hint of peach glowing at the horizon. When we reached the gate, Dominique spoke to the attendant on duty. Legal tender changed hands. Then we flew along the outer perimeter to a large lot designated as long-term parking for LAVs whose owners were off-planet.

We were up high enough that I saw over the fence that separated the LAV parking area and the one for larger, space-worthy crafts. Bulky public transports, ship carriers, and military vessels hunkered in the far back while smaller crafts, like skiphoppers and cruisers, parked in neat rows closer to the building. Drones patrolled the airspace around the fence. Each was kitted with an automatic blaster—the first shot would severely burn you, and the second would incapacitate you. When small ships were worth the price of a luxury home and large ships that of a resort—you didn't use kid gloves on thieves.

Dominique landed, popped open the gullwing doors, and everyone climbed out. We crossed the lot, following flashing arrows embedded in the pathway, directing walkers to the east entrance. Once we reached the building, Dominique held up her hand for us to stop.

I scanned our surroundings but found nothing of interest. Whereas the west and north sides of the R. Burns Interplanetary Spacedock were lined with plastiglass walls and balconies for viewing ships as they took off and landed, this side of the building was a flat, four-story wall.

Dominique's fingers flew through the air, navigating through holoscreens faster than my eyes could keep up. She slowed when she reached a blurry image of a rooftop with code scrolling beside it. "I looped the security feed from the camera directly above us. We have five minutes to get inside the building before the live feed kicks back in."

Goat nodded and ran his hands along the wall. Finding a minuscule crevice between the panels, he pulled himself up with only his fingertips and toes. Faster than I would have thought possible, he scaled the almost sheer surface.

That answered my question about why they called him Goat.

When he reached the top, he removed a rope ladder from his pack, secured his end, and tossed the other down to us. The six of us scurried up single file in more time than it took Goat on his own. The man had skills.

Willy brought up the rear. As soon as he swung his skinny leg over the ledge, Dominique signaled for us to follow while Goat pulled up the ladder. She halted at one of the lift maintenance shafts that dotted the roof and fidgeted with an access panel. It popped out with a soft whisper. On examination, the locking mechanism had been tampered with. Obviously, this wasn't the crew's first time gaining entrance this way.

I stuck my head inside the shaft and looked down. Four stories wasn't all that high, unless the drop was pitch black and you couldn't see the bottom.

Rizpah reached inside and tapped a ladder fastened to the wall. "Climb down. At the bottom, there's a door that opens to a short corridor. It's not far from where the *Fortitude* is parked and is only used to unload supplies. That's why we chose this shaft. It should be empty for the next hour or so. We'll ferry the electronics out by foot and back up the shaft."

"Electronics? *That's* what you're smuggling?"

"Of course. What else would come from Brione-2?"

"I don't know, drugs maybe? Weapons?"

"Tylo imports its drugs, same as we do. Weapons, sometimes. If we find a buyer looking for the real high-tech stuff, it might be worth it. But good power supplies, holoscreen cards, QE processors, and subspace comms are worth twenty times as much here as in Tylo if we can bypass the taxes and tariffs."

"Not a bad markup."

"It's less than what the government takes." Rizpah slung an empty backpack over her shoulders and secured the straps so it wouldn't bounce. "After you help transport the load back to the LAVs, you can return to the *Fortitude*. Dagy's our inside man on the ship. He'll secure you in the hiding place and let you out once you reach Brione-2." The bodyguard paused, as if debating her next words. "We don't normally transport humans. It'll be cold, but the flight's short. You should be fine."

"Lovely."

Rizpah nodded, ending our conversation. Her eyes once again took on their flinty edge from last night. "Let's go, people. Daylight's burning."

Chapter 12

RIZPAH SLIPPED OUT THE door first while the rest of us waited inside. Half still clung to the metal ladder since there wasn't much room on the floor. After a moment, she stuck her arm in and waved that the coast was clear.

No one wasted any time. Like a well-greased coupling, they slid past me and trotted down the hallway. Smooth and silent.

I turned to follow, and Iko grabbed my bicep, yanking me back. He pulled me close enough that the bitter remains of artificial coffee on his breath made my nose scrunch in self-defense.

He pitched his voice low, so the others didn't hear him. "I checked up on you last night. That shit you pulled on Andaress-4 is all over the news. It's only a matter of time before they hunt you down and drag you back in restraints."

"I'd turn myself in if it meant I didn't have to smell your breath anymore."

He shook my arm hard enough to rattle my teeth. "You should really be nicer to me."

"Why? So we can have more quality time like this? Hate to break it to you, but I'm only using you for your ride."

"Good luck with that, sweet cheeks." He released my arm and slapped me on the ass. "You're going to need it."

I fumed, but I didn't want to get into a pissing match. The crew had already disappeared around the corner, and Iko hurried to catch up.

"Jerk," I muttered under my breath. "May the void take you and swallow you whole."

A flash of remorse came and passed at my unkind words. He wasn't entirely to blame. I baited the guy. Sometimes, I just couldn't help myself.

I pulled the hood of my jacket over my head. The expensive ov-ex material would blow out my image on any visual recording devices, hiding my identity. It worked best for quick, in-and-out jobs. When security reviewed the recordings, all they would see was a big, white, useless blur. There were other ways to identify suspects—gait recognition, thermal reads, voice patterns, finger, toe, or palm prints, touch DNA, even ear shape—but nothing beat good, old-fashioned facial recognition.

We exited the building through a service door, and Dominique stopped us ten meters from the ship near a stack of cargo waiting to be loaded. The *Fortitude* was a midsized cargo ship in the arrowhead class, named so for its triangular-wedge shape and slate-gray exterior. It was ten times larger than the *Soteria,* but nowhere near the size of intersystem freighters. She'd happily transport two or three pods of dry goods or a few dozen passengers, but load her up too much and she'd never make it off the ground.

The sky had lightened to a pale blue with soft gray clouds sweeping in from the coast, and the first rays of Brione lit the land. We scattered ourselves among the crates, trying our best to stick to the shadows. Rizpah waited beside me, her full eyebrows drawn together in concentration as she scanned the loading area. Overhead, a drone silently passed, sending a shiver down my spine even though we weren't near the restricted zone.

I squatted low, my thighs aching as the minutes ticked by. Finally, a light-haired man in his fifties stepped to the edge of the ship's ramp. He mopped his brow with a rag from his coveralls and retreated inside.

"That's the sign. Let's go." Dominique's comm came over my cuff.

As one, our group hurried to the ship and up the ramp. The man waited for us inside the hull of the *Fortitude.*

"Dagy." Dominique inclined her head toward the mechanic before passing him a wrapped parcel the size of a data pad.

He tucked it inside his coveralls and scratched at his beard. "That her?" His chin jutted in my direction.

"Yes. Will it be a problem?"

"Shouldn't be, though I can't say it'll be a comfortable ride."

"Comfort is low on my priority list," I assured him.

"All right, well, we'll make it work then. The crew went to find some grub. I offered to stay behind while she refueled. We should be clear for an hour, but not much longer. Capt'n wants to get back to Tylo before the Asteroids' game starts."

"Yeah?" asked Rizpah, unbuckling her pack and tossing it to the floor. "You got credits on the game?"

Dagy shook his head. "Nah, they ain't playing for shit this year, not since Yaz got that bionic ankle. Still hasn't figured out how to run on the damn thing. Capt'n figures they're due for a spot of luck, though."

"Then let's not hold him up, aye?" Rizpah slapped him on the shoulder. The lean bodyguard was at least fifteen years younger than Dagy, but they had an easy camaraderie that spanned the age gap.

Dagy led us to a service hatch along the outer hull. He removed the floor panel, revealing a smuggler's slick—a hiding place that's easy to access but hard to find. The conduit tubes, wires, piping, and insulation had been removed or rerouted to create a space roughly one meter by one meter wide and three meters deep.

Iko grunted as he hefted the first box out of the hole. Willy took it and passed it back to Goat, who placed it carefully inside his pack. They repeated the process until each of our packs was laden with electronics.

I shifted mine around until the weight sat evenly across my back, then secured the chest and waist straps so it wouldn't bounce. The straps chafed at the base of my neck, but it couldn't be helped. I slung my messenger bag with my extra shirt, jacket, undergarments, LTs, and first-aid kit over the top of that. Altogether they weighed about thirty kilograms or dang near half of my body weight. The others did the same while Iko climbed out of the hole.

Dagy knelt and replaced the floor panel. He wheezed when he stood, the air rattling in his lungs. Not an uncommon affliction for people who worked at the docks and breathed sinnafuel exhaust all day.

"From here, we split into three smaller groups." Dominique paired us off: Goat with her; Iko with Willy; and Rizpah with me. It was a good mix. We had at least one experienced person on each team. She sent a comm to each of our cuffs, designating different routes back to the roof, complete with a map. Ours took us through the cafeteria. "Keep your hoods up and avoid security. Ov-ex material won't do you any good if one of them gets a solid look at your face."

Rizpah rested her hand on my shoulder. "We'll exit through the employee cafeteria. Keep your head down and your mouth shut, and no one will pay you any attention."

"Why don't we go back the way we came?" I asked. "We didn't pass anyone the entire way."

"Scared?" Iko sneered.

Dominique shot him a withering glare. "Before, we weren't carrying contraband. The most they could get us for was trespassing. Walking in a group wasn't risky."

"What she really means is," Willy interjected, "if you get pinched, we only lose a third of the merchandise."

"Yes, well, that too." Dominique's lips tipped up in a wolfish grin.

"Do you get caught often?"

Rizpah gave me a small push down the ramp. "Stick to the plan. You'll be fine."

My pack threw off my center of gravity, and I stumbled down the incline before catching my balance. Iko snickered as he passed.

Willy strode by me, the thrill of adventure shining in his eyes the way it only does for the young and naive. It probably hadn't occurred to him yet that he might do serious time in a detention facility if they apprehended him. Three to five years for legal items and up to twenty for prohibited tech like data skimmers, LAV boosters, or nonmedical body enhancements. I didn't trust that Lady Ilymechina's crew had been one hundred percent forthcoming with the nature of the cargo, so I was reserving a healthy level of skepticism.

Call me jaded.

Rizpah stopped beside me and watched the other two groups head off in different directions. "Come, this way."

As we approached a door marked RESTRICTED AC-CESS—EMPLOYEES ONLY, two security personnel flew toward us on a hovercart. Its lights flashed orange and blue, warning people to get out of its way. My heart rabbit-kicked against my rib cage, but they zipped by without sparing us a second glance.

I tugged my hood a little farther down around my face.

Rizpah held her cuff up to the door reader. The lock disengaged.

"You said the cuffs wouldn't work to get through secure areas."

"I said *your* cuff wouldn't work. Do I look stupid enough to break into a spacedock without a fully functioning cuff?"

Yeah, who would be that stupid?

She slipped through the door and motioned for me to follow.

Once inside, Rizpah guided me toward the left wing of the build-ing. We passed three people in the corridor, all too absorbed with their holoscreens to notice us. Signs hanging from the ceiling point-ed the way toward various hangers, loading bays, refueling stations, sinnafuel storage, security offices, and the cafeteria. I was grateful we didn't have to use the holoscreen map Dominique had provided, as nothing marked you as being out of place as projecting a map.

Soon, the smell of mass-produced food tainted the air. My stom-ach rumbled, reminding me that all I'd consumed in the last day was an order of crispers, a scone, and far too much caffeine. I must be desperate if powdered eggs and soy bacon sounded good.

As promised, the cafeteria wasn't busy. Islands of round tables dotted the floor. They were separated enough that occupants didn't have to make small talk if they didn't want to. Most people sat at the three tables nearest the end of the buffet where they could spot their friends in line and cajole them into joining the group.

We picked a path around the outer edge of the tables, steering clear.

The hair on the back of my neck prickled with awareness, and I was acutely aware of the illegal electronics in my pack, which had grown ten times heavier while we walked. I hadn't been this nervous since my rookie year. Even though everyone appeared focused on their plates or holoscreens, it felt like every eye was on me. As if, at any moment, someone would leap onto the table and shout, "Gotcha!"

Seconds later, we were through the cafeteria and in the back loading bay for food services. This area, too, was clear of spacedock employees, and I had to wonder if it was luck or exceptional planning by Lady Ilymechina's crew.

"There's another cargo lift over there," Rizpah said, pointing. "We'll climb up the shaft to the roof."

She, too, must have been feeling the strain of carrying her pack, because sweat dotted her forehead beneath her fringe of black bangs. We ducked into the mechanical room along the side of the lift. The only light came from the cracks around the door. I stared up the seemingly endless row of ladder rungs I'd soon be climbing.

Last check, I tightened the straps on my pack and wiped the moisture from my hands against my pant legs. I grasped the first rung and hauled myself up. Hand over hand, I climbed. It didn't take long for my thighs to protest, but I kept a steady pace until the start of the third floor.

"Hang on," I called softly down to Rizpah, who trailed me by only a few meters. I shook out my arms and took a deep breath to pacify my screaming lungs. Threading one elbow around a rung to secure myself, I readjusted my pack where the straps dug into my shoulders. Too much time in space had left me out of shape for this kind of physical labor.

I continued up the last flight to the top, popped out the access panel, and lowered it to the outside floor of the roof.

"Chintzy"—that's what I'd designated my new cuff—"record visual." I stuck my arm out far enough to do a one-hundred-and-eighty-degree sweep. "Play back recording."

Back inside the shelter of the shaft, my holoscreen lit up with an image of the roof. The graphics were atrocious and flickered in and out as they rendered the images. I kept a close eye for any signs of movement as the view panned from left to right. Three-quarters of the way around, I spotted Dominique and Goat hunched near another shaft.

"Open comm to Dominique." I waited a second for the link to establish. "We're on the roof. Safe to proceed?"

Dominique's head swiveled in my direction. "The others are already here. Looping the cameras now. Be prepared to run in ten, nine, eight . . ."

I scrambled out of the shaft and spun around to help Rizpah crawl through the small hole, but she had already slithered through and sat crouched beside the panel. We replaced the cover as Dominique counted down to one.

"Go!"

Rizpah shot out like a champion sprinter. She drew ahead of me, but not by much over the short distance. Iko and Willy came from the opposite direction and arrived right after us.

"Any problems?" Dominique asked. Everyone shook their heads. "That's what I like to hear."

At her signal, Goat pulled out the rope ladder from his bag, secured one end, and tied his backpack to the other end. He lifted it up and over the ledge of the building and carefully lowered it to the ground. The rest of us climbed down the ladder single file like ants on a log. I was last in line, and when my boots hit the ground, Goat untied his end from the roof and let the ladder fall. Rizpah gathered it in a bundle and stuffed it into Goat's pack while he free-climbed down.

Three minutes later, I stacked my share of the contraband into the back of a LAV beside Dominique's and Willy's bags. I stretched my neck from side to side and rolled my shoulders to work out the kink that had formed beside my shoulder blade.

The entire run took less than forty minutes.

Dominique claimed the pilot's seat and fired up the engine. Willy jumped into the copilot's seat. The LAV lifted off and its legs retracted into the hull. Sharp bits of sand whirled in the air as it rose. I stepped out of the way, shielding my eyes and nose with my jacket sleeve. When they sped off for the gate, Rizpah joined me.

"Iko will finish loading the rest of the bags while Goat and I help you back into the building. Goat will secure the ladder at the top. Dominique gave me the code to loop the cameras so you can get back to the shaft. After that, you're on your own. Find Dagy at the *Fortitude*. He'll get you into the slick and let you out once you reach Tylo. Do not leave until he comes to get you. The last thing we need is a crew member discovering our arrangement."

"I know the plan."

"Good. See that you stick to it."

I removed the data dot with all my research on Lady Ilymechina and the Seven Serpents from my bag but hesitated before handing it over. "How do I know that once I give this to you, you won't let security find me?"

"Lady Ilymechina gave you her word. I would rather die than betray her. Besides, you know about Dagy. If security apprehends you, you could turn him in and ruin a good supply chain for us. Of course, if you did that, you would also be admitting to smuggling in illegal goods yourself. This way, we both have an incentive to keep our side of the bargain."

I had to admit, that was well played. I handed her the data dot. "Thank you for your help."

"Don't get caught."

The three of us wasted no more time retracing our steps. Goat shimmied up the wall to set the ladder. He declined my offer to wait for him to use the ladder instead of making him climb back down again, claiming it was his favorite part of the job. He waited until I reached the shaft, then tossed the rope down and disappeared over the edge. I didn't know if Rizpah had fixed the cameras. No alarms sounded, so I took that as a positive sign.

I opened the panel and hurried down the ladder, mindful that the crew of the *Fortitude* would be returning. At the bottom, I almost opened the door, but froze when I heard voices. Two men, judging by the deep tones, sounded as if they were camped out, catching up on the morning gossip.

I didn't have time for that. I ran my hands down my face. *Think, think, think.*

"Chintzy," I whispered. "Show me the map of the spacedock again."

"Unable to process request."

Shitty cuff. I raised my voice as much as I dared. "Show me the map of the spacedock."

"Please specify which spacedock."

My brain about exploded. "The R. Burns Interplanetary Space-dock."

The same map Dominique had sent us earlier popped up in front of me. She must have gotten her hands on actual blueprints because it showed maintenance tunnels, service entrances, windows, doors—everything a greedy smuggler could ask for.

My eyes snagged on the viewing platform overlooking the ships and flight deck. I zoomed in on the west side, rotated the map, and spotted stairs in the northeast corner. Not ideal, but it would work.

Going back up the ladder, I found the second floor empty and exited the shaft. I pulled my ov-ex hood up and made tracks for the end of the building. Luckily, it wasn't far.

This wasn't a secure area. Passengers were free to watch ships taking off and landing. I held my cuff up to the reader, and the door to the outside slid open.

From up there, I could see the *Fortitude* parked in D5. A morning rush of commuters flowed in and out of the building. I was planning the least conspicuous path when I noticed two people talking right below me. One was a brassy-haired woman in a refueling-specialist's uniform.

The other was a tall man who cut a shockingly attractive silhouette in his black tactical pants and dark green DECA jacket. So, not a desk jockey. I hadn't expected him to personally come and get me, but apparently Grayson Wright was a boots-on-the-ground kind of agent. That was both admirable and frustrating. I would have preferred it if he'd given the task to an inexperienced minion.

My fingers curled into fists. Now what? I couldn't continue without being seen, and I didn't have time to go back to the lift before the crew arrived back at the ship. I closed my eyes and took a deep breath, willing the universe to provide an answer.

"Problem, sweet cheeks?"

My eyes snapped open to find Iko standing beside me.

"What are you doing here?" I asked in sotto voce. "You're supposed to be going to the drop house."

"Change of plans."

"Shh! Keep your voice low. See that guy down there? He's the agent from Andaress-4 who's looking for me."

Wright flashed his credentials to the specialist, and a holographic image of me floated between them. It cycled through a set of standard hairstyles, makeup options, and clothing designed to show possible changes in appearance.

"I know."

"You know?" I turned my head to see Iko's face.

"Yeah, I'm the one who told him you'd be here, ribbit."

My expression must have been priceless, because Iko snickered—right before he shoved me off the platform.

Chapter 13

I FELL FROM THE second level, twisting halfway to land on my side. My teeth clacked and air fled my lungs even though I slapped my arm to the side to distribute the force of impact. Falling three meters onto hard cement still hurt like hell.

Dazed, I shook my head and tried to get my bearings. Iko stared down at me from on top of the viewing platform. He gave me a rude hand gesture and retreated from view. So much for honor amongst thieves.

My head swung to the side. Grayson Wright and the refueling-specialist both stared at me. The woman's head swiveled from the holo to me, then back again.

I couldn't read lips, but I made out Wright say, "Shit," before sprinting in my direction.

Every bone in my body objected, but I scrambled to my feet and staggered toward the safety of the building. Wright trailed me by about ten meters, but he was gaining on me. I willed my legs to pump faster.

"Sinclair! Stop!"

I didn't waste my breath answering. It was hard enough pulling in oxygen as it was. Hopefully, my diaphragm just needed a moment to recover, and it wasn't something more serious, like a broken rib.

Blaster fire shot past me, biting into the pavement and kicking up a puff of dust. I swerved left and right, running in a zigzag pattern that wasted time but made me a harder target.

Another ten meters, and I'd reach the public access door. Once inside the spacedock, I hoped to lose Wright in the corridors, especially if Dominique's map still worked.

Drawing on a last reserve of speed, I lengthened my stride. I waved my cuff at the sensor, but before it opened, a second blast cut past me and took out the door reader. It exploded in a shower of sparks, and the acrid scent of burnt electronics filled the air.

Too late to stop, I face-planted into the door. Humiliation warred with panic. Panic won. My fingers pried at the door, trying to force it open manually. When it didn't budge, I pounded my fist against it and kicked it for good measure.

Smoke from the fried panel blew into my face with the shifting wind, stinging my eyes and making me cough. I spun around, searching for an exit.

"Give it up, Sinclair. You've got nowhere to go." Agent Wright stopped a few paces from me, his blaster half-lowered but ready to snap back up should I make a sudden move.

The morning sun crept up behind his shoulder, lending golden highlights to his hair and making me squint to see his face clearly. Dark shadows under his eyes and a day's worth of stubble told me he'd pushed himself to reach Clava so fast. He wouldn't give up easily. Not with my capture so close at hand.

I raised my hands to show I was unarmed.

"You're making a mistake," I said. "I didn't kill Jarrett, and you know it. Why are you wasting time pursuing me when the real murderers are still out there?"

"We recovered an encrypted communication between you and the victim days before his death that my tech can't break and your DNA all over the crime scene. You not only fled, but took extensive measures to avoid being questioned, including breaking into a secure facility, impersonating an agent, destruction of property, and assaulting an officer. And I'm sure I'll add to that list before we get back to Salin."

Well, when he put it like that . . .

"Circumstantial," I refuted. "There's a logical explanation for each of those. Jarrett was my closest friend. Of course my DNA is all over his place. I visited him a lot."

"I'm willing to hear you out," he said, removing a pair of augmented restraints from his utility belt and stepping closer. "But we both know that has to happen back on Andaress-4."

"Look, Wright, there's more going on here than Jarrett's murder. He stumbled onto something—something big. It got him killed, and there could be more lives at risk."

"Come in peacefully, and we'll talk about it."

I wanted to believe him. I really did. But if my former partner had taught me anything, it was that you could never truly trust a person, especially a DECA agent.

"I'm sorry."

"About what?" Wright shifted his weight to his back foot and glanced warily to the side.

"This."

I lunged forward, knocking his blaster to the side. He squeezed off a shot before it clattered to the ground, out of reach. We were too close for me to step clear, and the blast seared the outer edge of my arm. Scorching-hot pain lanced through my bicep. I swallowed a scream as brightly colored spots swam in my vision and my knees threatened to buckle. For a second, I almost gave in to the pain, but it wasn't a direct hit and he had set it to the lowest level.

Gritting my teeth, I followed through with an open-handed strike to his throat. He blocked it before I made contact, grabbed my wrist, and redirected my momentum into a one-hundred-and-eighty-degree spin. With his chest pressed solidly against my back and his arm banded around my shoulders, he cinched me tightly to his body.

He smelled like fresh soap and bergamot—and clearly I had a concussion from the fall if I was wasting time thinking about how nice he smelled.

Disgusted, I threw my weight against him, but his hold was unyielding. Struggling only made him grip tighter.

My cross-body bag twisted around between us. I slid my hand down my hip and slipped it inside, groping blindly for something to use as a weapon.

Wright juggled the augmented restraints into position. His hand slid along my waist, right below my breasts.

"Hey buddy, those aren't my wrists."

"And that's not my backup piece you're fumbling for."

My hand jerked out of my bag so fast I scratched myself on the metal buckle. "Fuck."

"Is that a bribe?"

"In your dreams."

"You're welcome to file a complaint with my superior back in Salin."

"That won't be necessary." I drove my heel into his shin and stomped on his foot. Anticipating the shock to loosen his hold, I bolted forward.

Or, at least, I tried to. My feet went airborne as Wright lifted me off the ground in a bear hug. I kicked wildly, hoping to catch his knee. He grunted as he shifted for a better hold. I pried at his fingers, targeting his weakest joints, and when that didn't do any good, I threw my head back and heard a satisfying crack when it connected with his face. That earned me a rough shake until I let go.

"Shit, Sinclair, you fight dirty," he said, setting me on my feet. "Calm down."

Never in the history of ever did telling a person to calm down result in them actually calming down. This time was no exception.

Luckily, Wright stood several centimeters taller than me, making my center of gravity lower than his. I jammed my elbow into his ribs and locked my hands onto his forearm, which was still wrapped around my chest. I bent my knees, threw my torso forward, and thrust my ass back into his pelvis. He grunted as I straightened my legs and twisted my hips to send him rolling over my shoulder and onto the ground.

I took one running step and was jerked off my feet. Wright had gotten a hand around my ankle from where he lay on the ground.

My forearms landed first, taking the brunt of the fall. The gash in my arm lit up until stars danced across my vision. Whoever promoted blasters as a humane option for incapacitating a person was a big, fat liar.

Wright yanked back on my ankle, drawing me closer. Something hard dug into my stomach. Another tug and Wright's dropped blaster popped free from under me. Wonder of wonders, it was still charged. I flipped over, using the opportunity to throw a kick at his head. He ducked out of the way, giving me time to dial up the strength.

The blaster emitted a high-pitched whine that every officer and agent knew by heart. Wright froze, his hazel eyes staring not at the end of the blaster but directly into mine. It was the moment every officer feared—having their own blaster turned against them.

"Don't make me do this." My voice was steady, but my eyes pleaded with him. "Just let me walk away."

His grip tightened around my ankle. "You know I can't do that."

It would have been easier to give myself up—to drop the blaster and let Wright take me into custody—but Cavender's betrayal still stabbed at my heart. There was no guarantee Wright wasn't just as corrupt. If I didn't see this through, Jarrett's killers might get away with it like they'd gotten away with the murder of Sorelsdotter's and Zairesh's murders. I couldn't let that happen.

"I'm sorry," I said and pulled the trigger.

"Psst," I peeked out from behind the door. "Dagy. Over here."

The mechanic stopped midstep and peered into the shadows. His pale-blond eyebrows rose to the middle of his high forehead. He shooed me back into the room and shut the door behind us.

Sweat dotted the man's hairline, and his eyes kept darting to the door. "How'd you get on the ship? Security's crawling all ov'r the place. Two DECA officers searched the ship."

"I know. I hid in the landing gear and watched for them to leave before coming inside."

"Pure luck they didn't find the slick. Thank goodness we got it unloaded in time. Lady Ilymechina would've had my balls in a vise." Dagy tugged at the collar of his coveralls. "This here's a lot more trouble than I signed up for. Find another way to Tylo."

My arm throbbed, my ribs ached, and I was developing a headache behind my right eye. I'd made it too far to stop.

Wincing, I swung my bag around to my front. It banged against my hip, notifying me of another bruise I hadn't cataloged yet. I pulled out one hundred in legal tender—half of what I had left—and waved it under Dagy's nose. "Will a bonus make it worth your while?"

"Uh-uh. Too risky." He shook his head, but his eyes never left the money.

I fanned the LTs, letting him see how many there were. "DECA's already searched your ship. There's no reason for them to come back. All you have to do is go ahead exactly like we planned."

Dagy shifted his weight from foot to foot.

"Or I can take my LTs and find another way. I'll be wanting the portion that Lady Ilymechina paid you for my transport, and you can explain to her why the deal didn't go through." I made as if to put the money back in my bag, but Dagy's hand on mine stopped me.

"Well now, wait a minute. Maybe we can figure something out."

I smiled and flipped my hand over so he could take the LTs. "That would be great."

An alarm buzzed twice over the speaker, warning the crew to prepare for takeoff. The ship lurched, and I stumbled sideways, bumping into the wall with my injured arm.

"Son of a—" I clamped down on the last word, waiting for the stinging to pass.

Dagy's eyes dropped to my bicep. Blood oozed out between my fingers where I was applying pressure. "You hurt?"

"Blaster burn grazed my arm."

He pulled a medkit from the wall and removed out a tube of regenerative salve and a square of GraftPatch.

"You know how to use these?" He handed them to me, along with a sterile pad to clean the cut.

"It's not my first scrape."

"I'll tell the capt'n I need to replace a janky switch in the cargo bay electrical panel. It'll knock out the cameras for a bit while I cut the power. Then we can get you into the slick." Dagy jerked his head in a nervous nod and left me to tend my wound.

The ov-ex fabric of my jacket stuck to my flesh where the blood had dried, and I winced as I peeled it away. I swabbed the wound with the sterile pad and squirted a healthy amount of regenerative salve on it to speed the healing process. The piece of GraftPatch synthetic skin tingled as it bonded to my flesh, creating a watertight seal.

Five minutes later, Dagy returned with a spare pair of insulated coveralls, a hat, and gloves. "Put these on. It'll be colder than an asteroid's backside in there."

After shimmying into the overalls, Dagy hustled me to the cargo bay. He pried open the floor hatch and lowered me in. Dominique hadn't lied. It was a tight fit.

Dagy wheezed between breaths from the exertion. "Once we get to Tylo, I'll wait for the cargo to be unloaded and for the guys to leave. Then I'll come get you."

"Just don't forget about me, okay?"

He ran a hand down his beard. "I didn't build this slick to transport people. Take off will be a bitch. No two ways about it. You hold on as best you can and try not to make any noise. There's no reason for the crew to be back here, but it'll look suspicious if I steer them away."

"It won't be a problem." Some of my stakeouts had lasted days. I could handle it.

He filled his responding nod with both pity and finality. It made me question my sanity at trusting my life to an organized crime ring. Then he replaced the floor plate, and it was too late to do anything about it.

I thought claustrophobia would be the worst part of being locked inside the smuggler's slick, but I hadn't counted on the utter darkness. Regular sounds intensified: every creak of the walls, every footstep overhead, every chitter of an unseen rat felt like a klaxon that would bring the crew running. I didn't dare turn on Chintzy's holoscreen for fear of its light leaking through the crevices.

Dagy had the forethought to add a small blanket and bucket with a lid. It was a six-hour flight, but I absolutely refused to use the bucket for anything other than sitting. I folded the blanket into a makeshift cushion and placed it on top of the bucket. Then I felt around for handholds to grab onto during takeoff and waited.

After what seemed like hours—but was probably more like twenty minutes—the engine powered up and we maneuvered out of the gate to the launchpad. I grabbed onto two pipes and hoped they wouldn't break loose.

Liftoff about shook my arms from their sockets, but I held fast for the eight minutes it took us to break orbit. It took another ten—I guessed—excruciating minutes for the *Fortitude* to begin her flight to Brione-2. Only once I felt us pick up speed did I allow myself to relax.

All my energy evaporated into the ether as my body succumbed to the aftermath of an adrenaline rush. Somewhere in my bag, I had an unappealing meal bar that I should eat, but that sounded like an awful lot of work. I compromised on a water pouch, taking only small sips. Even at room temperature and tasting like its biodegradable packaging, it washed away the foul taste in my mouth and soothed my sore throat.

Too bad it did little for my conscience.

It wasn't the first time I'd shot a person. By the void, it wasn't even the first time I'd shot an agent, but that didn't make it any easier.

If only I'd made it back to the *Fortitude* a little quicker or if Iko had kept his mouth shut, we could have avoided the entire incident. I'd be on Brione-2 and Wright, well, Wright would be safe and sound back on Vesen-1, sorting through hours of security footage. As close as we'd been, the blaster had knocked him out cold, but he'd still been breathing. I bet he'd wake up with one hell of a headache, though.

I lamented shooting Wright, but I'd done what I had to do. Something was very wrong with the Insight implants, and Tazza Industries was covering it up. If the deaths of Kelthea Zairesh, Thomas Rhinehardt, Silar Culpepper, and Ruana Sorelsdotter were true outliers, the company wouldn't have paid Cavender to tank the homicide investigations. My gut told me a lot more people would die if Tazza Industries continued unchecked.

The evidence had to be at its headquarters. I would find it and expose the company. They couldn't get away with endangering lives. I took an oath to protect and serve, and that didn't end just because I no longer wore the uniform.

Chapter 14

Scorching-hot air assaulted me the minute Dagy got me off the ship and onto Tylo's spacedock. The spare coveralls doubled as my disguise. He ushered me through the security check using a coworker's credentials, who he'd paid to call in sick the day before. We parted ways as soon as I could do so without drawing attention.

For the next half hour, I wandered the grounds between buildings. Signs flashed eye-catching advertisements from the ground up to the tenth story, tall enough to be seen by the multiple skylanes of LAVs flying overhead. I couldn't walk twenty paces without seeing one for the Insight. Tazza Industries must have spent a fortune on ads.

The one on my right featured a man in a business suit confidently making a banking transaction in a crowded spacedock. PRIVACY was written in bold letters across the top. On my left, another showed a confused thief trying to steal a woman's cuff, but of course, there was no cuff on her arm, because she had the Insight. A crowd formed around the would-be thief to laugh at him. SECURITY flashed above the actors. A new ad began. This time, two teenage girls chatted in a bedroom. They got up to leave, and the one wearing a cuff realized she hadn't charged it, so the battery was dead. Her friend—who was much prettier and more fashionably dressed—told her the Insight had a lifetime battery. CONVENIENCE.

I had to hand it to Tazza Industries, the ads were slick. Cuffs made everyday life a lot easier, but they weren't without their challenges. These ads highlighted some of the worst.

Beads of sweat formed on my forehead and upper lip and trickled down my neck to beneath my coveralls. Stars, it was hot. I circled and doubled back over my trail, choosing no particular order for my route. DECA agents would eventually pick up my trail, but I didn't have to make it easy on them.

When I couldn't take the heat anymore, I stepped into the shade of a building. I turned my back to the wind and spit into the red dirt. Sand felt like grit on my lashes and my teeth, and invaded every crack, crevice, and orifice in my body. Luckily, Dagy's uniform covered most of my skin, leaving only my hands, forearms, and face exposed to the punishing heat and ultraviolet light of Brione high overhead.

Brione-2 was not a hospitable planet. It orbited the inner ring of Brione, almost too close to bother terraforming. However, the bedrock was rich in rare earth metals and other materials highly sought after in the technology industry, so they plowed ahead anyway. Tylo was the only city of note, but temporary mining camps pockmarked the rest of the southern continent. They popped up long enough to strip the ground of its resources before moving on to the next dusty patch.

The high heat and thin atmosphere baked most of the moisture out of the air, leaving a thick layer of burnt-red sand covering the crust. Strong winds frequently whipped it high into the air to create weeks-long sandstorms.

Meanwhile, the humidity hovered around three percent. There were no lakes or oceans, only artificially created ponds encased in plastiglass domes to trap in moisture. All water came from reservoirs deep underground that was piped to the surface by a private company called Hydrolutions, the initial investor in Brione-2 and many other water-scarce planets.

My parents and I had only traveled to Tylo twice, despite its close proximity to Clava. Hotels and restaurants were expensive, and beyond taking a guided tour of an abandoned mine shaft, there wasn't much to do for fun. I'd visited a few times as an adult, mostly for work, and couldn't say I recommended it.

I held up my arm. "Chintzy, show me a map of Tylo."

A holographic map in the rough shape of a spoked wheel projected in front of me. Flashes of staticky light glittered across the map and grains of windblown sand passed through it. I moved closer to the building to try and block the worst of it.

The spacedock sat in the very center of the city. Since most everything needed to be imported, the cost of goods was high. Add in centralized water and environmental controls, and Tylo built up instead of out. The entire city was only three kilometers across, but the average building was over fifty stories high.

"Switch to 3D mode. Where is Tazza Industries' headquarters?"

The view of the map zoomed in, like a mini-me plummeting from the sky to ground level in the space of a second. Chintzy's graphics card was, well, chintzy. My stomach did a little flip-flop at the poor rendering.

An image of a building half a klick away blinked bright yellow with floors forty through fifty-three highlighted. The name Tazza Center and a list of occupants appeared next to it. No surprise, Tazza Industries' headquarters was at the top.

I turned off the map and weighed my options. All the buildings connected to each other via enclosed skybridges on every tenth floor. Hovercart rental stations dotted the pathways at regular intervals in case you were going a long distance or carrying something heavy. Restaurants, stores, and service businesses concentrated on those levels with housing and other commercial space filling in between.

It was a slick system that saved pedestrians from having to go out in the blistering heat to get from building to building, but it posed a problem for someone who didn't want to be spotted on a security feed. Namely, me. In a city built by tech giants, I assumed every square centimeter of indoor space was heavily monitored.

The safer course of action would be to stay outside as long as possible. LAVs flew in designated lanes between the buildings, but pedestrian traffic was light. No one wanted to stroll around in forty-degree heat.

I set off toward the building. Sweat rolled down my neck, gathering at my clavicle, between my breasts, and across my lower back. Red sand homed in on me like fleshflies to a dead body, burrowing into my scalp and under my nails. I wiped the back of my hand across my forehead to catch the sweat dripping into my eyes and it came away coated in a thick layer of grime. Yuck.

By the time I reached Tazza Center, I had a rough plan. Or at least, a plan on how to get a plan. I'd been half-assing my way through this operation so far, and it hadn't exactly gone well for me.

Fishing in the bottom of my bag, I came up with enough legal tender to either buy a new outfit or three cheap meals. My stomach rumbled and dinner won.

I entered the building adjacent to Tazza Center through a double set of doors. The cool, climate-controlled air hit me like a physical force. I unfastened the snaps at my neck and flapped the material to create air movement between it and my skin. I moaned in pleasure, causing an elderly woman passing by to do a double take.

The lobby was sparsely decorated with slate-gray floors, pale limestone walls, and a cluster of uncomfortable-looking chairs near an artfully positioned boulder on the south end. A large holovid took up the entire west wall. An ad for a luxury LAV ended and a larger-than-life image of Aurelian Tazza, the CEO of Tazza Industries, smiled down at me. A parade of beautiful actors followed: an office worker receiving a promotion, a runner listening to his music, a group of friends ordering drinks at a club, and a mother sharing a comm with her adult daughter and granddaughter. None of them wore cuffs. The vid blanked, replaced with spiraling text: *Insight. Look to your future.*

Strange that none of them were lying dead on the medical examiner's table.

My first stop was to a public restroom. After relieving myself in one of the private toilet cubes—Me: 1, bucket: 0—I stripped out of the coveralls and tossed them in the reclamator. They were too bulky to fit in my bag, and Rizpah's outfit blended in better.

I cleaned up as best I could using the sonic hand washer. It was tight quarters, but I stuck my hands under the mister, letting the soap-laced water vapor accumulate on my palms and patted it on my face. It was an awkward position, but I knelt in front of the speaker and twisted my head low enough for the sound waves to work their vibrating, scrubbing magic. I tried not to think too hard about how dirty the floor was.

Dusting off my knees and straightening my top, I looked into the mirror. A quick finger-comb got my purple hair back into place, but it could use a good shampoo. I added some heavy lip and eye color with my makeup brush and shrugged back into my wrinkled ov-ex jacket. Since they developed and manufactured the special fabric on Brione-2, it wasn't illegal to wear here and would hopefully keep most of the cameras from recording my image.

I took the lift to the fortieth floor and found a restaurant that offered tables beside the anti-radiation windows facing Tazza Center. Brightly lit holovid ads plastered much of the building's surface, casting a neon glow into the dusty air. This high up, the wide strips of red dirt separating the buildings looked like little more than bloody scratch marks on the planet's skin.

A low altitude vehicle flew by the window, startling me. Traffic lanes were higher in Tylo to avoid the dusty surface, which clogged engines and wreaked havoc on air purification systems. I watched it zip up another ten stories before veering left into the designated air space that helped keep accidents to a minimum.

"Chintzy, show me the menu."

"Unable to process request." The tinny, electronic voice grated on my nerves.

I missed Felix. We never had these kinds of communication issues. "Show me the menu for . . ." I looked for signage. "Tylo Tostadas."

"Unable to process request."

"Oh, for crying out loud." I tapped the display button, activating the cheap cuff's extra-large holoscreen. Gesturing like a madwoman with exaggerated swipes and jabs, people probably thought I was swatting at a swarm of bugs.

Finally, I found the restaurant's menu. Everything looked mouthwateringly delicious. The house special included free chips and salsa, so I ordered that and added a note to skip the cilantro. People swore it was delicious, but it tasted like soap to me.

Before placing my order, I had to participate in an interactive ad for the Insight neural implant by throwing a holographic cuff into a holographic reclamator like I was some kind of athlete. Tazza Industries was really laying it on thick with the advertising campaign.

It didn't take long for a server droid to bring out my dinner. I inserted a few of my precious LTs into the payment receptacle and a door opened, allowing me to remove a glass of water and a steaming plate of three vegetarian tostadas topped with crisp lettuce, juicy tomatoes, and gooey vegan cheese sauce made by blending locally grown potatoes and carrots with a few other imported ingredients. A basket of freshly fried chips followed, still sizzling from their trip through the deep fryer. I closed my eyes and inhaled the fragrant combination of chilies and cumin, trying not to drool. Classic comfort food.

The droid rolled back to the kitchen, leaving me to enjoy my meal. Starving, I wolfed down the first tostada and half the chips before coming up for air. That's when the heat in the salsa hit me. It started at the back of my throat, worked its way through my sinuses, and into my eyes. Tears threatened to spill until I blinked them back. Each inhale resulted in an ugly sniffle. Water only moved the pain around.

But it tasted so good.

I dabbed my eyes with the sleeve of my jacket and started in on the second tostada. The creamy bean topping on the corn tortilla soothed some of the pain. On the next chip, I was careful to scoop up a smaller amount of salsa.

Before rushing in to Tazza Industries, I needed to prepare. The virus I'd used to disable the satellite above Andaress-4 wasn't the only program I'd collected over my years in law enforcement. Jarrett used to like to reverse engineer them to figure out how they worked and how we could better stop them. Copies were stored on the *Soteria*'s server—a server with a back door. The only question was if I could access it with this cheap cuff.

I opened my holoscreen, trying to angle it in such a way that other diners wouldn't be able to read it—not an easy task, considering it was roughly the size of a red giant star. The first step was to connect to my ship over a secure channel. Thankfully, both Brione-2 and Ceti had fast and reliable subspace relay stations.

I'd instructed Felix to put the ship into lockdown mode, but I had a onetime access code that would give me a five-minute window to get in and get out. It was designed as a last-ditch safety measure that would allow captains to erase all their files or initiate a self-destruct sequence should the ship fall into the wrong hands.

"Reliance! You're back!" A computer-generated image of the ship's avatar popped up on the right side of my holoscreen. Chintzy's poor graphics card reduced the quality to a pixelated mess. Still, it was good to see his face.

"Hey, Felix. I'm just dropping in for a minute. I need a copy of that cloning program in the archive. Can you send it to me?"

"There are strangers outside. I made myself as quiet as possible without compromising essential functions, but they keep poking me and trying to get inside. It's very rude. Permission to engage self-defense measures?"

The *Soteria* wasn't a weapons ship by any means, but it did have a couple of sharp claws at its disposal. "No, I don't want you to hurt anyone."

His poorly rendered tail twitched, and I could feel him pouting over the subspace relays. "Fine."

"That's a good spaceship. Now, about that file?"

"Sending now."

It wasn't a huge file, but it needed to travel through subspace to get here from Ceti. Timing wise, it would be a close call, and every second the back door was open left the ship vulnerable to DECA.

As the seconds ticked by, Chintzy grew warm against my forearm. Its processor was being pushed to the limit.

"When will you be home?" Felix asked.

"I don't know. Soon, I hope."

"My power supplies are at ninety-two percent. What if you aren't back before they run out?"

Ninety-two percent battery life would keep the *Soteria* running for dozens of years parked on a moon and only running base systems. Leave it to a cat to worry about his food bowl going empty thirty years down the line.

"I promise somebody will recharge you before that happens," I reassured him.

The cat image settled itself into a "loaf" position, which I interpreted as acquiescence, if not agreement.

At four and a half minutes, the download finished.

"Felix, reengage lockdown mode and don't hurt anyone if they breach the hull. That's an order. I'll be back as soon as I can."

He slow-blinked, which was either a farewell or a signal lag resulting from the severed connection. Either way, the holoscreen went dark.

I blinked a few times myself to clear my eyes. Damn cat.

Installing the program on Chintzy took a few more minutes. It beeped when it finished. I went into the settings and keyed it to run the program when I tapped the outside of my cuff two times in quick succession.

I ate a few more chips and took the local temperature on the citywide implant program.

"Chintzy," I said, around a mouthful of tostada, "show me Tylo news sites featuring the word Insight."

"Processing." After a moment of hard chugging, it populated with a list of twenty different links. I sorted them by date and opened the first one.

It was a media statement released by Doctor Kandall Lourde, head of the bionics department at Tazza Industries, announcing the Insight's certification by the Interplanetary Board of Medical Devices. His name sounded familiar. It took me a minute to remember the medical examiner on Vesen-1 had said a Doctor Lourde was the surgeon who operated on Kelthea Zairesh before she died. The man leaped to the top of my list.

The second was a puff piece interview with Doctor Lourde on a local entertainment show with a live audience. I activated the holovid.

Doctor Kandall Lourde was a short man in his late fifties with pale, sallow skin, thinning and unruly dark hair, and sagging jowls. He walked across the stage, waved to the audience, and joined the host on stage. After a brief puff interview where he told the host he himself had an Insight, he demonstrated the implant by turning on lights, opening doors, and sending a communication to the host's cuff, which she displayed to the audience. They oohed and aahed and clapped with enthusiasm. Doctor Lourde smiled with the exuberance of a man finally receiving his due.

The third link displayed the application to the Interplanetary Board of Medical Devices to move the Insight past the initial trial stage. I checked the date. That was three years ago, around when Cavender covered up Zairesh's homicide. Having a dead client hit the news would have been rather inconvenient for Tazza Industries.

I searched for additional information on the studies cited in the application. Each link took me on a daisy chain of references that eventually all circled back to each other. Like a snake eating its own tail.

As I skimmed the last few entries—mostly advertisements featuring CEO Aurelian Tazza's holo-perfect headshot—a teenager and a woman carrying a young toddler walked by my table. The boy babbled, waving a small stuffed bunny around before chomping on its ear.

The teenager tugged at her mother's sleeve and pointed to my holoscreen. "That's it, Mom, that's an Insight! That's what I've been talking about."

"Don't be rude." The mother pushed down her daughter's arm. Jostled, the little boy filled his lungs and shrieked. With practiced ease, the woman bounced him on her hip and made shushing sounds. "I know what it is, honey, but that doesn't mean you're getting one."

"Ugh!" The girl's eyes rolled up so far her head tilted backward. "Faline's dad is letting her get one if she passes her quantum mechanics class."

"You're already passing quantum mechanics. I don't need to bribe you."

"So I'm being punished for being smart?"

"Your father and I bought you a brand-new cuff for your birthday. You're hardly suffering."

"That was six months ago! I'm going to be the only one at school who doesn't have an Insight. This is so unfair!"

"UNFAIR!" The toddler echoed his sister and threw the bunny to the floor by my feet in solidarity. He immediately regretted his decision and catapulted his little body headfirst after his stuffed animal. His mother caught him with a grunt. Stretching as far as his chubby little arms could reach, his eyes filled to the brim with tears.

Quickly, I scooped up the prized possession and handed it to him. "Is this your friend?"

Lip trembling, he stared at me.

"What's your friend's name?"

He sniffed. "Petey."

"You hang onto Petey, okay? We have to take care of our friends." The boy nodded and hugged the rabbit to his chest.

"Thank you." The woman gave me a tired, but sincere, smile.

"Don't mention it," I told her. "And stay strong about that neural implant thing. A mother's instincts are never wrong."

"Mom." The daughter dragged the word out to two full syllables. "We're going to be late. Again."

"All right, all right. Let's go."

"Finally." Three full syllables that time.

I couldn't make out the mother's response over the girl's stomping as they left the restaurant. Those were the people whom the Insight implants would hurt. Friends. Families. Children. None of them deserved to be lied to with slick advertising and bogus medical studies. Somewhere along the line, the system failed them.

Outside, sunlight gleamed off Tazza Center. Up there was the proof I needed to expose the company's lies. I would find it, take it to the authorities, and make them halt production while they reopened the cases of Ruana Sorelsdotter, Kelthea Zairesh, Thomas Rhinehardt, and Silar Culpepper. Once DECA corrected the cause of death, they could take that information to the IBMD. The Board would see that the devices posed a public danger and revoke its certification.

DECA would investigate Cavender and trace my former partner's finances back to Tazza Industries. If they bribed one agent, they bribed more. There would be comms and money transfers. Everything left a trail of digital dust they could track and trace.

Someone told someone to hire someone to kill Jarrett, and every last one of them deserved to rot in prison.

Chapter 15

I ALLOWED MYSELF A moment before gathering my things. After scraping my plate into the composter and returning the empty dish to the conveyor to be sanitized, I headed across the fortieth-floor skybridge. Built as convenient walkways, the plastiglass-enclosed walkways also served as parks and garden spaces. This one had hydroponic tomato vines strung from the ceiling to the floor along the outer walls that provided both shade and a pleasant fragrance to the air. Honeybee drones—the mechanical kind—buzzed among the blossoms, providing artificial pollination.

This high up, the enclosed bridge quivered as wind buffeted each building in a different direction. Expansion joints creaked beneath my feet. Locals bustled past, inured to the unsettling sway, while I stuck as close as possible to the middle line.

I wasn't afraid of heights. I just didn't see a reason to tempt fate.

The sun was setting, but a check of local time confirmed there was still an hour until the end of the first shift. It would be a good time to see if I could meet with someone at Tazza Industries. I didn't expect them to admit their product was faulty, but sometimes people let things slip when you caught them unprepared.

Floor-to-ceiling plastiglass panels marked the front entrance to the lobby of Tazza Industries. They were tinted a semitransparent bronze with a rippled water texture that complemented the whirls of gold in the cream-colored marble floor. One benefit of living on a mining planet was that stone was never in short supply.

Three receptionists stood behind a chest-high desk, each assisting a person. I took my place in the queue. A spot opened on the far left, and I approached the male receptionist. Late twenties, medium build, sharp nose, and sleek black hair tied back in a low braid. His name tag read Endicott.

Endicott waved his hand across his console, clearing the screen of the previous customer's information. "May I help you?"

"Yes, I would like to speak with Doctor Kandall Lourde. Is he in?"

He did some fast aerial scribing, pulling up Lourde's information. A glance down told me his office and lab were on the forty-seventh floor and that the holographer had not been kind in constructing his company profile image. Usually, they smoothed the wrinkles and subtracted a couple of kilograms. This one hadn't even bothered to remove the yellow mustard stain from Lourde's shirt.

"I'm afraid Doctor Lourde is unavailable," Endicott said with an apologetic smile.

"Are you sure? Doesn't that green dot right there mean he's in the office?"

Endicott frowned and cleared his holoscreen. "Doctor Lourde has noted that his schedule is closed until further notice. If this is a publicity inquiry, may I direct you to someone in our media relations department?"

I knew it was a long shot. "How about someone else in the bionics department? An assistant or a junior staff member?"

Endicott's smile lost a fraction of its friendliness. "May I ask what this is in relation to? So that I may best direct your inquiry, of course."

"Yes, I saw an interview Doctor Lourde gave about his neural implant. It's quite fascinating. I'm writing a paper on sensory substitution and would love to hear his thoughts on how the Insight could be used as a new method of interface." I'd totally stolen that from an article I'd read.

"Aren't you a little old to be in college?"

I smiled, baring my teeth. "It's a graduate course."

"Well, I'm afraid any information on the development of the Insight neural cuff would be strictly confidential and proprietary. I'd be happy to transfer all publicly available information to your cuff, if that would be of assistance."

At the edge of my peripheral vision, a tall man in an impeccable suit stepped out of a lift. It wasn't part of the main bank of lifts, which were behind the reception desks. It was off to the side and camouflaged as a wall panel. He turned his head, and I recognized the tanned face, perfect teeth, and overly styled blond hair. It was Aurelian Tazza, the CEO of Tazza Industries.

My sheer dumb luck left me . . . dumbstruck.

As he strode toward the exit, I turned my head to watch him pass. "Ma'am?"

"Hmm? Oh, no. Thank you, Endicott. Have a nice day."

This hadn't been part of my plan, but it was too good an opportunity to let pass. Quickly, I unfastened my ov-ex jacket and stuffed it into my bag. Rizpah's plain gray pants and long-sleeved shirt wouldn't pass as business attire, but it could aspire to professional. I'd have to take my chances with the cameras.

I quickened my pace to a power walk and held my bulging cross-body bag down with one hand to keep it from banging against my hip. Before I caught up to him, I slowed my pace and let my feet land heavy on the stone floor to lend gravity to my approach.

"Mr. Tazza? Mr. Aurelian Tazza?" Years of canvassing neighborhoods and interviewing witnesses lent a streak of authority to my voice. "May I have a word?"

He turned with a practiced smile that probably charmed the pants off reporters and women alike. "This really isn't a good time. Perhaps you could make an appointment?" He waved vaguely toward reception.

Shit. He must have an implant, because he wasn't wearing a cuff. On to Plan C.

I pulled on my best unimpressed-agent face. "There are at least four cases of your neural implant product malfunctioning and causing the user's death. Why hasn't your company reported them to the IBMD, and why haven't you made the public aware?"

He flinched, but only for a millisecond before the charming veneer returned. "You must be mistaken. The Insight has been rigorously studied and tested. I assure you, it is completely safe."

"Funny thing about those studies: I tried to get a hold of one, but they're nowhere to be found."

"You can hardly blame me for your lack of research skills. Now if you'll excuse me." Aurelian Tazza turned on his heel and strode toward the exit.

"Zairesh, Rhinehardt, Culpepper, Sorelsdotter," I called after him. Several people standing in line turned to see what the commotion was about. "Do those names sound familiar? They should. They're dead because of you."

Tazza spun back toward me. His eyes took on a vacant, faraway look for a moment before locking onto mine.

Across the room, a brawny security guard snapped to attention when his holoscreen flashed on with a communication. He bolted toward us, drawing a behemoth of a blaster as he ran. I'd seen pirate ships with smaller armaments than that gun. Working for an advanced tech company certainly came with perks.

A crowd of bystanders formed. Some held their cuffs out in our direction, recording the interaction. The hum of voices rose as they asked each other what was happening.

I raised my voice, so it carried over the noise. "The Insight kills people, Tazza, and your company is covering it up. People deserve to know the risk."

Aurelian Tazza took a menacing step toward me, his hand raised. My fingers curled into fists. I shifted my weight to my back foot and bladed my torso in case he intended to do more than jab a finger at me.

A bystander let out a gasp. Tazza took in his surroundings, reading the room and identifying the bad optics. In an instant, he dropped his hand and smoothed his face into an expression of tightly controlled calm.

The muscle-bound guard reached us. He was in his early twenties and had brown hair and light skin that looked artificially tanned. I bet he spent a lot of time doing arm curls at the gym.

"Sir?" he asked.

I stuck my hands in the air, knowing they couldn't legally hold me. I hadn't broken any laws—well, not here, at least.

"Sagi, this woman is causing a disturbance."

"Was it something I said?"

The guard holstered his gun when it became obvious I wasn't putting up a fight. He grabbed one of my wrists and brought it down behind my back. His palms were sweaty, and he smelled like cafaco, an addictive plant smoked for its stimulating effect on the body. Not illegal, but frowned upon at most workplaces because it gave you the jitters.

"You want to press charges, sir?"

"No, escort her off the premises and make sure she leaves."

"The exit's right there," I said. "I can show myself out."

"Tazza Industries owns this entire building. You are now trespassing on private property. I've entered your image into our system. If you come back, we will not be so gracious." Aurelian Tazza jerked his head toward the door.

Since Sagi didn't have any restraints, I dropped my other hand and let him maneuver me forward with a wrist lock. Once in the outer corridor, he kept a firm grip on me all the way to the bank of public lifts. He commandeered one, and only when the door shut did he release his hold.

I huffed and crossed my arms.

"Level One," Sagi said. The lift began its descent.

I surreptitiously tapped my cuff two times and counted the seconds in my head. *One, one thousand; two, one thousand; three, one thousand . . .*

Assuming it worked, the cloning program needed twenty-five seconds to connect to the nearest cuff, bypass the authentication protocol, and copy the data. During that time, my cuff couldn't be more than a meter from the source cuff. It would take an additional two minutes to complete the mirroring process and be functional, but the target didn't need to be within range for that part.

Twelve, one thousand . . .

The lift halted with a stomach-dropping certainty. Shit. With a soft, whooshing sound, the door slid open. I planted my feet.

"Come on, don't be a pain in the ass. It's almost the end of my shift." The big guy pushed against my back, but I dug in.

"Doesn't it bother you working for such a vainglorious asshole?"

Sagi gave me a long-suffering look. "He's a *rich*, vainglorious asshole, and as long as he approves my wages, I'll do as he says. So get out."

Twenty, one thousand . . .

I raised my hands, palms out. Chintzy warmed against my skin—a sign it was maxing out its processing power. "All right, all right. I'm going. No need to get your skivvies in a twist."

He marched me across the lobby. Even though I tried to stick close, I had no way of knowing if Chintzy had successfully completed the clone until I could get somewhere private to check.

We stopped at the door. "Look, I don't know what you hoped to accomplish with that little stunt up there, but let me give you a piece of advice. Aurelian Tazza is a god around here. He doesn't play by the same rules as people like us."

I looked him straight in the eye. "The rules exist because of people like him."

Sagi broke eye contact first, looking down at his boots. "Do yourself a favor and steer clear of this building, okay?"

I didn't press the point and strode out into the heat without a backward glance.

Chapter 16

Five hours later, I stood outside a fire escape door to Tazza Center cursing my cheap-ass cuff.

"Unable to process request."

I bit back a scream. "For the fourth time, just open the freaking program."

"Please restate the command."

Technology was getting worse. I would swear to it.

The sun set hours ago, and thanks to the quick rotation of Brione-2, heavy darkness already cloaked this side of the planet. Even though the temperature had dropped fifteen degrees from when I landed, sweat still soaked the long-sleeved shirt under my gray ov-ex jacket. The back of my knees felt slick, my socks were damp, and sand had somehow worked itself between my toes, the little gritty bits giving me blisters. I wanted a water shower so bad it hurt. I'd even settle for a shitty sonic one.

Giving up on voice controls, I turned on Chintzy's holoscreen. It cast a blue-white pallor over the door reader that had me looking over my shoulder while I navigated through the clone of Sagi's cuff. The program copied all the files from the source but wasn't sophisticated enough to duplicate the cuff's interface. It only gave me a master directory of files in alphabetical order.

My toe tapped against the ground as I pulled up file after file. The names meant nothing to me, so I was forced to open each one to see what was on it. Once I activated his security code, the reader should automatically pick it up.

There were a lot of holos of a cute, little brown-and-white dog. Like, *a lot*, a lot. Hundreds. Holovids of it doing tricks, too. More of a frail, older woman. His mother, perhaps. I skipped ahead.

Something made a clinking sound down the service alley between Tazza Center and the tower behind it. I stared into the dark for a long minute, but the only movement was from a large rat digging through a pile of trash, so I chalked it up to frayed nerves. If this stupid cloning program didn't open the door soon, I'd have to come up with a Plan D. Sooner than later, someone would notice me hanging around this fire exit and start asking questions.

The next file contained a shopping list dated three weeks ago: protein bars, pretzels, beer, dog treats. Part of my soul screamed inside of me. This could take forever.

Down the way, something cracked again. My heartbeat quickened, so that I had to concentrate to hear over the blood thumping in my ear. Another soft snap, farther away and higher that time. It was probably the buildings contracting as they released the heat they'd absorbed throughout the day, but my anxiety wouldn't accept that.

A soft beep from the door reader cut my musings short. The door slid open, and I gave myself a little fist pump in congratulations before hurrying through. It closed behind me and reengaged the one-way lock. I planned on getting out the same way I came in, but thanks to fire building codes, I wouldn't have to bother using a code to unlock it again.

Making sure my ov-ex hood was pulled up to keep my face blocked on camera, I began my steady climb up the forty-seven flights of stairs to Doctor Kandall Lourde's office. Since he was the surgeon who had operated on the first victim, I thought his office was the best place to start.

Around the twentieth floor, my thighs and glutes burned, and I couldn't recall the last time I'd done serious stair work prior to this week. Probably back when I was with the Department. The *Soteria* only had the one ladder between the lower deck and the bridge. I usually took in a good run whenever I was planetside and time allowed, but I clearly needed to step up my exercise game.

Unsurprisingly, the building owners didn't spend the credits to cool air in a rarely used section of the building. It was warm, stale, and rasped the back of my throat with every breath.

By the thirtieth floor, my second wind kicked in. My feet beat out a rhythmic *pat-pat-pat* as I hoisted my patootie up six hundred and thirty steps. Counting helped me focus.

At forty-six, I slowed to catch my breath and let my body recover. My thighs quivered from the workout, so I did a couple of quick toe-touches and calf stretches to relax the muscles.

Then I pulled up the same file that had gotten me into the building and held it up to the door reader of the forty-seventh floor. The lock clicked, and the door slid open.

I'd expected the floor to be swanky offices and conference rooms, but this didn't look like that at all. A spacious hallway ran the length of the floor. Sleek, white surfaces reflected pale-blue indirect lighting like morning light through fog. Strips of dim running lights curved gracefully along the left wall between head and hip height, guiding me toward a door at the opposite end.

This place didn't just say money. It said institutional money. I could break something in here and spend the rest of my life working to pay it off.

It didn't smell like an office either. I breathed deep through my nose, parsing out the scents. Cleaning solutions, astringents, ammonia, wet paper, and . . . rodent feces? When I was a kid, a friend of mine had a buckskin ferret for a pet, and her bedroom had that same odor.

To my right was a room separated from the hallway with a solid half-wall on the bottom with an opaqued sheet of plastiglass on the top. I slunk along the glass partition until I reached an opening, then ducked inside.

Four medical-grade beds sat along one wall, neatly made up with crisp, white linens and pillows that seemed to glow softly in contrast to the surrounding shadows. Around them, medical equipment sat at the ready. Hospitals weren't my thing, but I recognized a 3D imaging bed, a patient monitor, med dispensers, that tubular machine that I didn't know the name of that anesthetized a person, and a wall-mounted console near each bed. I nosed around the beds and machines but didn't see anything incriminating.

I stepped across the aisle through the only doorway on the left side of the hall. It opened into a lounge area. A stiff-backed sofa, molded chairs, and a dining table filled the space. There were two locked doors on either side, with the letters A through D above them. Sagi's code didn't have the clearance to access them.

My best guess was that Doctor Lourde used this floor to conduct clinical tests on patients, and this was where they slept. I debated knocking on each door but decided against it. They may be here for something completely unrelated to the Insight. Tazza Industries developed all kinds of tech products, from the medical field to military applications. Besides, a patient was unlikely to have the evidence I needed to take to the authorities, and they might call security if a strange woman woke them up in the middle of the night asking questions.

I tiptoed back into the hall and down to the next room, trying not to let my boots make squeaking sounds against the tile. The space had been kitted out like a physical therapy gym with a padded table, light hand weights, steps, balance beams, and a VR running simulator. Black-and-white mats with the Tazza Industries logo printed on them covered the floor, and plastiglass set to mirror mode lined one full wall.

A chart beside the door tracked the progress of "Subject C." A grid listed dates across the top and a series of exercises in the rows. The dates went as far back as two months. Early entries contained longer time records, higher repetitions, or the word "Pass." As the days progressed, the times got worse, there were fewer repetitions, and more Fails than Passes.

There weren't any charts for Subjects A, B, or D.

I put everything back exactly the way I had found it and continued down the hall. The stench of animal refuse grew stronger. I entered the last room and a chorus of squeaks and *wheek-wheek-wheeks* greeted me. Ten white rats and five brown guinea pigs stared at me from a row of cages. Their little whiskers twitched in a flurry of activity, trying to pick up my scent.

Four of the rats had their right front legs replaced with bionic limbs, each no bigger than my pinkie finger. The other six had electronic chips the size of my thumbnail glued to the back of their heads. A console below each cage displayed the rat's identifier, blood pressure, heart rate, and brain activity levels.

While I watched, one of the chipped mice walked over to its empty food bowl. Outside the cage was a lever-activated food dispenser with a tube running into the cage. My childhood friend had one of those for her ferret to help reduce food waste. But here, there was no way for the poor little rat to reach the lever.

The console below her listed her identifier as P3BL-5.

"Hi there, Pebbles," I whispered.

She scratched at the chip with her back leg, then sat back on her little haunches, and waved a paw up and down. At the same time, a stick by the dispenser pressed down on the lever. The dispenser made a whirling noise and five pellets dropped through the tube into the empty dish. She wolfed down the five pellets and then repeated the motion to get five more. The chip must be some type of simplified version of the Insight, allowing her to interact with the feeder via nerve impulses.

Four cages over, one of the guinea pigs ran back and forth across the length of its cage, its little nose wiggling frantically and glassy, black eyes darting every which way. Below it, the console showed his identifier was WLNT-89, and that he was being studied for appetite suppression and increased metabolism.

"Easy now. How about I call you Walnut?"

"Wheek-wheek!"

"Shh. Not so loud, fella."

He calmed down enough to sniff my fingers through the cage. The top of Walnut's head, neck, and shoulders had been shaved to bare skin, and I could see an incision mark down the middle with three neat stitches holding the sides together. Tiny scratch marks lined either side, and it was easy to see that he had been clawing at the incision with his hind feet. I was no guinea pig expert, but he looked thin. For a potato.

My heart ached for the poor little thing, but there wasn't much I could do for him. Even if I released him, I doubted he could survive long on his own.

I ventured deeper into the laboratory. Tables crowded the rest of the space. Half-completed projects lay in disarray so that it was hard to tell where one stopped and the next started. I scooted around a pushed-out stool to look at the contents. Dismantled cuffs, weapon parts, wires, chips, circuit boards, fuel cells, laser cutters, pliers, clamps, and soldering guns littered every available centimeter of workspace. Almost everything was broken down to its base components, and I wished I had a better grasp on current technology to make sense of it all.

A counter ringing two of the walls held different styles of bionic hands, arms, feet, and organs mounted on stands. Above them, a line of wall-mounted consoles sat silent and dark.

On the third table, I found a miniature version of the high-end blaster Sagi carried. Its guts were strewn about near the mechanical insides of a bionic hand. I circled around to the other side, trying to get a better look in the dim light. Every officer learned how to strip a blaster in order to clean and recharge it. While not the model I usually carried, I could tell some basic parts were missing like the barrel, trigger sensor, and energy converter.

"Shit." The expletive escaped before I clamped my lips shut.

Walnut gave a startled, "Wheek!" and ran inside his hut to hide.

Attached to the bionic hand's thumb and index finger were the missing blaster parts. Tazza Industries was developing bionic weapons. That violated at least twenty laws and every treaty Brione-2 had with, well, every other inhabited rock larger than a meteoroid.

Governments banned that kind of tech after the Ritruvian Uprising Massacre over eighty years ago. Once the overlaying skin grafts healed, they scanned as ordinary medical implants and were almost impossible to detect. Mercenaries—disguised as aid workers—had infiltrated a Ritruvian refugee camp and killed everyone. They estimated almost a quarter of the planet's nonfighting population was present, some five thousand people.

Jarrett's grandfather had been a small boy during the Uprising. He lost both his parents to the revolt over working conditions, although I didn't know if it had been to the massacre or one of the battles prior. It wasn't something you asked, but I knew it was the reason Jarrett had gone into law enforcement.

"Chintzy, initiate visual recording."

"Recording." For once, the cheap cuff understood my command on the first try. I walked the length of the table with my arm held out, pausing for a detailed image of the bionic hand, then backtracked to the rats and guinea pigs and got a recording of them as well.

"End visual recording."

"Confirmed. Recording complete."

Forget the Insight. That recording might convince the authorities to investigate Tazza Industries all on its own. A little extra evidence wouldn't hurt, though. I could only imagine the fleet of high-priced attorneys Tazza employed to keep his secrets hidden, and they would do their best to get this recording quashed.

The nearest console beckoned me. I checked the time. It had been nine minutes since I entered the floor. A few more should be okay.

I held my fist in front of the screen and splayed my fingers out quickly, like a starburst, to wake the console up. Immediately, it prompted me for a three-step passcode. A timer appeared at the top, counting down from twenty seconds. I didn't waste any time. An alarm would be tripped when the correct codes weren't entered. It wasn't even worth the time trying to guess them.

Seconds counted. I spun and sprinted for the door. My messenger bag swung wildly at my side. As if guided by an unseen force, it bounced off my hip, twisted, and snagged itself on the corner of the workbench, hauling me up short.

Pain shot up my shoulder and neck as I worked to unhook the bag from the completely smooth edge of the table. *How?*

Once free, I gripped the bag in one hand to keep it from catching on anything else and raced back down the hall toward the emergency exit. The sound of my boots pounding the floor echoed around me. As I neared the door, I raised my right arm so Chintzy could send a clear signal to the reader.

The dim lighting flickered twice, then flared to full power. Bright red washed over the running lights. An alarm blared, deep and grating, with an accompanying bass that rattled my rib cage.

The door didn't open. I waved Chintzy back and forth across the reader.

"No, no, no!" I pounded against the cold surface to no effect.

I ran through the floor plan in my mind. The only other exit was the main lift, which was what security would use to respond as quickly as possible. There must be maintenance shafts along the sides, like the ones Lady Ilymechina's crew used to sneak into the spacedock. If I could get to one of those, I could climb to a lower floor and take a skybridge to a neighboring building. That might work.

With no time to lose, I raced back toward the lifts. My hood fell back, exposing my face, but I couldn't slow down to pull it back up.

I didn't even make it to the laboratory before the door opened. Four guards poured out with blasters raised. I skidded to a halt, planted one foot, and tried to reverse course. My knees protested the sudden change in direction.

Twin blasts slammed into the back of my rib cage and my left shoulder blade, throwing me forward. It happened too fast to execute a proper breakfall, and my landing was sloppy. Pain lanced through my wrists and elbows, but it was nothing compared to the blinding heat engulfing my back.

I froze, terrified that moving would bring a fresh wave of pain. *It will pass*, I told myself, trying to recall how long targets remained incapacitated after being hit with a stun setting.

Two sets of hands lifted me by my biceps until my toes skimmed the floor. Splotches of color appeared in my vision.

"This is Michael. I have the perpetrator in custody."

"Copy that, Michael. Do you need assistance?"

"Affirmative. Have medical meet us at the lift on floor 47."

They half-dragged, half-carried me to Room D off the lounge area. It took three of them to lift me onto the bed. I got in a good kick at one guy's groin. He bent at the waist, hands shielding his family jewels and swearing enough to make an asteroid miner blush.

Face down with my shoulders and thighs pinned, I was doing a fair bit of swearing myself. The blond man with a beard who'd identified himself as Michael straightened my arm to the side. I felt the cold steel of augmented restraints lock into place around my wrist. The woman on my other side won the fight for that arm. Another set of restraints closed tight. After that, it didn't take much effort to secure my feet.

I jerked and felt the pinprick of a needle pierce the skin of my wrist. If I continued to resist, it would release a small dose of sedative into my bloodstream. The more I struggled, the more drug it would inject. At least, that's how they worked at DECA. Who knew what they loaded the syringe with here? And what the hell kind of place kept bed restraints on hand?

Michael took a knife from his belt, opened it, and held it a decimeter from my face. "We have to remove the material from your back to examine the wounds. I'm going to cut open your shirt. Hold still, unless you want to get nicked."

I was too stubborn to acquiesce verbally, but I stopped thrashing.

The knife ripped through the expensive ov-ex material. He laid both sides open like the fileted sides of a fish and went to work on Rizpah's shirt. Shards of pain flashed through me as he peeled the fabric off my burned skin.

None of the blasters I'd ever used had caused this kind of external damage on the stun setting. They spread out the energy hit. Incapacitate, yes. Knock a person out, sure. But not inflict an open wound like this.

Michael sawed at the material over my right arm until it fell away. He unfastened Chintzy and threw it to the floor, out of range.

I heard a commotion behind me but couldn't crank my head around enough to see. A woman—not the guard standing beside me—instructed someone to bring her the med kit from across the hall. Then a pair of comfortable white shoes and hospital-blue pants stepped into my view.

She poked at the edges of the wounds and tsked. "I am Doctor Yelena Adler. Your back has sustained significant injury. Do you consent to medical treatment?"

"N—"

"Let the record reflect the patient is unresponsive. Proceeding with treatment."

She removed a med dispenser from the kit the guard brought, inserted a drug cartridge, and jabbed the needle into my ass.

"Hey! That hurt." No one paid me much mind.

Whatever she gave me worked fast. A soothing numbness radiated down my legs and up my spine. It made my toes and fingertips tingle, and the pain in my shoulder and ribs subsided to a dull throb. My thoughts became foggy, and I bit my lower lip to keep my mind focused on the present.

"Who is she?" Doctor Adler asked, her back to me. She was short with thick chestnut hair twisted into a heavy knot, and she carried a few extra kilograms around her hips and thighs.

"I ran her face before you got here. Her name is Captain Reliance Sinclair, thirty-two, originally from Clava but transient for the last year. DECA on Andaress-4 flagged her last week, Priority Alpha."

"Fast work."

Michael folded his arms across his chest. "Mr. Tazza personally scanned her this morning after a brief altercation in the lobby. Her file was already in the system."

"I see." Doctor Adler tapped her finger against her thigh.

"Should I alert DECA?"

I fought my eyelids to stay open, even as they surrendered to the sedative.

The doctor turned toward me, her full brows drawn together in contemplation. "Hold off for now. Send a comm to Doctor Lourde. He'll want to hear about this opportunity immediately."

Chapter 17

I HELD PERFECTLY STILL as the beam of red light swept me from head to toe. I had to—Doctor Yelena Adler threatened to sedate me again if I so much as twitched.

The machine dinged, signaling completion. I scratched my nose against my shoulder. It started itching two seconds after the full-body scan began and hadn't let up for the last fifteen minutes. Plus, I needed to use the bathroom.

"We done?"

"Hmm?" Doctor Adler glanced over from where she stood in front of the oversized table console. A three-dimensional image of me hovered over the top, complete with skeletal, muscular, and vascular systems. "You may take a brief recess. I'll send someone to fetch you when you're needed."

I shuffled out of the med bay, through the lounge, and to the bathroom. After relieving myself, I leaned against the wall and gingerly pressed against the hard surface. They'd patched up my back with sutures and grade-A regenerative salve. It itched something fierce under the GraftPatch, but that meant it was healing.

The short guy had overstepped his rights to shoot me at such a high setting, but they were going overboard with the treatment. Probably worried about a civil suit.

When I exited, an older man sat on the couch. He hadn't been there a few minutes ago.

His hair had been shaved, but a fine fuzz of gray regrowth covered his dark brown scalp. He wore identical white patient scrubs as mine, but they hung from his emaciated frame like clothes on a rack.

I scanned the room but didn't see any staff from Tazza Industries.

"Hello." I circled around to the front of the couch. The walking restraints rattled with every step. "My name is Reliance."

"I know who you are, Captain Reliance Sinclair." He tapped the side of his head. "I saw you come in last night."

"Then you have me at a disadvantage."

His smile revealed a couple of missing teeth. "Everyone calls me Fax. You might as well, too."

I lowered myself into a chair across from him. Fax had probably been handsome in his youth, with broad facial features, full lips, and kind eyes the color of oak leaves in the fall. Years of sun and radiation exposure had leathered his skin, and sinewy muscles stretched across his arms. That kind of muscle came from years of malnutrition and rough living. Faded tattoos covered most of the skin on his arms and neck. A few were intricate, but many were simple stick-and-poke tatts.

He could be a miner—part of a surface-level crew. It was hard work and common enough on this planet, but if I were to hazard a guess, my credits would be on him being from the itinerant population. The tattoo on his forearm where a cuff would normally rest was of a circle with two parallel arrows running through it. It meant *hit the road* in the itinerant community.

"Are you a patient here? Are you here voluntarily?" I leaned forward and dropped my voice to a whisper.

"Well, now, that's an interesting question. I suppose I did volunteer. Don't know as leaving is much of an option anymore."

"Do you know how to get out of here?"

"I tried a few times, but it didn't do any good." Fax's eyes flicked side to side repeatedly, as if he were reading from a holoscreen, but there wasn't one. He wasn't even wearing a cuff. "They're coming."

"Who's coming?"

The guard from the lobby stormed into the lounge. I took stock of him again and revised my initial estimate of his age down to twenty-one or twenty-two despite his overly developed physique. His nails were chewed up, his knuckles scraped, and his whole hand shook with barely contained anger as he jabbed his finger toward me.

"So it's true. I didn't believe it when my boss told me someone broke in using my security code."

I shrugged apologetically. "Nothing personal."

"You almost cost me my job. My boss moved me back to hallway patrol."

"Is your boss the blond guy with the mustache? Do you want me to talk to him? Because I don't think he and I really got off on the right foot, what with him shooting me and all."

"You've got a smart mouth on you. Enjoy it now, because I bet that's the first thing to go when they turn your brain into swiss cheese." Sagi grinned at the blank look on my face. "I overheard the docs talking on my way in. They're not turning you over to DECA."

My mind raced. Why wouldn't they contact DECA? One comm and I'd become somebody else's problem. "What do you mean?"

Sagi shrugged one shoulder. "Sounds like they have other plans for you."

Doctors Adler and Lourde entered the lounge before I could get anything else out of Sagi. Neither of them came up to his shoulder, but Kandall Lourde still looked down his nose at the security guard.

"That is enough for now, Sagi. You may return to your rounds." Lourde turned to confer with Adler.

"Right away, Doc." Sagi lowered his voice. "Bet you wish you would have taken my advice now." Then he hurried off before the doctors could take issue with his continued presence.

Although neither wore cuffs, the doctors exchanged a quick series of aerial scribes that were so subtle I wouldn't have noticed if I hadn't watched them so closely. I assumed that meant Doctor Adler also had an Insight neural implant.

They reached some kind of consensus and presented me with a united front. Adler wore similar hospital blues as the night before, although she had braided her thick, chestnut hair and applied a fresh coat of crimson lipstick. It was a bold color choice for working in a lab.

Lourde wore a hip-length lab coat with a stiffly pressed collar, but the shirt beneath it was a size too large, wrinkled, and had an orange food stain near the top of his gut. Signs of a man engrossed in his work.

He tilted his head toward the old man on the couch. "I see you met Subject C. Remarkable, isn't he?"

Fax continued to stare at his socks, ignoring our conversation.

"We haven't really had a chance to talk yet," I said.

"Ah, well, I'm afraid he's not much of a conversationalist anymore. Still, making it this far is quite the accomplishment." Lourde gestured toward the D room. "Why don't we speak in your room, where it's a little more private?"

I didn't care for how he referred to it as *your room*. "How about you unlock these restraints first?"

Yelena Adler tsked. "Come now, you've put us far enough behind schedule as it is."

"Sorry, I hate to think I got in the way of your development of *bionic weapons*. That would make me so sad."

They met my sarcasm with looks more fitting on parents of rebellious teenagers. Fine by me. I tried to stomp off to the room, but the restraints made it more of a *swish-swish* as I hobbled by. Not nearly as dramatic as I would have liked.

The doctors followed me in, closing the door behind them.

I planted my feet shoulder-width apart and attempted to cross my arms over my chest. The restraints limited my movement, and I settled for clasping one wrist in front of me, hoping it portrayed more confidence than I felt.

"Why isn't DECA currently escorting me back to Andaress-4? I've been here for over twelve hours. That's plenty of time for the local office to pick me up."

As much as I didn't want to be in DECA's custody, these people were shadier than the backside of an asteroid and just as cold.

Lourde pulled out the chair from the small wall desk, unfastened the single button on his coat, and sat down. "We did not contact DECA."

"Why not?"

"I find it best to only involve them when absolutely necessary. Budgetary restraints." He rested an ankle on his knee. In his left hand, he held a metal stress cube, which he idly rolled between his fingers.

"Great. Unlock these restraints, and I'll get out of here."

"I'm afraid that won't be possible. You said some interesting things about my invention, and I would very much like to know how you acquired that information."

"I followed the money. It led to a corrupt DECA agent and a lot of dead bodies. My guess is, they're not the only ones."

The stress cube stilled in his hand. It *pop-popped* softly as he applied pressure with his thumb and then released it. "Once perfected, my invention will improve billions of lives."

"But at what cost?"

His face turned red, and his hand clenched around the metal cube. "You do not comprehend the magnitude of my research."

The suddenness of his anger surprised me, and I took an involuntary step backward. Adler seemed unperturbed, enthralled even, as she watched him with cow-eyed adoration. With visible effort, Lourde calmed himself and eased back in his chair. The click of the stress cube sounded loud in the now-silent room.

"Progress is not born of nothing. Observe, hypothesize, test, analyze, refine." He counted off the steps of the scientific method on his fingers. "We are currently in the testing stage."

"The data must come from somewhere," Adler added.

"Do you know many people died learning how to refine sinnalite, build warp drives, or colonize the first terraformed planets?"

I shook my head.

"Of course you don't. No one does. And more importantly, no one cares. It is irrelevant compared to the benefits. Humans have made no major technological advances for hundreds of years—not since developing warp technology and terraforming. Take my arm, for instance." He held up his right hand. The too-smooth skin and unnatural stillness marked it as bionic from the elbow down. "I lost it in an LAV accident as a youth. The model they gave me was the same model amputees had been using for over sixty years, and the one they continued to use until I developed a superior one in my twenties. This one is light-years beyond that. It barely requires a thought to control." His fingers snapped shut into a fist.

FTL travel, terraforming, bionic limbs. My brain had whiplash from the conversational change in direction. "I assume you're getting to a point."

"We, as a society, have become stagnant, and civilizations that are stagnant eventually die. But this"—he reached into his pocket and exchanged the stress cube for a small computer chip—"this is how we move forward. It is the first step in merging the best of humans and machines. When this chip is implanted into your brain stem, it intercepts the signals from your brain to your hand at almost the exact moment the command is thought. It eliminates the need for cuffs. I improved the signal response time by eighty percent over the latest gen cuff currently on the market."

My jaw dropped. Eighty percent? The tech world was forever chasing faster processing, faster connections, faster interfaces. It was the golden goose of technology. People paid through the nose for increases of three or four percent. I'd never even heard of such an advancement.

He looked pleased with himself.

"Eighty percent?" I repeated out loud, still somewhat stupefied. "But you still need a holoscreen to interact with programs."

"Not at all. It connects directly to your optic and vestibulo-cochlear nerves, using your own eyes and ears to interface."

I shook my head, refusing to let myself get distracted. "That didn't work out so well for Ruana Sorelsdotter, did it? Or Kelthea Zairesh? Thomas Rhinehardt? Silar Culpepper? Do you even remember the people your implant killed?"

"Yes, well, unfortunately, our early prototypes went to market with a few bugs."

"What's the fatality rate of a 'few bugs'?"

"Minimal. Less than five percent."

"Five percent?" My mouth hung open while I struggled with the math. "That's one out of every twenty recipients."

"Estimates are closer to one out of twenty-five experiencing serious injuries or fatalities for the current version. I've improved upon those early prototypes."

"How can you possibly justify that many deaths?"

"I have every confidence that the next generation of Insight will be down to a two percent fatality rate. We do not achieve progress without sacrifice."

"Don't give me any of that sanctimonious bullshit. Those people died horrible, painful deaths, and then Tazza Industries paid dirty officers to cover it up so the fallout wouldn't blow back on you." My mind flashed back to the documents on the data dot Jarrett had collected. "KaLo Research is the parent company of RMZ Incorporated, the entity that paid off my old partner. KaLo. Kandall Lourde. You named it after yourself."

"You've been busier than I thought." Lourde picked a speck of white fuzz from his pant leg and let it fall to the ground. "Obviously, Tazza Industries cannot be tied directly to any illegal activity, but I have received several very generous investments into my private research company."

"It's a smoke screen."

"Plausible deniability." He didn't even have the decency to look ashamed.

"And the bionic weapons in your lab?"

"Don't be naive. Research and development of bionic weapons never ceased after Ritru. We just do a better job of keeping it out of the public eye."

"You mean you kill anyone who threatens to expose you, like Jarrett Viorel."

Adler cleared her throat. "I believe we're getting off track."

Lourde glanced up at her and smiled. "Yes, of course, Doctor Adler. Correct, as usual. You see, Captain Sinclair, as you've so amply demonstrated, you know far too much for us to let you go."

Adler moved to the wall console above the desk. With barely a twitch of her fingers, it blinked to life, and a miniaturized version of my 3D body scan appeared.

"We need a candidate to test our newest version of the Insight. We call it the Intell. It's being developed exclusively for counterintelligence work, mainly for planetary governments, but it also has off-the-books commercial applications. Particularly, I've designed it with a state-of-the-art decryption program, code breakers, and electronic surveillance capabilities."

I could see how governments would be interested in that, and corporate espionage was big business, too.

Adler enlarged a chart showing the results of my body scan. "You are in excellent health and are within our target age range. We also believe your background in law enforcement would be advantageous for the unique functions of the Intell."

"But, again—and I really can't stress this enough—your implant *kills people*. Why, in the ever-loving void, would I let you put one inside of me?"

"You misunderstand." Lourde stood up and ran his hands down the front of his suit coat. "We already selected you as the next test subject. The implantation surgery is scheduled for this afternoon. It will take approximately two hours and Doctor Adler and myself will perform it."

"No, you can't do that!" I jerked my hands, chafing at the restraints.

"Tazza Industries manufactures much of the technology employed by law enforcement. We have access to all their systems. A simple search revealed you are a fugitive with no spouse or dependents, you work on a contract basis, and no one knows you are here." Adler ticked off my qualifications on her fingers. "That makes you an ideal subject."

The room suddenly felt a lot smaller and hotter than it had a moment ago. I shifted my weight from foot to foot.

"The procedure is inevitable," Lourde continued. "We've found that subjects who accept this going in fare better than those who resist. Doctor Adler believes the mind forms a protective mental barrier around itself, but we don't have enough data points to prove that conclusively yet."

Panic gripped me, turning my insides to stones and my thoughts to butterflies. All sense of reason took flight in a kaleidoscope of color behind my eyes, leaving me cold and hard inside.

I leaped at Doctor Lourde, knocking us both to the floor and sending the chair clattering across the room. The restraints limited my range of motion, so I decided on a chokehold. Crossing my arms at the wrist, I slid both hands along his flabby neck and under the collar of his lab coat. When they were as far back as I could reach, I fisted the material and pulled back in a scissoring motion, using my wrists and the fabric of his own jacket to cut the flow of blood and oxygen to his brain.

Needles from the augmented restraints stabbed into my skin at my wrists and ankles. I grunted and pulled harder.

Yelena Adler screamed for the guards, then kicked me twice in the abdomen with the pointed toe of her shoe.

Two men in black-and-white uniforms burst through the door. One was the blond, mustachioed guy who'd shot me. He wrapped his arms around my waist and lifted my lower half from the floor. I held on to Lourde with everything I had.

Lourde's face turned dark pink. Drool leaked from the corner of his mouth as he gasped for air, making choking sounds. His fingers dug into my palms as he attempted to pry them from his throat. Beneath me, his torso thrashed like a snake with its head trapped in a catch pole.

The sedative from the restraints worked into my bloodstream. A wave of vertigo crashed over me, followed by a shortness of breath and weakness in my limbs. Dimly, I was aware of my body being tugged backward. My focused narrowed to my shaking hands around his throat.

His hand movements lost their frantic edge, slackened, and fell to his side. The body beneath me went soft and limp.

My head dropped to my forearms, too heavy to hold up. Eyes closed, my breaths came in hot, heavy gasps.

More hands forced my fingers to uncurl, releasing the crushed fabric. Another pinprick of pain stabbed my neck. They rolled me to the side, abandoning me now that the sedative had taken hold.

The floor felt cool through the thin patient scrubs.

Beside me, Lourde wheezed, low and raspy. It was the last thing I heard before the drug pulled me under.

Chapter 18

Nightmares plagued my sleep.

My ship broke down midflight, leaving me stranded in the vast emptiness of the void. The engine was busted. I tried making repairs, but every time I reached for a tool, it turned into a mouse and ran away. Without the engine running, the ship lost heat. The metal walls turned so cold that touching them burned my fingers. My breath made icy puffs that glowed bright pink when I exhaled them.

Suddenly, I was on the bridge instead of in the engine room. I set my locater beacon and sent out a distress call. Felix jumped into the copilot's chair.

"Aren't you going to answer him?"

"Answer who?" I asked.

"Him." Felix raised a metal paw and pointed to my console. Then he licked his paw and used it to clean his face. It was very catlike and very unlike a ship's computer, especially because his tongue was a fixed piece of welded sheet metal.

The console lit up. "Rel? Is that you? You shouldn't be here."

My heart exploded and collapsed on itself like a supernova. "Jarrett? Is that you?"

His image materialized on the console in front of me. "Did you find who did this to me, Rel? Did you make things right?"

"I . . . I tried." My insides crushed with the weight of guilt. "I couldn't do it on my own. I needed you, Jarrett. I *still* need you."

Blood oozed down the side of his face, leaving a thick, red trail over his left cheek. "You messed up, and now more people will die. My death was meaningless. How could you let that happen?"

Hot, salty tears trickled from the corners of my eyes. "You were right about Cavender. He was a dirty agent. I know what they paid him to cover up."

A fleshfly landed in the growing hole of Jarrett's temple and burrowed inside. I wanted to throw up.

"None of that matters, Rel, not if nobody else knows. You always were stubborn, but I never pegged you for stupid."

"I'm sorry I dragged you into this. It's my fault they came after you." A sob broke through, and a flood of tears followed, blurring my vision. When I could, I dried my eyes with the edge of my sleeve. The console was empty. "Jarrett? Jarrett?!" I screamed. "Please, don't leave. Not again."

"You're an embarrassment to the agency. I knew you weren't cracked up for the job the moment I lay eyes on you."

I spun around, no longer on the bridge of the *Soteria*. We were in Ruana Sorelsdotter's house in Clava. My former partner's lifeless body lay face-up on the floor, three burn marks in his chest. The blaster was still warm in my hand.

His doppelgänger nudged the body with the toe of his boot. "Hell of a shot, though. Hardly felt a thing."

"Hal?"

"Sorry, I can't return the favor." Cavender raised his blaster and aimed it at my head.

Instinctively, I brought mine up as well, the same as I had the last time. Only this time, my hand was empty. My blaster had vanished.

So I ran. The house morphed into a hallway with slick tile floors and soft blue lighting. I ran, the end so far away it disappeared into the shadows, but I kept going. Sweat poured off me. My chest ached with the pressure of breathing. I slipped and fell, hurting my wrists and ankles.

Unable to get back up, I crawled on my elbows and knees. The walls shook and vibrated around me—the sound was so loud it was deafening. An earthquake? I covered my ears and screamed as voices boomed around me.

"She's coming out of it. Heart rate 170. Body temp 38.5 degrees Celsius. O_2 levels dropping."

"Push another three milliliters."

Then the darkness pulled me back under, and I slept.

A high-pitched whine pulled me from a fitful sleep. I rolled onto my side and ground the heels of my palms against my temples to make the headache go away. My first thought was that the *Soteria* must have drifted into an asteroid belt, and Felix had sounded the alarm. My second was that I couldn't feel the hum of the engines under my bed. That was enough to force my eyes open.

Thoughts and images from the nightmares flickered and vanished like shooting stars, leaving me unsettled as I sorted the dream from reality. Bright light blinded and disoriented me. I squinted, trying to get my bearings. Everything was a wash of cold blues and stark whites, not the familiar warm neutrals of my bunk on the *Soteria*.

Why didn't someone make the whining stop?

I tried to push myself up, got tangled in some kind of string, and flailed my arms, trying to get it off. Batting at it did no good. It was stuck to both my arms.

"Easy now," said a kind voice. "You're making it worse."

I jerked back and winced when every muscle protested the movement. "Who's there?"

"Relax, it's just me, Fax. I'm not going to hurt you. We met before."

Fax? Right, the patient in the lounge. Memories flooded back and shuffled themselves into some semblance of order, but there were a lot of gaps. I needed more information.

My eyes opened into thin slits. I immediately shut them again, waving vaguely at the source of the pain. "Too bright."

The lights dimmed. "There. How's that?"

I cracked one eye open, then the other. "Manageable."

Fax had pulled the desk chair over and leaned forward, bony elbows resting on his thighs, watching me intently. "You woke up. That's good."

Debatable. "You sound surprised."

"I'm no doctor, but I think it was touch and go for a while."

"What makes you say that?"

"Your heart stopped for a couple of minutes."

"Oh." I didn't know what to make of that. It was difficult to think over the whining noise. I plugged my ear with my finger, but it didn't help. "What is that awful sound?"

"Like your ears are ringing?"

I nodded and really wished I hadn't.

"Don't know. Near as I can tell, the implant picks up part of the floor's networking system."

"Can you make it stop?"

"I haven't figured out how to yet, but you get used to it."

"Really?"

Fax's face fell. "No, but I keep hoping."

"Is it . . . is it coming from outside or inside my head?" I felt stupid even asking, but I couldn't tell.

"Inside. They took me to a different floor once for some tests, and it was a lot worse."

"So it's done. They put one of those *chips* in my head?"

"Yeah."

I struggled to sit up again and regretted everything as stars exploded behind my eyes. *Blasted all! Shit, void, mother—*

"Hgnh." I grunted through the pain and made it all the way up. A wave a vertigo sent me clutching the bed rails.

My wrists and ankles were in augmented restraints, but they'd given me enough cording to adjust my position, scratch my nose, and stretch my legs. Gingerly, I reached back to touch the base of my skull. A swath of my hellaberry hair at the nape of my neck had been shaved off. In the middle was a finger-length scab where the laser had cut into my skull. It was still tender to the touch and left a foul-smelling residue of liquid on my fingers.

"You want some water?" Fax asked.

My mouth was parched, but I hadn't noticed until now. "Please."

Fax got me a tall glass of water from the lounge. I drained the entire thing in one go. The cold liquid hit my empty stomach hard, but it helped with the dizziness. Fax took the glass, refilled it, and brought it back to me.

"How long have I been out?"

"Two days."

I thought about that while taking a more restrained sip. "Why aren't you in restraints?" I jangled my arm bracelet for emphasis.

Fax sat back down, his knees making the soft creaking sounds that came with age. "Well, I suppose they know I don't have anywhere to go."

"Anywhere has to be better than here."

"Hmm," he nodded. "You may be right, but I guess I made my peace with it."

"How long have you been here?"

"Eight weeks, three days, and seven hours. It won't be much longer now, though. The headaches, they're getting worse." He shifted positions, grimacing until he got comfortable again. "I was having a string of bad luck, been having it for a long time, truth be told. I came looking for work, but the mining companies only wanted young people. Too old, too spent. I saw an advert looking for research subjects. They offered me a place to stay, food, medical care, and credits to boot. So I said, 'sign me up.'"

"Did you know they were going to give you a neural implant?"

He shrugged. "Didn't much care at the time."

"Were there . . ." I tried to think of a delicate way to phrase it. "Others?"

Fax stared silently at his soft-soled slippers for so long, I thought he wasn't going to answer me. "Three, as I know of. We all came in at the same time. They didn't make it long. The first gal didn't wake up from the surgery. That's why I was watching you so close, you see. This was her room. The second guy made it a couple of days before his chip malfunctioned. He'd been having real terrible headaches. I heard him at night. Crying, screaming fit to raise the dead sometimes. No one told us what happened, but they did the autopsy in the med bay. I don't think they realized we'd figured out how to turn the cameras on to watch."

"I'm sorry."

He absentmindedly rubbed his finger over the circle-and-arrows tattoo, then let out a deep breath. "Tate took it harder than me. All that information can be overwhelming. When his headaches started a few days later, well, he didn't want to wait to see how things played out. I found him the next day."

Beside me, the patient monitor kicked on, reading my vitals. Between one blink and the next, floating, white text began scrolling down the right side of my field of view. Heart rate, blood pressure, oxygen levels . . .

I threw my head back, but the text followed my gaze. "What is that?"

"Ah, that's the Intell connecting to the patient monitor. Scared the shit out of me the first time, too."

"How do I make it stop?" I tried swiping it away, but my hands passed right through the text.

"Haven't figured that out yet, either. Near as I can tell, the damn thing picks up every signal within range, whether or not you want it to. At least in here, the rooms are shielded from outside signals, like some kind of giant Faraday cage. Out there, it's enough to drive a person insane."

The text displayed like an augmented reality viewer, appearing to float in the air about half a meter in front of me. I reached out to touch "Heart Rate" but before my finger so much as twitched, the word enlarged, and a subcategory of information opened beneath it. It showed my blood pressure and heart rate stats over the last two days, the condition of my arteries and blood vessels, and a moving line graph of a real-time EKG reading.

I swiveled my head side to side, and the imagery moved with me. "Whoa."

Another image popped up, this one a camera feed on the left side of my field of view. The rendering was crystal clear and silky smooth. I recognized it as the hallway outside this room. In the feed, the exit doors at the lab end opened and Doctor Lourde and the security guard who'd shot me stepped out.

"Ah, that's my cue to leave," Fax said. "They probably wouldn't be too pleased to find me here." He rose, a little faster than his old bones would have preferred from the cracking sounds, and patted me on the knee. "You hang in there, now, you hear? I'll come back later."

I sat up straighter and covered his hand with mine. "Thank you."

Chapter 19

Unable to close the camera feed, I watched Doctor Kandall Lourde and the security guard traverse the hallway. My pulse quickened, and I took several deep breaths, trying to clear my head of the remaining fuzziness.

Lourde had ditched the suit for a pair of dress pants, a dark sweater, and a blue lab coat. I guessed that meant we were getting down to business.

He walked a few steps in front of the blond, mustachioed guard, not speaking to him or even acknowledging his presence. Rather rude, since that guy had saved his life the last time we were in a room together.

The image switched between angles as they passed the lab, the gym, and finally the med bay and lounge doors. My years as an officer combing through evidential recordings told me the cameras were motion-activated. Companies often used them to cut costs. I doubted that was the case here. Perhaps it had to do with the Faraday shielding Fax mentioned. Or, maybe it was to limit patient access to information.

My door slid open with a soft swoosh.

"Good, you're awake," Lourde said. "I've been waiting to move on to the next phase."

As soon as they stepped into the room, I was gut-punched with a barrage of unwanted information. If I hadn't already been sitting, my knees would have given out beneath me.

Data from the guard's cuff hit me first, overlapping the display from the patient monitor. The Intell made my cloning program look like a joke. It wasn't transferring a copy of the information but reading it straight from his device. Dozens of windows popped open, filling my vision with their data.

His name was Michael Hitz, and he had no qualms using his work-issued cuff for personal matters. A bevy of programs filled his quick viewscreen, including fifteen I recognized as interplanetary gambling sites. The most recently accessed one was for betting on fox hunters—fast, single-occupancy racing ships that chased a preprogrammed "fox" around a planetary system. It often required precision maneuvering through asteroid belts, daredevil slingshots around gas giants, and spectacular crashes as they tried to locate and capture the fox.

I stared at the program a second too long. It opened, releasing a flurry of ads with flashing lights, poppy music, and three-dimensional animations all vying for my attention.

My Intell tried to access Lourde's Insight implant, only it didn't get in. A security program blocked me. Another program opened on top of the camera feeds and medical readings, running lines of code so fast it nauseated me to look at it. The code breaker stalled at a firewall, then redirected itself, searching out vulnerabilities.

I shut my eyes, trying to block the words and images, but I still saw them. A thick spike of pain hammered into my brain from behind my right ear to the back of my eyeball. It was excruciating and worse than any migraine I'd ever experienced. I crumpled forward with a whimper, cradling my head in my hands and rocking my body forward and back. Genuine fear took hold as I thought for sure the implant had exploded inside my head.

The outside world receded until it was just me, the Intell, and the pain.

It lasted for minutes or hours, or maybe only seconds. My sense of time skewed. In an attempt to regain control, I employed a technique I used to cope with migraines. I imagined the spike as a physical thing, representing the pain. It was conical and made of slate-gray metal, rough hewn, and dented on the surface. The spike had wedged itself far into the right half of my skull. Every pump of blood from my heart felt like someone striking the end with a mallet, driving it deeper and deeper.

Far off in the distance, I heard someone scream. My throat burned, so I thought it might have been me.

In my mind's eye, I reached for the spike. It was buried deep, but the end stuck out above my scalp. With my fingernails, I scrabbled at the edges, slick with blood. I dug and clawed and pinched and tweezed until my fingertips found purchase. Then I pulled and imagined the tip of the spike retreating from behind my eye. The sharpest of the pains eased fractionally.

Slowly, I pried the fictional spike from my head. I poured all my attention on making the visualization as realistic as possible: the feel of the warm metal in my hands, the coppery smell of blood, and the sensation of it dragging across my skin. The more I focused on it, the less overwhelming the data dump from the Intell became. By the time I visualized the point of the spike sliding free of my skull, I had a handle on the pain. It still throbbed in the background, but I compartmentalized it and set it aside enough to deal with the Intell.

The implant, at its most basic level, was a computer. It ran programs, and programs could be turned off. All I needed to do was figure out how.

I didn't know enough about the hacking program to tackle it, but every two-year-old knew how to clear a screen of ads. The little leprechaun pelting handfuls of LTs at my face had to go first. I tried thinking commands like *close* and *end* and *shut down*, but none had any effect. My focus slipped, and the pain threatened to overwhelm me again.

I had to be missing something basic.

It was a neural impulse implant. Chintzy was a neural impulse cuff. They must both work on neural impulses—physical signals from the brain.

I reached for the leprechaun and flicked my middle finger against my thumb in the standard motion for closing a program. The flashing LTs blinked out of existence. I did the same on the next ad. After the first few, I realized it only took micro movements of my fingers to accomplish the task. I barely tapped my finger on the pad of my thumb to make it work.

As each one closed, my mind grew quieter and calmer. Finally, the only program left running was the one trying to access Lourde's implant. I shoved it to the side and fell back against the pillow.

"Nine minutes, fifty-seven seconds. That's an excellent baseline," Lourde said. "You may step outside now, Michael."

"Yes, sir. Holler if she gives you any trouble."

"I'm sure that won't be necessary. She couldn't hurt a mouse in her current state—which reminds me, we finished running the last set of labs on the test rats this morning. Tell maintenance to dispose of them by the end of the week. We'll need the cages sterilized and prepped for the next test group by Monday."

"I'll let maintenance know right away." Michael gave a curt nod and left the room.

The test animals? Walnut's whiskered face conjured in my mind. He'd been terrified, hiding in his little hut. I curled into a ball as much as my restraints allowed.

Lourde stuck his left hand—his biological one—into his coat pocket and I heard the soft *click-click* of the metal popping on his stress cube.

"An adjustment period is to be expected," he said. "The Intell processes data at a much faster rate than a traditional cuff. It will take time for your brain to adapt to the speed and volume of information." Lourde moved around my bed to the patient monitor. "Your numbers have stabilized considerably faster than our previous subjects. Any sensitivity to light or sound?" When I didn't answer, he slipped his hands into his pockets and rocked back on his heels. "You have a choice to make. You can either willingly participate in a study that will lead to the betterment of humankind, or you can be uncooperative, in which case I will extract the information through standard testing and observation. The choice is yours, but I will collect the data one way or the other."

I glared at him.

"Very well." His eyes unfocused for a second, and the lights flared to full power.

"Ah!" My hands flew to cover my eyes. "Fuck you."

"Eloquent. I'll mark that as a 'yes' to light sensitivity. Shall we test for sound, as well?" Without a pause, he clapped his hands beside my left ear. I shied away, but more out of startlement than pain. "Sound sensitivity only marginally increased. Very good. Can you move your fingers and toes?"

I gave him a three-fingered hand gesture.

"No difficulty with fine motor skills, I see. Do you think you can walk?"

Tough question. My legs felt like coiled fire suppression hoses, limp and rubbery yet heavy as hell. Also, like suppression hoses, it was as if they were filled with leftover chemicals from the anesthesia that needed to be flushed out. Exercise would help with that.

"Unlock these restraints, and I'll give it a go."

"After your previous outburst, the restraints will remain in place."

Lourde opened the door. At least, I assumed it was Lourde. He didn't have a cuff to wave in front of the reader, and the portion of my Intell working on hacking into his neural implant threw a fit. I minimized it again and shoved it back to the lower corner of my vision. The commands came easier as I got the hang of using smaller motions.

"Michael, I'm ready to move Subject E to the med bay for additional testing."

The surly guard returned, carrying a set of walking restraints. He snapped them on my wrists and ankles before unlocking and removing the ones chaining me to the bed. "Come on, let's go."

Sitting up triggered another wave of dizziness, but the not-so-subtle nudging of Michael's blaster over the GraftPatch on my shoulder encouraged me to work through it. I swung my feet over the edge and let them dangle. "Shoes?"

Michael grabbed a pair of soft-soled slippers from beneath the desk and tossed them on the bed. They were more like thick socks with anti-skid treads and straps to keep them from falling off. I slid them on and tightened the fasteners.

I shuffled out of my room, across the lounge and hall, and into the med bay. Fax was already there, sitting on a bed and facing a giant console. Something like a game played on it, and he appeared to be making the figures move using his Intell. I saw his fingers twitching with the minute movements I was coming to associate with controlling the implant. Doctor Adler hovered near him at one of the smaller consoles, inputting comments. Sagi stood to the side of the door, looking bored.

My Intell connected with every cuff, console, and medical device in the room. I staggered as if it were a physical blow. Immediately, I closed the programs until only Lourde's and Adler's Insights remained. My Intell refused to stop trying to crack their security measures, but at least I could move them off to the side. For some reason, it had yet to detect Fax's Intell, and that was fine by me.

"Sit." Michael pointed toward an empty bed. After I settled in, he positioned himself by the door near Sagi.

Lourde slid a console in front of me that was set up with the same program as Fax's. "Shall we begin?"

Chapter 20

I LOST TRACK OF the hours they kept me in front of the console playing training programs in the guise of games. The Department of Enforcement of Criminal Affairs used them—as did the military in a more strenuous capacity—so I wasn't unfamiliar with the concept.

At first, I resisted and refused to take part. At Lourde's direction, Michael turned his blaster to a low setting and used my legs for target practice. The energy blasts shouldn't leave permanent damage at that level, but they weren't designed for repeated use. I gave in when wisps of smoke rose from the synthetic fabric of my pants.

The beginning levels taught me the basic functions of the implant. Opening and closing programs, navigating the control settings, and aerial scribing. Unlike a physical cuff which was limited to reading the signals from whichever arm you strapped it to, the Intell allowed me to use both hands for inputting commands. My left hand wasn't as dexterous as my right, and the finesse required for aerial scribing with the Intell made me feel awkward and clumsy.

The ring finger on my left hand cramped, sending my character out the window of a ninety-story building. "Void be damned." I shoved the console away. That was the fifth time in a row.

"Imbecile! You must circle to the left," Lourde scolded. "The movement mirrors your right-hand commands, not clones it. Run it, again, from the beginning."

Fax reached over and patted my forearm. "It gets easier, kid. Try to look away from the command bar if you feel your movement going wild. That'll stop it from listening to your hands."

His screen flashed red as his avatar died.

Pop-pop, pop-pop. Lourde worked his stress cube. "You not only ruined your test, but you caused Subject C to fail his, as well."

"I'm tired, and my head is killing me. I need a break."

Michael stepped forward with his blaster drawn.

"You know, I could use a breather myself." Fax shifted in his seat as if he intended to swing his legs off the side.

Michael clocked Fax in the back of the head with the barrel of his weapon. "Nobody asked you, old man."

Fax fell back against the bed, one hand cradling his shaved scalp.

I jerked against my restraints. "Fax? Fax, are you okay?" He opened his eyes long enough to make contact with mine and gave the smallest of nods. I railed on Michael. "You have a problem; you take it up with me."

"Nothing would make me happier." Michael dialed up the power and fired a shot straight into my knee.

Lourde held up his hand. "That will do, Michael. How many times must I tell you? Not in the head."

"Sorry, Doc," Michael said, but he didn't sound sorry about hitting Fax in the head.

"Doctor Adler, please run a full diagnostic on Subject C's implant. Make sure it wasn't damaged. Subject E, you may have your break while we reset. But keep it short."

Sagi came over to help Adler transfer Fax to the 3D imaging bed while Michael put me back in walking restraints. I tried to catch Fax's eye again, but he turned his head toward the opposite wall.

Limping on my injured knee, I shuffle-hopped across the hall, used the restroom, and crawled into bed. In the quiet, with the lights dimmed to the lowest setting, I lay on my side and visualized the pain in my head as an inflated balloon slowing losing air. Unfortunately, the pressure didn't subside. My head felt like it wanted to burst open from the inside out. I sighed and rubbed my temples. The visualization technique could be hit or miss on effectiveness.

Sometimes, when I'd had stubborn migraines while onboard the *Soteria,* Felix would sit in the engine room until the heat warmed his metallic body. Then he'd snuggle behind my knees as I lay in my bunk. The warmth didn't do anything to mitigate the pain in my head, but out in the void, thousands of light-years from another human being, it was comforting to know I wasn't completely alone.

I missed that cat. And the *Soteria*. Home never felt so far away as it did that moment. After a few minutes, Sagi knocked on my door carrying food, water, and a strip of three medicine tabs. "I brought you something to eat." He looked around for somewhere to set the plate, but found nowhere. He held it out to me at arm's length. "Well? Do you want it or not?"

"Not." My stomach was both ravenous and revolted at the thought of food.

The security guard stood holding the plate and looking uncomfortable. "It's your own fault you're in here, you know. I warned you to stay away."

"If that helps you sleep at night."

"Hey, *you* stole my credentials *and* broke in here against the law. You don't get to be all high and mighty now."

I rolled over and sat up, letting my anger carry me through the pain. "So turn me into DECA. It doesn't give you the right to hold me against my will and treat me like one of those guinea pigs down the hall."

Even in the dimmed lighting, I saw Sagi's face flush pink. He dropped the plate on the bed, spilling carrot sticks and snap peas onto the blanket.

"Eat your damn food," he said and stomped out of the room, still holding my water.

I scooped the raw vegetables back onto the plate with the myco-protein patty sandwich. Sniffing, I detected hints of teriyaki, garlic, and ginger seasoning. My stomach would have preferred something blander, but I needed the protein to regain my strength. The first piece went down rough. I took small bites and made it halfway through the sandwich before calling it quits. Not sure when my next meal would be, I stuck the raw vegetables in my pocket to save for later. The tabs I left untouched.

Laying back down, I closed my eyes. My mind wandered to thoughts I'd been unwilling to face until now. Things did not look good.

What had I been thinking? This whole fiasco had been one poor decision after another, starting with not calling in Jarrett's murder the second I discovered his body. I wasn't some great vigilante, righting wrongs and fighting for justice. I was a former agent who investigated insurance claims for a living. High crimes and espionage were outside my skill set.

Sagi was right. I had no one to blame but myself.

And I'd gotten myself into a real jam this time. The exits were alarmed, the guards armed, no one knew where I was, and Lourde had confiscated Chintzy. Crappy cuff that it was, at least I knew how to use it and could have improvised . . . something. Then there was the chip in my head that would either drive me insane or fry my brain. There was probably a medical term for it, but I doubted I'd care much about technicalities at that point.

Maybe, like Fax, I should resign myself to the fact that I would die here.

The door opened, and Michael entered. His hand rested on the hilt of his blaster. "Break time's over, ribbit."

I opened my mouth to retort, but snapped it shut. What did it matter, anyway?

He switched me back to walking restraints, and as he locked them in place, he said, "I wish I'd known you were fucking law enforcement when I shot you. Nothing beats a little late night frogging." Michael made guns out of his fingers and pretended to shoot me.

I'd heard that—and much worse—over my years at the agency, but the intensity of his eyes told me he wasn't talking shit. They sparked the same as when an arsonist watched a fire burn. Just thinking about it made him light up on the inside and left me chilled to the bone.

For once in my life, I wisely kept my mouth shut.

We got to the med bay as Sagi was helping Fax out of his bed. The old man doubled over in a fit of coughing. When it finally eased, tiny red dots speckled his white shirt. An image of Jarrett's blood-spattered bedroom flashed unbidden to my mind. Sagi looped one arm around the frail waist and half walked, half carried Fax back to his room.

"What happened?" I asked, craning my neck to see around Michael's stocky frame. When I got no answer, I rounded on Doctor Lourde. "What did you do to him?"

"Subject C is performing below expected parameters. It is unfortunate, as that version of the Intell initially showed promising results."

"Fax. His name is Fax, not Subject C."

Lourde's eyes unfocused and the console beside him blinked on. He faced it and a file labeled *Subject E* filled the plastiglass screen. "I find designations keep an objective distance between test subjects and researchers."

"Sure. I'll designate you as Asshole from now on."

Michael slammed his fist into my shoulder, right where he had shot me three nights earlier. It drove me to my knees. "You will speak to Doctor Lourde with respect, ribbit."

I looked up from the floor, meeting him in the eyes. "Don't be jealous. I've got a special name for you, too."

He kicked me in the gut. I used my elbows to block the strike, but it still knocked the wind out of me.

Michael hauled me up by my bicep and shoved me onto the bed. "Not too smart now, are you?"

"That will do." Lourde swung the game console over to the bed again. After queuing up Level 3, he wheeled over another machine and positioned it a handspan from the side of my head. To me, he said, "Use both hands and try to complete the level this time. If you abort early, the results are invalid, and we will have to start over."

"And if I refuse?"

"Then Michael will shoot you again, and I'll have to find a new test subject. One who is more cooperative."

Michael's hand rested on the handle of his blaster. The corner of his mouth lifted in a half-sneer that implied he was more than willing to follow through with that order.

With little choice, I focused on the link between my Intell and the console. A simulation of a military intelligence building appeared. My goal, like the last time, was to gain access to an upper-level office and retrieve a file from a high-ranking official's console.

At least the game was entertaining.

Chapter 21

"Got you," I said, and tucked the golden chalice under my arm. I sprinted off in the opposite direction from which I'd come. I wouldn't make that mistake again.

My Intell projected a semitransparent map of the maze's floor plan in the upper-right quadrant of my field of view. "Overlay my coordinates." A pulsing dot appeared on the map. "Plot the shortest course to the exit." A line appeared, showing a zigzag path from my location at the heart of the maze to the exit.

A deep, guttural roar filled my ears, followed by the rapid *clack-clack* of two cloven hooves on stone.

I took two rights and a left, following the trail laid out for me by my Intell's mapping program. All the while, the sound of the minotaur grew louder until I sensed it was one turn behind me. Another ninety-degree corner, and I stumbled, dropping the chalice.

"Shit." Did I keep going and end with a failed mission or stop to retrieve the prize?

Too late. The minotaur entered the hall. Puffs of steam blew from its nostrils as it pawed the ground. I squinted. This was going to hurt.

It barreled into me, knocking me to the floor. A thousand pounds of pissed-off bull stampeded over me and then gored its horn into my soft belly.

Warning sensors flashed and clanged. Shocks of pain exploded inside my head.

I shut down the Minotaur program, leaned over the edge of my bed, and vomited. "Fucking-A, does it have to hurt so much?"

Doctor Adler grimaced at the mess. "The reward and punishment system is a proven training technique. Perform better and it won't hurt."

I rubbed my temple to soothe the headache that always came from using the Intell's hacking programs. "The minotaur didn't even live in a maze. He lived in a labyrinth. The least you could do is make it mythologically accurate."

"This was never my favorite of the ancient myths. I prefer the one about Pandora. She saved hope for humanity."

"Yeah, I'm not sure that's the lesson you should take away from that one."

She studied some readings on the wall console beside my desk and handed me four tabs. "I'm increasing your dosage."

At Fax's encouraging, I had reluctantly started taking the tabs. They eased the headaches and some of the other symptoms. "What's in these, anyway?"

The sound of a man clearing his throat drew our attention. Sagi and Michael—looking bored posted at the door in their rumpled black-and-white suits—snapped to attention.

Aurelian Tazza's eyes quickly passed over me. "Kandall, a word? Privately. I want a progress update."

"Of course, sir. Subject E, you may have a ten-minute break to stretch."

My feet tingled when they hit the floor, aware of the sudden rush of fresh blood to their digits. I arched backward to work my lower back. I'd run the training program for six straight hours. My brain felt like a vat of mycoprotein dough, mushy and lukewarm. Every muscle was tight, but I shuffled toward the door in my walking restraints before Lourde changed his mind.

"Have the medical staff at the new clinic completed their surgical training?" Tazza asked. "The latest report on wait times for the Insight was unacceptable."

"I have the numbers right here." Lourde spun around looking for an available console. Settling on the one beside Fax's empty bed, he called up a graph and beckoned Tazza closer.

My stamina for the physical strain the Intells put on us was better, but Fax had more experience and often beat me. Plus, he was tricksy for an old codger. Today, however, he'd only made it two hours before collapsing from exhaustion. Sagi had hauled him back to his room, and I hadn't seen him since.

As much as I would have loved to listen in on Lourde's and Tazza's conversation, their voices faded when Michael closed the opaqued, plastiglass door behind me. Tazza had stopped by every day for the last five days to check on Lourde.

I turned left, heading toward the emergency door at the end of the hall. When I approached, my Intell identified the door reader's electronic signal and opened a viewscreen. Immediately, the code-breaker program latched onto it. I minimized the program—because I'd learned how to do that—and let it spin its wheels out of view. A previous exploration had proved the program couldn't unlock the door and would only result in a bloody nose as the implant's computing power maxed itself out.

U-turning, I started off to the other end of the hall, wishing the leg restraints permitted a normal stride instead of awkward three-quarter length steps. A buzz of signals lit up as I approached the gym door and dropped just as quickly after I passed.

Fax thought they'd made the lab into some kind of giant Faraday cage to prevent us from contacting the outside world with the implants. The walls must be lined in aluminum mesh to achieve such good blockage, and I suspected the whine the Intell "heard" came from small leaks in the shielding. True Faraday cages were difficult to construct on a large scale. There had to be holes for plumbing, wiring, support beams, and doors, although windows weren't an issue, as I hadn't found a single one yet.

More signals bombarded me at the door to the lab. As near as I could figure, the Intell's range was about one meter from the doorways. Within a room, I'd been able to detect signals up to two meters from the machines.

I looked back toward the med bay. Neither Michael nor Sagi had followed me out into the hall, so I ducked inside. Even if I hadn't figured out an escape plan yet, the more information I gathered, the better chance I had.

A flurry of squeaks from the little test critters greeted me, but there were fewer today than before. Pebbles's cage was one of the empty ones, and I didn't realize I could care what happened to a rat, but there it was—a pang of sadness for the inquisitive animal.

It took a second to sort through the signals, turn off what I was able, and minimize everything else. The effort made my temples throb, but I was getting faster at the delicate aerial scribing.

Walnut poked his head out of his hut, his little buck teeth showing beneath a pink nose and white whiskers. He was kind of cute for a rodent. His coat was a soft, nutty brown with a white patch that started on his forehead and ran between his eyes, over his chunky cheeks, down his neck, and across his belly.

I took a carrot stick from my pocket and dropped it inside his cage. My Intell picked up information from the chip implanted into his tiny, pea-sized brain. Walnut's heart rate increased, as did areas of his brain associated with hunger, curiosity, and decision making.

He spent a few seconds sniffing the air, then scurried out and dragged the carrot back to his hut. Crunching sounds and happy purr-trills filled the quiet room. When he finished, Walnut wiggled his butt back out.

This time, I held a pea pod out to him. "Here, Walnut. Come and get it."

After a moment's hesitation, he accepted it from my hand and nibbled the end. I pet him gently between his ears, being careful not to touch the incision with the scratch marks all around it. He paused his munching, thought it over, and decided he enjoyed being petted. My Intell didn't tell me that, but he leaned into my fingers and didn't try to run away.

Something gave way inside of me. I couldn't do much to improve my current situation, but maybe I could improve Walnut's. He didn't deserve to be disposed of like a worthless piece of trash because Lourde had finished playing with him.

I opened the connection between our implants further and rummaged through his program. His chip provided basic info on his health and regions of brain activity. There was also a control that allowed the researcher to stimulate or depress particular areas to provoke a desired response. In Walnut's case, the implant suppressed his appetite while simultaneously stimulating his metabolism. The implications sank in. If they marketed the Insight as a weight-loss device, they'd sell billions. Trillions.

Screw that. I turned off all the controls, allowing Walnut's appetite to return to its natural state. Then I added in some fake data to make it appear that the guinea pig had a heart attack and died.

Taking a large handful of food nuggets from the dispenser, I put them in my shirt pocket. Walnut wheeked and ran to the nearest corner, putting his paws on the wall and hoping for food to drop from the sky.

"Shh." I reached both hands in to keep my restraints from clanging on the cage. "We have to be very, very quiet. Can you do that?"

He was too big to carry out of the lab in my arms without being seen, so I untucked the front of my shirt and carefully hid him in a roll of the fabric next to my belly. I concealed the bulge of his body and supported his weight by clasping my hands in front of me.

Then I went into his chip's program and found the command that would stimulate the *predator, hide from danger* part of his brain. He buried his face in the nook between my arm and stomach and went still.

"This is only for a couple of minutes," I whispered. "I know it's scary, but trust me, it's better than staying here another night."

As a last step, I deleted the information from the console below his cage, so it looked like maintenance had already disposed of him. I hurried down the hall, hoping I hadn't been gone so long that Michael would come looking for me.

Walnut and I made it to my room. I turned off the stimulation to his brain telling him to hide and pulled him out from under my shirt.

"Easy now," I said, giving him a reassuring stroke along his back. "We need a place for you to stay where the mean, old scientist won't find you."

And kill you. But I didn't tell Walnut that. He was having a hard enough day.

I set him on the bed with a few food nuggets and searched the room. There was a minimalist bathroom which supported only the bare basics of human hygiene, a desk, chair, bed, and cabinet closet. I opened the closet and found a change of sheets, two sets of patient uniforms identical to the one I wore, and my cross-body bag crumpled on the bottom.

My hands shook as I snatched it from the shelf. It felt light and a quick rummage revealed they'd removed everything of value: Chintzy, the data dots, and anything close to resembling a weapon. Still, I took comfort in holding something familiar, and it smelled like home when I hugged it close.

I tied the bag to the bedframe and hung it over the edge of the mattress facing the wall. With my pillow pushed up, I couldn't see it at all. I added the rest of the nuggets and pea pods into the interior pockets, which I left open.

"Come on, Walnut." I made little scratching noises with my nail against the sheet.

He waddled over to investigate the bag.

"What are you doing in here?" Sagi asked from the doorway.

I spun around, tripping on the grippy bottoms of my socks. Had he seen Walnut? Resisting the urge to break eye contact to check on the critter, I moved over to the cabinet and began rummaging around the shelves. "I'm looking for something to bandage up my neck. It feels infected."

"Let me see." Sagi stepped behind me, close enough for me to see stray pieces of white dog hair on his uniform. "I don't know about infected, but it is pretty red. Wait here." He came back a minute later and applied regenerative salve and a fresh GraftPatch over the incision.

"Thanks."

"Yeah, well, Doc can get pretty focused when he's working."

"Don't you mean kidnapping and torturing?"

Sagi's brows furrowed. "He's doing great work here—*we're* doing great work. Tazza Industries is going to change the galaxy."

"With bionic weapons? Sure."

"By merging humans with machines. The best of both parts. Doc says the implants and bionic tech are going to help us evolve into a better species."

"Do you really believe that?"

"He's the smartest guy I ever met. If he says so, then it must be true."

"If his ideas are so great, then why has every inhabited planet banned the development of bionic weapons? Technology should not exceed humanity."

Sagi didn't say anything, but I saw him chew over the thought. He escorted me back to the med bay where Lourde queued up a training program. Adler stood in the far corner with her back to me, but I heard the clinking of a bottle against the stainless-steel countertop.

Fax's bed was still empty. He'd become violently ill three hours into training and had to be taken to his room. Even though I was worried about him, I was glad he was getting some rest.

I settled into my spot while Lourde positioned a new machine behind my head. A padded metal ring folded down over my forehead and locked into place. The pads extended inward, sandwiching my head between them to the point I couldn't move.

"What is this?" I asked, my voice shaky.

"This program will focus on the connection between the Intell and your optical nerve. In order to record your physical responses, we must first manually stimulate and stain the nerve."

Doctor Yelena Adler walked over carrying a syringe. She removed the cap revealing a long, thin needle and held it in front of my eye. "Do not move."

"No!" I grabbed her hand with mine and threw my weight against the ring. It held fast.

We struggled. Adler was stronger than she looked and unfettered by augmented restraints. As I strained against her, twin pinpricks stabbed the insides of my wrist. It wouldn't take long for the sedative to hit my system.

I whimpered as anger and fear gave way to a feeling of helplessness. My arms quivered and tears rolled unbidden down my cheeks.

Michael reached me first. He pressed the muzzle of his blaster against the outside of my thigh and squeezed the trigger. An electrical shock rolled through my body. My fingers spasmed, releasing Adler's hand. She stumbled backward with a gasp, and I hoped she felt the shock, too.

Sagi wrapped his arms around mine, wedging his shoulder beneath my chin. A mix of sweat and stale cafaco hit my nose. Below him, Michael pinned my legs to the bed with his body weight. Between the two of them, the ring contraption, and the sedative, resisting was a losing proposition.

I ceased struggling, but couldn't stop the tears once they'd started.

Adler tugged her coat straight and smoothed back a wisp of hair that had come free. "Really, Ms. Sinclair, this is all quite dramatic."

A magnified, three-dimensional image of the internal workings of my head appeared on the console in front of me. As Adler got closer, a rendition of her hand and the syringe appeared on the screen. She used her index finger and thumb of her left hand to hold my eyelid open. They were cold and hard against my flushed skin.

I watched in fascinated horror as the sharp tip of the needle crept toward my eye. Centimeters away, it dipped below my vision. On the console, I saw it press into the white of my eye, below the golden-brown of my iris. The sclera dimpled and then the needle punctured the surface with a hot flash of pain. Everything blurred.

Adler pulled the needle out and straightened.

I blinked rapidly, but my left eye continued to water. It was impossible to tell if the tears were obscuring my vision or if Adler had damaged the eye itself. Instinctively, I squeezed it shut, although any damage had already been done.

On the console, an inky-blue fluid shot through my left eyeball to the optic nerve at the back. It traveled all the way to the center of my brain before stopping.

Lourde leaned over the console, obstructing my view. His fingers aerial scribed the motion to enlarge the view. "Very good, Doctor Adler. You bypassed most of the vitreous humor this time."

The short brunette straightened her shoulders and brought herself up to her full height, clearly pleased at the compliment. "Thank you, Doctor Lourde. As with most motor skills, practice improves technique." She retrieved a second syringe from the counter and bent forward until her face was level with mine. She held up the needle for me to see. "A pity I only get to practice on two at a time."

Chapter 22

Walnut poked his head out of my bag, whiskers twitching. His implanted chip automatically read his brain activity levels and fired off a report to my Intell. *Curiosity, hunger, anticipation.*

Sagi had left another plate of food on my bed, tossing it down and leaving without speaking to me. Again. He'd avoided any kind of conversation since our chat three days ago.

My dinner included a serving of bright-green miniature apples, which I'd saved for Walnut. After all the staff left for the night, I pulled one out of my pocket and offered it to the guinea pig. He snatched it from my fingertips and ran back to his bag to enjoy his treat in private. Without the chip suppressing his appetite, the little guy was a regular food composter, and nothing seemed to fill him up.

"How long do you think you can hide him?" Fax asked from the doorway. His hand clung to an IV pole for support so hard his knuckles stuck out pale and knobby through papery skin. The IV was new and meant the daily hydration supplements they'd been giving him weren't enough anymore. He visited me every night, each time looking a little worse.

I gave him a weak smile. "Longer than you can keep hiding that you're not eating."

He dropped a handful of apples onto my blanket before settling down on the desk chair with a soft groan. "Can't keep it down anyway, so what's the point?"

"Are your headaches getting worse?"

"The tabs don't help much anymore. It's near constant now. Can't eat, can't sleep. It's getting so I can barely think straight. Not sure how much longer I'll be able to haul these old bones over here to check on you."

"You shouldn't overexert yourself for me."

Fax swatted the air with his free hand in a *nonsense* gesture. "I'd rather die hobbling over here than lying on my back staring at the ceiling."

"Don't talk like that."

"It's coming, sugar. Only a matter of time now. I wish . . ."

"Wish what?"

"Well, I suppose I'd like to talk to my brother one last time. We had words at our father's funeral. It was the last time we saw each other."

"How long ago was that?"

"Must be about ten years now, eleven maybe."

"Where is your brother now?"

"Still on Mars, I suppose. You'd probably call it Sol-4, but my family's been there since the first colony."

"A Martian, huh? I've read some old stories about them. Aren't you supposed to have antennae and green skin?"

He snorted and raised the hem of his pant leg. "I got the skinny arms and legs at least."

"What does JJ mean?" I pointed to the tattoo above his ankle.

Fax scratched his salt-and-pepper beard. "Jeremiah Johnson. It's been a long time since anyone's called me that, but I guess I didn't want to forget." He saw my confusion and continued. "Fax is my moniker. Short for Face the Facts. I wasn't cut out for factory work. My boss knew it and told it to me plain. Best advice I ever got."

"So you left home?"

"I have the wanderlust. Spent the last sixty-odd years exploring the galaxy. Been to about every inhabited planet and made many wonderful friends. Never regretted a single day. Being in here, though, it sure makes me miss the sky. Clear blue or roiling mad with storm clouds or, heck, even black and speckled with stars outside a porthole, she always reminded me there was more out there to see."

It was a loss I empathized with. I'd give anything to be on the *Soteria* with Felix again. Even though it'd only been a couple of weeks since I left the ship on Ceti, it felt much longer.

Fax scooted his chair closer to the bed and patted my ankle over the blanket. "Bring out the little rodent. I sure love watching him play."

I made a clicking sound to call Walnut out. He spotted Fax and turned his glossy, black eyes to me, his chip sending out data that he was nervous. I scratched the white spot in the middle of his forehead, right above his eyes.

Fax held up one of the miniature apples he'd brought. Walnut was highly food motivated and easily bribed. He waggled out quicker than you would expect something that potato-shaped to move. The proffered fruit disappeared with three juicy chomps of his sharp buckteeth. Two more apples followed as Fax nudged them in front of the tiny suction tube.

"Keep bringing him treats, and he's going to follow you back to your room," I warned.

"His incision is healing nicely. Looks like he finally stopped scratching at it. How's yours doing?"

I touched the lump on the back of my neck. It was hot to the touch, and every so often I caught a whiff of something sour. "No improvement. Adler gave me a shot of something yesterday, but I don't think it helped."

"You taking your tabs?"

I nodded. "Not at first, but Adler caught me tossing them in the reclamator and threw a fit for throwing off her numbers. Now she stands over me and watches while I take them. Did they ever tell you what's in them? She won't tell me."

Fax shook his head and wiggled another miniature apple at Walnut. "Naw, not that it would mean much to me if they did. They help with the headaches, though—or at least, they used to."

Camera feeds from the main entrance popped on in both our heads, showing us that the door reader had flipped to unlock. Fax's worried eyes met my own. Someone was coming.

I stared at a particular point to the bottom-left of my field of view, which triggered voice activation of my Intell. "Time." A clock appeared. 2200 hours. "Have they ever been here this late?"

"Just that time you busted in. Then they all came running." Fax pulled himself up with the aid of the IV pole. "Guess our visit will be a little short tonight."

I sent the *predator, hide from danger* command to Walnut's chip. He didn't waste any time beating a hasty retreat into his bag. I scooped up the miniature apples and dumped them into one of the inside pockets.

"Try to get some rest tonight," I said to Fax. "And please try to eat something."

He left, making it halfway across the lounge before I turned my attention back to the camera feeds. Five people walked down the hall: Doctor Lourde talking furiously and emphatically waving his hands, three security guards wearing a black-and-white Tazza Industries uniform, and Lead Agent Grayson Wright.

I sat up straighter and tested the range of my restraints. What was Wright doing here? Had he been working with Lourde the entire time? That would explain the zeal with which he had hunted me across the galaxy. With me out of the way, he could rule Jarrett's murder a burglary gone wrong and sweep it under the rug, like Cavender had done with his cases. I should have set that blaster to maximum and killed him when I had the chance.

My hands itched for a weapon. Despite convincing Lourde to let me take daily walks up and down the hall, I'd been unable to procure anything to turn into a shiv, garrote, or cudgel.

Lourde's raised voice reached me, even through the closed door. "You cannot remove her from the premises. She is participating in a highly confidential and sensitive study."

My door opened. Lead Agent Wright strode through first, with Lourde unsuccessfully attempting to squeeze past the agent. The heavier-set male guard followed them in while the thinner male and female guard waited in the lounge.

Lourde's scraggly hair was unkempt and frizzy, like he'd been sleeping, and he wore a light sweater in place of his lab coat, whereas Wright looked like he didn't even remember what sleep was and that suited him just fine. The guard brought up the rear, making my room feel cramped.

Both Wright and the guard carried traditional cuffs. My Intell chomped through their security measures within seconds. I closed out the programs as quickly as I could. Now wasn't the time to get distracted. I threw the window with Lourde's Insight into the background. As usual, my Intell refused to give up on cracking it.

Wright brushed aside the doctor, his attitude announcing his authority as much as the forest-green jacket he wore. "You have a copy of my interplanetary warrant for Captain Reliance Sinclair. That supersedes any claim you might have on her continued presence."

"I don't agree with this. It hasn't been signed by a Brione-2 judge," sputtered Lourde. The sagging skin around his jowls quivered.

"That is unnecessary. The Treaty of Alpha Bohn-ri covers extradition of fugitives wanted for felony crimes. Both Andaress-4 and Brione-2 are signing members."

"I've contacted our attorneys."

"My badge number and DECA office are on the warrant. That should be all the information they need."

"Excuse me," I interjected, "but will someone tell me what the hell is going on?"

Wright smiled at me the same way a predator smiled at its prey after a long and satisfying hunt. It had less to do with me and more about seeing victory within his grasp. "I'm placing you under arrest for the murder of Jarrett Viorel."

"You are doing no such thing! Subject E—Captain Sinclair is very sick. Without our medical attention, she may die."

I snorted. I was probably going to die either way.

Wright used a master key to unlock me from the bed and placed his own augmented restraints on my wrists. "The prisoner is now in my care. If required, I will see that she gets proper medical care from a licensed facility."

Lourde rounded on the guard. "Do something! That's what they pay you for."

The guard took a hesitant step toward us. His pudgy cheeks blanched as he assessed Wright and came to the obvious conclusion that he was no match for the seasoned agent.

Wright's hand hovered over the blaster strapped to his belt. "I have an extra set of restraints for anyone who attempts to interfere with my lawful arrest of Captain Sinclair."

"No, sir," said the guard, raising both hands. No doubt this would be his last day at Tazza Industries.

I stood up, not sure if my situation was improving or not, but hoping some good could come of it. "Lead Agent Wright, there's another patient here being held against his will. Can you take him, too?"

"You're holding others?" Wright asked Lourde.

"In the past, yes, but volunteers only, like Ms. Sinclair. They signed consent forms."

"I did no such thing."

"Would you like to see them? I can send the documents to your cuff right now." Lourde's eyes went unfocused, and Wright's cuff alerted him to an incoming communication.

My Intell intercepted it before Wright activated his holographic screen to view the document himself. It was a stack of medical study applications, consent forms, and power of attorney appointments. All signed and dated by me.

"Those are forgeries," I contested. "And they have no bearing on Fax."

Wright's eyes locked onto mine, testing the truth of my words. He turned toward Lourde. "Show me the other rooms. If someone is being held involuntarily, I will alert the local authorities. This is their jurisdiction."

We trudged across the hall and into Fax's room. Except he wasn't there. The bed looked hastily made, and they'd cleared the room of any sign of him. The other two guards were nowhere to be found.

I rounded on Lourde. "What did you do with him?"

The doctor ignored me and spoke to Wright. "Like I told you, Ms. Sinclair is very unwell. She suffers from hallucinations and paranoia, among other things. She is our only patient at the moment."

"No, that's not true," I said, but Wright was already ushering me toward the door. "He's here somewhere. They couldn't have moved him far."

Wright grabbed me by the shoulders and spun me to face him. His hazel eyes bore down on me. "I spent the last three weeks chasing you from one side of the quadrant to the other. I have haggled with a pawnbroker, fielded damage reports from foreign offices, and been stonewalled by a smuggling ring. You, personally, have punched, thrown, and *shot me*. And I had to explain to my superior how a multibillion credit satellite was incapacitated by an insurance claims investigator. Now, if you don't mind, I would like to go home."

His right eye twitched, daring me to speak, but even I wasn't that dumb. I nodded my acquiescence.

"Thank the fucking stars." To Lourde, he said, "If you want to register a complaint or challenge jurisdiction, you have my information."

Lourde fumed but had no more moves to play.

We got as far as the door to the hallway before I stopped. "Wait! My bag. It's tied to my bed."

Wright closed his eyes, and I imagined him counting to ten in his head. "I'll need the prisoner's personal effects."

The remaining guard hurried back to my room and retrieved my bag. He handed it to Wright, who slung it roughly over his shoulder.

I winced and sent another stimulation command to Walnut to stay hidden. His heart was racing, and the fear areas of his brain were lit up like a cockpit console during an emergency landing. I wished I could comfort him—that we could comfort each other. The truth was, I didn't know if where Wright was taking me was any better than where I was. Murder was a capital offense. Although it hadn't been enforced in over a decade, Andaress-4 still carried the death penalty.

Wright escorted me to the end of the hall. As soon as the door to the lift room opened, I knew I was in trouble. This wasn't like walking into the med bay and getting hit with signals from a couple of cuffs and a dozen machines. This was . . . indescribable. Without the shielding protection of the Faraday cage around the floor, hundreds—thousands—of signals slammed into me, and my Intell greedily accepted them all.

I fell to the ground, screaming and clutching my head in the fetal position. Voices argued above me. A spate of new communications popped into my head. Emergency comms, top priority. They quickly disappeared under the onslaught of new information.

Rough hands jostled me at my back and knees. I didn't dare open my eyes, but I felt my body lifted and carried a short distance. Flashing lights, more jostling, the hum of a crowd, and then I was set down. I tasted blood and suspected another nosebleed. They happened when the Intell worked too hard.

An engine vibrated. My stomach dipped as we lifted off the ground and sped forward, and my body identified the familiar motion of a hovercart, even if my mind was too busy to process it.

Moving faster was better. Most electronics had a short transmission range, and we blew past them before my Intell latched on. My stomach took the opportunity to empty its contents onto the floor.

The cart came to an abrupt stop. I hazarded a brief glimpse of my surroundings and saw the front doors to the Tylo Municipal Hospital. My Intell started collecting signals: cuffs, door readers, cameras, lights, comms, holos, and the citywide net.

The last thing I remembered before blacking out was a nurse rushing toward us with a hoverchair.

Chapter 23

THIRTY MINUTES LATER, I woke up in a blind panic of flailing arms and hyperventilation. Thankfully, no one was in the hospital room to witness the embarrassing display. My headache was epic but manageable, no doubt thanks to a heavy dose of meds pumping into me via an IV tube. It attached to my arm right above the single wrist restraint securing me to the bed.

My Intell registered signals from hundreds of medical devices, but only a smattering of cuffs. That suggested an intensive care unit. I silenced the most obnoxious signals and then searched for a master off switch within my Intell programming. No human could function with that kind of continual bombardment of information. Lourde must have included an off switch. He was sociopathic—maybe even psychopathic—but he wasn't stupid.

I chided myself for not figuring this out earlier. The shielding around the lab limited the signals and simply turning off the programs as they popped up had been sufficient. Unless I planned to go for the mentally unfit defense at my trial, that approach wouldn't work anymore.

The Intell's administrator hub contained dozens of applications. Most I couldn't even guess as to their purpose. Tech had never been my thing. They could come standard on nerve impulse cuffs or be entirely unique to the implant.

Jarrett would have spent five seconds scrolling through the list and told me what I needed to do. A spot in the center of my chest ached at my friend's memory, but I set it aside with all the other things I didn't have time to deal with.

I flipped through the list and, after some trial and error, opened a program called Display Application. In it, I found a setting for Notification Only Mode. I toggled it on and closed out. Immediately, all the pop-up windows disappeared from my view. In their place, a small box appeared at the top right of my view. As my Intell detected a new signal, its name flashed briefly in the box, then disappeared. Not perfect, but a vast improvement.

Once I could think and see straight, I took stock of my surroundings. It was a standard hospital room with one bed, one chair, and one exit. Terrible lighting. Strong notes of antiseptic and industrial-grade soap. I felt for the subtle sway of the building, but there was none. Its absence probably meant I was on a lower floor.

I looked out the window and saw it was nighttime. Bright lights from advertisements on the building next door flooded the room. The largest one touted the RELIABILITY benefits of the Insight, complete with a three-story high smiling face of Aurelian Tazza. Even in the hospital, I couldn't escape him.

My over-the-shoulder bag lay on a chair near the door. I found Walnut's signal. He was sleeping; the chip telling me he was in the middle of a REM cycle, and I hoped it was a pleasant dream.

Across the hall, a patient snored so loudly they must have been in that kind of deep sleep you only achieve while heavily medicated. Hospital staff hustled by, chatting with a sense of familiarity and efficiency. Their cuffs triggered notifications to my Intell whenever they got within eight meters, but blissfully did only that.

Someone had changed me into a fresh set of white patient scrubs. These had cold metal snaps down the front of the shirt and short sleeves. Standard slate-gray socks with grippy bottoms. I patted my hips and smiled. Pockets.

I didn't feel any new holes, other than from the IV. My blaster wounds had a fresh piece of GraftPatch. They may even have given me a once-over with a sonic shower wand, because my skin smelled like oranges and rosemary. The soap at Tazza Industries was reminiscent of the goop I used to clean grease off the engine parts on the *Soteria*.

Tentatively, I patted the back of my head at the incision. The swelling had reduced significantly and was no longer hot to the touch. That was one good thing, at least. I lay my head back on the pillow, closed my eyes, and watched the steady blipping of Walnut's heart on his EKG display to calm my nerves.

I needed to come up with a plan to convince Grayson Wright he had the wrong suspect before he recommended charges to the city attorney. Lourde had taken all my proof—the data dots with the recordings from Jarrett's apartment and the information Jarrett had left me, as well as Chintzy, which contained the recording of the bionic weapons. He'd also removed the weapons parts before I'd woken up from the implant procedure, so I hadn't had an opportunity to rerecord them with my implant. Or to reassemble a blaster and shoot him in the face with it. Not that I had fantasized about that or anything.

A notification flashed in my top right field of vision. Wright's cuff moved within range.

He paused in the open doorway, and I could feel the weight of his eyes. The smell of hot, artificial coffee wafted over, tickling my nose.

Wright took a drink. "I know you're awake. Your nose is twitching."

I opened my eyes. Wright was an impressive figure. He leaned his shoulder against the jamb, one foot casually crossed in front of the other, with the toe of his boot resting on the floor. His blond hair looked darker under the harsh lighting. So did the shadows under his eyes.

"Did you bring me some?" I asked, sitting up.

"It's not very good. Pretty awful, actually."

"Worse than what passes for coffee at the precinct?"

One side of his mouth lifted in a half-smile. "Nothing's that bad."

"Glad to hear they're upholding universal standards."

Wright swallowed another mouthful, then handed me his half-full cup. I shrugged. Agent cooties were the least of my worries, and caffeine was caffeine.

My eyes watered a little. "Oh, wow, that tastes as bad as it smells." Wright reached to take the cup back, but I wrapped my fingers around it protectively. "Did I say I didn't want it? I haven't had caffeine in *days—no weeks*. Believe me, it's better for both of us this way." I braced my stomach and took another drink. "How did you find me?"

"I received an anonymous tip that you would be at the space-dock on Brione-2."

"Iko."

Wright dipped his chin in acknowledgment. "Nothing is truly anonymous if you know where to look. It took my tech person a little time, but she tracked it back to Iko. You have some interesting friends."

"It's more of a frenemy situation."

His lips split into something that almost classified as a smile. "I can be very persuasive when I want to be. Iko gave me the identifier on the cuff they gave you. We traced it to Tazza Center before the signal died. Agent Singh secured a warrant and Agent Leahy spent a lot of hours looking at security feed and found you being escorted out of Tazza Industries and in the alley behind the building later that night."

"I guess I owe them one."

"You can thank them at your court hearing."

Heat flared in my chest cavity, which had nothing to do with the coffee. "You have the wrong person."

"That's what they all say. The doctor said you'd be fit for transport in an hour. They treated your infection from whatever that thing is you had Tazza Industries stick in your head. We're just waiting on the discharge papers."

"I didn't ask for the implant. Those volunteer forms Lourde gave you are forgeries. He kidnapped and falsely imprisoned me."

"Or he aided and abetted a fugitive, providing you a hiding place until the heat died down."

"He performed medical experiments on me!" The hot coffee sloshed over the edge of the cup and burned my fingers. I bit my lip to keep from yelping and transferred the cup to my other hand, shaking hot coffee off the first one.

Wright shook his head, took the coffee from me, and handed me a tissue from the medical supply station. I sopped up what I could and gave it back to him to throw in the reclamator along with the now-empty cup.

Taking a deep breath, I tried again in a calmer tone. "Tazza Industries developed a neural implant that takes the place of nerve impulse cuffs."

He tilted his head toward the window. "It's hard to miss the ads."

"What they don't tell you is that not everyone is compatible with the device. Lourde expects between two and five percent of recipients to reject the implant—to die. To him, that's an acceptable loss for the advancement of science."

"Tazza Industries must have IBMD approval for its program. Why would it jeopardize that by conducting off-the-book experiments?"

I ran my finger along the incision line at the base of my neck. With the swelling down, I could feel that the regenerative salve had finally started doing its thing and knitting the skin back together. "What they put in me is something different, a next generation product. I don't think they intend to sell it to the public."

"To what end?"

"Military. Black market."

Wright folded his arms across his chest. "Let me see if I have this straight. One of the galaxy's leading technology companies—a company worth hundreds of billions of credits—is risking it all on some potentially faulty hardware. Why would it do that?"

I cocked one eyebrow. "To be worth thousands of billions of credits? People do irrational things for that kind of money."

"That's quite the conspiracy theory, I'll give you that, but don't you think it's a little convenient that you show up at their lab needing a place to hide at the exact same time as they're looking for someone to test their product out on?"

"No, it wasn't convenient at all. I followed the money. Investigating 101. Try it sometime." My voice rose. I knew arguing wouldn't help me get my point across, but it was preferable to reaching out and smacking him upside the head, which is what I wanted to do.

"If what Kandall Lourde is developing wasn't safe, the IBMD would never have sanctioned it."

"Unless Tazza paid them off."

He chuffed. "So now the Board is in on it, too?"

"Yes! Maybe." I shifted uncomfortably, tugging at the one restraint tethering me to the bed. I needed to move. "Security caught me while I was searching for evidence."

"By breaking and entering a private facility."

"Well, you know what else I discovered? Lourde is developing bionic weapons."

Wright's eyes hardened and between one heartbeat and the next, he'd closed the distance between us. He leaned over me, caging me between his arms and invading my personal space. Like Jarrett, Grayson Wright was tall and broad-shouldered. Early settlers of Ritru-6 had been genetically modified to withstand the stronger gravity and punishing conditions of the rocky planet. It was only one of many atrocities done to the miners, and their descendants still bore their effect.

His voice dropped to a gravelly whisper. "That's a serious claim. You have proof?"

I swallowed hard and shook my head. "Only what I saw. I made a recording, but Lourde confiscated my cuff."

Wright stayed there, scrutinizing my face for tells. As much as I wanted to shrink back, I held my ground and met his stare. The seconds ticked by. A storm of emotions gathered behind his eyes, but otherwise he remained perfectly still. Finally, he broke, stepping back with an audible breath.

"Your great-grandparents?" I asked after the silence became too much. It was a guess, but that would be about the right generation for the Ritruvian Uprising Massacre eighty years ago.

At first, I didn't think he was going to answer me. His eyes looked past me to the window for several long moments. "My great-grandmother flew supply ships in from the neighboring planets. She was pregnant and away on a run to Ritru-5 when the massacre happened, but my great-grandfather was still on Ritru-6. He worked in the refugee camps building temporary housing pods. We don't know exactly how he died, but his name is on a memorial plaque near one of the camps."

"I'm sorry."

"It's not an uncommon story on Ritru-6. Almost everyone has at least one relative who died in the massacre."

"Perhaps not, but it's your story, and it still matters."

Wright's eyes returned to me, and they'd lost their faraway look. "Even if everything you said is true—and that is a very big if—it is no defense against your murder of Agent Viorel."

"Jarrett was a good friend. My best friend. He stumbled onto the money trail while doing me a favor. Tazza Industries paid agents to cover up the deaths of patients that died after receiving the implants."

"Now the Department is in on it, too? Next, you'll be telling me *I'm* a part of the conspiracy."

I didn't say the thought had crossed my mind, but he must have read it on my face. "You're a real piece of work, Sinclair, you know that? Let me give you some advice, not that I think you'll take it. Come clean at your hearing. Be honest, be remorseful, and ask for leniency. If you don't waste the court's time and can avoid dragging DECA, the IBMD, Tazza Industries, and whomever else's name through the mud, you might get life instead of lethal injection. Hell, you might even see a few years of freedom at the end of it."

"Maybe if you'd do your job, *ribbit*, you'd be hauling Jarrett's actual killers into court instead of me."

"What did you call me?"

"You heard me."

His right eye twitched. "I'm getting another cup of coffee. We'll leave as soon as the doctor gives the go-ahead."

Wright left, but I heard him stop and talk to a woman out in the hall, their voices too muffled to make out their conversation. After a minute, the conversation ended, and Wright continued on toward the cafeteria.

A short brunette in a doctor's blue, thigh-length coat entered the room. She read from a large holoscreen projected in front of her—probably my chart. I'd have thought a doctor could afford a better model cuff than that.

She closed the door behind her and turned off the projection. My heart slammed into my breastbone like I'd hit warp speed.

"Can you believe I used to use this antiquated thing?" asked Doctor Yelena Adler. "I had to dig it out of my storage. It barely powered up."

"What are you doing here?" My eyes raked the room for some kind of weapon. Unfortunately, Wright had done a thorough job of removing anything sharp or pointy.

"That implant in your head represents a decade's worth of proprietary work. We can't afford to let you walk away with it, not when we're so close to securing a contract. You might take our research to a competitor." Adler reached into a pocket of her lab coat and removed a med dispenser preloaded with a drug cartridge. "This may sting a bit."

My first instinct was to muscle my way out of the augmented restraints tying me to the bed, but wonder of wonders, I'd finally gotten it through my thick skull that fighting against a sedative was a losing battle. Whatever I did, it would be without the use of my arm.

Adler approached on my left side.

I kicked my legs free of the blanket and drew them up to my chest. "You don't think there will be an investigation if I die strapped to a hospital bed?"

She tsked. "Suicide. A careless nurse left a med dispenser filled with Dilazadol near your bed and, rather than face judgment for your crimes back on Andaress-4, you tragically took your own life."

"There are cameras. They'll know that's not how it happened."

"Tylo Municipal Hospital is one of Tazza Industries' clients. We disabled them to install a vital security update."

Adler lunged, making a grab for my arm.

I flipped onto my left side, twisting my hips and using the momentum to power a roundhouse kick into the woman's shoulder. She grunted and stumbled forward, crashing into my IV pole and sending it clattering to the ground. An alarm sounded.

Adler caught herself on the edge of the bed. As she hauled herself back up, I punched the side of her head. The angle was poor, and my position made it hard to put much force behind it. She jerked back, giving me space to regroup.

A bald nurse ran in and froze in shock as he took in the scene.

Adler, face wild and hair in disarray as large clumps tore free of her bun, turned to the nurse and injected him with the Dilazadol. The effect was immediate. His blue eyes rolled up, exposing the whites, and he fell face-first across the foot of my bed with a jarring thud.

We both stared at the dead man for a second, then at each other.

Adler dropped the med dispenser and pulled a compact blaster from the small of her back. "This isn't as clean, but it will have to do." The blaster whined as the charge amped up. She stepped forward and pressed the muzzle to my temple. "At least this way I won't have to retrieve the Intell later. It'll be fried beyond recognition."

I ripped the IV needle from my arm and stabbed it into her eye.

Adler reeled back, screaming. Blood dribbled down the side of her face from beneath her fingers.

I rifled through the nurse's pockets and found a master key for the augmented restraints. Quickly, I inserted it into the base of the lock and heard a click. The band popped open, and I scooted off the bed.

I grabbed my bag off the chair, feeling the familiar heft of a sleeping guinea pig tucked inside. Poor little guy was in for a rude wake-up call. I slung the strap over my head, gripped the bag in one hand to keep it from bouncing too hard, and dashed through the door. Behind me, Adler let out an enraged bellow.

Startled faces of staff and patients watched as I sprinted down the hall. There weren't any signs or arrows pointing toward the exits, but the rooms all had numbers in the three hundreds. I stared down and to the left to activate the voice command on my Intell. "Connect to the Tylo Municipal Hospital's private network." A view window popped up on the right, making running challenging. Immediately, the decryption program opened and did its thing. This hospital had nothing on Lourde's training program. "Find a map for the third floor."

The Intell's search bot combed through files. After several seconds, it returned with the building's design schematics from the maintenance department.

I dodged around a cleaning cart parked outside a patient's room and bumped into a nursing assistant because the design schematics blocked her from view.

"Hey!" the woman admonished, righting herself.

I hazarded a glance over my shoulder.

Adler exited my room and shoved through the lookie-loos clogging the hallway. One hand covered her left eye. The other held her blaster.

I kept running.

A chorus of exclamations rose in my wake as I split my attention between reading the map and avoiding obstacles.

"Overlay map with current location icon." A red dot appeared in the upper corner. "Zoom in." The map size increased to a readable level, and I identified the nearest set of emergency stairs. Adler would expect me to go down to ground level, so I planned on going up to the tenth floor and taking a skybridge to the next building.

A hallway branched off to my right. Agent Wright was strolling back, a steaming cup of artificial coffee in his hand. He saw me, dropped the coffee, and engaged pursuit.

Well, he was going to have to get in line, because Adler was closer.

I rounded a corner, my less-than-grippy socks causing me to slide into and bounce off the wall. The stairwell was halfway down the row. I double-checked the schematic and used my Intell to open the fourth door on the left.

Or what should have been the fourth door. There were only three.

A new wall spanned the width of the hall, cutting the floor in half. Construction equipment littered the floor and a temporary sign read, *Bionic Limb Rehab Center Coming Soon.*

Shit. The schematics were out of date.

I spun around as Adler turned down the hall. She slowed to walk, hands shaking as she held out the compact blaster in a bloody, two-handed grip. Smears of bright red streaked her right cheek. Her other eye burned with hatred.

She fired.

I ducked, but it went high and wide, scorching a black hole in the brand-new wall. Either she was a bad shot, or the lack of an eye was screwing with her depth perception.

Adler stalked closer. "I should have let Michael finish you the night you broke into the lab."

Behind her, Wright turned the corner and zeroed in on Adler's blaster. "Halt! Law enforcement. Show me your hands."

The doctor spun around one-eighty, blaster still held chest high.

"No!" But I was too far away to do anything about it.

Her finger squeezed the trigger—either out of malice or surprise—sending a volley of energy charges in a wide arc toward Wright. He dove to the side and returned fire.

I threw myself to the ground and covered the back of my head with my arms. A flashback of the night my partner tried to kill me threatened to overwhelm me, but I shoved the memory down, concentrating on the here and now.

Between my elbows, I watched Adler stagger back from the force of impact and collapse to the floor. Her chest rose and fell in shallow breaths, but the rest of her lay motionless. Not dead, just stunned.

Walnut! My fingers wormed into my bag and brushed against a lump of warm, fuzzy fur right before he bit me. Rightly so, I totally deserved that.

Wright rolled up to a crouch, weapon still trained on the unconscious doctor. Our eyes met over her body and the muzzle slid seamlessly to my heart.

"Take your hand out of the bag. Slowly," he directed.

I did as he said, spreading my fingers wide so he could see I hadn't pulled a weapon.

"Hands behind your head."

Again, I complied, lacing my fingers together and touching my nose to the floor.

Wright stood and kicked Adler's blaster out of reach. He tapped his cuff. "Sophie, base level med-ex of the subject."

A blue light from his cuff swept over Doctor Adler. "Examination complete. Subject is unconscious due to electrical shock. Non-life-threatening abnormal heart rhythm detected. Moderate burns to upper chest cavity. Severe visual impairment of left eye. Immediate medical attention recommended."

Wright rolled her onto her back and locked a pair of augmented restraints around her wrists.

"Sophie, open voice comm to Tylo DECA Liaison Officer Boel Tademan."

A hard-edged woman's voice came on. "Tademan here. Agent Wright, I'm getting reports of blaster discharge at your last known location. Please tell me you didn't come all the way from Andaress-4 to shoot up my hospital."

"I'm at TMH, third floor, with one suspect down and one in custody. Requesting a med team and backup for a prisoner transport."

"Med team is en route. Two officers will meet you at your location. Do not leave the premises. They will escort you to the spacedock."

"Close comm." He strode over, his standard-issue boots coming into my peripheral view. They were damp and reeked of burnt coffee. "Friend of yours?"

"Employee at Tazza Industries. Works under Lourde. Apparently I'm a loose end that needs tying."

He made a noncommittal grunt. Then his tone softened as he squatted beside me. "Are you injured? More injured than ten minutes ago?"

"No, she took a shot but missed."

Wright snapped his backup handcuffs around my wrist and brought it to the center of my lower back. His grip was firm, but not rough. Then he brought my other arm down and secured it with the second bracelet. With a physical key, he double locked the steel handcuffs so they wouldn't become too tight. And also so I couldn't pick them.

"Up." He lifted me to my feet by my biceps.

Three hospital personnel guiding a hoverchair hurried toward us, two medical staff and a security guard. One of them turned on his cuff's holoscreen and aerial scribed a few commands that flattened the hoverchair into a gurney. He lowered it to the floor, where the other two rolled Doctor Adler onto it. She groaned at the jostling, the first sign she was waking up. Wright gave instructions she was to remain restrained throughout the examination. The bed rose to waist height, and they rushed her off.

"We need to leave," I said. "Tazza sent Adler in first, probably because she would blend in with the staff and could get rid of me without raising suspicion. That's off the table now. They'll try again, and next time they won't be so subtle about it."

"Don't worry, I've requested backup. You'll have an armed escort all the way to the spacedock."

"Yeah? And who's going to protect me from the escort? Tazza Industries has people inside the Tylo DECA office. Lourde practically bragged about it."

"Again with the conspiracy theories."

"How else did Adler know which hospital you took me to and which room I was in? I assume you followed standard procedure and checked me in under an alias."

"Of course."

"In less than an hour, she procured a lethal dose of Dilazadol and a backup weapon, located me, and timed her attack for when you were out of the room."

Wright rubbed a hand across his face. "She may have acted alone, or someone at the hospital may have tipped her off."

"Or someone at the precinct. What about that liaison, Tademan?"

"Officer Tademan has been less than helpful, but no more so than any other interplanetary liaison. No one likes another dog digging in their sandbox."

"Are you willing to take that chance? Because I'd rather not." I shifted to stand directly in front of him. "We go to your ship right now, and I'll give you my word I won't cause any trouble."

He rocked back and rubbed a hand down his jaw. "Sophie, open voice comm to Tylo DECA liaison Officer Boel Tademan, again."

She answered with an exasperated tone. "I'm busy Agent Wright. You aren't the only agent I'm babysitting today."

"Redirect backup officers to the subject's room. Have hospital security release her into their custody once she clears medical. They can contact me for a full report."

There was a long pause. "Officers are two minutes out. Hold until they arrive. Under no circumstances are you to leave the hospital. Is that clear?"

I cocked one eyebrow.

"Agent Wright, is that clear?"

Wright swore under his breath and ended the comm. He removed his DECA jacket and placed it over my shoulders so that it covered my white patient garb and partially concealed the handcuffs. "This doesn't mean I agree with you."

"But you don't disagree, either."

"Move," he said, and pointed back toward the main exit. I didn't need to be told twice.

Chapter 24

"THAT'S A GOOD COPY, sir," said a young woman with an Andarian accent. They tended to speak quickly and punch the hard consonants. "I'm sending the updated files over subspace now. Check the second account I flagged. You'll find it interesting."

"Thank you, DeAjamae," Wright replied. "We'll be on our way as soon as the transfer is complete. Have Ravi prepare the case file for the city attorney."

He ended the audio comm and swiveled his pilot's chair around to face my cell. His ship was a standard, city-issued cruiser, complete with two holding cells, more kilometers on the warp drive than a civilian ship ten times its age, and at least five smells I didn't care to identify. The *Soteria* was newer and sleeker, but some days I missed flying one of these old frog legs. What they lacked in style and grace, they made up for in power and speed.

I sat sideways on the narrow bed with my back against the wall, feet up, and knees bent. Pain meds from the hospital still coursed through my system, keeping my ever-present headache to a tolerable level.

The trek to the spacedock had thoroughly ruined my hospital socks, so I'd discarded them in a pile on the floor. My feet were bare and tender, but for the first time in days, I was restraint-free. It felt wonderful to stretch my limbs unfettered.

I rubbed at the abraded skin around my ankles, studying Wright while I waited for him to talk. He unfastened his green DECA jacket and shrugged out of it. Underneath, he wore a long-sleeved charcoal shirt that fit snuggly around his arms and chest but fell in loose folds over a toned abdomen. Muscular without being bulky. Early signs of crow's feet bracketed sharp, intelligent eyes. Together with the fine lines around his mouth, they told me he was probably quick to laugh. Not that he'd done much of that in my presence.

No, he'd been stubbornly quiet as he escorted me to the nearest hovercart rental station, procured a vehicle, and drove us straight to the spacedock. It hadn't been quite the madcap dash I'd made on Andaress-4, but the word "asshole" had been used liberally by pedestrians as they scrambled out of our way.

That was fine. My head still reeled from the fight at the hospital. Adler had almost killed me and would have succeeded if Wright hadn't shot her. He'd saved my life. I didn't know how to process that, other than to acknowledge that maybe, just maybe, my plan to do this on my own needed reevaluation.

Wright tossed the jacket over the copilot's chair, eased back, and laced his fingers behind his head. It was a deceptively relaxed pose I didn't buy for a minute. "All right, Sinclair. You've got five minutes while we wait for the file transfer. Tell me about the doctor and why I bypassed fifteen regulations getting you off-planet?"

"Yelena Adler worked under Lourde. It was her idea to use me as a test subject for their new implant, which they call the Intell. If I had to guess, I'd say they thought she'd blend in with the hospital staff the easiest. Or maybe she drew the short straw, who knows?"

Wright rocked in the seat. "For argument's sake, let's say there's a vast cover-up going on. Walk me through your conspiracy theory, from the beginning."

I took a moment to collect my thoughts. This was my one chance to convince Wright. I still wasn't sure if I could trust him, but he was my best shot at getting the charges dropped, identifying Jarrett's actual killers, and rescuing Fax. No pressure.

"Tazza Industries is developing bionic technology. The Insight neural implant is their commercial product, but it's not as far along in development as they're leading people to believe. Jarrett found multiple cases where recipients of the earlier prototype rejected the implant and died."

"Agent Viorel worked as a digital forensic analyst. Why was he investigating Tazza Industries?"

"It was a favor for me."

That piqued Wright's interest. "Explain."

I folded my arms and rested them on my knees. "You've seen my file and the reason I left DECA. My former partner—"

"The one you killed?"

"It was a clean shot—self-defense—but I couldn't let it go, even after leaving the Department. It never made sense why Cavender shot at me. We were new partners, but we had a decent working relationship. I'd had dinner with him and his wife, and we'd put back more than a couple of beers after some bad shifts. Hell, I even dog sat for him once. Cavender had been with the Department a little over two years. He transferred over from Vesen-1. There wasn't much for scuttlebutt on him other than Command had passed him over for a promotion. He took a lot of leave to help with his sick mother-in-law and didn't meet the hourly requirements to sit for the exam."

"How does Viorel factor in?"

"Jarrett and I worked together in Clava before he transferred to Salin. We stayed friends, and he offered to see if he could dig up anything." I paused, lost in the memory. If I could go back in time to that moment and tell Jarrett to forget it and leave well enough alone, he'd still be alive.

Wright's voice dragged me back to the present. "What did Viorel find?"

"Credits. A company called RMZ Incorporated made four large deposits into Cavender's account. RMZ is a subsidiary of KaLo Research. I later confirmed KaLo Research is owned by Kandall Lourde and backed by Tazza Industries. The deposits coincided with four homicide investigations Cavender led, including the one he and I worked on when he took a shot at me. Three of the victims had Insights, and I bet the fourth one did, too. I don't know how much Jarrett pieced together on his own, but he had those case files and

Cavender's financials on a data dot hidden in his boot heel when he died."

"Remind me to add crime scene contamination and tampering with evidence to your list of charges."

I scowled. "Moving on. I believe the company got wind that Jarrett was poking around and had him killed before he could expose them."

"And the bionic weapons fit in, how?"

"Well, I cloned a security guard's cuff to get access to Lourde's laboratory."

Wright's face scrunched up like I'd physically caused him pain. "Identity theft, breaking and entering. Is there a law you haven't broken?"

"Yeah, okay, it sounds bad now, but it was the only way I could get my hands on hard evidence."

"It never occurred to you to bring this to DECA? You used to be a void-be-damned agent."

My bare feet hit the cold floor as I stood up. "I didn't know who I could trust! This all started with my partner being in Tazza's pocket."

"All right, all right." Wright made a placating gesture. He leaned forward to rest his forearms on his thighs. "Get to the part about the bionic weapons."

"I was just getting there. Lourde's lab had a bunch of bionic limbs and disassembled weapons parts. It looked to me like he was trying to merge the two. It's possible he's also trying to combine them with the neural implant. There were some lab animals with bionic limbs that would show he is at least exploring the possibility." I let that sink in a moment. "If a person had both an Intell and a bionic weapon, there would be no stopping them."

"What's special about the Intell?"

"For starters . . ." I used my Intell to bring up the ship's operating system and navigated to the holding cell's command panel. Since I'd flown this model before, I knew exactly where to look. My cell door unlocked with a loud clank. I opened it and stepped through.

Wright was on his feet in an instant. Two quick steps and he had me pressed face-first against the wall, my wrist and elbow torqued behind my back. His pressure was firm, but not painful. I didn't resist.

"Relax, big boy. If I wanted to cause trouble, I wouldn't need to leave my cell to do it. I'm in your ship's system and past your security protocols. The Intell allows me to access things even you can't, override safety protocols, and bypass your commands. From the moment I entered, I could have changed the flight coordinates, cut off life support, or sucked you out an airlock. Passwords, firewalls, encryptions, access codes—they're all irrelevant." My fingers twitched, and I plunged the bridge into darkness for effect.

His grip on my elbow tightened, and he pressed his body harder into mine to keep me pinned between him and the wall. The fine hairs on the back of my neck rose as he lowered his lips to my ear. "What have you done to my ship?" he ground out with tightly reined constraint.

One breath, two. I brought the lights back on. "Imagine what I could do if I also had a bionic weapon. You can't feel them during a pat down, and they are undetectable to a body scan. I could've killed you before you made it out of that chair. I could infiltrate government buildings, assassinate dignitaries, stage a coup. You'd never see it coming."

He released me and stepped back. His expression told me he finally grasped the implications of what it meant if this technology got in the wrong hands. "Fuck."

"There's something else you should know." I reached under his chair and removed a circular disk no bigger than a data dot. "Your ship is bugged. I disabled this one when we boarded, but there may be others too far away for me to detect. My bet is that someone at the local DECA precinct is on Tazza's payroll. Probably multiple someones. Who else would have access to your cruiser?"

Wright took the listening device from me. His mouth opened to speak, but his cuff chimed. "Incoming transmission."

For the first time since I'd met him, Wright looked unsure of what to do. "Can you sit back down for a minute while I process this?"

I plopped down in the copilot's chair. We both knew there was no point in putting me in the cell. Hopefully, he wouldn't put me back in the augmented restraints. My Intell had no tricks against mechanical locks, but I didn't see a reason to point that out.

"Transfer complete," his cuff said.

"Sophie, display the file on the main console," he instructed his cuff.

"That's my bank account statement," I said. Agent Leahy had highlighted the last entry.

"Twelve days ago, twenty-thousand credits were deposited into it from RMZ Incorporated. Care to explain?"

I felt the progress I'd made with Wright slip away. "It's Tazza covering its tracks."

He looked skeptical, but he also held the listening device in his hand. Placing it in the reader tray, he instructed Sophie to give him the specs. It came back as being manufactured by Tazza Industries. No surprise—at least, not to me.

"Take me back to my ship on Ceti," I said. "Lourde may have taken my cuff with the recording of the lab on it, but the original data dot I took from Jarrett is back on the *Soteria*. You can see the files for yourself." He hesitated, so I pressed further, appealing to his law-enforcement side. "It adds less than a day to our return. If I'm telling the truth, it provides you with additional evidence. If not, then you caught me in a lie, which only makes me look worse. You have nothing to lose."

He thought it over and nodded. "Sophie, send a comm to the DECA office on Ceti informing them we'll be arriving and request that we have access to the *Soteria*, which is currently in impound. Then recalculate our flight path to that moon."

"Communication sent. Coordinates reconfigured."

My mouth dropped. I hadn't actually expected him to go for it. Maybe there was hope for Agent Grayson Wright yet.

He buckled his harness and motioned for me to do the same. "Is there anything else you want to tell me before we go?"

I looked over at my bag and bit my lower lip. "Yeah, one other thing. How do you feel about guinea pigs?"

Chapter 25

A LOCAL OFFICER MET us at the Ceti spacedock. Wright instructed her to have someone from the tech department scan his ship for any bugs we'd missed. I'd disabled four additional ones, but there were only so many places I could access while in the vacuum of space.

It was early morning and Nephali-4, the planet Ceti orbited, hung large and gleaming in the predawn sky. Violent storms raged across the gas giant's surface, creating beautiful swirls of golden yellow-and-white clouds that were visible with the naked eye.

Wright had forgone the augmented restraints while we were on the ship, giving me the freedom to roam. Walnut, however, he confined to quarters inside the cell. After an hour of complaining about me bringing a rodent on his ship, Wright stalked over to his bunk and returned with a lidless container, a packet of dehydrated fruit chips, and a worn shirt. He thrust the bundle at me without a word.

Walnut had taken an immediate liking to the shirt, burrowing his way through the folds until he situated them the way he liked. Dopamine saturated the little pleasure centers of his brain. I'd emptied my bag of guinea pig refuse into the reclamator and almost chucked in the messenger bag, but it made for a convenient carrying case for Walnut, so I hung on to it.

Now that we were on the moon, though, the augmented restraints went back on. Wright wasn't taking any chances, particularly since we'd be on the *Soteria*. The impound was on the far side of the spacedock, but the pleasant view and weak gravity made for a jaunty trip. It had been a while since I'd enjoyed any length of time outside.

Too soon, we passed through the impound gate and an older DECA officer, far past his prime, directed us to the *Soteria*. Wright thanked him and ushered me to the back of the lot.

"Agent DeAjamae Leahy is the digital forensic analyst on my team," Wright said as we approached my ship. "She had a few choice words about whomever set up your security system. She flew here and worked on it for a full day without making any progress. I pulled her off when I received word you'd escaped detainment on Vesen-1 and needed her help to track you there."

I made a noncommittal grunt and let my eyes roam over my ship, noting where they'd forced open the cargo hatch lock. They'd done a makeshift repair, but it wasn't pretty. The new weld left a splotchy patch of shiny-gray solder dripping down the door. Sedwaro would throw a fit if he knew, since the ship was technically still in pawn, and that would be nothing compared to the righteous indignation I'd be getting from Felix.

Speaking of, a notification for Felix popped up in my head. I made the connection and opened the window to his interface.

"Reliance! It's nice to see you back in one piece. That's more than I can say about my poor hull. Did you see what those filthy people did to me? They used a blowtorch. A blowtorch! I couldn't even send out a repair bot because of the lockdown mode."

"Hey, Felix—"

Wright looked around, clearly confused since the computer's voice was only in my head. "Who are you—"

I held up a finger. "—It's good to be home. Lower the cargo door, please."

Wright side-eyed me until the lock disengaged with a solid clunk and the cargo door groaned before beginning its descent. It settled onto the pavement, rocking the ship as its weight distribution shift-ed.

I marched—as much as one can march in reduced gravity—up the ramp. "You coming?"

He made it to the top in four exaggerated bounce-steps and paused, quartering the cargo bay and scanning for threats. I'd done the same, but other than the hoverbike still secured in its rack, I kept this area pretty empty. Occasionally, I needed to repossess a LAV or other damaged property before I could authorize a claim to be paid out, but that was unusual. Most of the time, it wasn't worth the cost of the sinnafuel to haul them back, so I sold them locally to get what credits I could out of them and apply that toward the balance owed.

Satisfied, Wright folded his arms across his chest and rocked back on his heels. "Where can we access Viorel's files?"

"From the bridge would be easiest. The original is difficult to access, but I have copies on the ship's system. We can start there." We crossed the bay to the ship's midpoint and stopped at the ladder leading up to the second level. "You know, this would be easier if you took off the restraints."

"I'm already giving you a lot of leeway, Sinclair. Don't push it."

Using an awkward grip and sliding motion with my hands and elbows, I maneuvered myself up the ladder. Wright stayed at the base until I made it to the top, and I wondered what he would have done if I had fallen. Catch me or watch me go splat?

Walking onto the bridge was like coming home, in every sense of the word. All the familiar dents and scratches on the control panel, the squeak in the second-floor panel that I'd never managed to fully tack down, the distinct smell that was a mix of metal, cleaning products, late-night dinners eaten in front of the console, and . . . me. I soaked it all in, hoping this wouldn't be the last time I stood here.

Felix jumped down from the copilot's chair, sending it spinning. His joints creaked from inactivity, but nothing a little oil couldn't fix.

"Felix, this is Lead Agent Grayson Wright. Wright, meet Felix."

Wright jumped back, eyeing the mechanical cat warily. "You didn't tell me the ship had an avatar."

"Seddy threw him in as an incentive when I bought the *Soteria*. He said he couldn't bear the thought of me 'roaming the vastness of space with naught for companionship but the cold light of the stars.'" I snorted. "Seddy waxes poetic if he thinks it might push a sale."

Felix sat directly in front of Wright. The top of his head came up a little past the man's knee. A beam of blue light shot out of his right eye as he scanned Wright from head to toe. "I added Lead Agent Grayson Wright to my memory. Designation?"

"Friendly. Crew access. Authorization Sinclair-Foxtrot-Mike-Lima-Ten-Four."

Wright's eyebrow rose.

"What? I wasn't in a good place when I bought the *Soteria*. Things had happened. Snarky authorization codes were chosen."

"I didn't say anything."

Felix's tail whipped across the floor. "We're taking on crew members? And he's the best you could find? He looks clumsy. And loud. We should restrict him to the common areas."

"You just don't like new people. Agent Wright is here to help. He'll be looking over the information we got from Jarrett."

"Jarrett always brought me system upgrades."

"Your ship's computer is very opinionated. I can't imagine where it gets it from." Wright sidestepped the cat to sit in the copilot's chair. Felix blinked and swiveled his head to continue watching him. "Does he always stare like that?"

"You're in his chair," I said, powering up the electrical system.

"Can you make him stop?"

I jerked my head to the side, and Felix jumped up to lay in his recharging station. From there, he had a good view of the entire bridge and could see down the hallway, as well. Next to the copilot's chair, it was his favorite spot. "Happy?" I plopped into the pilot's chair and booted up the system.

"Not even close."

There was no need to enter my authentication codes. My Intell automatically notified me as each device came to life. The pain meds from the hospital wore off, and my headache came back with all the additional information being processed. I sent Felix a silent command to sweep the ship for any foreign objects or codes and made a mental note to ask Wright if we could get my migraine tabs before leaving.

I scrunched my bare toes against the cold metal floor. And a pair of shoes.

The main console screen blinked on. I pulled up Jarrett's files and sent the command access over to the copilot's half of the control panel so Wright could look through the documents at his own pace. He opened Kelthea Zairesh's file and settled in. Some things made more sense now than when I'd first read through them, so I opened a file and started highlighting key information and making notes on the salient bits. We worked in companionable silence for the next hour. I tried my best to keep my guard up. Even though Wright seemed on the up and up, there was still a chance this was all an elaborate ruse. I didn't know how deep the corruption ran. The longer we sat there, the harder it became. He'd rescued me from the lab, kept Adler from shooting me, and been open-minded enough to come retrieve the files. Now he combed through them like he took my side of the story seriously.

It was hard to keep pushing him away, when it would be so much easier to let him in.

Without environmental controls running for the two weeks, the *Soteria* was hot and stuffy. In concession, Wright rolled up his sleeves and undid the short row of buttons at the collar of his shirt. He leaned over the control panel, resting his elbows on the padded ledge as he swiped back and forth through the documents.

I tried not to stare, but the idea of him inside my ship, when weeks ago I'd violated multiple laws to avoid that exact thing, struck me as ludicrous. A laugh burbled up from deep inside that I couldn't stop.

It started small and grew until my laughter echoed off the walls. Soon, my ribs ached, and I had difficulty pulling full breaths into my lungs.

Wright arched one eyebrow like I'd lost my mind.

"It's just . . ." I gulped in air, trying to get a hold of myself. Tears streaked down my cheeks. I had to use both hands to wipe them away because of the restraints, and that sobered me up. "It's just that this is not how I pictured this month going."

Wright's cuff flashed with an incoming communication. He held up one finger to indicate he needed a moment and opened the comm while I fought down another bout of laughter.

A hologram materialized of a junior officer with short, dark hair and a wiry build. "Sir, this is Officer Torres with forensics. I'm afraid I have bad news regarding your cruiser. We found several tracking devices on the hull and a virus in the operating system. It's a nasty one. It'll take some time to figure out how to disable it. A day, maybe two."

"Can you tell me anything about it? What it does? Who put it there?"

The junior officer shook his head. "Not yet, but I'll give you a full report when I can."

"Contact Agent DeAjamae Leahy on Andaress-4 and keep her apprised of your progress."

"Copy that, sir." The comm blinked out.

Wright rubbed his hand across his jaw, thinking. "I wish we had these documents at the start of the investigation. If Viorel was gathering these, it gives motivation to another party to silence him. We swept his apartment and workstation but didn't find anything connected to this. You were our only lead."

Valid concerns or not, my actions had handicapped their investigation. "What did you think was my motivation?"

"You were in a long-distance relationship. He broke it off or maybe you came to visit, discovered he was seeing someone else, and shot him in a fit of rage."

"A crime of passion?" That threw me into another fit of laughter. "We weren't lovers. He thought of me as a little sister. A bratty one."

Wright's eyes roamed down my body, causing me to flush. "I doubt that. There are cryptic entries in his schedule and gaps where he went back and deleted previous entries. We didn't find any references to a partner, so we thought, with you visiting so often . . ."

"We were close, but not like that. He wasn't seeing anyone seriously that I know of. His last relationship ended badly, and he was taking a break. I thought that was partly why he agreed to help me—to give him something else to focus on for a while, you know?"

"We didn't find any hint of past relationships. His comms with you were the most frequent contact he had with anyone."

"Yeah, well, like I said, the breakup was messy. If Jarrett didn't want any reminders of it, he certainly knew how to delete his old comms and erase some holos. Look, Jarrett was a good man and an excellent agent. He deserves justice." I leaned forward, forearms on my knees, and looked Wright in the eye. "After all this, do you really think I killed my best friend?"

Wright held my gaze for a long moment, then turned back to the documents displayed on the console. "No, I've had doubts since I interviewed Sedwaro. He was astonishingly loyal for a pawnbroker. He was adamant that while you could be rash and bullheaded, you had a good heart."

"That sounds like Seddy."

"He also mentioned that you were a buzzkill at mah-jongg."

I snorted. "That's because he cheats, and I don't let him get away with it." Thoughts of the quirky pawn broker in his bright-orange, stingy brim hat coming to my defense made me smile. "So why chase me down?"

"Because innocent people rarely run, and you fled the scene of the crime. And you shot me."

"You shot me first!"

"It barely grazed you, and my blaster was on its lowest setting. You shot me in the head. I woke up in the back of an emergency LAV with a concussion."

He had a point. "So, where does that leave us?"

"I can't release you from custody until we verify the authenticity of these documents, but I'd like to take you back to Viorel's apartment and see if you notice anything we missed. Anything to point us to the actual killer. A suspicious corporation isn't enough. We need to know who pulled the trigger."

"Killers," I corrected. "There were at least two. We should leave right away. As much as I want justice for Jarrett, the sooner we identify the hired assassins, the sooner we can trace them back to Tazza Industries. Fax, the other test subject who was with me, may not have much time."

"I'll have to requisition another ship."

"Or we could take mine. The *Soteria* is fully charged and fueled."

"Are you sure Tazza Industries hasn't bugged her as well?"

"Felix?"

The cat swished his tail, making a whisking sound across the metal wall. "As if I'd allow a bug on me."

Wright opened a comm to Officer Torres. "Officer Torres, you can take your time with my cruiser. I'll be transporting the *Soteria* back to Salin's impound lot for further analysis by my team."

"Yes, sir. I'll send the forms over to you right away."

"Can you have my personal affects transferred to the *Soteria*?"

"Of course, sir."

"Uh-hum," I cleared my throat and twitched my nose.

Wright growled under his breath, but the corner of his mouth flickered into a smile, just for a second. "Officer Torres, there will be a guinea pig in the holding cell. Be sure to bring it as well."

The young man's smile wobbled, and his brows squeezed together in confusion. "A . . . a guinea pig, sir?"

Wright cut the transmission. He reached across and unlocked the augmented restraints. "Don't make me regret this."

While we waited, Wright's stomach growled. "I don't suppose you have anything to eat in here."

"There might be a hellaberry bar in the kitchen."

He grimaced. "Pass."

I reached below the console and pounded a fist against a loose panel, popping it out. A silver flask and tumbler lay nestled in the bottom corner. "Then how about a drink?"

Chapter 26

We dropped out of warp at the edge of the Andaress system and coasted past the sixth planet. I fired the reverse thrusters to slow our momentum. Felix estimated we'd reach the fourth planet in about fifty-five minutes.

"I would kill for a hot-water shower." Wright raised an eyebrow at me. I winced. "Poor choice of words, but you know what I mean. Sonic showers get the job done, but they never leave you feeling squeaky *clean*."

"There's time before we land if you want to grab one now."

"Can't. I busted a gasket on a pipe coming from the gray-water tank."

"DECA sealed Viorel's apartment, and it'll be too early when we arrive to get authorization to enter. My place isn't far from the spacedock. We can wait there until the office opens, get something to eat, and you can use my shower, if you want."

That sounded reasonable. If we broke the seal without authorization, any evidence Wright collected would be inadmissible. I'd already botched things by taking the data dot, but there was a chance the court could still admit it. Best-case scenario, though, would be to find the original source in Jarrett's apartment.

"That works. I'm going downstairs to pack a change of clothes and feed Walnut."

"Take the cat with you. He's creepy."

Felix flicked his tail, the overlapping scales sliding smoothly to create a whip-like effect. It lashed into Wright's ankle above the top of his boot.

Wright jerked his foot up before Felix could get him a second time. "Fucking cats."

"He's just an avatar," I said, but silently agreed with him. Felix's creator had done an amazing job with his personality program. At least he'd never barfed oil on my bed.

Felix followed me off the bridge and nimbly jumped down to the lower level while I took the ladder. He landed with a loud thud and clank of shifting parts before loping off to the common area with his stilted rocking-horse gait.

Walnut gave an excited *wheek-wheek-wheek* when I entered the kitchen. His little pink feet pressed against the wall of his new enclosure as he stretched to touch his nose to my finger. The kitchen no longer had a counter, and the copilot closet was missing its plastiglass shelves, but it was worth it to give Walnut extra room to run around.

I scratched behind his ears. When this was over, I would figure out a way to give him the run of the ship. It's not like he could get lost so long as I could connect to his chip.

Walnut's food and water bowls were low, so I topped them off with rations from my dry goods supplies. He needed fresh fruits and vegetables, but that would have to wait until I could restock. Nothing perishable had survived the stay in impound. Even my mycoprotein starter had died. I needed to purchase another batch before going on a long flight, but that was getting ahead of things.

"Want to come pack with me?" I took his nose twitch as a yes and lifted him from his enclosure. Walnut scrambled up my shoulder and sniffed the back of my ear.

It tickled, so I gave his soft, warm fur a good pet before carrying him to my room and depositing him on my bunk. Enclosed on three sides with a ceiling high enough for a person to sit up comfortably, it made for an ideal guinea pig playground. Walnut went to work scoping out the corners, the crease between my pillow and the wall, and the underside of my blanket.

"Felix, I need you to set up an additional monitoring program to include Walnut's food and water dishes for when I'm away from the ship. I'll connect his chip to the *Soteria* so you can track his health as well." Pulling up the program with my Intell, I made the link. Then I checked on Walnut to make sure it hadn't caused him any stress. It hadn't.

The metal cat stared at me with unblinking eyes. "I am a physical manifestation of the *Soteria*'s central computer and a sophisticated piece of technology. I do not babysit rodents."

"Well, from now on, you do. You're going to have to get over your programming and be the bigger computer. I'll leave an extra bowl of food and a water pouch by his cage and move a chair over for you to reach it."

Felix's head tilted to the side. "The *Soteria*'s programming includes vermin extermination as part of its safety protocols against transporting invasive species."

I stopped playing blanket monster with Walnut. "No." I pointed my finger at the oversized cat. "There will be no exterminating Walnut."

No response.

"Felix?"

"I was only informing you of my capabilities."

"Mm-hmm. Walnut, you have my permission to poop in Uncle Felix's box of spare parts."

Walnut gave a happy chirp.

I crawled into the bunk and sat cross-legged with my back against the wall. Walnut waddled over and climbed onto my lap. Not to be outdone by a rodent, Felix hopped up and lay by my side. The mattress dipped appreciably under his weight, and I used it as an excuse to lean into him. My fingers slid from his head to his back. His outer covering was made of thousands of overlapping scales. While not soft like cat fur, they were soothing to stroke—more akin to the cool, supple skin of a snake.

Felix engaged his rumble box, which caused his body to gently vibrate and hum in his designer's imitation of a purr. He could be a pain in the ass sometimes, but he was my pain in the ass.

The *Soteria* had been my home for the last year, and Felix my family. Not that I didn't have other family—the stars know my mom had tried—but after everything with Cavender and leaving the Department, I'd pushed her and everyone else away. Even Jarrett to some extent, but he'd been too mule-headed to let it stand.

Was I correct to keep Wright at arm's length or just falling into old habits? Yes, his single-minded pursuit of me had been a serious thorn in my side, but he'd also gotten me out of Lourde's lab and prevented Adler from shooting me. Those were two very big pluses in my book.

And what were my options, really? I could take control of the ship, but then what? Maroon him on the nearest habitable planet? Jettison him into space? I'd tried taking on Tazza Industries by myself, and it hadn't gone well. I had no credits, Seddy held the deed to the *Soteria*—which was technically still in impound—and the Intell might fry my brain at any moment. Not exactly the makings of an avenging superhero.

I thunked the back of my head against the wall. The one thing that had become abundantly clear was that I couldn't do anything until Wright dropped the charges against me. Even if he wouldn't help me after that, at least my assets would be unfrozen, and I could move around freely without an arrest warrant hanging over my head. And Wright could restart his investigation with all the information he should have had from the start.

Walnut worked his way up to my shoulder and sniffed at my ear. His whiskers tickled my neck, making me laugh and kink my neck to the side in an attempt to get away. My Intell picked up happy signals from his chip. I hoped he liked his new home. The reverse thrusters fired again, rumbling through the ship. My body lurched forward until the inertia dampeners kicked in. We were nearing Andaress-4.

I set Walnut back on the bed and grabbed an old backpack from my closet. Into it went a change of clothes, a jacket, and a couple of emergency LTs I had stashed in a hidey-hole—enough to buy lunch at a food cart, but not much else. My migraine tabs were in a drawer beside my bed, and I shoved the entire pack into the backpack.

"Agent Grayson Wright requests you strap in," Felix said, jumping down. "We are entering low orbit and will land shortly."

"Thanks, Felix." I returned Walnut to his fortress. There wasn't time to make it to the bridge, so I unlatched the jump seat from the common room's interior wall. The straps of the five-point harness were tangled, since I never used this seat. It took a minute to sort them out and get locked in. "Tell Wright I'm secured for landing."

Central Command must have bumped us to the top of the priority list, because Wright took the *Soteria* down immediately. He was a decent pilot, and we made the shift from hurtling through space to hurtling through atmosphere with as little banging around as possible. Ten minutes later, I heard the landing gear extend and felt the ship come to rest on solid ground. I unbuckled, grabbed my bag, and walked to the cargo area to meet Wright.

"I don't have a LAV at the spacedock," he said. "I could order an auto-LAV or . . ." He glanced over at the wall with unadulterated longing. "We could take your hoverbike."

I looked at the bike. She was a beauty. "As long as I pilot."

"Technically, you're still in my custody."

"Technically, you can't appropriate my property for your personal use."

"You don't know where I live."

"You could tell me."

He gave the bike another long look. "Please?"

Dang, but I needed him on my side. "Fine, but if you scratch her, you're paying for a full repaint."

"Deal."

Wright caressed his hand along the smooth lines from her fuel capsule to her seat before swinging a leg over and powering her up. She purred to life with a satisfying rumble. "Cymbeline SR8?"

"SR9 plus a few after-market upgrades."

I took two helmets from the storage rack and tossed him one before donning the other. The viewscreen lit up on the inside of the shield with information from the bike: weather conditions, speed, altitude, pitch, traffic targeting, map, comms, music. My Intell threw up a flurry of notifications for the same things, giving me a weird, double-layer effect if I opened any of them. On second thought, it was probably wise I didn't pilot the bike until I got a little practice in.

Wright spun the bike around in a smooth circle while I punched the manual release for the cargo door. He revved the engine, and as he passed by, I grabbed his shoulder and swung up behind him. We exited straight out and up, leveling at three meters above ground.

I glanced over my shoulder. Felix sat at the edge of the ramp. "Be a good boy, and I'll bring you a treat," I told him over the comms.

"What?" Wright twisted his head around to ask me.

I laughed to myself realizing he only heard my side of the conversation and connected the comms between our helmets. "Felix. He likes cables: long ones, short ones. He drags them all around the ship. I find them everywhere. No idea what he does with them."

Beneath my hands, Wright's body shook with silent laughter. "Have you checked under the couch?"

We landed on the rooftop in the old part of town as the sky entered the blue hour, that hazy time when it was too light to be night but too dark to be day. Salin hadn't yet woken. Most of her citizens still slept in their beds, although the windows of a few early risers glowed brightly to usher in the dawn.

Wright's building looked to be built with chalky-gray regolith bricks and held together with grit and obstinance. I felt an immediate kinship. This close to the spacedock, the building would have been in the first wave of construction on the terraformed planet. It may have once been a storage facility or maybe a small manufacturing plant. Now it had been converted into housing for those wanting to live nearer to the city center.

The roof had a cozy little patio area with a wooden table and six mismatched but comfortable chairs set up near the ledge. Miniature lights hung on strings between potted poles and leafy, green vines climbed up the wall to the stairwell, providing shade from the desert sun and making it an unexpected garden retreat. I bet the view was spectacular at night.

Wright held his cuff to the door reader, and the lock clicked open. "Sophie, lights on." He waited for the darkness to disappear, then held the door for me. "Coming?"

I tore myself away from the view and ducked inside. The stairs were old-fashioned wrought iron, which matched the other architectural features of the building. Iron was sturdy, easy to mine, and it didn't require a high level of manufacturing skill like modern materials, making it an ideal choice for early construction. The industrial black paint on the balustrade had worn over the years, leaving smooth metal beneath my fingers.

Once we descended below the roofline, the stairway opened to a two-story room with an open loft plan. It wasn't at all what I'd imagined. In my mind, I'd pictured an efficiency apartment similar to Jarrett's, but with fewer consoles and more sports memorabilia. Maybe a kickboxing bag in the corner. This place was far too nice for an agent's salary.

Instantly, my previous suspicions returned. Was Wright on Tazza's payroll? If so, why the charade of arresting me and stunning Doctor Adler? A hard knot worked itself into my stomach.

Warily, I paused on the narrow balcony and let my Intell gather what it could. There were fewer signals than I expected, just the standard suite of network-connected cooking appliances, plumbing, electrical, temperature, plastiglass windows, and a home console.

I didn't see any physical threats, either. It was basically one large room. A massive, arched window dominated the middle of the outside wall, with shelving and artwork on either side. He'd left the regolith brickwork bare in some places and partially plastered in others. A comfortable living area with plush chairs and a giant couch dominated the bulk of the space. I leaned over the railing to peer into the kitchen. A long island separated it from the living room. Minimal but high-end appliances ran the length of the wall with warm, honeyed butcher block for countertops.

Andaress-4 didn't have a thriving lumber industry like Brione-5. Salin, in particular, was mostly too arid for large trees. The counter-top alone would have cost a fortune. I'd been to my captain's house once back in Clava, and even her place hadn't been this nice. How did Wright afford it?

"Do you entertain much?" I kept my face turned so he wouldn't see my skepticism and continued down to the first level.

"Mostly on the weekends. Ravi and I aren't from here. DeAjamae is, but her siblings have all moved away. We're each other's family."

"It's a great space for it, what with the private rooftop access."

"I added it shortly after I moved in. A buddy owns a remodeling company. They ripped out the staircase from an old bar and asked if I wanted it. My landlord was amenable to me installing it and the access door, since it improved the property value."

"Your friend just gave it to you?" In my experience, no one ever gave you something for nothing.

"He takes payment in sweat equity whenever he needs extra help." Wright tossed his bag on the leather couch and headed straight for the kitchen. "You hungry? There wasn't much to eat on your ship."

I followed behind him and inhaled the rich, earthy fragrance of real leather coming from the couch. The rug beneath my boot was dense and plush. Expensive. No way he earned enough at DECA to pay for all this, friend or no friend. My gut turned. Something didn't add up, and I feared I'd misplaced my trust in another DECA agent.

Wright slowed to grab a whisk and wooden spoon from a ceramic container near the sink. I caught up and stepped into his personal space, forcing him to turn and face me. He was tall enough that I had to lift my chin to look him in the eyes.

"Is Tazza Industries paying you to bury this investigation?"

His eyes widened, then narrowed into flinty shards. "You've got to be fucking kidding me. Now you think I'm in on it?"

"This is a pretty swanky apartment. Where'd you get the credits for it? It wasn't working for the Department."

"That's real rich, Sinclair, considering you're the one with Tazza's cutting-edge technology in your brain."

My face warmed and probably flamed pink from all the blood rushing to it. "When did Tazza contact you? After you caught Jarrett's case, or have you been on the take all along?"

"Just because your old partner was dirty doesn't mean every other agent is, too."

"Not every agent, only the ones covering Aurelian Tazza's ass. First, your department doesn't notice that one of their agents was missing for four days. Then you try to pin Jarrett's murder on me. You didn't expect me to escape and find the connection to Tazza Industries, though. That's why you dogged me all around the quadrant. You had a personal stake in keeping me quiet."

"As if anyone could keep you quiet." Wright ran a hand through his hair, disheveling the strands until they stood on end. "Look, Viorel took an unexpected leave of absence that week, citing a family emergency, which is why no one noted his absence. You fled the scene. We had every reason to believe you'd murdered one of our own. Hell yes, we had a personal stake in it. And let's not forget that you shot me. In the face." He pointed at the red burn mark still covering his temple.

"You lived, didn't you? And none of that explains how you can afford this apartment. If not Tazza, then how?"

"Anyone ever tell you have trust issues?"

"Lots of times. Usually right before they stab me in the back. Quit evading the question."

Wright's eye twitched. He stepped back and dragged his hand down his face. When he looked at me again, the heat had cooled in his eyes.

"My parents are foreign dignitaries. They own the apartment. Andaress-4 doesn't do much trade with Ritru-6, so they're not here all that often. It was falling into disrepair, and I agreed to fix it up in exchange for rent when I moved to Salin. It's not a secret, although it's not something I generally advertise, either. Being a diplomat's kid—even an adult one—can have its limitations."

I looked around the room, noticing for the first time that the regolith brick-and-plaster walls weren't an aesthetic choice, but that the plaster was flaking from the walls. Holes dotted the walls where framing for walls had once been attached. The butcherblock countertops had been recently refinished, but I could tell they were old by the knicks and scratches, and the rounded edges that had been worn smooth through use.

"Limitations, huh? Like having to work extra hard to prove you weren't just given a job? Like chasing a suspect to four other planets and breaking her out of a high-security medical facility?"

"Something like that. Although to be fair, it was three planets and a moon."

"Anyone ever call you anal-retentive?"

"They usually just shorten it to ass." Despite my anger a minute earlier, I found myself snorting at his joke. Wright smiled, and my gut did a little flippity-flop.

"Hey, we have an hour before I can get the paperwork rolling. Why don't you grab a shower, and I'll make us breakfast. You like omelets?"

"Sure, but no mushrooms. I've had enough mycoprotein to last me a lifetime."

Wright pointed to the back of the apartment where a platform bed took up half the space and a partitioned-off room took up the other. "Bathroom's over there. Help yourself to anything you need."

"Aren't you worried I might escape?"

"Are you planning to?"

"No."

"Then I'm not worried."

I went into the bathroom and locked the door, leaving Wright gathering fresh vegetables, eggs, and cheese on the kitchen island.

That was something I missed about living planetside; access to real, unprocessed food whenever you wanted it.

Looking around, I realized why Wright wasn't concerned about me running. No doors. No windows.

"Funny," I said, loud enough for him to hear me, and got a pleasant laugh in return.

The bathroom was small but well appointed, with patterned tiles in charcoal gray on the floor and muted white in the shower. A plastiglass shower wall was set to clear. His sink—a water–sonic combo—was bowl shaped and sat on a weathered, wooden table with turned legs that must have been another salvage piece. Above it hung a round, three-dimensional mirror.

I swept the space with my Intell for recording devices before stripping down naked. I eyed the door, then the clear shower wall. "Engage opaquing." The plastiglass shimmered and rippled, settling into a frosty, heathered-gray tint. Satisfied that even if Wright barged in, I'd have a second to grab a towel, I stepped into the shower.

A soapy mist shot out at me from high, mid, and low spigots on three of the walls. It smelled like bergamot and sun-ripened limes. I rotated and raised my arms so that the soap reached every square centimeter of skin and hair. The mister shut off and a high-pitched tone sounded for thirty seconds, loosening the dirt and oil from my skin until they bonded with the chemicals in the soap and fell to the floor.

"Water on, thirty-eight degrees, half pressure." The shower head above me turned on and released a gentle rain of warm water over my head. I tilted my head back, letting the water stream over my face and through my hair. Thinner jets of water erupted from the wall spigots. They hit every bruised muscle, strained tendon, and aching joint with eerie precision. When my body adjusted to the temperature, I pulled my face out of the stream and increased it by two degrees.

Pleasure resonated throughout my entire body. Man, I loved a hot shower.

Conscious that while purified water wasn't a luxury item on most planets, it also wasn't free. I reluctantly switched off the water and dried myself with a fluffy white towel from the shelf beneath the sink.

I pulled on a clean pair of olive-green pants, a belt, and a fitted black sweater with three-quarter length sleeves. The absence of a cuff on my forearm left me feeling a little naked, but my jacket would cover it. It was early fall, and the morning would be cool, especially on the salt flats. My boots were a little rugged for the look, but after spending more than a week in nothing but hospital socks, I craved something substantial on my feet. I'd forgotten to pack toiletries, so I finger-combed my hair and left it to air dry.

Wright set two plates on the table alongside two cups of coffee. The real kind. As I sat down, he slid a steaming omelet from the pan onto my plate and topped it with diced tomatoes and chopped parsley. "Ham and cheese."

"Thanks."

He watched me eat the first bite, then turned back to the stove to cook his own. Butter sizzled as he cracked three brown eggs into a bowl and whisked them together with a splash of cream. "Tell me about Viorel. Help me get into his head so I can search his apartment from a fresh perspective."

I chewed and thought about how best to answer. "Jarrett liked puzzles. It wasn't the who or the why of a crime that intrigued him. It was the how. That made him a good digital forensic scientist, but he could get so wrapped up in making the pieces fit he forgot to look at the big picture."

Wright poured the eggs into the pan and added ham, shredded white cheese, salt, and pepper. "Motivation is what makes a person dangerous. You think he got wrapped up following your old partner's money trail and forgot to watch his back?"

"He shouldn't have had to. It was *my* job to watch his back." And that was the crux of it, wasn't it? I may not have pulled the trigger, but I was still the reason Jarrett had died.

For a long moment, the only sound in the loft was the sizzling eggs and the scrape of Wright's spatula as he flipped the omelet in half and slid it onto his plate. He turned off the stove, set the pan to cool, and pulled a stool over to sit kitty-corner from me.

"This job comes with an inherent set of risks," he finally said. "Every rank-and-file officer has come to terms with the fact that death is one of those risks. Our best hope is that if it has to be, then our death will be in service of the greater good. That it will mean something."

I thought about the corruption in DECA that Jarrett had uncovered, of the people like Sean Rhinehardt and Waverly Culpepper who would finally receive closure, and of the hundreds or thousands of would-be patients who would not be subjected to defective implants.

Would Jarrett have sacrificed his life for theirs? Without question.

Wright's comm flashed with an incoming message. He opened his holoscreen and skimmed it. "I have authorization to search Viorel's apartment. We can leave right away."

I shoveled the last bit of cheesy egg into my mouth. "Let's do it."

Chapter 27

I appreciated the stark beauty of the morning sun over the salt flats on the ride from Salin to Jarrett's apartment in the outer district of Brin. In the distance, ragged mountain peaks ringed the basin on three sides. During the rainy season, the entire basin filled with a shallow pool of water that reflected the cloudless blue sky like a mirror. When the rains stopped, the naturally arid climate and scorching sun evaporated the water, leaving the pristine white salt to bake and crack into rough geometric patterns. From the air, it looked like nature's most complicated jigsaw puzzle.

Wright decreased our speed as we dropped from the main skylane of traffic to the city streets of Brin. The bike protested with a rumble I felt through my calves, thighs, and hips before settling into a lower gear.

Today wasn't a market day, so the streets were relatively quiet. We landed in the small LAV lot behind Jarrett's building, primarily used by his neighbors and customers of the first-level shops. It was still early enough that finding an open space wasn't an issue. We secured our helmets to the magnetic locks on the side of the hoverbike and climbed the stairs.

Wright pressed his hand to the biometrically secured door of Jarrett's apartment. We waited a full minute while it analyzed a sample of his touch DNA and compared it to the list of authorized personnel. It flashed from orange to blue, granting us entry. Like the augmented cuffs Wright had put back on me, this was another type of technology that my Intell couldn't circumvent.

My DNA was already all over the apartment, but Wright made me put on the disposable booties and gloves anyway. We would drop them in an evidence bag when we left.

We stepped in. As the first person inside, Wright automatically swung right around the far edge of the door. I swept left through the opening. Standard operating procedure for entering a potentially hostile room. I didn't know how much help I'd be without a blaster, but old habits died hard.

The apartment looked the same, except for where forensics had collected evidence. They'd marked sections where they scanned for DNA or prints and removed the busted console from the floor. They probably took the pieces back to the lab for examination. Jarrett's body would be at the morgue office, the autopsy complete, and held in cold stasis until the investigation closed. They would release it to his family for cremation, as was their tradition on Ritru-6.

"Lights on," Wright said. Half of the wall sconces were broken, but enough remained to give us decent light to search by. "Take the kitchen. I'll start in here."

Kitchen stretched the definition of the word. Jarrett was more of a street cart/delivery kind of guy. He told me once that he found cooking too time consuming. You had to buy the food, bring it home, store it, pull it back out, prep it, cook it, eat it, and then clean up and empty the reclamator. I secretly suspected he was just bad at it and couldn't stand his own cooking.

He had all the standard appliances, and each one pinged my Intell, wanting to connect. The refrigerator pinged last, warning me that a container of sweet-and-sour chicken had gone bad. As I read the message, the O and U in the word *sour* twisted into an unrecognizable shape. My right temple throbbed, and for a second, I worried the connection between the Intell and my optical nerve had been damaged. Then my peripheral vision blurred as if I were looking through a glass of milky water.

Relief and dread washed over me as I recognized the early signs of a migraine. Under normal circumstances, I'd lie in a dark room for an hour and practice my visualization techniques, but it had taken too much to get here. I couldn't leave now. If Wright didn't find something today, I doubt he'd come back again. I rummaged in my backpack for my migraine tabs and placed two under my tongue. If I caught it soon enough, it might not progress much further.

I started with the lower cabinets. One contained bags of snack food and a box of hellaberry protein bars, another some dusty, mismatched pans, and the rest held an assortment of cables, adapters, battery packs, cases, tape, ties, lubrication oil, and a miniature tool set with three-quarters of the pieces rolling around the bottom of the cabinet. No data dots. My hands were filthy when I finished, and I was grateful for the gloves.

Next, I searched the upper cabinets, which held more cups and plates. They extended higher than I could reach, so I hopped on the counter to examine the rest and the tops of the cabinets. Nothing but dust bunnies.

Light streamed in from the window, making me squint at the brightness. Five percent of my vision was lost in the smudgy area of the aura. I climbed down more carefully than I'd climbed up, making sure my feet were steady before transferring my weight.

The migraine made looking at anything straight on arduous, but I painstakingly combed through the kitchen by keeping my eyes constantly shifting. Why were data dots so tiny? And black? They should be florescent orange and the size of dinner plates.

Moving past the cupboards, I checked for loose floor tiles, in the air vents, under the lip of the counter, along the windowsill, and inside the refrigerator. Other than a questionable taste in craft beer, I found nothing out of the ordinary.

"Kitchen's clear," I said, turning back to the common area. "You know, this would be a lot easier without the restraints."

"I'm sure it would." Wright stood up from a pile of couch cushions he'd been digging through. He smoothed out a crumpled piece of paper in his hand. "The techs missed a betting stub for one of the local fox hunter races that didn't pay out, but it's probably nothing. Did Viorel gamble?"

I shrugged. "Jarrett caught a match now and then. I think he rooted for the Quasars."

Wright dropped the ticket into an evidence bag, sealed it, and tucked it into his jacket pocket. "Bathroom or bedroom?"

Even though I'd be fine never stepping foot in Jarrett's bedroom again, it was the room likeliest to contain clues as to the identities of the assassins. "Bedroom."

We split again. Inside the bedroom, the techs had taken the chair, bindings, and other movable items in the immediate area of the crime scene for processing. Blood spatter still stained the floor, walls, and dresser.

Plastiglass lay on the floor below the window I'd broken to escape, but someone had patched the hole with a temporary seal. Random drops of blood were smeared and dyed purple where techs had taken samples for rapid DNA analysis. Since Wright hadn't found other suspects, I assumed the blood had all come from Jarrett.

My vision loss increased to about fifteen percent. It left me light-headed and nauseated. I shoved another migraine tab under my tongue and hoped it kicked in soon.

I worked my way around the perimeter of the room. Jarrett's dresser took some time. I pulled out each drawer, rifled through every pocket, ran a finger along each seam. By the time I reached the bed, Wright came in.

"Nothing in the bathroom. Where haven't you looked?"

Not the best news. We needed to find something that tied Tazza Industries to Jarrett or Wright would have no cause to investigate them, and I'd still be the prime suspect.

I sat back on my heels and wiped the sweat from my brow with my forearm. "Take the closet. The bed is almost done."

He opened the door and my Intell picked up a flood of notifications. I wobbled as pain shot through the base of my skull. Wright's hand on my shoulder steadied me until I got myself back under control.

"I'm fine. Your techs missed something electronic in the closet, though."

Reluctantly, Wright let go, but he waited until I stood up to return to the closet. We moved the clothing to the bed and stared at the bare walls.

"You're sure?"

I twitched my finger to open the notifications and regretted it instantly. "Yeah. It's big, like an entire console or something."

Wright ran his hand along the surface of the wall and rapped his knuckles first on one side, then the other. "Hear the difference? The inside could be coated with a thin layer of lead."

He shut the door, and the view window in my head blinked out. He opened it, and the window popped up again, along with all the previous notifications.

Pain stabbed at my brain. When he made to close it again, I put my hand over his to stay him. "Stop. The signal is definitely coming from inside the closet."

We knocked on the walls, lifted the rod, and ran our fingers around the trim casing. Then Wright dropped to his hands and knees and felt along the floor.

"Sophie, torch mode."

A beam shone from his cuff, and I added that to my list of things the Intell couldn't do. I needed to carry a light source with me. Wright twisted his arm so the cuff lay flat against the floor. The angle of the light caught against ridges in dust lines, throwing them into harsh relief. It revealed faint smudges of finger and handprints concentrated near the right wall.

Wright took a knife from his pocket and used the blade to test along the floor panel. It slid smoothly until about the middle, then tinged against something metal. He tapped it and applied firm pressure. With a click, a latch released, and the floor panel lifted.

Inside, Jarrett had turned a narrow cavity between two joists into a hidey-hole. A black box the size of my hand sat at the bottom.

"It's a server." Wright took a quick holo, noting the location and a brief description for the record. He tried removing the box, but it was hardwired in and only lifted out a decimeter before running out of wire. A smaller second box was connected to the first. Its screen lit up on the top requesting an eight-digit passcode. Sixty seconds appeared on a timer beside it and began counting down.

At the same time, my Intell notified me of a new signal. "You need to get out of here. Jarrett booby trapped his server."

Wright froze. He had been inspecting the wires in order to disconnect it from the floor. "What do you mean, booby trapped?"

"I mean that when that timer hits zero, it's going to go boom."

"That's great."

"Come again?"

"This must be what we're looking for. He wouldn't have gone through the effort unless it was important."

"Did you miss the part about it going boom? Because that's the most important part."

He rotated the box, so it was right side up. "Can we guess the code? Any ideas?"

"None. Jarrett wouldn't have made it easy to guess." I hated it, but he was right. Jarrett wouldn't have gone to these lengths unless whatever was on that server was important. The time ticked down to fifty seconds.

"Then we leave it."

"Go. I'll stay and disarm it."

"Can you do that?"

"I think so. I had training." The basics. In the academy. Ten years ago. My instructor had strongly recommended calling in a specialist team to perform a controlled detonation, but that wasn't an option with less than a minute on the clock.

Indecision warred on Wright's face, but he unlocked and removed the augmented restraints and let me take the server and knife from him. He backed out of the closet. "This is as far as I'm going."

Sweat beaded on my brow, but I couldn't make him leave the apartment. Gently, I removed the cover plate and got my first look at the explosive. It was crude by modern standards, but that didn't make it any less effective. He'd used a pea-sized ball of sinnalite compound as the explosive material. Standard dilution ratio would give it a blast radius of about one-and-a-half meters. In the partially enclosed closet, the force would concentrate and funnel out the open door. Two-and-a-half meters? Three? *If* he used a standard ratio.

"The common room would be safer," I tried again.

He aimed the light down over my shoulder to help me see. Forty-one seconds left on the timer.

It would really help if this damn migraine would go away. A squiggly, C-shaped aura had formed around the right half of my field of view. Like the visual output from my Intell, it didn't matter if I closed my eyes. The rainbow-speckled aura wouldn't go away.

Okay, Rel, think this through. You just need to focus.

Easier said than done. Stress aggravated migraines. Nothing I could do about that, but I visualized stuffing the pain into a box and shoving it off to the side to deal with later.

I needed to tease the components apart without triggering the bomb. My fingers trembled as I nudged the internal guts around to see all the parts. A thin coat of the sinnalite compound was smeared on a metal plate. No easy way to remove it.

A wire was soldered to the plate. I traced it back to a cylinder the length and width of my pinkie finger. Inside the cylinder would be the switch and initiator.

Four wires ran out the other end. Blue and green wires ran into the floor. One had to be the power supply hooked up to the apartment's main electrical system. I guessed the other went to a backup battery but couldn't tell for sure. No way to cut them without getting electrocuted. The other two wires—white and yellow—led to the server where the countdown timer would signal the switch to trigger the initiator, which would set off the explosive. One was real, one was a dummy. No way to tell which was which. Cut the wrong one—boom.

My only option was to crack the cylinder and separate the switch from the initiator. I glanced at the timer. Twenty seconds.

With the knife, I slit the length of the cylinder—being careful not to cut too deep—and then repeated the process on the opposite side.

Shimmying the tip of the knife into the cut line, I held my breath, and wiggled it back and forth until the casing snapped.

Inside was a type of switch I'd never seen before. I twisted my head around, trying to get a solid look with what remained of my vision. There should be a physical connection between the switch and initiator, but it looked like one solid piece.

I rubbed my forehead against my jacket to wipe away the sweat threatening to drip into my eye. Fuck, it was hot in here.

The timer read six seconds.

"I can't disarm it!"

Sucking in a deep breath, I followed the white and yellow wires back to the server in my left hand. There was a fifty–fifty chance of picking the right one. Or the wrong one. Whichever way you wanted to look at it. My right hand vacillated between the two wires. I'd only get one shot.

My gut nudged me toward the white wire. I gripped the server tightly in my left hand and pressed the blade against it with my right. Then I closed my eyes, and—

Wright grabbed me by the waistband of my pants and hauled me out of the closet. We fell through the doorway, with Wright landing on top of me. His chest and arms formed a protective shield around my head.

A concussive blast rocked the apartment, setting my ears ringing. Wall sconces shattered, raining shards of plastiglass over us. Shelving and artwork crashed to the floor. Acrid, gray smoke billowed from the closet. Instinctively, I curled into Wright, burying my face against his chest.

An alarm blared, a crescendoing *wooOOOP, wooOOOP, wooOOOP* that signaled the activation of the fire suppressant system. Nozzle heads descended from the ceiling and squirted fluffy pink foam over the entire room.

"Reliance?" Wright lifted his weight from my body. His voice sounded muffled and distant, even though he looked like he was shouting.

I coughed and wiped a gob a pink foam from my face that had dripped off Wright's head. "Ow."

"Are you hurt?"

"Only my pride." I groaned, rolling out from beneath him. My brain protested the movement. "You?"

"I think the bed got the worst of it." He looked over his shoulder at the ruined frame and mattress, now sopping wet with foam.

"Void be damned, Wright. Hold still."

I rose on one elbow and squinted to focus my vision. Carefully, I picked out a piece of plastiglass embedded in the back of his neck. The cut wasn't deep, but a few centimeters to the right could have caused serious damage.

"Thanks." He touched his fingers to his neck. The tips came back bloody. "I better call this in."

"You do that."

I collapsed back down and shut my eyes while he contacted the office. That had been a close call. Too close. If Wright hadn't pulled me out when he did, the techs would be scraping little bits of me off the walls.

Wright ended the comm. "My team is on the way. They're bringing a medic along to check you out."

"I'm not the one who's bleeding."

"You also haven't gotten off the floor yet."

Fair point. "What's wrong with the floor? I happen to *love* the floor. It's quite comfy."

A derisive grunt was his only response.

With much effort, I convinced my body it was time to move again. By the time I'd hauled myself to my feet, Wright was surveying the damage done to the bedroom. I joined him near the remnants of the bed. Foam coated everything from the ceiling to the floor. The chemicals would break down over the next hour, leaving nothing but a fine residue of dust. At the moment, though, it looked like we stood inside of a cotton-candy cloud.

"How did you know the server was rigged?" he asked.

I tapped my temple to indicate the Intell. "A device named Butcher of Bellarouxdonda activated when you lifted the server from the hole. I doubted it could be anything good."

"The Butcher burned his crime scenes, destroying both evidence and witnesses. That's why he was never caught."

"Jarrett was fascinated with that case. He used to study old case files trying to work out how the Butcher did it."

"But why would he set an explosive on his own equipment?"

"He knew someone was onto him. That must be why he wanted to meet away from his apartment. Maybe he figured anyone coming after that data wouldn't be a very nice person."

"If it was that important, he should have reported it immediately." Wright's tone was laced with judgment that made my skin bristle.

"Maybe whatever was on it made him think he couldn't go to DECA." I could tell that concept didn't set well with Wright. He didn't buy it when I gave it as my reason for running from him, and he wasn't buying it now. A few years ago, I probably wouldn't have either, but I'd learned the hard way that DECA wasn't the bastion of integrity it held itself out to be. I held up my hand between us and unfurled my fingers to reveal the palm-sized server I'd managed to hold on to when Wright had yanked me from the closet. "I guess there's only one way to find out."

Chapter 28

THE CURVY BRUNETTE COCKED her head to the side, evaluating. "I thought you'd be taller, and more, I don't know, grrr!" She curled her fingers like claws and growled. "You don't look mean at all."

Agent DeAjamae Leahy had arrived ten minutes ago, and Wright briefed her on the morning's events. She was the same height as me, although where my build could most graciously be described as athletic, she had proportions that made lingerie designers weep tears of joy. Her long, natural curls were a rich mahogany threaded with hot-pink highlights that perfectly complimented her skin tone. Unlike my botch-job of a cut and color, she'd gone to a salon. A fancy one.

I caught myself reaching up to touch my own indigo hair that had been first chopped with cheap scissors and then partially shaved during the implant surgery and yanked my hand down. "Um, thanks?"

She shrugged as she dug a portable console out of her bag and set it up on the kitchen counter. "It surprised me when Grayson filled us in. We spent a lot of time thinking of you as the bad guy. It's a little hard to shift gears."

"Sorry to disappoint."

DeAjamae laughed. "No, no. It's not that. I just had this mental image of a hardened criminal, living life on the edge, leaving nothing but pain and destruction in her path."

I snorted. "You don't spend much time in the field, do you?"

"Don't need to. I can see everything from right here." She slid a secondary cuff onto her right forearm and splayed her fingers in a bursting motion to wake up her portable console.

A bright-blue holoscreen projected upward from the box and pinged my Intell. The assigned name designated it as an official DECA console. Part of me wanted to open it and take a peek around, perhaps find a copy of my file and scroll through it. However, even though Wright seemed onboard with the pro-Reliance plan, it hadn't escaped my notice that he hadn't officially dropped the charges yet.

That was where things got complicated. Before, I couldn't help seeing the programs and files my Intell accessed, but I'd gotten better about controlling what it opened. Without getting DeAjamae's permission, it would be wrong to snoop. Besides, my first impression hadn't exactly been a stellar one.

"We're lucky you saved the server," she said, connecting the black box to her console with the cable she'd dug out of her bag. "The case got dinged up, but the insides seem undamaged."

It had been in my hand when Wright yanked me from the closet, and I'd instinctively held on. Hopefully, when he threw himself on top of me, his body had shielded it from the blast.

"Do you need me to do anything?"

"Naw, I got this."

Excellent. The migraine tabs had kicked in, dulling my headache, and returning most of my vision, but the light still bothered me. I uprighted a kitchen chair and dragged it to a darker corner before sitting down.

The front door opened. Wright and another man stepped through, talking about the case. The new guy was in his early thirties, had dark eyes, wavy black hair, and a long-distance runner's build. He scanned the room, stopping when he got to me.

"You must be Reliance Sinclair," he said, flashing a charismatic smile and extending a hand. "Your holo doesn't do you justice. I'm Agent Ravi Singh."

Finally, someone with a little common sense.

We shook. His grip was firm, but rough calluses on his fingers belied the otherwise manicured look. "I wish we were meeting under different circumstances."

"Are you kidding? You've barely been planetside for two hours and you've already blown up a building. I can't wait to see what the afternoon brings."

Behind Ravi's back, DeAjamae stuck her finger down her throat and mimed gagging motions.

I bit back a smile. Wright pretended not to notice his team's antics.

"Hey, lover boy, did you bring me the thing I asked for?"

Ravi fished a bag of roasted, spiced cashews out of his pocket and tossed it to DeAjamae.

Wright cocked one eyebrow. "*That's* why you were late?"

DeAjamae funneled a handful into her mouth. "How often do we get to Brin? Plus, you know I don't work well on an empty stomach."

"Where are we on the server?" Wright asked.

"Setting up a virtual sandbox now. I don't want to risk triggering any other surprises the victim may have left." There was a hint of admiration in her voice.

Ravi passed around a second bag of cashews while we waited. They were good. Salty with a kick of heat from garlic and Sahara pepper and still warm from the roasting barrel. I'd had them before when I visited Jarrett. We'd played VR games late into the night, drank his terrible beer, and talked about everything except the old days. I knew he kept in touch with several of our former coworkers, but he never brought them up.

My mouth went dry, and the next time the bag circled, I waved it off.

The progress bar on DeAjamae's holoscreen blinked twice, signaling it was complete. She cracked her knuckles. "Okay, let's see what we've got."

Wright and Ravi crowded behind her, leaving no space for me in the small kitchen. The only sound was DeAjamae's soft whispers as she unconsciously read to herself.

"What's that?" Ravi pointed at the screen.

DeAjamae swatted his hand down. "Nothing. Quit interrupting."

I stood and paced to the far side of the room. Suddenly, I had more energy than I knew what to do with.

"Huh, interesting," she mumbled to herself, and used her free hand to tuck a loose curl behind her ear. "Where is the . . . oh, uh-huh. Now why would he . . .? Oh, piss off, you little fucker. Why? *Why* would you do that? Asshole!" Fingers on both hands stabbed at the holoscreen. "No. No, no, no. That's not what I said. I don't have time for this bullshit. Seriously, this is ridiculous. There's nothing there. That's not how it fucking works. Oh, wait, that was clever. Mm-hmm . . ."

"Well?" prompted Wright after several long minutes, giving voice to what we were all thinking.

DeAjamae jumped. "Sorry. Yeah, so this server is on a totally different system than the rest of the victim's consoles. There's some pretty cool shit on here from a technological standpoint. Top-of-the-line software. Maxed out on the upgrades. Most of the files are individually encrypted. It'll take a while to access them."

Wright ran a hand through his hair. "Can you tell what's on there? There has to be something for him to go to all that trouble."

DeAjamae tapped a nail against her tooth and stared at the screen. "I can't do a deep dive until I'm back to the office, but going off the file size and type, we've got some standard text docs, some graphics, holos. Audio—those could be voice comms or music. Wait, this could be something. These look like visual recordings. Daily entries dating back . . ." DeAjamae flicked her finger in an upward motion, causing the screen to scroll to the bottom of the list. "About three years."

I moved closer but still couldn't see around Wright's shoulder. "That's when Jarrett moved here. A position opened with a bump in rank and pay, and he couldn't turn it down. Can you open them?"

"No, like I said, they're encrypted. I'll get the decryption program running. If we're lucky, it'll finish by the end of the day. No guarantees, though."

I chewed my lower lip. This was one of those moral gray areas. More like charcoal, if I was honest with myself. DECA had great decryption software, and I had every bit of faith that they would get through Jarrett's security measures. Eventually. So what would it hurt if I gave it a little nudge?

Not giving myself time to talk myself out of it, I opened the window to DeAjamae's portable console and eased into her virtual sandbox. That was already beyond my computer skills, but all I had to do was hitch a ride on her work and let the Intell do the rest. Decryption was its specialty.

She had the recordings open on the screen. I found the batch that included the video file dated the day of Jarrett's death and let the Intell latch on. It would be wrong to say the Intell was gleeful about the task, but it attacked the encryption program with a certain vim and vigor that was close. My head still felt like a loose ball bearing had been knocking around inside it during a rough reentry, and this didn't help. I staggered back to the chair and plopped down.

"Central Command to Reliance." My attention snapped back into place. Ravi waved his hand in front of my face. "Hey there, starshine, you back with us now?"

I minimized the windows and blinked a few times to refocus my eyes. "Sorry, I zoned out for a minute."

DeAjamae's console dinged. "No shit. We're in. I guess the security measures weren't all that strong after all."

Wright gave me a loaded side-eye but didn't question our good luck. At least, not out loud.

We gathered around. By mutual consensus, DeAjamae enlarged the projection and played the recording from the day Jarrett died.

A three-dimensional image of a darkly lit common room appeared. It was eighteen hundred hours by Universal Standard Time, which made it late evening local time.

I leaned forward. "It's a surveillance video of this apartment. He must have a hidden camera."

"You're right," Ravi said, comparing the projection to the room behind us. "I didn't recognize it with the furniture all right side up." He carried the chair I'd been sitting on to the bedroom door, stepped up, and ran his fingertips over the trim. When he got to the end, he dug his nail into the wood and pulled out a micro-camera. A thin green wire ran from it back into the trim. "Looks like he removed the nail and fed the wire through in its place."

"The closet is on the other side of that wall," Wright said. "Viorel ran the wire behind the frame, along the floor joist, and into the server."

As fascinating as that was, I was more interested in what the camera had recorded. "Can you advance the recording?"

DeAjamae obliged, skipping ahead until we saw movement.

Jarrett's front door eased open. Two men entered, one short and compact, the other tall with a muscular upper body. Both wore dark clothing, ov-ex caps, and had blasters holstered at their hips. The ov-ex material caused the camera to overexpose the area around their heads, turning them into useless, white blobs.

They cleared the apartment and set to work, tossing the place. Minutes passed. They searched every nook and cranny of the common room. The tall man tried logging into Jarrett's console but couldn't get around the passcode. After that, they moved into the bedroom, out of sight of the camera. More minutes passed with only the occasional glimpse of an arm or the white blur of an ov-ex cap.

My heart ached as I watched Jarrett walk through the front door. He had a sandwich in one hand and scrolled through his messages on his cuff's holoscreen with the other. A glob of sauce dripped onto his shirt. There was no audio, but I could lip-read "damn it" from fifty paces.

My hands clenched, nails biting into the soft flesh of my palms. I wanted to run to him, scream out a warning, something.

He looked up and noticed the state of his apartment.

Both men rushed from the bedroom, blasters drawn. The camera was almost useless from that angle. The taller one was mostly out of frame, but I thought the shorter one carried a Kismet-8 blaster. Top of the line and expensive. They weren't amateurs.

Jarrett put up a good fight, but they'd taken him by surprise and had him outnumbered and outgunned. He took the tall man to the ground with a leg sweep. They scuffled.

Jarrett got around the man's back and put him in a headlock that would have knocked the guy out if the short man hadn't hit Jarrett in the back of the head with the butt of his blaster.

My friend slumped, knocked out cold.

I decided the short man was the one in charge. He nudged his accomplice in the side with his foot when the taller man sat up, catching his breath. There was a heated exchange of words, and the tall man clambered to his feet. More arguing, and then the tall man grabbed Jarrett by the feet and dragged him into the bedroom with the short man following behind.

Seconds ticked by on the console's clock. The camera jiggled as if something hit the wall. The back of a shirt came into view, then disappeared. A light turned on. Shadows passed back and forth, and then the taller guy came back out. He retrieved a chair from the kitchen table—the mate to the one I had sat on earlier—and carried it into the bedroom.

No one came back out for the next twenty minutes. Even though we couldn't hear anything, I knew from how I had found Jarrett that they were torturing him. Then the tall man searched the common room for a second time. He ransacked the couch cushions, coffee table, holoscreen, gaming console, kitchen cabinets—everything Wright and I had searched. It didn't look like he had found anything, either.

He slunk back to the bedroom. A few more minutes passed, and the short man took his place. This guy headed straight to Jarrett's console. The screen lit up, requesting a passcode. No surprise. The man stormed back into the bedroom.

I watched with my heart in my throat as shadows passed across the light in the door. My eyes blurred, but I swiped a finger under them and forced myself to watch.

The short man returned, streaks of blood covering his knuckles and forearm. The console rejected the code he entered and put itself into permanent lockdown. A brief warning flashed before the whole screen went dark.

Oh, Jarrett, why didn't you give him the damn passcode?

In a fit of rage, the short man ripped the console from the wall and stomped on the screen. Broken bits of plastiglass scattered across the floor. The heel of his boot found the delicate hardware inside and ground it into the floor.

Beside me, DeAjamae swore under her breath.

He stormed back into the bedroom.

There was a bright flash, and the camera shook. A hollowness filled me, and I knew deep down in the marrow of my bones that Jarrett had died in that moment. From the time the men attacked him until his death, forty-seven minutes had passed. That was a long time to be in pain.

The tall man ran from the bedroom to the bathroom. One hand clutched at his stomach and the other covered his mouth. A minute later, he walked out, wiping his mouth against his sleeve. His ov-ex cap had slipped off, but his back was to the camera.

His partner met him in the common room. They stood facing each other, arguing. The tall man made exaggerated hand gestures, pointed at the bedroom, and shook his head.

The short man's hand settled on the butt of his blaster, now holstered at his waist. He said a few more words and then the tall man backed off. Threat received. They headed toward the front door, but before they got there, the tall man looked back at the bedroom one last time. As he did, a shaft of light from the window caught the side of his face.

I inhaled sharply.

DeAjamae paused the recording and drew a circle around the head with her middle finger. "Running facial recognition."

"There's no need," I said, scrubbing the tears from my cheeks with the palm of my hand. "I know who they are."

Wright's hazel eyes pierced me. "Who?"

"Sagi Barros. He works security for Tazza Industries and was one of the guards who held me captive. I'd bet anything that the other man is his boss, Michael Hitz. The build and body language match, along with the general air of assholeness." Anger welled up from the pit of my stomach, roiling and turning until I thought it might burst through my skin. I spotted a torn cushion on the floor and kicked it across the room. "It didn't occur to me they'd use in-house personnel. I assumed they'd contracted the hit out. Void be damned, I was in the same room as those bastards! I should have killed them when I had the chance."

Kicking the pillow didn't make me feel any better, so I let the couch have it with a low front kick. The feet squeaked against the floor as it lurched away from me. I kicked it again, sinking all my energy into it. Something inside splintered with a satiating crack. My foot pulled back for another go, and then Wright was behind me, pulling me back from the edge of sofacide.

"They would have killed you, too. Is that what Viorel would have wanted?"

I spun to face him, chest heaving and breathing hard through my nose. "I should have tried. It's what he deserved."

"Viorel deserves justice, not revenge." Wright rested his hand on my shoulder. The warmth and weight grounded me. "Deep in your heart, you believe that, too. That's what made you a good agent."

"In case you haven't noticed, I'm not an agent anymore."

Wright held my gaze for a long time, and I wondered what he saw in my eyes. I hoped it was fury.

"No. No, you're not. And more's the pity." He let his hand drop from my shoulder and stepped back.

"Is this enough?" I asked, pointing toward the frozen image of Jarrett's murders. "Is this enough to arrest them?"

"Barros, but not Hitz. It's enough to bring them in for questioning, though."

Ravi gave me a sympathetic smile. "Agent Viorel was one of our own. Believe that we want answers, too."

"DeAjamae," Wright said, "send a copy of this recording to forensics and have them go over the apartment, again. Test any place they touched for DNA. Tell them to swab the bathroom sink if they have to. I want physical evidence tying Barros and Hitz to the apartment."

She started packing up her portable console. "Got it. Now that I have names, I'll go back over the digital evidence again. Traffic cameras, spacedock records, everything we have. This is the first real solid lead we've had so far. It's a good thing, Reliance."

"We do this by the book, and we build a case that sticks. I'm requesting an interplanetary warrant for Barros." Wright crossed to the other side of the room and tapped his cuff. "Sophie, open a direct comm to Judge Xiao's clerk."

The storm raging inside me subsided enough that I could see a patch of light through the clouds. What was done was done. There was no going back. And DeAjamae was right; now we knew who killed Jarrett and where to find them. That was so much more than we knew an hour ago.

Michael and Sagi weren't the only ones responsible, though. Someone ordered them to come here, and they needed to be held accountable, too. Lourde was involved. No doubt about it. But did he orchestrate the entire thing himself, or was someone else pulling the strings?

Chapter 29

WRIGHT'S TEAM DIDN'T WASTE any time. By the time the judge signed off on the warrant to bring Michael and Sagi in for questioning, we'd already loaded our bags onto a cruiser. I'd barely had enough time to hock a few trinkets from the *Soteria* in exchange for an auto feeder and install it in Walnut's cage. Thankfully, Wright agreed to let me remove a few items once I pointed out that the only alternative was bringing Walnut with us.

Wright had dropped the charges against me, but the ship was in impound until all the paperwork cleared. Even after that, it still belonged to Seddy until my assets were unfrozen and I got it out of pawn.

Stars, I only had a few days left before my month with Seddy was up. I needed to send him an update to let him know his money was coming.

We slept in uncomfortable shifts on the two-day flight to Brione-2, pooling our data about the suspects and running through scenarios. A successful interrogation began long before you asked the suspect the first question and having a game plan increased the chances of obtaining useful information.

Ravi leaned his elbows on the table, the sleeves of his white shirt coming dangerously close to the red sauce of his spaghetti. "I still say our primary focus should be on Hitz. Given his and Sagi's height difference and the size and locations of the blood spatter voids, he was most likely the one who pulled the trigger, so he'll be the most likely to want to save his ass by making a deal. Plus, his position gives him the best access to the information we want. If we can get Hitz to confess that Lourde or someone else at Tazza Industries gave the order, Judge Xiao won't have any problem issuing additional warrants. It'll be like the Robidoux case."

"But Agent Viorel was one of ours. Arresting his actual killer should be our chief priority," DeAjamae argued. "Barros is younger, less experienced, and won't lose as much by flipping on the company. He'll be easier to break, even if he doesn't know who gave the order."

"What do you think, Sinclair?" Wright asked. "Based on your personal experience with the suspects, which one will be more likely to give up the information we want?"

I took a bite of spaghetti and mulled over the question. DeAjamae had a point. As the only one visible on the recording, Wright had already obtained an arrest warrant for Sagi. He could take Sagi straight to Salin to await trial but doing that meant we wouldn't get a shot at the bigger prize. If Wright got either man to admit being directed by someone at Tazza, then we could follow that lead as far as it ran. However, any delay in our departure meant more opportunity for something to go wrong and possibly returning to Andaress-4 empty handed.

"I would focus on Michael. Jarrett dedicated his entire life to helping people. He'd want us to do everything we could to get the Insight off the market."

"Agreed," Wright said. "If there's a chance of opening a full investigation against Tazza Industries and shutting down the Insight program, then it's worth the risk."

DeAjamae snagged a piece of garlic toast from the basket. "Okay, I can tell when I'm outvoted. Let's talk logistics. Where are we doing this? Home, work, precinct?" She took a bite of the toast and grimaced. "Yuck. How do you survive on this rehydrated stuff?"

I shrugged one shoulder. "Extra garlic."

"Questioning them at home would catch them off guard," Ravi offered. "They'd have less time to prepare their stories."

Wright shot that idea down. "Too many variables we don't know. DeAjamae got their addresses, but that's it. We don't know the layout or who else might be there."

"Michael is going to feel the most secure at Tazza headquarters," I said. "It's his own little fiefdom where he's the head of security. And I can't see Aurelian Tazza letting Michael or Sagi be questioned on the premises without a roomful of attorneys at the table. My vote is that we pick them up before they get to work and use interrogation rooms at the local DECA precinct."

"It's a good plan," Wright said, "but our liaison with the Tylo office hasn't been helpful so far. I doubt we can count on much local support."

DeAjamae swirled a forkful of 3D-printed spaghetti noodles into her sauce. "I can handle the recordings and biometric feedback. As long as they lend us the facilities, we shouldn't need any of their personnel."

"What about Barros?" Ravi asked.

I thought about my interactions with Sagi. "He's deferential to Michael, Lourde, and Aurelian Tazza. I think he'll respond well to someone he perceives as an authority figure."

Ravi speared a mycoprotein meatball and used it to point at Wright. "That means Grayson will handle the interrogations. DeAjamae will be busy on the tech end, and I'm too pretty to play the stern lawman." He leaned toward me and stage whispered, "They save me for when they need to charm someone."

DeAjamae threw the hunk of garlic bread at him.

"What?"

"You're incorrigible, that's what."

"Kids, kids," Wright interrupted. "Focus, please."

They settled down, but I didn't miss DeAjamae sticking out her tongue at Ravi when Wright turned his back. The three of them shared an easy camaraderie, and my heart panged at the bittersweet memories it dragged up of my days at the Department.

We spent the next hour ironing out the details. It was exhausting work and came with no guarantee we'd made the right choices.

The cruiser dropped out of warp and entered the outer edge of the Brione system. From this distance, the star looked like most other stars in the galaxy, but my heart gave an extra thump as I watched it grow larger and brighter on the main viewscreen. I grew up in this system, and despite recent events, it would always be home.

DeAjamae held off sending our notice of extradition over the subspace relays, but she couldn't tactfully delay once we entered the Brione system. If there was a leak in the Department, the clock was ticking on how fast Tazza Industries learned we wanted to question its employees. We couldn't risk them getting to Sagi and Michael before us and making them disappear.

Wright brought us in hot. My body lurched painfully against my harness as inertia warred with the reverse thrusters. Across the aisle, Ravi sat with his eyes shut and fingers dug fervently into his armrests. We passed by Brione-5, my homeworld, and then Brione-4 and 3, small, rocky planets with no atmosphere, before Wright fired the thrusters again to slow us enough to enter Brione-2's orbit. Tylo's Central Command wasn't pleased with our hasty entry, but DeAjamae shot them our credentials and they cleared a parking spot for us in the gate reserved for law enforcement.

Ravi and I grouped outside the ship. Within moments of stepping off the ship, a thin layer of sweat and red dust coated my arms and face. It was near midday in Tylo, with Brione shining high overhead so the skyscrapers ringing the spacedock did little in the way of providing shade. A strong wind whipped between the buildings, but rather than offer cooling relief, it kicked up clouds of stinging sand and forced me to squint to protect my eyes.

A surly officer from DECA greeted us at the gate. Her bronzed skin was so lined and weathered by the harsh sun that it was difficult to determine her age.

"Lead Agent Grayson Wright?" she asked Ravi.

"Agent Wright is still on board." Ravi extended a hand. "I'm Agent Ravi Singh."

"Officer Boel Tademan," she said in a clipped tone, ignoring Ravi's hand. "I'm your liaison for the duration of your stay in Tylo. You're searching for citizens Michael Hitz and Sagi Barros?"

"They're suspects in a homicide investigation on Andaress-4." Ravi transferred a copy of the warrant to her cuff.

"Is this the homicide that brought Agent Wright here a few days ago? He'd have saved your department some credits by picking everyone up at the same time, but maybe Salin doesn't have the same budgetary issues we have here in Tylo." She gave me a once-over. "You look familiar."

She probably recognized me from the hospital security footage, even though I'd been in scrubs and running for my life.

Ravi shifted to the side, partially blocking me from her view. "We received new information."

Officer Tademan took her sweet time reading every word, even though it was a boilerplate warrant and we were all sweating our asses off. "Unfortunately, we're underresourced this week and won't be able to provide additional assistance."

"Not a problem." Ravi gave her one of his most charming smiles. "We can manage on our own."

"Yes, because that worked well the last time your commander was here. I'm still receiving complaints from the hospital staff." She signed off on the warrant receipt. "As requested, I reserved two holding cells and interrogation rooms for you in Precinct Six. See that you mind your manners while you're here. You may have been extended jurisdiction as a courtesy, but you are still a guest in my city. I expect regular and prompt reports."

Wright exited the cruiser, carrying an oversized duffel bag of DeAjamae's equipment. He nodded to our liaison. "Officer Tademan. We appreciate your cooperation. As you can imagine, we're eager to get going. Please send Agent Leahy your local files on both suspects. It would surprise me if they hadn't had prior run-ins with DECA. I request the use of two hovercarts for the duration of our stay."

Officer Tademan's lips thinned. "That can be arranged."

"That's appreciated." He walked through the gate and set the bag of equipment onto the back of Tademan's hovercart, then clapped his hands. "Let's go!"

DeAjamae hurried out of the ship, carrying two more bags with the straps crisscrossed over her chest.

Ravi locked the cruiser's hatch and helped her into the back of the cart before hopping in beside her. Wright slid into the driver's seat and started the engine.

Tademan opened her mouth to object.

I snagged the seat next to Wright as the cart lifted. "I guess we're commandeering her cart?" My voice was pitched low enough that Tademan wouldn't hear.

Matching my volume, Wright said, "Well, we're not waiting around for her to requisition one. Something tells me we'd be filing for our pensions by the time it arrived." Wright smiled and waved to the agent. "Thank you, Officer Tademan. You've been most helpful."

Chapter 30

Wright dropped DeAjamae and me off at the precinct while Ravi and he picked up the suspects. We set up shop in the viewing room.

DeAjamae linked her cuff to the wall of built-in consoles and turned them all on. Her teal-tipped nails flew as she reconfigured the screens to her liking with spare parts she removed from the bag she carried with her everywhere. She pulled up the controls for the interrogation rooms and ran a diagnostics test on the sensors to verify that everything was in working order. Once satisfied, she checked her comms for messages.

She muttered a string of incomprehensible curses under her breath.

"Problems?" I asked.

"This is such fucking bullshit. I'm about to go nova on these incompetent space worms. The records department *still* hasn't sent me the files on Hitz and Barros. How long does it take to transfer two files? Less time than it'll take me to walk across the precinct and shove my foot up their ass, that's how long. They've got five minutes to get their shit together." She fired off a tersely worded comm before hopping her butt up on the table. "Hey, you got anything to eat? I'm starving."

"We ate on the cruiser."

"That was like, three hours ago."

I fished a smushed hellaberry bar from the bottom of my bag and offered it to her.

She crinkled her nose. "Pass."

I smoothed the packaging and checked the expiration date. "It's fine. Probably."

"I'll let you know if I get desperate." DeAjamae's cuff chimed, signaling an incoming comm. She glanced at the sender, then hopped off the table. "Finally."

A minute later, she was absorbed in her task of transferring Michael's and Sagi's files onto the interrogation room's system. I recognized the focused look as one I'd seen on Jarrett's face many times and knew better than to interrupt, so I leaned back in my chair and kicked my feet up on the table to wait.

On my fourth pass of counting the cracks in the ceiling panels, Ravi sent us each a comm notifying us he had arrived with Michael.

I took a sip of artificial coffee obtained from the break room and grimaced at the burnt taste. Bad coffee wasn't something I missed about working for DECA. "Are you ready?"

"Just give me one sec . . ." DeAjamae brought up camera feeds for both interrogation rooms and holding cells, each on their own holoscreen. A fifth screen she used to queue up the files Wright might want to use during questioning. "We're all set as soon as Wright gets back with Barros."

We watched Ravi stuff a dusty Michael into a holding cell. On the screen, Michael circled the small room, testing the door and checking the security features. When he spotted one of the camera lenses in the center of the long wall, he looked directly into it, held up his middle three fingers and flicked them around in a *fuck you* to the camera.

"Classy," DeAjamae observed.

"He's not used to being the one locked up," I said. "He enjoys being in charge. Wright will have to walk a tight line. Come on too strong, and Michael will clam up. Too weak and he won't have a reason to talk."

"You don't think he'll talk once he sees the recording?"

I thought back to my interactions with Michael. He had a superiority complex and enjoyed lording power over me. "He'll cooperate as long as he thinks he's getting information out of us. Once we show him what we have on him, I bet he'll demand an attorney."

Ravi joined us. He tossed his jacket on the table and stood in front of the nearest climate-control vent. Red dirt covered his face, and dark patches of damp fabric clung to his upper back. "Man, it's hot on this planet. There's a dust storm rolling in. Isn't that supposed to block the sun and cool things down?"

"This is cool for Tylo," DeAjamae said.

"Why didn't you take the skybridges?" I asked.

He pulled at the sticky fabric to circulate air under his shirt. "The second hovercart Officer Tademan procured for us broke down. My options were to wait fifty minutes for a replacement or walk. There wasn't a direct path via the skybridges, but we were only three buildings away if we dropped to ground level."

Ravi used the hem of his shirt to wipe grit from his eyes, and I didn't miss the way DeAjamae's eyes fell to his toned, tanned stomach before darting back to her screen.

"I may never feel clean again," Ravi griped, and raked his fingers through his black hair to shake out the sand.

"The restroom's down the hall on the right," I said. "I spotted it when we came in."

"Thanks. Send me a comm if Grayson gets here before I get back."

"Hey, if you pass a vending machine, pick me up something, huh?"

Ravi took DeAjamae's request in stride. "I'll do you one better and see if I can sniff out the cafeteria and grab us lunch."

"My hero."

Ravi smiled as he backed through the door. "She only says that when I bring her food."

The brainy analyst stuck out her tongue. "That's because it's the only time you're useful."

The next ten minutes dragged on. DeAjamae worked on the rest of the encrypted files from Jarrett's server. It had taken a lot of willpower on my part not to nudge the process along with my Intell, but she'd expressly forbidden me from doing so when I'd brought it up on the flight over. She was confident she'd crack it, and information accessed by a DECA employee using tested and reliable technology would hold up better in court.

Movement from the camera in the second holding cell caught my eye. Wright escorted Sagi into the room and slammed the door closed. The big man retreated to the fixed bench along the wall and sank down. Shoulders rounded and head in his hands, Sagi seemed resigned to his fate.

"Oh." DeAjamae tore herself away from the console with a smile stretched across her face. "I didn't have time to tell you earlier, but I tracked down that payment Tazza Industries made to your bank account. They falsified the dates. The funds didn't transfer until *after* Grayson arrested you. You're totally in the clear from that end."

The guys walked in. Wright tossed two cuffs—each carrying a Tazza Industries logo—onto the table. My Intell pinged, telling me they belonged to Michael and Sagi.

"See what you can find on these."

"On it." DeAjamae scooped up the cuffs and deposited them on her makeshift workstation. She linked them to a console and began sifting through the information.

"Who should we start with?" Ravi asked Wright, dumping three sandwiches on the table and handing one to DeAjamae. He'd scrubbed the sand from his face and hands and made a passable attempt at drying his shirt, but there was only so much you could do in a restroom.

"Michael Hitz. We'll give him a few more minutes to worry about what we have on him, but I want to let him think he's still one step ahead of us. I plan to give him enough rope to hang himself with." Wright took off his forest-green DECA jacket, undid the buttons at the top of his shirt, and untucked the hem from his waistband. He ran his fingers through his sandy-blond hair to muss it up. "One overworked, underpaid, and slightly inept agent coming up."

"Not really much of a disguise," Ravi joked. He held up his hands as he backed toward the door. "Kidding, boss, just kidding. I'll put him in Room A and Barros in B."

"It might not be helpful," I prefaced, "but Michael likes to gamble."

Wright glanced at DeAjamae. She aerial scribed a few commands and nodded to verify what I said was true. "He's got at least eight betting programs on his cuff."

"Thanks. Sinclair, stay here in the observation room with DeAjamae. Officer Tademan has suddenly found herself a lot less busy than she initially claimed to be. She's now demanding updates every twenty minutes. While I dropped the charges against you, I'd like to avoid a prolonged discussion with her about the situation if I can. It's best if you stay out of her way. If you think of anything else, tell DeAjamae, and she can get word to me."

With that last instruction, he left for the interrogation room.

I sat in front of the panel of consoles and watched Wright barrel into Michael's room. His eyes were glued to his cuff's holoscreen, reading Michael's file as if he hadn't memorized it on the flight over like I knew he had. Without looking up, Wright hooked a foot around the chair leg and scooted it out so he could sit.

Michael gave him a once-over. A sneer tugged at the corners of his lips, making his mustache twitch. He relaxed back, stretched his legs out in front of him, and crossed his feet at the ankles.

Wright closed the holoscreen and acknowledged Michael for the first time. "Mr. Hitz? Thank you for coming in. My name is Grayson Wright. I hear you had some transportation issues on the way over. My apologies for the inconvenience. Thirsty?" Wright set a water pouch down on the table and pushed it toward Michael. "I don't know how you Tylonians deal with this heat."

"You get used to it." Michael tore off the corner with his teeth, tipped his head back, and squirted the water into his mouth.

"All the same, we appreciate your cooperation."

"Always happy to help a fellow industry professional, but your man put me in a holding cell like some criminal."

"He did? Something must have gotten screwed up on the paperwork. You didn't have to wait too long, did you?"

I could tell Michael wanted to be mad, but Wright's expression sold his story.

"No, it's all good. Let's just get on with it, yeah?"

"I need to ask a few basic questions for the record. You know how it is."

Michael's chest puffed at the implied compliment. "Yeah, yeah, of course. Gotta go by the book. That's how I do it, too."

"Name and address?"

Michael rattled off the information, calm and collected. These were baseline questions, designed to give Wright a chance to observe Michael's body language with no stress applied. Wright continued with questions about Michael's age, place of employment, and favorite sports team.

Behind the scenes, DeAjamae used the room's built-in sensors to measure Michael's body temperature, heart rate, and pupil dilation. The chair recorded shifts in his weight distribution. She wouldn't interrupt Wright midquestioning with the information, but it could prove helpful when analyzing the recordings later. Changes in behavior from the baseline could reveal when the subject felt stressed. Stress could indicate lying or which topics he wished to avoid talking about. Or it could mean nothing at all. Innocent people felt stressed talking to law enforcement all the time. For now, Wright had to rely on his own observations to feel his way through the interrogation.

It was more of an art than a science, really, and none of it was admissible in court. Even if all the signs were there, we still needed a confession.

On the screen, Wright rubbed at the back of his neck. "Do you know why we asked you here today?"

"Yeah, that other guy said it was about a crime that happened off-planet."

"We're from Salin on Andaress-4. We have spacedock records showing you visited about a month ago."

Michael's breathing stopped for a full two seconds. He swallowed hard, the lump of his Adam's apple bouncing up and down. "Don't know how I can help. I was only there on a layover. Thought I might go see the salt flats, but I spent most of my time at the bar."

"Which bar was that?"

"The Salt Pig." His answer came too quick.

"You're sure? It was almost a month ago, and we have a lot of bars."

"Yeah," Michael doubled down. "It's close to the spacedock."

"The one with the mural of pigs in suits on the back wall?"

Michael's foot jiggled under the table. He sat up and tucked his feet under his chair. "Yeah, that's the one. Cheap beer."

Beside me in the observation room, DeAjamae snorted. "Lie. That mural is at The Wallow. The Salt Pig's walls are plastiglass so you can see the vats for their craft beer in their back room. There's no way he could have missed that. And their beer is anything but cheap. To cover our bases, though, I'll send a subspace comm to our office to have the owners of both bars send us the receipts and recordings from that night. That should prove Hitz wasn't there."

"Good, good." Wright nodded, like it all made sense. "You said you were at the bar all night. Can you be more specific? What time did you get there?"

"I wasn't really keeping track."

"Take a guess. Before sunset? After? Was it still light outside?"

"Sometime around 1800 hours. What's this all about?"

"Well, Mr. Hitz, there was a murder. We're hoping you saw something that could help us out."

Michael shifted in his seat. "I don't know anything about that."

"Do you recognize this man?" Wright waved his hand at the wall console and a holo of Jarrett in his formal DECA uniform appeared. It was professionally taken with the official DECA Seal of Office hovering behind his left shoulder. All officers had one to be used for press releases, commendations, or funerals.

Michael barely looked at the holo. "Can't say as I do."

"You see that?" DeAjamae pointed to a graph on a side console. "The camera angle isn't great, but the sensors are showing rapid fluctuations in weight distribution on the chair. He's bouncing his knee. A lot."

"Burning off excess energy," I agreed. Inwardly, though, I cringed. Wright was moving too fast.

Michael was a bully, brash, and full of himself, but he wasn't stupid. Wright would tip his hand if he wasn't careful.

Wright stood up and approached the wall console in the interrogation room. "His name was Agent Jarrett Viorel."

All expression dropped from Michael's face, leaving only a stony mask in its place.

My mental groan cut short when Officer Tademan stormed into the viewing room. A few strands of blond hair had come free from her low ponytail, and her clothes looked disheveled, as if she had been running.

"What's going on?" Her eyes darted to the camera feeds on the consoles. "You already started the interviews?"

DeAjamae crossed her arms. "We started the *interrogations* about ten minutes ago."

"You were supposed to wait for my authorization."

"No. No, I don't think so. This is our case. You're only assisting with the logistics."

Tademan huffed and tugged at the bottom of her coat. "You should have notified me."

"Consider yourself notified."

"I don't know what kind of department you run in Salin, but this is not how we do things in Tylo." Tademan scowled, turned on her heel, and stormed out.

"Well, that went well," I said.

DeAjamae unwrapped a sandwich and took a bite. "I don't think she likes us very much," she said between mouthfuls.

I turned back to the camera feed in time to see Wright exiting the interrogation room. He'd left the holo of Jarrett on the wall console for Michael to think about.

There was a brief pause, and then Wright entered Interrogation Room B with Sagi. He'd straightened his uniform, slicked
back his hair, and walked into the room like he owned it. Sagi
was young and used to taking orders. I'd seen him defer to both
Michael and Doctor Lourde on numerous occasions without
question. He hadn't struck me as the rebellious type, so we
thought he'd respond best to an authority figure.

"His heart rate is already elevated," said DeAjamae, stuffing
the last of her sandwich into her mouth. She nodded to my
untouched sandwich on the table. "You going to eat that?"

"Where does it all go?" I eyed her curvy but toned figure
before shoving the sandwich across the table. If I ate like that,
my ass wouldn't fit in my captain's chair.

She snagged it off the table and unwrapped it. "Good metabolism. Big Momma says I should enjoy it while I can, because once
I hit thirty, it's all over." She wiped mustard from the corner of
her mouth and pointed to the console. "Here we go."

Wright paced the length of the room while Sagi squirmed in
his seat. After a full minute of silent observation, Wright folded
his arms across his chest, a stern look on his face. "I'm going
to ask you some questions, and I expect you to answer them
honestly. Can you do that?"

Sagi nodded.

"You're going to have to speak up."

"Yes. Yes, sir."

"That's good. Now, state your name for the record."

"Sagi Barros. That's S-A-G-I B-A-R-R-O-S." He looked to
Wright for approval.

Wright nodded and ran Sagi through the same baseline questions he had asked Michael, but Sagi was so nervous it was
difficult to get a good read on him.

The young guy wiped his palms against his thighs. He glanced
anxiously up at Wright. Gone were all traces of the bravado I'd
grown to expect from him, and he bore little resemblance to the

cocky guard extolling the virtues of modern science to me only a few days earlier.

"I'm investigating a murder that took place on Andaress-4, and I think you can help me."

"Murder?" The young man's voice cracked. "No, you have the wrong guy. I couldn't help you with anything like that. I'm nobody."

"Oh, I doubt that very much, Sagi."

"How long will this take?" he asked and rubbed at the back of his neck. "I'm going to be late for work."

Wright smiled, but it wasn't a real smile. "I'm glad you mentioned that. Let's talk about your job. What kind of work do you do?"

Sagi sank about five centimeters into his seat. "Security. Mostly watching the front entrance."

"What else?"

"I can't say."

Wright glared down at him. "You have to do better than that, Sagi."

"No, really. They made me sign one of those papers says I can't talk about what I do."

Wright's brows furrowed. "A nondisclosure agreement?"

"Maybe?"

"Now, why would a glorified hall monitor need an NDA?"

"How should I know? I needed the job. They had me fill out a bunch of forms. I didn't ask questions. Maybe I should contact someone at work. I can't lose my job."

Wright leaned down, both hands flat on the table. "You're going to lose a lot more than your job if you don't start answering my questions."

Even over the camera feed, I could see Sagi's face blanch. He looked about five seconds away from pissing his pants.

Wright was pushing him too far, too fast. We talked about Sagi needing an authority figure to open up to, but Wright was coming across as more of a bully with a badge. I watched as Sagi physically shut down. His shoulders slumped, and his gaze turned vacant.

Wright asked a few more questions, but it became obvious Sagi wasn't going to answer. He must have sensed things had gone off track, too, because he leaned down over Sagi with both hands on the table. "I'm going to give you a few minutes to think about how you want the rest of this interview to go. When I get back, I hope your answers will be more forthcoming."

Then he pushed off the table and walked toward the door, out of view of the camera.

Chapter 31

WRIGHT STORMED BACK INTO the observation room. "Where did we go wrong? Because neither one of them is talking."

Ravi drummed his fingers against the table. "Maybe Hitz is more loyal to Tazza Industries than we thought he was."

"Tazza's lawyers could have coached him before we got here," DeAjamae offered. "They had to think something like this might blow back on them."

"If that were the case, wouldn't he have asked for legal representation when you picked him up?" I asked.

"Not necessarily." Wright paced to the opposite side of the room and turned. "They may think that whatever information he discovers about what we know is worth the risk of him incriminating himself. Just because he's loyal to the company doesn't mean the company is loyal to him."

DeAjamae pulled up the sensor readings from Interrogation Room A. "He's not as calm as he looks. Elevated heart rate, quick, shallow breaths, and his eyes keep darting to the door. Hitz might think he has the upper hand, but something you said rattled him."

"I don't care what they offered him, Michael is still out for number one," I said.

Wright stopped pacing and ran a hand through his hair. "So, we shift tactics. Go after him hard and convince him that Tazza Industries is letting him take the fall for the murder and washing their hands of him."

"I'll see if I can dig up anything on his cuff that can help," DeAjamae said, turning back to her wall of consoles. "Written comms, audio recordings, meetings in his calendar."

"What about Barros?" Ravi asked.

I checked on the console displaying Sagi's room and watched the young man crumple in on himself. His elbows hit the table, and he held his head in his hands like it carried the weight of the world. I saw something we hadn't expected. Unlike Michael, Sagi still had a conscience.

"He feels guilty," I said, and pointed at the holoscreen. "Look at him."

Wright came up behind me to view the console over my shoulder. Ravi and DeAjamae crowded in at the sides, pressing Wright into my back.

DeAjamae made a slow fist, causing the camera to zoom in on his face. "He looks scared."

"As he should, with a murder charge hanging over him," Ravi added.

I tried not to fidget as I waited for them to see it. "Not just scared. He feels shame, regret over what he did. See how he's shut down? He's not looking to escape. It's almost like he's resigned to whatever happens next."

The more I stared at the holoscreen, the more evidence I saw. He was several weeks past due for a haircut, and he'd bitten his nails down to the beds. His shirt, which he typically wore snug across his muscular chest and arms, hung with slack in the material as if he'd missed his last few sessions in the gym.

"He's lost weight in the last month," I continued, "slacked on his personal hygiene, and he smokes cafaco—a stimulant—to stay alert. Maybe he's having trouble sleeping."

DeAjamae nodded. "Insomnia can be a symptom of anxiety."

Wright stepped back, and I suddenly felt chilled in the absence of his body heat. "All right, I'll bite. Barros is feeling stressed—not eating, not sleeping, not taking care of himself. Guilt is riding him hard. How do we turn this to our advantage?"

DeAjamae swiveled to face us. "If you were my mother, you'd tell him how proud you were of his important job in the big city, even if it means he only gets home to visit once a year. And then you'd sob dramatically."

"Dirty," I said.

She smirked and shrugged. "I need Exploration Day off, and I'm not taking Big Momma's guilt trip all by myself."

"None of us will be going anywhere if we don't figure out how to get a confession out of Barros," Wright said.

Ravi straightened from where he'd been stooped in front of the screen. "He needs someone he can take his problems to, open up to. Someone who will make the problem go away."

"Less drill sergeant, more father figure," DeAjamae said.

Wright ran his fingers through his hair as he thought on it. "It can't be me. I've burned my bridge with Barros."

Ravi raised his eyebrows. "Me?"

"Sinclair." Wright's head dipped in my direction.

DeAjamae pursed her lips. "Yeah, that tracks."

My heart kicked hard against my chest. "How would that even work?"

"We'll hire you as an interrogation consultant."

DeAjamae's eyes lit up. "That's right! You have all those training certificates in your file."

"Well, yeah," I hedged. "I took the courses when I was prepping for the agent test."

"If he's going to feel guilty talking to anyone, it's going to be you," Ravi added.

"You're our best shot, but I won't ask you to do anything you're uncomfortable with." Wright said. "Do you think you can handle it?"

I thought it over. Hal had conducted most of our formal interrogations while I watched from the observation room, but I'd done plenty of informal ones in my time undercover. Getting informants to talk was how I'd built most of my cases. And true, Sagi had been one of the people who held me captive in the lab, but I could set aside my personal feelings to get the job done.

"Only one way to find out."

My Intell easily bypassed the electronic lock to Room B, and I slipped into the room.

Sagi had fallen asleep slumped forward in his chair. His head rested on his folded arms, a curl of brown hair falling forward to hide his eyes. It was almost hard to believe this was the same man who'd held me down while Doctor Adler shoved needles into my brain.

The first time a suspect had fallen asleep on me in an interrogation room, I'd found it strange, but it happened often enough that it no longer surprised me. Sagi had been keyed up for a while, thinking about what he'd done and if we had enough on him to send him to jail. Given a few minutes to relax, the resulting adrenaline crash left him physically exhausted.

My next move determined how the rest of the interrogation would go. Part of me—a large part—wanted to yell and scream and beat the ever-living shit out of him for his role in Jarrett's death and helping Lourde hold me hostage. But that would only make him shut down further.

"Hey, Sagi."

His head jerked up, blinking in the harsh light. Smudges of pale purple darkened the skin beneath his eyes.

It took a moment before he recognized me. Then his shoulders stiffened. He groaned and covered his face with his hands.

For this to work, I needed his full attention. I shoved the table toward the far wall, causing him to sit up or risk falling over. The metal legs grated against the floor, and I grit my teeth against the void-awful sound. Then I dragged the chair forward so not even empty space served as a barrier between us.

I took a deep, audible breath through my nose and exhaled through my mouth. Again, and again. Slowly, I lowered myself into the chair, positioning myself such that Sagi had an open line to the door. I didn't want him feeling trapped; I wanted him relaxed. Psychologically, a clear escape path should make him more comfortable.

Another deep breath—a little less obvious—and another. Slow and calm. Humans naturally gravitated toward homeostasis, and it didn't take long for Sagi's breathing to mirror my own.

Sagi stared at me in open-mouthed confusion. "What are you doing here?" He glanced around the interrogation room. "Do—do they know you're in here?"

"Agent Wright thought it might be best if you and I had some time to talk—to clear up any misunderstandings before he writes his report."

"Hey, that stuff at the lab. That wasn't my idea. I was just following orders. I told you to stay away, but you didn't listen."

"I know. I'm not here to talk about that." Not yet, anyway. "Why don't we start over? Get to know each other better."

He snorted. "What? Like you wanna grab a beer, or something? Spring me out of here, and I'll buy."

"Let's start with something smaller. Like, what's your dog's name?"

"Huh? You want to talk about my dog?"

"You have one, don't you?"

"What's Jazzy got to do with anything?"

I used my Intell to bring up a holo of the shaggy-haired pooch on the wall console. It was from his cuff that DeAjamae had linked to the system.

"She's cute. Bohn-ri Terrier?"

"Part that, part something else."

"Is she a rescue?"

Sagi's brows furrowed, but that was okay. If I could get him to talk about his dog, it should induce positive emotions that would help transition him out of the state his confrontation with Wright had caused.

"She was a skybridge dog. Used to hang out in one of the park areas, begging for food. One day she followed me to the lifts, and I brought her home."

"Does Jazzy do any tricks?" I already knew she did. He had at least ten thousand holovids of her on his cuff.

"Yeah, she's pretty smart. She can ride a hoverboard by herself. I mean, I have to control it, but she stands on it without help."

With a little prompting, Sagi rattled off a few more of Jazzy's tricks. That was the thing about guilty suspects. They would often talk about anything else if it meant they didn't have to talk about The Thing.

While he rambled on, I watched for nuances in his facial expressions and body language to establish a baseline. I gently nudged the conversation back on track.

"Do you have someone to watch her while you're at work? A dog walker or something?"

"My mom. It's good for them to get out during the day."

"Good for them?"

His knee bounced, and he gnawed at a hangnail before answering. "Mom used to work in the refineries, and the chemicals made her sick. The air is fresher in the skybridge parks, though. Easier to breathe. Walking Jazzy helps. It gets her out of the apartment."

"She lives with you?"

"For now. I'm saving up to get her her own place with a nurse."

"Hmm, that sounds like it would be difficult on a security guard's salary."

I opened a viewscreen with my Intell and searched his holos for ones with a woman and his dog. Several dozen popped up, all with the same dark-haired woman. She looked the right age to be his mother, and they shared the same heavy brows and bright-blue eyes.

"The company's been decent to me. When my boss found out about Mom, he let me pick up extra shifts."

"Your boss. You mean Michael Hitz?"

Sagi's chair squeaked as he shifted and leaned back. Was he distancing himself from the thought of Michael? There was no single behavior—no upward glance or touch to the mouth—that would tell me he was guilty. Instead, I watched for minor changes in his body language indicative of stress.

Finally, Sagi nodded. "Yeah, hey, can I go yet? It's hot in here."

He clearly didn't want to talk about work. I approached from a different angle. "I'll try to hurry this along, but I need you to be honest with me. That's really important, because I can spot a lie a light-year away." I scooted the chair right in front of him, so close that our knees almost touched and I could smell the cafaco on his shirt. "Three days ago, I left the lab with Agent Wright and went to Andaress-4. Have you ever been to Andaress-4?"

He licked his lips and swallowed hard. "I think so. I mean, yeah, sure, on vacation or something."

"Or something?"

"Yeah, it's one of those layover stops, isn't it? People go to see the salt flats."

Interesting. That was almost verbatim what Michael had told Wright. Had they rehearsed their story in the event the authorities ever questioned them?

"Why do you think Agent Wright brought you here?"

"He said something happened to some guy back on his planet, that my company might know something about it. I guess because it's such a big company or something like that." Sagi's eyes drifted toward the door, unable to maintain contact.

Someone did something somewhere. Classic specificity avoidance. Time to disabuse Sagi of that notion.

"*That guy* was Agent Jarrett Viorel, a friend of mine. *Someone* murdered him in his home on Andaress-4 a month ago. Funny, it turns out *you* were on Andaress-4 at the same time."

"I was?" His voice hitched, and his eyes darted to the door.

"You don't remember? Agent Wright has you on a recording in the same neighborhood."

Air wheezed through his nose as his breathing quickened. "Oh, oh, sure. Yeah, you said a month ago, right? I didn't see anything like that."

"Now, Sagi, you and I both know that's not true." I switched the holo of his dog to the one of him in the apartment without his ov-ex hood. Blood spatter covered the front of his shirt and thighs, and his facial features were clear as day. There was no doubt it was him.

His whole body lifted four centimeters as the muscles around his ass clenched. "Shit."

My voice sharpened. "Why were you in Viorel's apartment? Don't lie to me."

He chewed at his thumbnail, his teeth making sharp little snaps as they slid off the nubs. "It was supposed to be a quick break 'n' take. In and out. Michael knew from my background check that I'd done a little time for that as a kid. The guy wasn't even supposed to be home."

"But he was."

"He walked in on us, and then everything happened so fast. Michael said we couldn't leave without the data. I . . . I took him to the bedroom."

My stomach clenched, but I kept my voice soft. I rested my hand gently on his forearm. "What happened in the bedroom?"

Sagi's face pinked as tears welled in the corners of his eyes. His words tumbled out. "We killed him. Shot him in the face. I didn't know, didn't mean to—We were talking. Roughing him up a bit, yeah, sure, okay, but I didn't think Michael would—I thought he was just trying to scare the guy. Then it was over. Just like that. There was nothing I could do. I swear, there was nothing I could do." A great hiccupping sob rolled through his large frame. "What did I do?"

I squeezed his arm. "This is important, Sagi. I need you to tell me who pulled the trigger."

"What does it matter? We were both there."

"It matters, Sagi. Who pulled the trigger?"

He took his time regaining his composure, but when he did, his voice was steadier. "It was Michael, but my hands are just as covered in blood as his."

As if to prove his point, he raised his hands and stared at his open palms.

"Sagi. Sagi, look at me." His head slowly lifted, revealing watery blue eyes open so wide I could see the whites all the way around them. "Why were you in Viorel's apartment? Who told you and Michael to go there?"

His lips pressed into a thin line as he shook his head. "No, no, I can't say."

"Why can't you?"

"If I tell you, he won't help her!"

"Her? Your mom? Who won't help your mom?"

Tears made his eyes shine like glass, but he shook his head.

I pulled a more recent holo of his mother—one where her body looked frail, but her spirit still shone strong. "Does your mom know about—"

"No! She's got nothing to do with this. I just needed the extra credits to cover her treatments. We'd already gone through her savings."

The woman in the holo wore a soft sweater—possibly for the extra warmth or possibly to hide her thinning frame. She had a kind smile, gentle crow's feet, and laugh lines at the creases of her mouth. She looked like a nice person. I took a gamble.

"No one's blaming your mom, but would she accept the help if she knew what you had to do to get it?"

Sagi stared at the holo, and suddenly his twenty-two years looked much younger than his cocky persona usually led you to believe.

"He said the stuff he was working on had the potential to cure her, that machines could take over when her body failed. If I helped him, he promised to get her into the early trials, and he gave me a bonus for the extra time."

"Who?" I knew who the slime bucket was, but I needed Sagi to say it.

"Doc. Doctor Lourde."

"How did you help him?"

"Nothing big at first. Running errands. Making deliveries and pickups in a few shadier areas of the city. After a while I helped out in the lab. A few of the volunteers tried to leave early and Doc told me to 'persuade' them to stay so the trial wouldn't be ruined. Then some guy had hacked into Doc's system and stole documents showing payments made to members of the IBMD. If it got out, the whole program would get shut down, including the parts that could help my mom. We were supposed to destroy the files. I'm sure Doc never meant for anybody to get hurt. That was all Michael." Near the end, he'd started shaking his head back and forth, his body unwilling to go with along with the lie.

"It didn't concern you?" I asked. "That Doctor Lourde was paying off the Board?"

"He said that was how big business was done. I never—I mean, I didn't do well in school. Doc, he's real smart. If he says that's how it's done, then that must be how it is."

"What he did was illegal. He paid off someone at the IBMD, because the Insight isn't safe. Some recipients reject the neural implants and die."

"I don't believe you."

"Sagi, you know it's true. You saw the test subjects who were there before me. None of them made it out alive. How can you be positive that Doctor Lourde didn't order Michael to kill Agent Viorel?"

He shook his head vehemently. "Doc only wants to help people."

"What about the subjects who were there before me? What about Fax? What did Lourde do with him after I left?"

"I . . . I don't know. Michael told me to move him to the forty-ninth floor right before that DECA agent arrived. Fax started screaming as soon as we got on the lift. I got him to the room, and Doctor Adler gave him a shot with a med dispenser that knocked him out. That's the last time I saw him."

My stomach clenched, remembering my first experience outside the shielded walls of Doctor Lourde's lab. It had been disorienting and excruciatingly painful.

I stuffed my feelings down deep so I wouldn't lose my shit on him. "Sagi, listen closely because this is important, okay? It's your face on that holo. At a minimum, Agent Wright has you on accessory to murder. That's thirty to forty years in prison on Andaress-4, if you're lucky; life, if you're not. You've got one chance to get ahead of this thing. You'll do time no matter what, but if you give Agent Wright something he can work with, like information on someone higher up the food chain, he might put in a good word for you with the city attorney." I changed the holo again, this time to one of Jarrett's tortured body the forensic techs had taken before sending him to the morgue. "Come on, give me something. Who ordered the hit on Jarrett Viorel?"

Sagi stared at the holo, transfixed. "I was making my rounds like normal. It was the start of my shift. Doc was in his office, and I overheard him talking about a security breach. I slowed down to listen in, because nobody'd filled me in about any problems. Doc told the other guy we'd been hacked, and the project was in danger. The other guy was furious and yelling. He said there were too many credits on the line to stop now and he wanted a permanent solution to the problem. Then he left. I ducked into the med bay so he wouldn't see me. When I came out, Michael and Doc were in the hallway. Michael told me to go home and pack an overnight bag because we had a special assignment. I didn't realize what he meant by a permanent solution until it was too late." He dragged a knuckle under his eyes. "I'm so stupid."

"Who was the other man?"

Sagi trembled from head to toe. "You're sure they'll take me to Andaress-4? I won't go to prison here?"

I nodded. "A cruiser is sitting at the spacedock, waiting to take you back."

"It was Mr. Tazza. Mr. Aurelian Tazza."

After he said it, relief visibly washed over him—and over me. We got it. DeAjamae could send the recording back to the judge in Salin, and we could get warrants for Kandall Lourde and Aurelian Tazza.

Everyone who had a hand in Jarrett's murder would be brought to justice.

The door opened, and Wright walked in. He hooked his thumb toward the door.

"Mr. Barros," he said, taking my seat in front of Sagi. "I'd like to go over a few more details with you."

Chapter 32

I GLANCED AT SAGI one last time before exiting the room. He still wouldn't meet Wright's eyes, but his back was straighter, and his shoulders had relaxed as if a great burden had been lifted from them. Letting go of secrets could be funny that way.

The door closed behind me, leaving me alone in the empty hallway. I sagged against the wall, closed my eyes, and blew out a shaky breath.

We got it. We got the confession.

A notification from my Intell flashed, alerting me that the hallway camera had activated. Probably DeAjamae checking on me. I pushed myself off the wall and waved at the lens, then double-timed it back to the viewing room. DeAjamae and Ravi stood in front of the consoles, eyes glued to the screens.

Ravi greeted me first. "Way to go, Reliance!"

DeAjamae's pink curls bobbed up and down. "That was awesome. The only thing missing was popcorn."

"Do you think it's enough to get arrest warrants for both Aurelian Tazza and Doctor Lourde?"

"Filling out the paperwork now," DeAjamae said. "The judge won't be thrilled with a civilian conducting the interrogation, but the recording is good. We'll have to wait and see. It's early afternoon there, so hopefully we'll get a response soon."

"Can you add in a separate search for my friend Fax?"

She shook her head. "Barros didn't say anything that could give us jurisdiction, but if we see him there and he tells us he wants to leave, we can help."

I pursed my lips but nodded. The warrant would give us permission to search the lab, and Fax had to be there. There was nowhere else to put him.

"What happened with Michael?" I asked.

Ravi grimaced. "He demanded an attorney. Tazza Industries is sending an overpaid suit as we speak."

"So Aurelian Tazza knows we're here."

"Afraid so."

We needed as much evidence against Tazza Industries as we could get to bolster the warrant requests. I'd thought about Sagi's confession and had an idea about what was on Jarrett's encrypted files.

"How much do you want to bet that Jarrett found proof that Lourde or Tazza bribed someone at the Interplanetary Board of Medical Devices? It's the only thing he would have taken such measures to protect."

"That would make sense," Ravi said. "They would have destroyed it the second they got their hands on it."

DeAjamae scowled. "I still haven't been able to hack into it. I need dedicated time to work on it, but I've been a little busy."

"How about letting me take a crack at it?" I pointed at my head and then made woo-woo magic fingers at it.

DeAjamae shared a look with Ravi and shrugged. "Well, we do have a legal right to access the information, and Wright did hire you as an official consultant."

"I say go for it," Ravi agreed.

"Just don't manipulate any of the data once you unlock it, okay? Let me take it from there."

"You got it." I located the problematic files in the sandbox on her portable console and set my Intell's decryption program loose on them. DeAjamae looked at me expectantly. "This could take a little while. I don't exactly know what I'm doing."

"Oh, sure, of course. I'll keep working on these forms."

Ravi moved his chair over beside her. "Let me give you a hand with that."

Their shoulders almost-but-not-quite touched as they huddled in front of the holoscreens together, discussing word choice and which areas of the interview to highlight.

My eyes shut, blocking out the light. Minutes passed. The space between my temples throbbed in time with my heartbeat. I'd felt the beginnings of a headache as soon as we landed in Tylo. Not only was the city densely populated, but a conglomerate of tech companies founded it. If it ran on electricity, emitted a signal, or connected to the net, the people of Tylo had embraced it with an unabashed fervor.

So far, I'd handled the influx of information, but something about running the special hacking software made my Intell run hot. Hopefully not literally, because I didn't relish the idea of slow-cooked brain stew. Running the program taxed me physically, though, and the side effects worsened once Lourde's medication had worked its way out of my system—headaches, light sensitivity, nausea, dizziness, and a sort of high-pitched whining sound that no one else heard.

A new viewscreen popped up and flashed bright green. Decryption key identified.

I sat up so fast my head spun.

"You okay?" Ravi handed me a tissue and tapped at his nose. "You have a little . . ."

I blotted my nose with a tissue. It came away smeared red with blood, and I added nosebleeds to the list. "Thanks. The Intell found something."

"Yeah?" DeAjamae spun around from the consoles.

"I'm sending over the master decryption key now." Focusing took some effort, but I pushed the key to her cuff.

"Hunh. That's what it needed? But that doesn't make any sense." She made a wide swiping motion, clearing the screen in front of her, and brought up a single new program. A few flicks of her fingers, and she was lost in her task. Her voice dropped to a low mumble as she argued with the console. "No, I didn't tell you to do that. Over there. No, no. Right there. Right. There. Why are you not doing the fucking thing I told you to do?"

I relaxed as my neural implant shut down the decryption program on its own. My head ached, and DeAjamae could handle the rest.

"Thirsty?" Ravi tossed a cold hydration pouch into my hand.

"Thanks."

The water had a faint metallic taste from the packaging but was cool and the electrolytes gave me a much-needed boost. I heaved myself to my feet and dropped the empty pouch and bloody tissue into the reclamator.

Behind me, DeAjamae continued to berate her console. "Shit. Why aren't you highlighting? Yes! Finally. Fuck. Why was that so hard? Thingamajig, make a backup copy in case this outdated piece of trash crashes."

"On it, D!" She'd augmented Thingamajig with the cheerful, high-pitched voice of a character from a children's holovid popular about fifteen years ago. I flashed back to Sparkle's tinny voice and cringed.

When I turned back around, Ravi was studying me. "What?" I touched my upper lip to check if my nose was still bleeding. It wasn't.

"Nothing," Ravi said. "Glad you were with us today, is all."

"Got it. Got it!" DeAjamae interrupted, pumping her fist in the air.

On the screen was a comm from a high-ranking member of the Interplanetary Board of Medical Devices. It was too far away to read from my seat at the table, but I made out the words generous, fast-tracked, and approval. Below that was a number ending in a lot of zeros.

"What did you find?" asked Ravi.

"It's a comm from Doctor Benedict Rennali of the IBMD accepting a very hefty donation from KaLo Research on behalf of his own private company, the Rennali Foundation." On a separate console, DeAjamae pulled up the Tylo net and searched for the foundation. "Their mission statement is something vague about helping kids with Engelkirk-Pryzblya disease. I bet if we dig into it, we'll find it's a sham corporation."

"KaLo Research is Doctor Lourde's company," I said. "The one used to pay off my old partner."

"Through another shell company, but essentially, yes. At the very end, Rennali says he's delighted to inform Doctor Lourde that Tazza Industries' new neural implant was fast-tracked for immediate approval and that they waived the requirement for a phase-two trial."

Ravi whistled. "No wonder they didn't want this comm getting out."

"Hopefully the judge agrees this is enough probable cause to get us a search warrant for the premises and arrest warrants for both the good doctor and his boss." DeAjamae attached a copy of the comm to her new warrant request and sent the entire package to Andaress-4 over the subspace relays. "Now we wait."

The door opened, drawing our attention. Wright strode in, unfastened his jacket, and threw it onto the back of a chair. "Report."

Ravi straightened. "Hitz lawyered up. I officially placed him under arrest and had him moved back to a holding cell until we're ready to put him on the cruiser. The suits will probably want to talk to him before we take off. I'll ask that Barros be placed in a separate holding cell."

DeAjamae pulled up the comm she'd found in Jarrett's files and showed it to Wright. "I sent a copy to Salin over subspace and requested search and arrest warrants."

"Excellent work. Ravi, I want you to prepare an update for Tademan, but don't send it until we get the warrants. Ask if she can provide support to secure the perimeter and execute the searches."

"On it."

"DeAjamae, see if you can get a schematic for Tazza Industries' headquarters. I don't want to go in blind. Sinclair, help her fill in any blanks if you can."

She'd barely accessed Tylo's city records department when her workstation beeped, notifying her of an incoming comm. She aerial scribed to the communication program. "That was fast. It's from Judge Xiao's clerk. He caught the judge on recess from a trial. We got the warrants."

Chapter 33

WRIGHT FLEW THE HOVERCART through the fortieth-floor walkway as fast as possible without running over anyone. Officer Boel Tademan refused when Ravi asked her to provide backup, citing limited resources.

I sat in the back seat beside Ravi, staring out at the blur of flashy advertisements plastered over the walls. The sound of the engine cutting off snapped me back to the present, as did the flood of electronic signals that bombarded my Intell. Cuffs, communicators, building maintenance systems—the amount of tech passing in, through, and around Tylo was staggering. Literally.

A wave of vertigo passed over me. Hurriedly, I tacked all of them down, except the one connecting to Tazza Industries' internal network. I hadn't yet figured out how to turn off the automatic search-and run-setting on my Intell's hacking program, but seeing as how this was the company that had developed it, I felt zero qualms letting it do what they designed it to do.

The hovercart's landing feet barely extended before Wright, Ravi, and DeAjamae jumped out of their seats. DeAjamae rummaged in her backpack and pulled out four palm-sized surveillance drones. She pressed a button on each of their backs, activating their dragonfly-like wings.

"Thingamajig," she instructed her cuff, "pair drone navigation controls to Wright, Singh, and Sinclair. Set to record." The drones took up position behind our shoulders. She swiped her hand over her jacket sleeve's transparency panel and activated the holoscreen on her cuff. A window opened, showing live feeds coming from each drone. She nodded to Wright. "Good to go."

We strode through the floor-to-ceiling plastiglass doors of the lobby with drones in tow. I fell into step beside Ravi. His naturally gregarious face was as hard and cold as the marble slabs beneath my feet.

The male receptionist with the braided black hair was working again. He stepped from behind his desk to block our path to the elevators.

"May I be of assistance, officers?" His smile faltered as his eyes passed over the green uniforms until finally resting on me. Recognition passed over his face. "This woman is barred from Tazza Industries' properties. I must insist that you leave."

"She's with us," Wright said, not even slowing down as he shouldered past the man.

I glanced at his name tag. Endicott. Right.

A few quick aerial scribes by DeAjamae brought up an image of the search and arrest warrants on her holoscreen. She wasn't shy about the magnification, either. With a flick of her wrist, she transferred a copy to the large holoscreen behind the reception desk.

Customers waiting in line craned their necks for a better look and murmured among themselves. The other two receptionists scrambled to take it down.

My Intell picked up a comm from Endicott calling security, but we were already past him and crowding into the lift. Another comm pinged as the door slid shut. I looked directly at the notification and tapped my middle finger twice to open it.

"The receptionist warned Lourde and Tazza that we are coming for them," I said, paraphrasing the brief message.

Ravi looked to Wright. "Which floor?"

"Sinclair, best guess as to their location?"

"Best guess or best *educated* guess?" I asked.

His right eye narrowed but didn't quite twitch. "Educated guess."

Since the Intell had already tapped into the building's network, I pulled up the program that would show me the security feeds. It was the same program the lab used, but with a bunch more cameras and sensors.

A spike of pain lanced through my right eye as dozens of viewscreens popped open all at once, flooding my vision. I swayed at the sudden loss of my surroundings until a firm hand at my elbow steadied me.

"You all right?" Wright asked.

I nodded sharply to show I was okay. "Just give me a second."

Scanning over the camera feeds, I tapped my index finger on my thumb to close each one that didn't contain the information I needed. "There. Aurelian Tazza is in his office on the top floor. There's a camera pointed at his assistant's desk. I can see him through the door. It looks like he's packing his things. He's going to run."

"What about Lourde?" Ravi asked.

I flicked through the screens, searching for the little weasel's face, but not finding it. "If he's here, he must be in his lab on the forty-seventh floor. It's self-contained. The cameras there aren't tied to the main system."

Wright rubbed a hand across his jaw. "Floors forty-seven and fifty-three," he instructed the lift.

"Singh. You and I will take Tazza. Leahy and Sinclair go to the lab. Take Lourde into custody if he's there. If he's not, execute the search warrant and make sure nothing is removed or destroyed. I want anything we can tie back to the murder taken with us. The warrant doesn't cover bionic weapons, but document anything in plain view."

"Yes, sir." "Yes, sir." "Aye, sir," we acknowledged in unison, my Clava protocols differing slightly from theirs.

"I want check-ins every ten minutes. If your comms aren't getting through, get your ass out to this lift and make contact. Am I clear?"

"Yes, sir," DeAjamae said. "Everyone's comm should be set to channel seven-sierra-foxtrot. It's secure."

The doors opened. We moved into the small antechamber. She and I stepped out, leaving the guys to continue up to the top floor.

"The Intell doesn't work on the lab doors," I said.

"No problem. I got this."

She went straight to the locked door reader. Her cuff linked, and she entered the override command granted to us via the warrant. It beeped, then blinked red. Her finely sculpted brows drew together. She reentered the command code. The light remained red.

"Jackass. Why are you not doing the thing I told you to do?" She swung the backpack from her shoulders, dug out a green cable, and used it to connect the reader to a port on the side of her cuff. "You have one job. Do the fucking job."

I reached out with my Intell, but the same firewall that prevented me from leaving also kept me from entering.

"Anytime," I prodded. "We're losing the element of surprise here."

"Working on it." DeAjamae's lips moved silently as her fingers flew across her holoscreen.

The light blinked to blue.

"Good job," I said.

"I didn't do anything yet."

The door opened with a gentle whoosh. A young man with a crop of florescent orange and green spiky hair rushed through. He carried a large box filled with electronic equipment. His head twisted behind him, shouting to an unseen person at the end of the hallway.

"I'll be right back, I'm going to dump these in the incine—" He ran into DeAjamae, crushing the box between them. His eyes widened at the badge hanging from a chain around her neck. "—rator. Oh, sorry, um, Officer . . ."

"*Agent* Leahy of the Andaress-4 Department of Enforcement of Criminal Affairs. Let's take this back inside, shall we?"

Carrot-top clutched the crumpled box to his chest. "I was taking this out. My boss wants me to—"

DeAjamae glared down at him. She stood half a head taller than him, not even counting the extra centimeters her mass of pink and brown hair added. "I wasn't asking."

His face paled, and he peddled backward into the hall. "Right. Yeah. Okay."

As soon as the door shut behind us, the shielding built into the walls cut off the barrage of signals pinging my Intell. There were a couple of sources still active on the floor, but the levels were nothing compared to outside. My spine straightened, as if a heavy pack had fallen from my shoulders. It felt like breaking through a planet's thermosphere into weightlessness, but my relief was short-lived.

The entire floor was in slash-and-burn mode. It was clear they'd been at it for a while. Someone had tipped them off that we were coming much sooner than the receptionist's hasty warning. My bet was on Officer Boel Tademan. She'd been giving us nothing but roadblocks since we arrived.

To my left, the lab had been emptied. The experimental bionic limbs and parts were gone. Rows and rows of cages sat empty, doors open. All except one. In it lay a mound of furry bodies. Their wires and tiny artificial limbs had been removed and discarded. Thoughts of Walnut's twitchy little nose and tiny pink feet flashed through my head, and I was glad he was safe on the *Soteria* with Felix watching over him.

DeAjamae ushered the employee to a bench in the lab and told him to sit. He sucked in a breath as if to yell to his coworkers. DeAjamae held her finger to her lips in a shushing motion and tapped a poison-green fingernail against her blaster. He slumped back down without a word.

"Hey," she said, tossing me a pair of restraints from her bag. "You remember how to use these?"

I caught them in midair. "Not something you really forget."

"Remove his cuff and secure him to the table."

A quick pat down didn't turn up any weapons or tools he could use to escape. I secured his arms around the table leg, which was bolted to the floor, then unfastened his cuff from his forearm and tossed it to DeAjamae. She popped it into an evidence bag and set it on the counter.

We walked into the hall where we heard two people talking at the far end. I gave her a quick layout of the floor.

"The left side is where all the work is done: experiments lab, rehab gym, and med bay. On the right is a community space for the patients with two rooms on either side. No windows. The door to the emergency stairwell is locked."

"Stay behind me. We'll secure the ones in the med bay, then search the rest of the floor." She handed me a stack of four more restraints.

I nodded. "Watch your blaster setting. My friend might still be here. He's old, and they haven't taken good care of him."

We hurried down the hall, letting the drones scan the empty gym and patient lobby before moving past them. As we neared the med bay door, we heard the soft whirring of a disk eraser. It was punctuated by the shrill screeching of metal being ripped apart by a shredder.

"Fuck." DeAjamae powered up her blaster until I heard the familiar soft whine of a full charge and rushed into the room. "D-E-C-A. Hands where I can see them."

Two people looked up in surprise. The woman—midfifties, a little soft in the middle region, with shoulder-length, cotton-candy hair—dropped the strip of data dots she had been feeding into the disk eraser and shot her hands up over head. The man—late twenties, stocky build, with a bald scalp and twin ridges of body modifications extending back from his forehead—panicked and bolted for the exit. Unfortunately, the only door was the one we currently occupied.

I braced for impact, lowering my center of gravity and readying my hands to tackle him as he passed.

DeAjamae had other ideas. She squeezed off a shot, hitting him in the right shoulder. He cried out, clutching his injured joint.

"Did I say run? No, I don't think so. I said put your freakin' hands up." She marched over to him. "Dumbass. Now why did you go and make me discharge my weapon? Do you know how many forms I'm going to have to fill out? Effing pain in the ass."

I snapped the restraints on the woman, who didn't put up a fight. "Does he need medical attention?"

DeAjamae poked around his shoulder with her fingernail. He didn't flinch, but he did a fantastic impression of a skulking dragon. His body mods rose from dull mounds to sharp peaks—responding to the flux of chemicals his body was dumping. They were nicknamed mood mods, although most users didn't put them on their heads.

"No, my blaster was on low. Didn't even blister the skin."

"It still fucking hurt," the man snarled.

"Don't worry, big fella. The stinging will pass in a minute."

DeAjamae frisked him, removed a small pocketknife and his cuff, and secured him to a medical bed rail. She spotted the restraint straps already there and quirked an eyebrow at me.

"Like I said, I wasn't here voluntarily."

DeAjamae tossed me another pair of restraints. I followed her lead and steered the female employee toward the next bed. For the first time, she resisted, digging her heels in, and pushing back against me. It took exerting extra leverage against her shoulder joint to gain her compliance. Once on the bed, she scooted to the end as far as the restraint allowed. As I stepped closer, I saw what had her so freaked out.

"Agent Leahy, you better look at this."

"What is it?" she asked, coming up beside me.

"Blood, and it looks fresh." I tried to swallow the lump in my throat but found my mouth had gone bone dry. "This is Fax's station."

"Okay, don't jump to any conclusions. It's not that much blood, and this is their medical bay. He could have cut himself. This might not even be his blood."

I rounded on the woman. "Where is he? Where is Fax?!"

"Wh-who?"

"Subject C."

Her faced flushed, bringing it dangerously close to matching the shade of her hair. "He ... I ... Well, Doctor Lourde said the subject was in so much pain. It was the humane thing to do."

"No. You're lying."

"Bastard son of a sow," DeAjamae muttered under her breath. "Go. I'll finish up here."

I sprinted to the hall.

"Fax!"

Two seconds and I'd crossed into the common room. It was lit only by a dim strip of blue lighting ringing the ceiling. A thin trail of blood drops led to Fax's door, where a soft light glowed around the edges. I hurried, weaving between the couch and stiff-backed chairs, and threw open his door.

A soft, "No," escaped my lips as the air rushed from my lungs. It felt as if I'd been sucker-punched in the diaphragm. My knees jellied as I closed the distance between us, and I gripped the edge of his bed to keep from collapsing.

Fax's body lay in what should have been an uncomfortable position—torso bent at the waist, arms akimbo, and an emaciated leg dangling over the edge. One pant leg was scrunched up to his knobby knee and the grippy-soled sock on his foot was twisted halfway around. It was undignified, and he would have hated it.

His face was turned toward the door, as if he'd been waiting for me. The assholes hadn't even had the decency to shut his eyes.

Only years of working crime scenes kept me from reaching out to him, from holding his hand one last time. Instead, I forced myself to breathe through the pain and analyze the scene.

Bright-red blood soaked the pillow beneath his head. They'd killed him recently—probably when they got the tipoff that we were executing the arrest warrant. That matched what the female employee told us. With Adler already arrested for attempted homicide, Michael and Sagi in custody, and Tazza and Lourde on the run, there wasn't anyone else intimate enough with the program left to keep it running, even in the short-term. Fax was a liability, a loose end. Disposable.

I only hoped that they had ended his life before removing the Intell chip from his brain stem. They hadn't been neat about it.

Tears burned the back of my eyes, and my jaw quivered with the effort of holding them in. "I'm sorry, my friend. I failed you, too."

He'd died without seeing the sky again, and now he never would. Gently, I reached over and closed his eyes. Protocol be damned.

Rubbing a knuckle across the corner of my eye, I turned to leave. There was nothing more I could do for Fax here, but I could make damn sure the people responsible for his and Jarrett's deaths answered for their crimes.

I sucked in a quaking breath to steady my traitorous legs. There would be time to grieve later.

My return to the med bay was slower than my exit. DeAjamae looked up from behind the holographic imaging bed when I entered. She had two screens running, despite a panel being removed from the side and wires spilling out like disemboweled guts. Carrot-top sat on the third bed, staring at his shoes.

"Your friend?"

I shook my head. "What have you learned?"

She gave me a sympathetic look, then hooked her thumb toward the employee she'd brought down from the other end of the hall. "Not a whole hell of a lot. Billy here says we just missed Lourde. He removed the hard drives from several of the consoles and gave the order to destroy the rest. I shut down one disk eraser, but there's a second still going."

I rounded on Billy. "Where is Lourde now?"

His already pale face blanched even further. "I don't know."

"Think harder."

"Uh, maybe he said something about getting the backup files?"

"And where are those kept?"

"In the data storage room."

"Which floor?" Impatience lent a harsh bite to my words.

Billy shrank down until his ears touched his shoulders. "Forty-one."

I turned back to DeAjamae, who held a twisted hunk of metal up to the light and squinted at it. "That's only six floors down. Let's go."

She dropped the piece like it offended her. "No, we need to give Wright an update, and I have to kill this disk eraser, or it'll eat through whatever is left in here. They've already destroyed half the electronic files—possibly more. I don't know what I can salvage. Ask Wright how he wants us to proceed."

"But we should—"

"Look, arresting Lourde won't do any good if we don't have the evidence to make the charges stick. Report back to Wright. It's his call."

"Copy that."

I raced down the hall with the drone flying after me. The door still wouldn't open, so I lifted the evidence bag with Carrot-top's cuff from the counter and used my Intell to hack into the cuff. A moment later, the door to the lift antechamber opened. Once again, a myriad of signals from the building's network hit me hard. I wasted precious seconds sorting through them until I found a security feed showing me Doctor Lourde. It was only the back of his head, but I'd recognize his frizzy, scraggly hair and stooped shoulders anywhere.

I opened my comms to channel 7SF. "Wright, this is Sinclair."

The sound of rushing wind filled my ear, then Wright's voice came over the connection. He was practically shouting to be heard over the background noise. "Wright, here. Report."

"Lourde isn't in the lab. We found three employees destroying evidence. One civilian dead on arrival. Agent Leahy has the employees under restraint and is attempting to stop any further loss of data."

"Any leads on Lourde's whereabouts?"

"One employee talked. I verified Lourde is on the forty-first floor using the building's internal security system."

There were some muffled words I didn't catch. "Wright? Can you repeat?"

His voice came back stronger, but I could barely hear him over the revving of a ship's engine.

"We're on the roof now. Tazza has a private dock up here with a fox hunter class ship. If he takes off, he'll be out of the system before we get back to the spacedock. Tazza is the bigger fish. Go back and help Leahy secure the lab."

"Let me go after Lourde." Images of Jarrett's tortured body and Fax's lifeless eyes invaded my mind. "He has to answer for his crimes."

"No, it's too dangerous without a partner. If something goes wrong, you won't have backup."

"Please, we've gotten this far. Don't let him get away with murder."

There was a long pause, then, "Reliance Sinclair, under the Department of Enforcement of Criminal Affairs statute 42.07(b), I grant you emergency officer status for the apprehension of Kandall Lourde. Go, and don't make me regret this."

Chapter 34

THE FORTY-FIRST FLOOR WAS an empty, nondescript warren of offices. Scuffed paint, harsh lighting, and outdated art on the walls were a stark contrast to the glossy, plastiglass partitions and high-tech equipment of the lab. This floor wasn't for clients or high-paid execs; it was for the data-pushers and worker bees that kept every company chugging along.

A quick scan of the security feeds didn't reveal Lourde, but there were plenty of blind spots among the maze of offices to exploit, especially for a man with his own neural implant. I needed to find him before he got out of the building.

Carrot-top thought Lourde was in the data storage room. I looked down and to the left, activating voice controls on my Intell. "Access program Minotaur. Find building schematics."

A set of architectural plans popped up. I opened the file for the forty-first floor and tried not to trip while walking and reading at the same time.

"Set to transparency mode and overlay my coordinates." A pulsing dot appeared on the map. "Plot the fastest course to the data storage room."

A line appeared, running from my current location to an interior room near the center of the building. I took off at a fast jog.

The hallway started off relatively empty, but soon the familiar dings of comm notifications drifted out of every office door. Chatter rose and employees stuck their heads out, jerking back as I ran past. Word of DECA's presence at the company was making the gossip rounds, and every excited message sent a notification to my Intell. My ears rang with pings only I could hear.

It took a minute and a half to zigzag my way through the connecting halls to the data storage room. An electronic lock barred access, but it wasn't kitted with the same protection measures as the door readers in the lab. I stared at the palm-sized reader until my Intell latched onto it. A tendril of pain wrapped itself around the back of my eyes, causing one eye to water in the corner. Within seconds the light turned blue, and the pressure eased.

Cool air smelling faintly of ozone rushed out as the door opened, and a bank of overhead lights blinked on. Four rows of floor-to-ceiling racks of computer equipment filled the space. Thick ropes of tightly bound cables snaked from the machines over the floor, where they plugged into the wall.

No Doctor Lourde, but I found a conspicuously empty slot in one of the server racks. Disconnected cables dangled out the front, like something had been yanked out in a hurry. Likely he'd been here already and removed the entire device with his backup files rather than spending time to transfer them to smaller disks.

I ducked out of the room, wishing I knew how to reprogram the door reader so that only DeAjamae had access, in case I was wrong and the files were still there.

Lourde had a head start on me. He had to assume that we'd be watching the lifts and main exits. That left the roof—which Wright and Ravi had covered—and the emergency stairwells as his only options.

I enlarged the window with the schematics, laying one hand on the wall for balance as another wave of dizziness swept through me. The closest stairwell ran down the eastern side of the building.

"Plot the fastest course to Stairwell J."

The directional line flashed on. I took off running, rounded the first corner, and bumped into a personal hoverchair parked outside an office door. Cursing, I shrank the map so I could better see where I was going.

A man saw me coming and stopped smack-dab in the middle of the aisle to gawk.

"Move!" I motioned to the left as I veered right. He stumbled against the wall as I shouldered past him.

I wound around several more corners before reaching the outer wall of the building. Anti-radiation tinting turned the sunlight streaming through into a soft bronze. From there, it was a straight shot to a door marked STAIRWELL J where my location dot merged with my destination dot. I pushed through the door.

The temperature inside the stairwell was easily ten degrees warmer than the climate-controlled main areas. The air was stale, dry, and smelled like feet.

I paused, listening. From far below came the steady *clap-clap-clap* of dress shoes on cement.

My heart leaped, a surge of adrenaline slamming it against my rib cage.

The door swung shut with a loud bang. Below, the footsteps stopped, then resumed at a faster pace.

I took the stairs two at a time, angling my body so the balls of my feet found firmer purchase on the narrow steps. Friction from the handrail burned my hand as I used it to slingshot myself around the landing and down to the next flight.

DeAjamae's drone still flew beside me. The controls weren't easy to manipulate while running, but I managed to send it ahead of me and bring up the viewscreen from its live feed without breaking my neck falling down the stairs.

Ten floors down, it reached a portly, middle-aged man with thinning hair huffing his way past the thirtieth floor. Slung over his shoulder was a large cloth bag.

He glanced up as the drone buzzed him, and I got a clear shot of his face.

"Open group channel," I huffed out between jarring steps. Man, my knees hurt. "Suspect located in Stairwell J heading down. In pursuit." Then I set the drone to auto-follow Lourde.

He tried briefly to wrest control of the drone from me, but my Intell was quick to shut him down. If we'd been in the lab, it may have been a different story, but he was distracted and running scared, and that worked in my favor.

Floor thirty-nine, thirty-eight, thirty-seven. They came and went much faster than when I'd climbed them to break into the lab. That felt like a lifetime and a half ago.

"Give it up, Lourde!"

A clattering noise was his only response. It sounded louder, closer. I was gaining on him.

Round and round we descended. I let gravity help where it could, jumping the last three, sometimes four steps of every flight. My knees and ankles ached from the awkward angle and abrupt landings.

As I reached the twenty-third floor, a door creaked open below me, sending a gust of even hotter air swirling up the shaft. Outside air? He was still seventy meters off the ground!

I checked the live feed coming from the drone. It hovered in the stairwell, a large sign with a bold number 20 visible behind it. My wrist rotated, causing the drone to spin in a slow circle. Lourde was gone, but at the 180-degree mark, a second door came into view. It was labeled, "LOW ALTITUDE VEHICLE PARKING."

Shit.

A commuter lot. And he'd ditched the drone by locking it in the stairwell.

"Open the group channel. Suspect in LAV lot on the twentieth floor."

Wright responded immediately. "Wait for backup. Ravi can meet you in five minutes."

Five minutes! Was he insane? "I'll be happy when he gets here, but we don't have five minutes. I'm continuing pursuit."

By then, I'd made it to the twentieth floor. I reset the drone to follow me and held the door for it to fly through after me.

Strong winds buffeted me from the side. The lot had screens at the edges to block sand from blowing in, but some made it through anyway. It drifted into ankle-deep piles along the wall and at the base of every support pillar, and a thin, red layer coated every vehicle.

I jogged out, listening and scanning for signs of movement. About fifty paces down, another door opened. A woman stepped out, holding the edges of her jacket together. She bent into the wind and walked to a jet-black hoverbike in the third row. She removed a helmet from the saddlebag and threw one leg over the bike.

Dismissing her, I kept going, eyes darting under and between vehicles. Two rows over, an engine rumbled. I darted across the aisle in time to see Lourde's profile before a powder-blue, gullwing door lowered shut. The ground vibrated as his LAV powered up. Twin thrusters with flashy black covers rotated into takeoff position and fired, lifting the craft half a meter into the air so the landing gear could retract.

He looked out the window and our eyes made contact.

"Get out of the vehicle!" I shouted. Not that he could have heard me.

Lourde pulled back on the joystick. The LAV rose and swung out into the aisle.

"Shit. Shit, shit, shit, shit, shit." Why couldn't I have gotten here two minutes sooner?

I closed the rest of the distance and leaped. My fingers latched onto the step bar—now half a meter over my head—and held on as my weight caused the LAV to list dramatically to one side.

Lourde spun the ship in a tight circle. Centrifugal force flung my legs out from under me, and before I could haul myself up onto the bar, my thighs and ass crashed into the cockpit of a parked family-sized LAV.

Stars exploded across my vision. Plastiglass cracked beneath me. A high-pitched alarm sounded. My fingers slipped from the step bar, and I flopped to the ground like a sack of mycoprotein powder.

I rose to my hands and knees as Lourde accelerated, expelling a cloud of sulphuric sinnafuel fumes. Coughing, I climbed to my feet, using the side of the damaged LAV for support.

My Intell flashed a notice of an incoming audio comm on the group channel.

"Status update," Wright requested.

"Suspect is in a personal LAV. Light blue, quad occupancy, black after-market thruster covers. He exited the garage and is heading toward the city center."

"He'll be trying for the spacedock. I don't have authority with Tylo Central Command to get flights grounded. I'll request Officer Tademan have a transpo vehicle meet you in the parking lot."

I limped toward the exit, rubbing a hand over my right hip where it smarted. Lourde was slipping away from me. I could feel it. Even if she agreed to it, Tademan would probably insist on bringing in a requisitioned LAV from the DECA office with all the forms properly filled out, signed, and witnessed by an authorized officer. By that time, Lourde wouldn't only be off the planet, he'd be halfway across the Brione system.

My stomach turned at the thought. Or maybe it was the headache catching up to me.

The woman with the hoverbike pulled her helmet off and ran toward me, waving her arms. "Oh my stars, are you okay? I saw that man fly into you. Do you need me to call for help?"

I looked from the woman to her hoverbike and smiled. "Wright, never mind the transpo. I have a better idea." Then I turned to the woman. "Ma'am, I'm going to need to commandeer your bike."

Chapter 35

THE BLOWING SAND WAS fine up here—more of a powder, really, creating a rusty haze that grew murkier the farther down I looked. I made out the glow of advertising signs on the ground level. More signs clustered around each skybridge, creating a striped pattern of lights across the city buildings. In between those were four levels of skylanes transporting tired commuters home from work.

DeAjamae's drone flew high overhead around the fortieth-floor level, transmitting a bird's-eye view of traffic directly to my Intell. Tylo was laid out like a wheel with the spacedock at the center. A series of concentric rings expanded outward with eight straight spokes connecting them. Tazza Center was in a posh business district along one of the middle rings. It was the heart of rush hour and high winds pushed pilots into the upper skylane tiers to avoid damage to their LAVs caused by swirling sand. Airspace in the ring was nose to tail vehicles.

My borrowed helmet's visual display created a weird double image with input I received from my implant, so I shut it off. Beneath me, the hoverbike purred. She was as tricked out as a bike could be. A real beaut. Sleek lines, upgraded suspension, and a hell of a kick out of the starting gate. I shouldn't have expected anything less from an employee of Tazza Industries. High-tech was their business.

I wasted precious seconds picking out four blue LAVs within my search perimeter, then zeroed in on the one with the flashy black thruster covers. It darted off the main airway onto a side lane, but not before I locked the drone to its signal.

If Officer Tademan had provided us any resources, I'd have set up a perimeter to block Lourde in. We'd either flush him out or search building by building until we found him. Since that wasn't an option, I would have to track him down myself and hope the team caught up.

"Suspect heading southwest on Sunset," I reported after checking a map I'd accessed on Tylo's city net. Sunset was one of the main spokes with a direct east–west path to the spacedock.

I hit the throttle and wobbled at the sudden jolt. It was my first time piloting since getting the neural implant, and having the control visuals on my eye versus on the visor took some getting used to. The bike growled as I slid into the third tier of skylane traffic. I blasted around a bulky delivery vehicle only to pull up hard seconds later when three LAVs camped out across the entire lane from building to building preventing anyone from going past them. Horns blared behind me, but they did nothing to encourage the LAVs to higher speeds.

Swearing, I dropped to the second tier skylane where I could fly faster. The hoverbike sputtered as fine grains of sand were sucked into the engine, but it sprang forward when I asked for more speed.

Visibility became limited the closer to the ground I flew. Two-hundred-meter buildings turned into nothing but neon blurs on either side.

Like a shark, I cut through the deep, searching for my target's silhouette against the lighter sky. The drone kept pace far above, my shadow a bare ripple to its mechanical eye. I used its feed to track Lourde's position in relation to mine. He was five blocks ahead, moving at a good clip but not flying recklessly—perhaps trying not to draw attention to himself. Twice he slowed as if preparing to turn off, but sped back up to the speed of traffic at the last minute. At this rate, he'd make it to the spacedock in less than ten minutes.

I leaned forward over the energy cells, flattening my torso against the bike to reduce wind drag. One by one, I passed the LAVs above me.

"What the—"

A holovid sign popped out of nowhere. I braked hard and swerved left, almost smashing into it.

The closer we got to the city center, the narrower the space between buildings became. Unwittingly, I'd drifted too close to the building on my right, and the sign's flashing lights only cut through the sand the last four or five meters. Half my vision being blocked with maps and camera feeds didn't help.

Righting myself, I twisted back hard on the throttle to make up time. The bike responded with an enthusiastic growl. Each cross path came progressively faster as the rings got smaller and smaller. As the traffic above me slowed to allow for merging vehicles, I steadily closed the distance between Lourde and myself. Five blocks became four, then three, then two.

Beneath my helmet, sweat dripped down the side of my face. I hadn't turned on the climate control and didn't have time to figure out how. Perspiration beaded on my upper lip, and when I pressed my lips together, copper tinged its natural salty taste. I sniffed. Another nosebleed. Hastily, I closed out the city map, my comms, the drone control, and every other program I could to forestall passing out.

Lourde was less than a block ahead of me. I made out the shape of his LAV, even if it was only a dark splotch against the lighter sky.

He slowed, this time actually taking an exit.

Were we that close to the spacedock or was he heading somewhere else?

I took the corner sharply, taking my hand off the throttle but not braking. When I was directly below Lourde, I hauled back on the handlebars, rotating the twin thrusters downward, and shooting up at a steep incline. I leveled out a few meters behind Lourde's port side. Gauging it worth the risk, I allowed my Intell to break into his LAV's communication system and opened an audio channel.

"Kandall Lourde, you're under arrest. Land now and turn off your engine."

"Who is this? How dare you interfere with my LAV's system," he said and closed the channel.

I tried forcing it open again, to no avail. Lourde may not have an Intell, but certainly knew how to block one. No matter, he wasn't the first unwilling suspect I'd brought in.

But maybe the first one on a hoverbike.

No longer concerned with stealth, his LAV shot out, trying to pull away. I stuck on him, hugging his port side and crawling up level with his thruster. Then I sucked in a deep breath, laid my hoverbike on its side, and engaged the thrusters at full blast.

They both fired, expelling tremendous amounts of hot gas and sinnafuel exhaust straight into Lourde's rear port side. The force knocked his LAV off center, causing it to swerve suddenly to the left and sink into a tailspin. One wing clipped my rear end, rocking me hard. I steered into a controlled spin and followed Lourde down.

My hoverbike hit front-end first, sending jarring pain up my arms to my shoulders. It flipped and hurtled me to the ground. I rolled half a dozen times, tucking my chin and elbows tightly to my body, before coming to a rest several meters away.

"Son of a sow's teat," I said, borrowing one of DeAjamae's more descriptive phrases, and pulled off my helmet. My headache was worse, but at least the dizziness was fading fast. In the future, I'd leave the aerial takedowns to fully encapsulated vehicles only.

Lourde crashed on the other side of the street. His LAV's emergency landing gear had kicked in and deployed a safety parachute. The landing would have been bumpy but survivable.

Dark blue splotches of oily sinnafuel coated the sand leading up to the LAV. Its starboard side hull had crumpled inward, and the whole craft listed heavily to that side. Smoke trailed from the engine compartment, only to be whisked away in the wind. I kept a watchful eye for any sparks that might set fire to the fuel.

"Suspect has crashed near Sunset and 7th Circle, ground level."

"Copy that. Tazza is in custody," Wright responded. "We're at least six minutes from your location. Sinclair, be careful."

As I approached, the port side gullwing popped open. It stuck at the one-third mark and refused to budge, even after Lourde beat against the frame with his shoulder and legs. He gave up, and soon after, a man's dress shoe and pant leg wiggled out the bottom, then a second. I waited as the rest of him slid out like the slimy trail of snail's snot that he was.

Lourde crumpled into a heap with his back resting against the powder-blue side of his LAV. A strap was wrapped around one wrist. He tugged it, and a cloth bag fell to the ground beside him with a dull *thunk*. From that distance, I saw a jumbled mass of cables, boxes, and mechanical parts—all things he had taken from the lab and, hopefully, the backup files.

Even though it had been a controlled descent from a low altitude with a low risk of injury, he patted down his body parts, seeming to reassure himself that everything was intact. Then I remembered he'd lost his arm in an LAV accident as a child. He looked a decade older and a great deal frailer than he had as the all-mighty king of his lab.

The LAV created enough of a windbreak that we could talk. "This is it, Lourde. The end of the line for you and your experiments."

He looked dazed, eyes unfocused, and movements sluggish. I stepped closer, and he finally registered my presence. He raised his bionic arm, as if to stop me. The fingers opened and closed in halting spurts instead of the smooth motions I was used to seeing. He worked his mouth as if chewing something sour, but remained silent.

"Nothing to say? This might be the first time I've ever seen you speechless."

A notification popped up that someone was attempting to access my implant. So, not confused, just using his Insight. I set up a block that should keep him out of my head.

His lips twisted and pulled back, revealing his yellowed teeth. "Subject E. You've been practicing."

"I had a little free time in between uncovering your paper trail to the IBMD and squeezing a confession out of Sagi. It turns out the security features on this implant are top-notch."

"You are performing above expectations for being outside the shielded lab for so long. Piloting a hoverbike is not something I would have tested for several months. This version of the Intell must be close to production-ready."

"This isn't a fucking performance review!"

"We should have disposed of you that first night, but Yelena convinced me to keep you. Our previous subject had expired quicker than expected, and we required a replacement. Your arrival seemed fortuitous. I never imagined you would be such an affliction. None of the prior subjects created near as much trouble."

"I'm real broken up about that."

"Tell me, how is the Intell performing? I see the nosebleeds have worsened. That's expected, since you discontinued the medication."

I swiped the back of my hand under my nose, and it came back red. Now that I'd stopped moving, Tylo's inexhaustible supply of signals were pinging my Intell, again. It had been used more in the last hour than in my entire time held captive in the lab.

"It's worth every drop of blood to see you answer for murdering my friend."

"Ah yes, your friend. That was a miscalculation on my part. Wasting away at a dead-end job. No family, no one to miss him. Well, no one of consequence, anyway. How was I to know there'd be this much fuss over him?"

"Jarrett Viorel was a decorated agent. The youngest digital forensic analyst in the Clava office. He put hundreds—thousands—of criminals in prison."

"Nothing he did *mattered*. Incarcerate a criminal and there will just be another to take his place. My work will advance the human species into the next stage of evolution. Human and machine, existing together as a cohesive unit. It's not even comparable."

"He pieced together your scheme. You rushed your product into trial, and when your faulty implants killed the customers, you paid dirty agents to cover up their deaths. Then you bribed a high-ranking member of the IBMD to get your Insight fast-tracked for approval."

"Per usual, you vastly oversimplify the issue. That's why Subject C prevailed over you on the puzzle exercises."

"His name was Fax, not Subject C. He was an old man, an itinerant for fuck's sake. He was no threat to you. You didn't have to kill him."

"That phase of the experiment had to be prematurely concluded. You have yourself to thank for that. Pity. All that wasted data."

I kicked the bottom of his shoe. "Get up. You're under arrest."

He made no move to comply, so I bent down to grab him by the elbow and force him to stand. That's when he attacked. Not physically, like I'd readied myself for. No, he flooded my Intell with hundreds, thousands of streams of information. It was as if the entire Tylo net was cramming itself into my head.

I screamed and fell to my knees, clutching my head. *Fastfastfast* I shut down what I could, attempting to stem the flow of information. How had the bastard gotten around my block?

This was worse than when Wright removed me from the lab, but I refused to pass out. Gritting my teeth, I called up the systems manager and traced the flux of data back to its source.

Scuffing sounds and a soft groan came from my right side. Lourde was getting up. I scuttled back, creating distance.

There! I found the opening he'd used and locked it down. The pressure inside my head eased immediately. That's when I heard the familiar high-pitched whine of a blaster reaching full charge.

Lourde swung his bionic arm up, only it wasn't the arm he normally wore. He'd swapped it out for the prototype bionic weapon I'd found on my first night breaking into the lab. Synthetic skin fell away from his finger, revealing the tip of the muzzle.

I dove into him, grabbing his shirt with one hand and hooking my other arm around the inside of his thigh for the start of a fireman's carry throw. I yanked down. He tipped forward, unbalanced, and I took all his weight across my shoulders as I drove my leg forward and completed the throw with a twist of my hips.

He let out a startled exclamation as he flipped ass over tin cups and fired a wild shot that only missed me by millimeters. It struck a holovid sign behind his LAV, sending a shower of smoke and sparks into the air.

Lourde landed flat on his back with a gasp. I followed, pinning his chest to the ground with my body and scrambling to get control over his bionic arm. He bucked beneath me with more force than I expected from a man of his age and stature. I rode it out, letting him expend his energy fighting my body weight. Meanwhile, I twisted around until our chests were perpendicular and I got a solid grip on his bionic limb. The entire thing was heated to an unnatural level.

I brought my knee up to his ribs with a fast strike. He grunted and flung a handful of sand in my face. Blinded, I shifted my weight and drove my knee in harder. My other hand pounded into the joint at his elbow where the bionic arm attached to his body.

The metal frame bruised and bloodied my knuckles, but I heard something crack. It loosened and wobbled. I grabbed it with both hands and rolled off Lourde. Momentum and torque tore it the rest of the way off.

Lourde bellowed, and I couldn't imagine that having your arm ripped off felt good, even if it was mechanical. I thought about Jarrett's tortured body and the gaping hole in the back of Fax's head, and I stopped caring if Lourde suffered.

I scrambled back, the bionic weapon now pointed at Lourde's center mass. Unlike DECA-issued blasters, Lourde hadn't burdened this one with safety features. All I had to do was figure out how to fire it. Lourde had an Insight. Credits to crispers, he'd designed it to work with an implant.

Hot air seared the inside of my lungs as I greedily sucked in oxygen. My sides heaved in and out, but I kept my hands steady. I directed the Intell to make the connection. It did so happily.

My hand opened and closed; the bionic hand opened and closed. I pointed my index finger; it pointed its index finger. I thought about shooting Lourde in the head; it shot an energy charge that sailed a decimeter above his worthless noggin.

Lourde raised his arms high in the air.

"Fucking asshole." I rubbed my face against my shoulder to clear the sand from my eyes. "On your knees."

"You won't shoot me," Lourde said with a smirk. "I'm unarmed, as it were."

"You're not as clever as you think you are. Look around. Who's going to see? It'd be your word against mine, and you'd be dead." For the first time, Lourde seemed unsure. "Ruana Sorelsdotter, Kelthea Zairesh, Thomas Rhinehardt, Silar Culpepper, Jarrett Viorel, Fax, and all the test subjects that came before me. Even if you didn't pull the trigger yourself, their deaths are on you. So go ahead. Tell me why I shouldn't end you now and save the galaxy a whole heap of trouble."

"I gifted you with the culmination of my life's work. The Intell is technology light-years beyond what anyone else has developed. Not even Aurelian Tazza has this level of technology."

A laugh burbled up from somewhere deep inside of me. It was loud, uncontrollable, and wholly inappropriate. "You think this thing inside my head is a gift? I suppose you expect me to say thank you. I wouldn't hold my breath."

He pushed his bag toward me. "I made backups of my research. I abandoned the hardware but that can be rebuilt. Improved, even. With your new capabilities and my knowledge, we could make a fortune. Any government, rebel faction, or corporation would pay handsomely for our services. My dear, the opportunities are endless. The galaxy is ours to take and reshape."

"You aren't even the slightest bit remorseful, are you?"

"Why would I be remorseful? My research will have profound effects on humankind for decades to come. They will laud me as the father of modern bionics. My name will be in books. They will dedicate entire classes to teaching my method. You are too close to see it yet, but mark my words, it will happen."

My mental finger hovered over the trigger command. The bastard couldn't even summon up the humanity to feel sorry for what he did—for the people he hurt. He deserved to pay for what he did. He deserved to die.

But that wasn't my choice to make. Lourde deserved a trial where his crimes would be made public and the families of his victims could receive some sense of closure. The system would work, if only because I would be there ensuring it did.

"Kandall Lourde, as an emergency officer for the Salin Department of Enforcement of Criminal Affairs, I'm placing you under arrest for the murder of Jarrett Viorel. You may remain silent if you so choose. If you choose to speak, your words may be entered as evidence in trial. You have the right to an appointed attorney or one of your own employment." Then I linked to the shared comm. "Sinclair, here. Lourde is secure. You can send that transpo now."

Chapter 36

"Do you want to see a doctor?" Wright asked, handing me a wad of gauze to shove up my nose. "We can make the time."

"No, I've had bad luck with Tylo hospitals."

"But you will get this looked at when we get to Salin, right?"

"I can, but I'm not sure a doctor can help. There's not much precedence for malfunctioning neural implants."

His fingers under my chin turned my head side to side. "Are you hurt anywhere else?"

"Bumps and bruises. Nothing serious. The headache is the worst part."

Wright removed a med dispenser from the kit and popped in a cartridge of low-dose pain killer. "This might help. Roll up your sleeve."

My breath caught in my lungs, but I hopped onto the table and scrunched the sleeve of my short-sleeved shirt over the top of my shoulder. His hand was gentle but firm where he placed it to steady my arm. I focused all my attention on that instead of the looming med dispenser. Adler had given me a lot of shots at the lab, and gentle wasn't a word I used to describe her.

"Are you going to leave your hair purple?"

"I haven't really thought—"

The needle prick was hot, fast, and over before I knew it.

"Tricksy," I said, pulling down my sleeve.

He shrugged, but the corner of his mouth lifted into a half-smile. "You've given a lot of shots?"

"Too often. In a different life."

People in the medical field rarely made the jump to law enforcement, so my credits were on the military where basic first-aid training was mandatory. Fifteen years ago, Ritru-6 had been in a border dispute with its sister planet Ritru-2 over an asteroid belt. I didn't recall the details, but that was the right timeframe for Wright to have seen action. I wouldn't have guessed that career path for a diplomat's kid.

Wright handed me a biohazard bag and a fresh roll of gauze. I removed the saturated wad from my nostril, dumped it in the bag, and applied the fresh roll. My nose hadn't stopped bleeding since he'd picked up Lourde and me from the crash site, although it slowed once we got back on the ship and there were fewer signals to contend with.

"How long until Ravi returns from the precinct with Michael and Sagi?" I asked. We'd already secured Aurelian Tazza and Kandall Lourde in one of the two holding cells on the cruiser. Thankfully, they both only had the Insight implants and couldn't use them to break out of their cell as I had with the Intell. I guess they hadn't been willing to test the newest technology on themselves.

"Any minute. Officer Tademan swore she'd have them processed and ready for transport by the time Ravi got there."

"You don't think she'll drag her feet? She hasn't been helpful so far."

"I'm guessing she won't want us looking too hard into her performance now that Tazza is under arrest."

"You think she's dirty, too, don't you?"

He lifted one shoulder. "At this point, nothing would surprise me." My smile must have betrayed my thoughts because his eyes narrowed, and he pointed his index finger at me. "That wasn't a challenge. I've had enough surprises for the time being."

"Spoilsport."

Wright put the med dispenser, gauze, and scissors back in the first-aid kit. He leaned against the counter after snapping the kit back into place. "You did good today."

I dropped my eyes and hoped the scrapes and bruises on my face hid the flush I felt rising to my cheeks. "You have a good team. Everyone works well together. I'm glad you let me help."

"I mean it, Reliance. The interrogation, apprehending Lourde—it was solid work. It's a shame you left the Department."

"It was more like they left me."

"How so?"

The part of my heart that was still raw from how my coworkers had pulled away from me bristled and shied away from Wright's question. Learning why Cavender turned on me began the healing process, but the wound hadn't yet scabbed over.

I sighed and scooted my butt off the table. "Never mind. I'm just tired. Thanks for patching me up."

Correctly reading my cue, Wright straightened from the counter. "Are you okay on your own? There are a few things I need to check before we take off."

"Go." I made a shooing motion with my hand. "I'm going to sit here and enjoy the pain meds when they kick in."

To prove my point, I grabbed a water pouch from the cooling unit, sat down at the table, and propped my feet up on the chair across from me.

He nodded and walked toward the door that led to the bridge. "You should, you know," he said, looking back. "Keep your hair purple. It suits you."

My eyes followed him down the short hallway. He cut a fine figure, that Lead Agent Grayson Wright. When I looked for it, I saw the stamp of the military ingrained in the straightness of his spine and the measured cadence of his walk. He had an economy of movement—no energy wasted and always at the ready. That dedication to duty looked a lot more appealing on this side of the line than it had a month ago when I'd first encountered his unflinching resolve.

He disappeared around a corner. I scrubbed my palms across my face before tearing open the water packet. The cold liquid rinsed the gritty feel of sand from my mouth, but I still tasted dirt after draining the pouch. I should've grabbed two.

I tossed the empty pouch to the end of the table and closed my eyes. This was the first chance I'd had to rest since arresting Lourde. The adrenaline rush had long since worn off, leaving me exhausted. The pain med started kicking in, dulling the ache in my shoulder from when I'd hung from Lourde's LAV and he'd slammed me into another vehicle. Or it could be from crashing the hoverbike. Hard to tell.

Today had been a key day in bringing Jarrett's and Fax's murderers to justice, but it wasn't over. The city attorney still needed to review the evidence and make a formal decision on whether she would prosecute. If she did, the four men would either strike plea bargains or go to trial. The media would be all over a high-profile defendant like Aurelian Tazza. I would need to testify.

There would also be paperwork. So much paperwork. That was one thing I didn't miss about working for the Department.

I yawned. The last couple of days felt like flying through a supernova, hurtling at light speed from one reality to another. In three days, I'd gone from captive to criminal to emergency-appointed officer, and soon I would be back to a regular citizen. It was a lot to absorb.

Reliance Sinclair, Insurance Claims Investigator sounded boring by comparison.

A wave of homesickness washed over me as I thought about Walnut, Felix, and the *Soteria*. Things wouldn't go back to how they were. How could they? But I had a home and a family. Maybe boring wasn't so bad.

The floor rattled beneath my feet. Wright was powering up the engine. Ravi must have made it back without any hiccups. My Intell rapidly fired alerts and notifications at me as the cruiser came online. Systems were all a go. We could take off as soon as Tylo's Central Command gave the okay.

There was a jump seat in the common area that I could strap into, but I tossed my empty water pouch into the reclamator and headed for the bridge. That was where Ravi and DeAjamae would be in case Wright needed help, and strangely, it was where I wanted to be, too.

Chapter 37

WRIGHT RAISED HIS GLASS. "To another case closed. Cheers!"

"Cheers!" Ravi and DeAjamae clinked their glasses against his.

My whisky glowed like liquid honey as the twinkle lights shone through it. "Sláinte."

The alcohol warmed my belly, warding off a chill breeze sweeping in from the bay. I breathed in the salty air. For a moment, it reminded me of home back in Clava. Except in Clava, it would probably be raining. Here in Salin, the sky was so dark and clear that both moons shone bright silver overhead. I relaxed back against the padded chair and nibbled on a piece of dark chocolate. *Real* chocolate topped with smoked sea salt.

We'd arrived back to Andaress-4 early this afternoon. Lourde had complained loudly and incessantly the entire trip. Tazza kept silent, but a team of his high-priced attorneys met us at the gate. They'd already filed a data dot's worth of objections ranging from lack of jurisdiction to insufficient evidence to some obscure section of a treaty involving merchant rights. The city attorney requested I remain in Salin until she decided whether she needed me to give immediate testimony.

DeAjamae suggested we celebrate. Wright offered his rooftop terrace and liquor cabinet. She brought a crudités platter, cured meats, and a mild cheese that complimented both. I picked up a box of fancy chocolates for dessert. Ravi came bearing an old guitar. He volunteered to play if DeAjamae would sing. She'd confessed that she sang at a club downtown a couple times a month.

I ate my fill and licked my fingers clean while they argued over favorite bands. Walnut waddled across the table and bumped his head against Ravi's hand. The man obliged by scratching the guinea pig behind the ear.

"He's hoping you'll give him something to eat." I didn't need to check Walnut's neural implant to know that. The little bugger was insatiable.

DeAjamae slid the half-demolished crudités platter across the table to Ravi. He held up a fresh snap pea and gave me a questioning look.

"Just not the dip or mushrooms. Lucky critter can't handle fungi or mycoprotein in any form. He eats more fresh food than I do."

"Got it." He held out the pea. "Come on, little guy."

Walnut rose on his hind legs, his sniffer-twitcher working double time. Ravi let him have the treat after a mock tug-of-war, and Walnut made quick work of nibbling it to shreds. The pea hadn't stood a chance.

"How's the little guy adapting to life on a spaceship?" DeAjamae asked.

"Better than Felix, my ship's computer avatar. Apparently, when his programmers based his personality on a cat, it included a strong dislike for all things rodent."

Wright laughed. "Not an undesirable trait on a ship."

"Sometimes I go down to the mess area and find Felix staring at Walnut in his cage. It's creepy."

DeAjamae made a stack of cheese cubes and popped the top one in her mouth. "Want me to see if I can tweak his program? I've never worked on a ship's avatar before. Might be fun."

"You sound like Jarrett. The last time I let him look at Felix's insides, he programmed him to knock my coffee cup off the bridge's control panel whenever I set it down."

She snorted and tried to cover it with a fake cough.

"Sure, laugh now, but it took me weeks to figure out what was going on. It only happened when I was out of the room. At first, I thought something was wrong with the anti-grav system. Then

I thought the stabilizers were buggy and ran three full diagnostic scans. Then one day I walked in and caught Felix mid-act."

Ravi broke a carrot stick in half and gave it to Walnut. "Can you scold an avatar?"

"Not successfully. He jumped down and walked through the puddle of coffee, trailing pomegranate-sized paw prints across the bridge floor." I held up both hands—middle fingers and thumbs touching—to emphasize how large his metal feet were.

Everyone laughed, and a warm feeling washed through me at the memory.

I took the moment to step away from the group and check on Felix. Wright's apartment was close enough to the spacedock where the *Soteria* was parked that my Intell could communicate with Felix.

"Hey, Felix." A computer-generated image of the mechanical cat appeared in my mind's eye. He yawned, displaying a set of sharp titanium canines that looked far more ferocious than they were in real life. "Did you mess with your graphics settings again?"

His mouth snapped shut. "You were gone for a long time. I got bored."

"I see. Well, they look great, buddy." A rusty purr-rattle transmitted over the link. "I'm going to pick up a few groceries now that my accounts are unfrozen. Do I need to get anything for the ship?"

"We could use a new extension cable for the hydroponics light."

"What happened to the old one?"

"It, uh, sort of got shredded."

"Felix!"

"I said I got bored!"

My face scrunched. At least he'd picked an inexpensive one. "All right. I'll be back in a few hours. Try not to chew on anything else until I get there."

I severed the connection and blew out a breath.

"Everything okay?" Wright asked. He was stacking empty plates on a tray by the door.

"It's fine. Nothing a quick trip to the hardware store can't fix." I picked up the remaining glasses and added them to the pile.

"Thanks." He motioned for me to follow him over to the railing.

Salin was beautiful at night. The breeze carried with it the low hum of air traffic, and someone's dog barked the next block over. I stared off into the distance and was pleased to spot a few stars above the city lights.

He leaned his forearms against the railing and looked out over the rooftops. "Have you decided what to do with Fax's remains once they are released?"

"Fax once mentioned an estranged brother on Mars. I figured I'd start there."

"I've never been to the Sol System."

"Me either. I thought I'd take a week, see if I can find his brother. Maybe stop at Earth while I'm in the area. They say everyone should see it at least once."

"What are your plans after that?"

I swirled the whisky in my glass, watching the amber light reflect on the surface. "Contact the insurance company I worked for, I suppose. See if I still have a job. Seddy wants me to resume my payments now that the *Soteria* is out of impound."

"He's quite the character."

"Eh, he's not so bad once you get to know him. But don't let him talk you into playing mah-jongg. He cheats worse than an ex-boyfriend."

"I'll keep that in mind." Wright tossed back the last of his drink and faced me. His hazel eyes looked browner in this light, warmer and more intense. "What if you didn't have to leave Salin? What if there was another option?"

"Another option?"

Wright glanced at the others, still absorbed in their own conversation. He took a step closer and lowered his voice. "My lieutenant wants my team to follow up on Tazza Industries' bionic weapon development. It violates the Treaty of Alpha Bohn-ri, of which Andaress-4 and Brione-2 are both members. Ravi and DeAjamae are sorting through the files we seized, but so far, our only proof is the sample you removed from Lourde's person. The higher-ups are concerned about how advanced the research is and who Tazza planned to sell the weapons to. We need to find out how far it goes." Wright paused and leaned down. "She also agreed to add additional personnel to my team. The job is yours, if you want it."

I eyed my near-empty glass, wondering if I'd had too much to drink. "You're offering me a job? After..." I waved my drink vaguely at the world. "... everything?"

"It's probationary. You'd start as an officer."

"Even with this thing inside my head? I don't know if it can be removed."

"That was one of my selling points. You have personal knowledge and vested interest in the case."

"I shot you."

"Are you trying to talk me out of it?"

"No! I mean, maybe? This is a lot to take in."

Over at the table, Ravi plucked a string on his guitar and twisted the tuning knob until the note rang true. He strummed a few chords before settling on a familiar tune made popular a few decades earlier. DeAjamae hummed a couple of bars, then joined in on the chorus. Her voice was raspy and well suited to the song. They looked happy. Even Walnut had found a cushion to curl up on and was sending signals of contentment.

To be a part of a team again. A real team. My pulse quickened at the possibility.

"Did you talk to them about it?" I asked.

"It was a unanimous decision. Does that mean you accept?"

"I guess it does."

Wright grinned. "This should be fun."

***

Continue Reliance's story in
ON IMPACT (Reliance Sinclair, #2)

https://www.amazon.com/dp/B0F99YL27N

They turned me into a weapon. Now I'm the only one who can stop them.

When an assassin kills a Ritruvian official using an illegal bioweapon, the galaxy teeters on the edge of war. My team must locate the remaining weapons and shut down Tazza Industries, the company that developed them.

I have history with Tazza. Six months ago, they used me as a test subject, implanting a cutting-edge chip into my brain designed for espionage and covert operations. Instead of killing me, it gave me a deadly advantage—and a purpose.

To take them down and avoid an interplanetary war, I'll need to confront my darkest fears—and trust the lethal skills I never wanted.

THANK YOU FOR READING
ON IMPULSE!

I would love to know what you thought of Reliance and the gang.

If you enjoyed the story, please consider leaving a review wherever you purchased the book or on your favorite review site, like Goodreads or Amazon. Indie authors depend on reviews like yours to help find new readers so we can keep writing the stories you love.

Don't Stop Now!

Dive deeper into the world at heathertexle.com

★ Curious about Reliance and Jarrett's adventure to take down Lady Ilymechina? Get the *FREE* short story right now!

★ Find bonus content like book club questions, inspiration boards, and more!

★ Be the first to know about new releases, deals, and upcoming events!

Acknowledgements

Writing a book is often done in solitude, but it is by no means a solitary pursuit. Many people helped shape its final form.

First, I thank you, the reader, for taking a chance on a new author. A book is only truly complete once someone has read it. There are many ways you could spend your time, and I'm honored that you spent it with me.

This would not have been the same book without the excellent guidance and advice of my editor Kat Betts of Element Editing Services (elementeds.com). Her skill and compassion in working with a wide-eyed, first-time author cannot be overstated.

The folks at MiblArt (miblart.com) did a fantastic job designing the cover and bringing my story to life. Likewise, the very talented Giselle K. did an outstanding job on the interior illustration of Reliance.

A big thank you to my mentor and kindred spirit, author Elicia Hyder (eliciahyder.com) for her inspiration, advice, and sneak peek at the publishing roadmap. The journey seemed much less daunting with your light shining on the path.

Although she doesn't know me, author Chloe Neill (chloeneill. com) inspired me to write my first book after I attended one of her signings. You never know when you may touch someone's life.

To my friends and beta readers Rosa, Tawnie, Shawn, and Dee Dee for their unwavering love and support: thank you. Without your patience, gentle prodding, and thorough redlines, this book may still just live on my computer.

I am forever grateful to my elementary teachers, Ms. Thuestad and Ms. Gallagher for instilling in me a lifelong passion for learning. Because of you, I still look at the world with a sense of wonder and curiosity.

Thank you to my parents. You not only supported my dreams but gave me the tools to build them.

And finally, thank you to my husband, Justin, who has more faith in me than one person deserves. You told people I was a writer before I dared admit it to myself. You are my firm foundation, I couldn't have done this without you. Merk!

About the Author

Heather Texle is the award-winning author of the *Reliance Sinclair* science-fiction series who finds inspiration in the quirky, weird, and I-can't-believe-that's-true things. With a lifelong passion for learning, Heather is fascinated with the creativity and ingenuity of the human spirit. She also adores a good conspiracy theory.

After graduating college, Heather moved to Minnesota where she attained her law degree and continues to live with her husband and two cats, Mew and Spots. Despite once being stranded in the Gulf of Mexico on a burning cruise ship, she loves to travel and can often be heard muttering "I miss Scotland" on cool, rainy days. Her debut novel, *On Impulse*, won the 2023 Minnesota Author Project contest for Adult Fiction.

For more information about Heather and her work, follow her online on FaceBook, Goodreads, and BookBub. You can also sign up for her newsletter and receive a free *Reliance Sinclair* short story at heathertexle.com.

Giselle

www.ingramcontent.com/pod-product-compliance
Lightning Source LLC
Chambersburg PA
CBHW071230300726
48975CB00002B/359